AINSLEY ABBOTT ~ KAT ALEXIS
M.A. ELLIS ~ HELEN HARDT
KELLY JAMIESON ~ AMBER SKYZE

BODY SHOTS
Amber Skyze

Got tequila? Sierra does, and Reed isn't afraid to use it. He's determined to do shots on every inch of her skin, but Sierra has insecurities preventing him from exploring intimate areas. Her insecurities won't stop her from lavishing *his* body with the heady liquor though.

Ten years ago an accident tore Sierra Allen and Reed Walker apart. Now a chance encounter has them burning for each other. A bottle of liquor and a pool table has this duo ready to quench their thirsts with one night of body shots. But will one night be enough?

SHAKEN AND STIRRED
M.A. Ellis

Susanne is one final challenge away from winning a national beverage competition and reaching the pinnacle of her career—a management position with a very wealthy client. She's intent that nothing will stand in her way. Not even the drop-dead-sexy cowboy who sidles up to her at the hotel bar.

Lucifer Treyton Ryder is under express orders from his uncle to find Susanne and do whatever it takes to have her disqualified. Trey plans to take her to bed and keep her there until the security team discovers them together. It's against the rules. It's a foolproof plan. Until the auburn-haired beauty shows more than a passing interest in a bit of *yee-haw* rope play.

Before Susanne realizes what he's about, Trey has her hands expertly bound and she's forced to make a choice—play it safe or allow the devilishly tempting man full rein for an evening of uninhibited loving? A "perfect" stranger and kinky sex? Susanne's about to make a choice that could cost her everything.

SLOW AND WET
Helen Hardt

Jillian loves her gorgeous bronc-busting boyfriend, Dale. She just hasn't told him yet. After a satisfying romp, she walks naked into Dale's kitchen, shocked to find another hot cowboy. Travis likes what he sees and is eager to take up where he and Dale left off four years earlier—as two men giving one woman the ultimate pleasure.

To please Dale—and herself—Jill agrees. Under the Wyoming summer sky, she yields to the desires of both men. They cover her in her favorite beverage, Dale's homemade honey-lemonade, and lick every drop from her body. But will this erotic encounter with four strong hands, two delectable mouths and two determined men lead to what Jill ultimately wants—Dale's love?

SET ME UP
Kat Alexis

Indigo Larsen can finally live her dreams of exploring the world. Her first stop is Ireland, where on a dare she accepts the Tongue of Truth liquor. The sex that follows is passionate and more exotic than anything she's ever imagined. Waking up the next morning on Aedan Ciaran's naked lap with his hard cock inside her is more than disconcerting. Convinced the liquor is the cause of her predicament, Indigo tries to leave.

What's a leprechaun to do? Why, bring out all the luck he can find in hopes of loving his way into Indigo's heart.

SEXPRESSO NIGHT
Kelly Jamieson

After a disastrous D/s relationship nearly destroyed her, Danya swears she'll never go back to that lifestyle. She tries to deny the dark hunger rising inside her, a craving to be pushed, taken to the edge, until the night she ends up at Karma Coffee for Sexpresso Night. She discovers how sensual and sexy coffee can be—and how sensual and sexy barista Carter Jarvis is.

Carter senses gorgeous Danya wants to let go of control with a man. When they end up back at his place "for coffee", she submits to him so beautifully he knows she's meant to be his. Carter seems perfect for her—not wishy-washy, but not a sadistic pervert. The true test comes the night he shows her his BDSM playroom.

JEMIMAH'S GENIE
Ainsley Abbott

The promised toast Jemimah Murphy offered her deceased grandmother was one she'd never forget. As her great-great-grandmother's homemade elderberry wine trickled down her throat, a poof and flash sent her reeling and the most delectable man she'd ever seen suddenly appeared. Brian, she discovered to her utter amazement and delight, was her personal genie.

Brian's reason for existence was to pleasure Jemi and fulfill her deepest sexual desires. His fiery lovemaking introduced her to passionate, sensual experiences she'd never believed possible.

But the magical wine diminished each time Jemi summoned her lover, and both Brian and Jemi knew their perfect fantasy would inevitably have to end. Unless...

An Ellora's Cave Romantica Publication

www.ellorascave.com

Wet

ISBN 9781419962486
ALL RIGHTS RESERVED.
Body Shots Copyright © 2009 Amber Skyze
Shaken and Stirred Copyright © 2009 M.A. Ellis
Slow and Wet Copyright © 2009 Helen Hardt
Set Me Up Copyright © 2009 Kat Alexis
Sexpresso Night Copyright © 2009 Kelly Jamieson
Jemimah's Genie Copyright © 2009 Ainsley Abbott
Edited by Helen Woodall and Pamela Campbell.
Cover art by Syneca.

Trade paperback publication 2011

With the exception of quotes used in reviews, this book may not be reproduced or used in whole or in part by any means existing without written permission from the publisher, Ellora's Cave Publishing, Inc.® 1056 Home Avenue, Akron OH 44310-3502.

Warning: The unauthorized reproduction or distribution of this copyrighted work is illegal. Criminal copyright infringement, including infringement without monetary gain, is investigated by the FBI and is punishable by up to 5 years in federal prison and a fine of $250,000.
(http://www.fbi.gov/ipr/)

This book is a work of fiction and any resemblance to persons, living or dead, or places, events or locales is purely coincidental. The characters are productions of the author's imagination and used fictitiously.

WET
ଛ

BODY SHOTS
Amber Skyze
~11~

SHAKEN AND STIRRED
M.A. Ellis
~83~

SLOW AND WET
Helen Hardt
~171~

SET ME UP
Kat Alexis
~215~

SEXPRESSO NIGHT
Kelly Jamieson
~265~

JEMIMAH'S GENIE
Ainsley Abbott
~347~

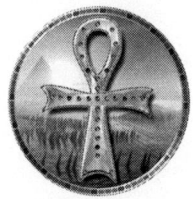

BODY SHOTS
Amber Skyze

Dedication

I'd like to dedicate this book to a dear friend who passed away in January. She was my best friend for a long time and then we had a falling out. We lost touch with each other for over twenty years. I always dreamed about ways we'd reconcile, but all those dreams were shattered when she lost her battle with cancer. She's survived by three daughters and a husband. Their marriage was a true life fairy tale. They met as teens and fell in love. They were together for over twenty-five years. It's through her passing I realized life is too short to live with regrets. Forgive your enemies and follow your dreams. Live for today because tomorrow may never come. While I never got to say goodbye I can follow my dreams. I'm going to continue to write stories of true love, the kind Lisa lived.

Acknowledgments

I'd like to thank my family for continuing to support my crazy writing life, especially my husband who reads every single story. My dear friends who buy my books—you know who you are. And the fellow authors who help promote my work as release day approaches. Without you, writing wouldn't be the same. And my wonderful editor, who makes my work shine! She's truly a blessing.

Trademarks Acknowledgement

The author acknowledges the trademarked status and trademark owners of the following wordmarks mentioned in this work of fiction:

Corona: Cerveceria Modelo, S.A. de C.V. Corporation

Jet Ski: Kawasaki Heavy Industries, Ltd.

Chapter One

Reed Walker leaned his massive frame against the wall. His leg bent, his boot-clad foot tapped against the wall to the rhythm of the bass drum. He stuffed his hands in his pockets, as his eyes gazed upon the singer crooning the soft rock ballad. She was gorgeous by every standard of the word. Long flowing black hair, dark mysterious eyes, her arms sleeved in tattoos. Dressed only in black leather pants and a matching leather bra, her rock-hard stomach revealed she worshiped the gym but Reed wasn't here for the singer. She wasn't his type any longer. Another time, another place maybe. Not tonight. Tonight, he was here for the owner of the bar.

Looking to make some extra cash doing something they loved, Reed and his fellow band mates decided to reunite after a ten year hiatus. Reed, having always been the businessman of the group, took on the task of going to different bars and clubs to see if they were interested in adding his band Foul Play to their lineup.

When he walked into Crimson Nights he thought he was walking into a dream. Never in his wildest imagination had he thought he'd come face to face with the only true love of his life—Sierra Allen.

The look on her face when he walked up to the bar and asked to speak to the owner was one of shock. Like seeing a ghost. And that's how he felt. Oh, she'd cut off most of her long red hair but she couldn't deny the scar on her right cheek. It had faded some over the years and she tried covering it with her hand most of the time they spoke but he knew it was her. She told him her name was Laura but Reed knew better. Those haunting green eyes couldn't be mistaken.

He went along with her charade, though it killed him deep inside. She had run away from him after the car accident without so much as an explanation. The weeks he spent by her side, holding her while she cried over what she felt was a deformed face. The painful recovery from the shards of glass that cut her, when the windshield shattered. He stood by her side, loving her, wishing he could take away her pain. Wishing it was him who suffered instead of her, only to have her up and vanish when she was released from the hospital.

Now she was pretending she didn't know him. It didn't make sense. He'd let her go a long time ago but this time he wasn't going to leave without finding out why. It was the least she could do. She owed him an explanation.

She shocked him when she agreed to let his band play. He fully expected a flat-out "no". Why would she want his band playing there if she was hiding her identity? Was it a ploy to make him believe she was this Laura she pretended to be? Or was she feeling the connection too? If it was to prove her charade, she was sadly mistaken. Reed wasn't stupid enough to be fooled by a haircut or name change.

Reed would wait until the night was done and the bar empty before he confronted her but he would and when he did, Sierra had some explaining to do.

He scanned the crowd. The place was full of drunks. There was a table full of college-age guys looking like they had been served one too many. They were getting rowdy and Reed had a feeling before the night was through there'd be trouble. He eyed the group of young guys doing shots. They were hooting and hollering to the singer requesting she flash them some boobs.

Reed cringed. It wouldn't be long. He cased the bar searching for any signs of a bodyguard. Nothing. What was Sierra thinking? She couldn't possibly run a bar without the help of bouncers. What did she do when patrons got out of hand? She couldn't wait around for the local police to come. Christ in this small town it could take forever.

He swigged the ice-cold Corona and reverted his attention back to the bar. She was laughing and carrying on with a group of women sitting at the bar. She looked happy. A small stab of pain filled him. In some ways he wished she wasn't so happy. He wished after all these years she regretted walking away from him, disappearing without so much as a goodbye. But that didn't seem the case. Just the opposite.

He did notice from their brief conversation that she wasn't wearing a wedding band on her left hand. That was a promising sign. At least there wasn't a husband for him to contend with. Because Reed was determined to get his answers and get this woman out of his every waking thought once and for all.

"Come on, bitch. Stop teasing us and show us those boobs." One of the drunks shouted as he moved closer to the stage. He threw his drink at the singer, splashing the cold liquid all over her.

Reed pushed off the wall and rushed through the crowded tables to where he stood.

The singer continued with her song, ignoring him, adding fuel to the fire. He tried getting up on stage when Reed lunged forward, tackling him.

"Get the fuck off me, asshole," he cried. His arms attempted to lash out, punching Reed.

Reed pinned him down and looked him square in the eyes. "I'll let you go if you agree to keep your hands to yourself. You and your buddies pack it up and call it a night. You hear."

"Fuck you. Who died and made you boss?" He spat at Reed.

Reed wiped the remnants of saliva off his face, before punching the jerk in the jaw.

"Ouch!" he cried.

Blood dripped from the kid's bottom lip. "I'm warning you one last time. You get up, get the hell out of here or I'll have to hurt you."

"Fine. We'll leave."

Trusting him, Reed climbed off him and helped him to his feet. "Now move along."

At this point the music had stopped and the entire bar watched, waiting to see what would happen next.

As the kid started to walk away, Reed bent and picked up a small towel sitting atop one of the speakers, turned and tossed it to the singer.

She smiled.

"Business as usual," he said.

She nodded and directed her band to start back up.

Reed headed toward the wall he'd been leaning against for the last hour when someone jumped on his back.

"You can't mess with me you son of bitch. You obviously don't know who I am."

It was the stupid drunk kid. He had his arm hooked around Reed's neck, trying to choke him. Reed bent forward, flipping the kid onto his back. He pressed the heel of his boot against his neck.

"I don't give a rat's ass who you are. I told you to leave and I wasn't kidding."

Tables were pushed out of the way and a crowd surrounded them. This had the potential to get really ugly and Reed knew he could be outnumbered. His band mates hadn't arrived yet and he wasn't ready to take on more than this kid but he would if it meant the safety of the other people in the bar.

Luck was on his side and someone had called the police. Two officers barged through the crowd took one look at the kid lying on the floor. The older one spoke.

"Johnny, what kind of trouble have you gotten yourself into now? Your father isn't going to be happy."

He picked the kid up off his sorry ass.

"Tough. I don't give a shit what my father thinks," he said, wiping off his clothes. He lunged toward Reed taking another shot.

Reed ducked. "Easy there tough guy."

Two officers grabbed him and carted him off. "Let's go see your father, Johnny."

"Yeah, let's go see about your jobs, assholes."

The kid was full of piss and vinegar. Reed didn't envy the officers their job. He was obviously a spoiled punk. Reed watched as his buddies followed close behind the officers. They didn't seem to feel the need to jump in and help their friend. Lucky for Reed.

Reed noticed everyone was looking to see what he would do next. "Show's over folks."

He stomped off to his wall, while the crowd cheered for him. They shouted their thanks. When he returned to the same position against the wall he waved his hand in thanks.

As quickly as the ruckus started the crowd returned to normal. The crowd went back to talking in whispered groups while the singer belted out a rock tune.

Tucking a strand of his shoulder-length blond hair behind his ear he felt her eyes on him.

A glance over at the bar proved correct. She was standing wiping a glass dry with a white dishtowel staring intently at him.

"Thank you," she mouthed.

He nodded, gave a quick smile and turned his attention back to the stage. He'd deal with Sierra or Laura or whoever the fuck she was calling herself these days later. Right now he wanted to finish his beer and concentrate on the night ahead.

Sierra shivered. Why had she agreed to let Reed and the other members of Foul Play, be part of the lineup at her bar? She was beginning to believe that along with lying to him about who she was, this was one of the dumbest ideas she had. But when he entered her bar, she panicked. So she resorted to the only thing she could think of—being someone else. They say everyone has a twin in the world. Ha! What were the chances of having a twin with the same scar on her right cheek? Slim to none.

And what if someone blew her cover? Everyone knew her by Sierra. Would she make it through the entire night without someone calling her by her legal name? Highly unlikely. So why had she risked it all and agreed to let him back into her life, even for one night?

Because she couldn't say no.

It didn't matter that ten years had passed. No. He still held a place in her heart and she couldn't refuse him. And it was a good thing she hadn't. She didn't know what would have happened if he weren't here tonight. No one else stepped up to Johnny when he got out of hand. No one but Reed. And Sierra feared he might find himself in a heap of trouble down the road. Johnny McCoy didn't take kindly to being challenged. Topped with the fact Reed had made him a laughingstock. He'd likely be out for blood. No one intimidated him. Until Reed. And his daddy might not like it too much either. But Reed had no clue who his father was. He stood up and took out the trash so to speak. Sierra always let Johnny and his friends do as they pleased. After all he was the son of the sheriff. She couldn't mess with that. Not if she wanted to keep her liquor license.

She was very thankful for Reed's help, she just hoped it didn't come back to haunt her, in the form of Sheriff McCoy.

* * * * *

When Lita's band finished Sierra watched the singer as she made her way to Reed. The two seemed to be chatting easily. Jealousy filled Sierra as Lita laughed at something Reed was saying. Would they hook up before the night was over? She wasn't sure she could handle something like that. She wasn't ready to witness Reed with another woman but she couldn't begrudge him happiness either. Oh why had she agreed to this mess? The least she could have done was scheduled them for a different night, when Lita wasn't there. Because Lita was beautiful. All the men drooled over her. Normally she didn't seem interested but tonight she did.

A twinge of pain seared her heart as Lita reached out and touched Reed's arm. He pulled her into a hug, their bodies lingering longer than a friendly embrace. She tried shaking the anger and feelings of betrayal overwhelming her. He wasn't hers. He never could be.

Foul Play finally went on stage and Sierra breathed a sigh of relief. Reed would be busy and couldn't catch her staring at him and Lita. The few times he came to the bar, he caused her heart to flutter. But he immediately returned to Lita.

She ran her finger over the scar. It was her reminder that no man would look at her the same. She was damaged goods. Yes, the scar had faded over the years. The plastic surgeon had done the best he could at the time but it didn't erase the disfigurement she'd lived with all these years. And the other scars. The ones hidden by her clothes. She had to live with the horrific memories of the accident. Though the nightmares weren't as frequent, she sometimes pictured the moments after impact and Reed wasn't beside her. He'd landed in the backseat when the driver's seat tore out of the floor. He was the lucky one. This was the one time *not* having a seatbelt on saved a life.

She often wondered how she might have fared if she hadn't been wearing a seatbelt. Would things have been different? Would she have run away? It didn't matter. The simple fact was she didn't fare well and she had scars.

Sierra tried dating. What a mistake that turned out to be. The rude comments of some of the men she'd dated over the years had sent her into a depression. No man wanted to see her body a second time.

The scene with her last date played over in her mind whenever she thought about trying to date again. The look on Bruce's face was etched in her mind, when he'd looked at her in disgust and asked, "What the hell happened to your stomach?" He'd looked like he wanted to vomit at the sight of her scars.

Sometimes she thought she would too. But they were her demons and it was her life.

She'd resigned herself to the fact that she was never going to get married, settle down and have a family. No, she was going to live a lonely existence as a bar owner the rest of her life.

She poured herself a vodka and seven while listening to Reed's band play. Tonight was about facing the last of her demons. Reed Walker.

If she thought him being on stage would be a distraction, she was sadly mistaken. It took two songs before he began singing the one song she had pushed to the back of her memory. The one she'd long since buried. It wasn't like she'd forgotten about it, she just didn't want to remember.

"That love of a lifetime. A love to stand the tests of time."

His soft voice mesmerized her. This was her song. The song he'd written only for her. The promise they would be together forever. Until the accident.

"I love you now, as the first time I laid eyes on you. Time will never change what I'm feeling inside. Oh…"

She squeezed her eyes closed praying he didn't say her name. Praying he'd removed her name from the song.

"Sierra," he finished.

Her lids snapped opened to find him staring intently at the bar. A single tear slid down her cheek. Their eyes held locked on each other and in that moment Sierra knew she'd made the biggest mistake allowing Foul Play and Reed Walker back into her life.

* * * * *

The one night she needed Henry to lock up the bar, he couldn't.

"Sorry S...boss. Wife's not feeling well. She needs me to stop at the twenty-four hour pharmacy and get her some medicine. You know I would do it."

She knew he was struggling with his decision to leave her alone with Reed. Although, she didn't give him all the details, he knew enough to know she didn't want to be stuck alone for a single moment with him.

"I know, Henry. Don't worry about it. Get home to Dawn," she said, letting him off the hook.

She didn't need him feeling guilty for her mistakes. His wife needed him and *she* should be his priority, not Sierra. And besides they weren't completely alone.

She ushered him out the front door, locking it behind him. The members of Foul Play were breaking down their equipment and loading it into a van they had driven around to the back door.

Sierra turned off some of the lights so people would know she was closed. She paced behind the bar, cleaning the counters, putting away clean glasses and emptying peanut bowls. Overall the night had been a success. Patrons packed the bar. The beer and liquor flowed all night. She'd have to put in an emergency order for a few things in the morning.

Morning? Who was she fooling, it was morning. Two in the morning to be exact. The band had stayed on stage longer than expected. The crowd kept cheering for more each time they'd tried to call it a night. She hadn't stepped in. She let them decide if they wanted to continue playing. She was making a ton of money, so she didn't mind.

Tomorrow she would be tired but that was the nature of the business.

"We're just about done loading the van," a voice said behind her. Chills ran through her body.

Damn. Plastering a smile on her face she turned.

"Great night."

"Thanks for giving us a chance."

"Anytime." She slid an envelope across the bar. "You guys rocked the house."

"The band before us was pretty hot too. That singer was on fire."

Jealousy surged through her. Was Reed interested in Lita, with that to-die-for body and that killer voice? What guy wouldn't want to get to know her better?

"Lita's incredible."

"Yes, she is. Hey, do you mind if I have a beer or are you shut down for the night?"

Her head told her to deny him but her heart trumped her. "Sure, one Corona coming up."

She went to the cooler and removed the beer. She reached for a slice of lime and stuck the wedge in the opening. "Here you go."

He pushed the wedge into the beer with his thumb and then licked the juice from his finger.

She groaned, imagining that tongue on her, tasting her.

"Something wrong?" Reed asked.

She shook her head, realizing he'd heard her groan. "Just remembering something I have to do tomorrow."

She stood there uneasy. She didn't want to make small talk with him. She wanted him to drink his beer and get a move on. Because if he stayed she was going to continue to wonder if his lips were still as baby soft as they were ten years ago. Or if they felt like butterfly wings tickling the skin when he kissed her stomach. She had to forget about things like that and about Reed. One look at her stomach now and he'd be running for the door, like all the others.

She'd saved him from a lifetime of misery and disgust when she disappeared. Because she knew Reed would have done the right thing and stuck by her but she also knew he wouldn't be able to stand looking at her body every night when they went to bed or made love. It was disfigured and flat-out gross.

"Hey Reed, we're all set. We're gonna take off."

"I'll catch up with you tomorrow to square up, Tim," he said, holding the money envelope up for his band mate's view.

"Sounds good."

They waved goodbye and closed the door tightly behind them.

Why was he lingering? He should be leaving with his band mates, not sticking around her bar. She wanted to lock up, finish cleaning and escape to the safety of her apartment. Away from him.

He returned his gaze to her. He was undressing her with his hazel eyes. She could feel the power of his stare.

She darted away from the bar toward the back door, out from under his gaze.

"You can finish your beer but I have to lock this door. Don't want any stragglers roaming in thinking we're still open. I'll just be tidying up. Don't pay no mind to me." She started wiping down tables and rearranging chairs, anything to keep busy.

She heard his footsteps. Fuck! He was headed in her direction. Pretending she didn't hear him or sense his closeness she continued brushing peanut shells onto the floor, where she'd eventually sweep them up.

"We're alone now." His fingertips brushed over the small of her back, where her tank top had ridden up, exposing a small area of skin. "You can be honest now. I know your name is not Laura. God, Sierra give me some credit."

His voice was pleading, not angry, like she'd expect.

Slowly, she turned. They were face to face. She stepped back hitting the top of her legs against the table. Nowhere to run. Like a trapped animal. She couldn't flee. Yes, this was the biggest mistake she'd ever made. Somehow, some way she had to get herself out of this mess.

"Listen, Reed." She turned her eyes away. What could she say? What lie could she concoct to get him to leave her alone?

He closed the minimal gap between them, sucking the air from her lungs. He reached out touching her face.

"Admit it. Tell me you're not Laura."

She crumbled under his touch. "I'm not Laura."

Chapter Two

"Oh dear god," he said, gathering her in his arms. "I've missed you so much."

She struggled to free herself from his grip. This was the reason she didn't want to admit the truth. This was why she wanted to pretend she was someone else. She didn't want to deal with him. She didn't want the questions or the pretend sympathy.

He released her and stepped back. "What's wrong?"

"Reed, it's been ten years. A lot has changed in that time. I'm not the girl who left. I'm not that person anymore." *I'm not the woman you loved,* she wanted to scream. Yet she couldn't deny she still had feelings for him. Ten years hadn't erased those feelings. How she wished it had. But the truth was she loved Reed as much as she did the day she walked out of his life—for what she believed was forever.

She moved to the side and started to walk away.

Reed grabbed her arm, twisting her around.

"Don't give me that bullshit, Sierra. I know you. I can see the pain in your eyes. And I can also see the love."

She shivered, hating his ability to read her. Her pain was from the fact she couldn't stop loving him. She hoped he'd have moved on by now. Married and settled down. But part of her was relieved to know he hadn't.

"Reed..."

His hands pulled her face closer. His lips descended, capturing hers. She didn't resist. She accepted his kiss. When his tongue invaded her mouth, she parted her lips, allowing him access. She knew she should push him away. Instead she wrapped her arms around his neck, pulling him closer, devouring his mouth hungrily.

His arms enveloped her waist lifting her off the ground. She felt his bulge through his pants. It throbbed against her stomach.

She whimpered. It'd been so long since she felt a man inside her. So long since she had sex. Thoughts of having Reed inside her consumed her. Blinded by desire, she lost her grip on reality. Her legs snaked around his waist.

"Fuck me, Reed," she whispered between kisses.

His mouth froze.

What the fuck? Why was he stopping? Wasn't this what he wanted?

"Are you sure?"

"Yes," she said, before sucking his lower lip into her mouth. She nibbled and released it. "One hundred percent positive."

Holding onto her ass, he carried her over to the bar. He set her down on a stool, picked up his beer and took a long swig.

"Got any tequila?"

"Behind the bar." She hitched her thumb back. "Second shelf next to the vodka."

"Don't move." He dragged his lips across hers.

She tapped her fingers against the side of the bar stool, wondering why he needed the tequila. She swiveled the chair around to see what he was doing. He found the tequila easily per her instructions, now he was ransacking the bar.

"Can I help you find something?" Her amusement was only going so far. If he didn't fuck her soon, she might change her mind.

"Lemon?"

"Middle of the bar, in that little cooler type thingy. Salt is down near the cash register."

Maybe a few shots was exactly what she needed to cool her burning skin. His touch electrified her.

He moved around the bar, collecting all the items he needed. Placing them on the counter one by one he asked, "Have you ever done body shots?"

"No." Though she'd seen some youngsters doing it a few times. She'd never understood what the big deal was.

"No time like the present to try your hand at it." He filled a shot glass full of the golden liquid. "We'll start off at your neck and work our way down."

His finger trailed down the front of her shirt over her skirt resting on her hot spot. Moisture pooled in her pussy from his faint touch.

"When do we get to the part where you fuck me?" It was a bold statement but she didn't care. It was all she could think about. His penis was bulging against his pants. He was ready. Why hold things up with shots?

"Soon. Very soon."

Her pussy ached.

He moved the strap of her tank top down over her arm, exposing her bare shoulder. His tongue rolled over her shoulder blade.

She trembled.

He sprinkled some salt on the spot he licked.

"Umm, this is going to be irresistible," he whispered.

"I was hoping it would be something better than shots," she retorted.

Reed lifted her chin and smiled at her. "Don't worry, Sierra. I'm going to fuck you. I promise. Over and over again. You'll be begging me to stop."

She grew weak under his touch. How many years had she waited to hear those words flowing from his lips? Now here she was, her body being used as a temple for shots.

"Okay," she whimpered.

"This nestles in here," he said, guiding the shot glass into the vee of her shirt. "I need you to push your beautiful breasts together for me."

She did as he instructed. Holding the shot glass between her breasts.

"Open wide," he said, holding the lemon in front of her.

"Why?" she protested.

"Humor me?"

She opened her mouth.

"Now, lightly close your teeth around the wedge, ever so gently."

She did.

"Perfect."

He bent, taking her earlobe in his mouth, sucking.

His warm breath sent chills racing through her body. He released her lobe and moved down her neck, leaving tiny kisses along the way.

"God you're beautiful," he whispered, before taking a nip of her shoulder. "I'm going to have fun with this body all night long."

Sierra tilted her head back giving him better access to her neck.

His tongue swiped the salt off her shoulder. He quickly moved to the shot glass resting in the vee of her shirt. His hands pressing against hers he squeezed her breasts tighter, lapping up the liquid in the shot glass and then he captured her lips, sucking the lemon. Juice dripped down her chin and he licked it away.

Tingling sensations filled her body. An orgasm was building. How the fuck was that happening?

She couldn't wait any longer to find out. Ridding her mouth of the bitter lemon, she tossed it aside, before she removed the shot glass from her shirt, which she also tossed on the bar. Grabbing hold of his belt buckle she tugged on it, until it loosened. She pulled it free from each loop and tossed it on the stool next to her.

She unbuttoned the top of his pants. Licking her lips, she had one thought in mind. His cock filling her.

Reed thought he was going to explode when he touched her skin. So soft and delectable. She was the same only more mature. He remembered the feel of her like he'd kissed her skin just yesterday.

"What are you doing?"

"Taking what I want." Her hand slid into the back of his pants. She squeezed a handful of his flesh. "I love this ass."

He tilted his head to meet her eyes. "Sierra, are you positive this is what you want?"

"Never been surer about anything in my life."

He shrugged. "Hot damn."

There was no waiting or taking his time anymore. She claimed she knew what she was doing and saying, who was he to argue? He hitched up her skirt exposing a perfectly trimmed pussy. She wasn't wearing underwear.

He placed her back on the stool.

Sliding his jeans down over his hips, he fumbled in the pocket, searching for the packet he'd purposely tucked in there earlier.

He tore a condom off and jammed the rest back into the pocket. Quickly he ripped the foil package and sheathed himself. One swift step and he was nudged against the opening to her pussy ready to fill her. Her juices pooled between her lips, inviting. Her pussy was ready.

"Any second thoughts?" He didn't want her having any regrets for what was about to happen. Because once his cock submerged into the depths of her cunt there was no turning back. Reed knew he wouldn't be able to stop once he was inside the woman he'd loved so long ago. The woman who still haunted his dreams.

Biting her lower lip she shook her head no.

Without hesitation he filled her.

She gasped.

"Sierra?" He didn't want to hurt her, in his desires to become one.

"Take me," she wrapped her arms around him. Nuzzling his neck, kissing him.

He moved closer, deeper.

She coiled her legs around his waist, giving him better access to her soaked pussy. The urge to jam his cock into her repeatedly, until he was spent, intensified but he didn't want to be that naïve schoolboy, so he fought the demands of his penis. He rocked his cock back and forth slowly, savoring the feel of her tight walls clenching against his cock. As he glided in and out, her pussy cemented what he already knew — they fitted perfectly together.

She arched her back and dipped her head back. Her hips moved picking up the rhythm he set. Her body fought against his need to go slow. She wanted him fast and hard, like the young man he used to be. Instead of denying the urges any longer, Reed matched her tempo and built on it.

He placed two strong hands on the bar, steadying himself. The taut muscles in his ass flexed as he pumped into her. The stirrings of his orgasm took over as blood filled his hard penis. He was going to come.

Sierra must have sensed his closeness along with her own orgasm budding. She removed her arms from around his neck and gripped onto the barstool, pushing her pussy, forcing him to go deeper.

His balls tightened and his seed began to work its way through his penis. Reed's fingers whitened as his grip tightened on the bar. Losing all sense of reality he pumped wildly into Sierra, as the walls of her pussy contracted against him. Draining him.

Reed released his hold on the bar and gathered Sierra in his arms. Her head fell against his chest, her breathing labored. As he struggled to catch his breath he prayed she wouldn't walk out of his life again leaving him hurt and confused.

Sierra knew once the intensity of the orgasm subsided that she had made a mistake. Having sex with Reed was a huge no-no. He was off limits for so many reasons. Her feelings for him, for one. After all this time she thought for sure she was over him. But the sex only proved her wrong big-time.

Ready to tell him this was a mistake and he should leave she looked up into his eyes. The eyes, brown speckled with green, had lost that haunted look from earlier, and it had been replaced with excitement and content.

She didn't have the heart to hurt him just yet. Hope lingered. Maybe she wouldn't have to hurt him.

Sweat glistened on his brow. She wiped it away with her finger.

He bent kissing the tip of her nose.

"That was incredible. You're incredible."

She buried her face in his chest afraid to look him in the eyes. "Yes, it was."

Her heart was breaking inside. She was torn between leading him on and wanting him in her life. And not only to fill the void of sexual satisfaction, though he did that well. She had walked away for a reason. A reason she had to remember or it could cost her her heart.

"Something wrong?"

He detected the trace of fear in her voice.

"Everything's right," he consoled. "Perfect."

Sliding out of her he deposited the condom in the garbage, behind the bar. He tugged his pants up leaving them unbuttoned. He wasn't done with her yet.

"Another shot?" he asked, holding up the tequila.

Her smile was forced. Was she regretting her decision? He sure as hell hoped not. He couldn't get enough of her and he was about to show her.

"How about the proper way this time."

Her nervousness didn't go undetected. She didn't want to do body shots, fine. He could do them the old-fashioned way. For now.

He filled two glasses. Handed her the salt. "You first."

She accepted the shaker and wet the back of her hand with her tongue. Then she sprinkled the salt on the wet spot.

Reed stood in front of her holding her shot along with her lemon. Her hand shook slightly as she reached for the glass. She licked the salt off, downed the shot and sucked the juice from the lemon in less than thirty seconds.

"Yuck!"

Reed chuckled. "Don't like the taste?"

"No," she said, through a pinched face. "Never have."

"Something else I can interest you in?"

She shook her head. "Not of the liquid form."

Was that an invitation? Had she given him the green light to continue this night or morning? It had to be three in the morning at this point but who was keeping track? Not Reed.

She hadn't fixed her skirt, leaving her pussy still exposed and ripe for the taking.

"How about something in the hard form?" His cock pulsed and grew harder just thinking about being inside her again.

"I...I think you might be on to—"

He eased her legs apart.

She moaned.

He knelt in front of her.

The scent of her arousal filled his nostrils. A scent so familiar. One he had longed for.

"Hand me the bottle of tequila please and the shot glass." He didn't look up at her, instead his eyes feasted on her swollen pussy lips and the swollen nub waiting—no begging—for him to suck it.

She handed him the bottle along with the shot glass, no questions asked.

He felt her eyes watching him as he poured more liquid into the shot glass. He dipped his finger into the glass, pulled it out and wiped it across her clit.

She flinched.

"Does it hurt?" He searched her face for any signs of pain.

"No. It's cold yet hot and burning but in a good way."

He blew lightly on her clit.

She shuddered.

He spread her lips open. Moving closer his tongue darted out, flicking the nub, the taste of tequila tingling on his tongue.

For Reed there was nothing more erotic then covering a woman's body with tequila and licking every last drop off. He tried ignoring his throbbing cock. He didn't want to rush into her again, not just yet. He had to taste her, to feast on her luscious honey. Then he would fuck her over and over until she was begging for mercy.

Lifting her foot, he kissed her muscled calf. He kissed his way up to her knee where he lingered. Her body quaked when his lips caressed the back of her knee. *Still ticklish.* He smiled remembering her pleasure spots. At one time he knew every inch of her body as if it were his own. He spent many nights caressing her feet, her breasts and kissing those hidden spots that turned her on so much.

Until that damned accident.

He shook the memories from his mind. There would be time for discussing the accident later, now he was a man on a mission and that was bringing Sierra to another mind-numbing orgasm.

He dipped his finger into the liquid then glided it into her wet folds. Sliding his finger in and out he covered her labia with the heady liquor.

His tongue pressed against the inside of her thigh.

"Salt," he requested.

She obliged and he sprinkled her thigh lightly.

"Lemon."

"Where could you possibly put that?" Her voice was indignant.

"Oh you'd be surprised at the places you can fit a lemon wedge." He held out his hand, giving her a wink.

Her eyes flashed uncertainty as she handed him a wedge.

"Trust me, you'll enjoy this."

She leaned against the back of the stool. "If you say so."

Was she doubting him? Reed loved nothing more than a challenge. He would show her just how much fun body shots could be.

The lemon fit nicely in the folds of her vagina. He still had perfect access to her clit. The magic button he would play with bringing her all sorts of excitement.

Once again he dosed her nub with tequila.

Licking the salt off her thigh, he pulled her clit between his teeth, flicking the nub with the salt. The mixture of salt and tequila invaded his mouth.

"Oh! My! God!" she cried.

Satisfaction filled him as he continued his assault on her clit. Her hands grabbed a hold of his hair and she pushed his head closer, demanding more.

He didn't disappoint. He sucked harder as her cries grew louder.

She was nearing a climax. He slid his finger into her waiting pussy. Slipping past the lemon, which he would use shortly, he finger-fucked her while lapping her clit. Her hands raked his hair, her legs enveloped his body.

One digit became two, the lemon wedge fell out. Reed no longer cared about the wedge. The only thing that mattered was bringing her to sweet orgasms, one after the other.

He didn't have to wait long until he felt the walls of her channel contracting against his fingers. Her breathing grew heavy and her moans more intense.

A few flicks of his tongue as he continued sucking and she was racing headfirst into orgasm. Her body shuddered against his fingers and mouth.

"Holy shit!" she howled.

"Now that's how a body shot is done," he said, resting on the backs of his heels, a wicked grin on his face.

Over and over she felt her pussy contracting, as multiple waves of orgasm rode through her, like a stampede of horses, trampling her body. That was the most delightful orgasm she'd ever experienced. He rocked her world. She couldn't argue, he knew his way around a body shot.

When she finally caught her breath she leaned forward and dragged him into a lazy kiss. She tasted the mixture of tequila and her juices on his lips. It tasted right. He was right, body shots were better than she'd ever dreamed.

Their tongues danced playfully as they explored the other's mouth. Her body was overheated she wanted to feel him inside her again. How could that be? He'd already filled her, then the orgasm he'd given her with his tongue. How could she possible be ready for more? But she was. She couldn't get enough of him.

She released his mouth. "Fuck me again, Reed."

Standing, he reached deep into his pocket pulling out a string of condoms.

"You've come very prepared." She smiled.

"Never leave home without them."

She snatched them from his hand and ripped one off with her teeth. "May I do the honors?"

He let out a low whistle. "Absolutely."

Wow. Who was this woman offering to sheath him? This wasn't like her, the shy timid Sierra. She was acting like a wanton woman but she liked taking what she wanted and the way he made her feel. She wanted to get to know this part of herself better.

Sierra shimmied off the barstool, pulling her skirt back into place.

"Tsk. Tsk. Tsk."

"What's the matter big boy?" she asked, hooking her fingers through his pant loops and dragging them down. "Afraid of the big bad wolf?"

"Not at all. I welcome her," he growled, as her hand wrapped around his shaft, stroking softly.

"Do you welcome this?" she asked, before swiping her tongue over the tip of his penis.

"Shit."

"And how about this?" She took the head of his cock in her mouth, gently sucking.

"You're killing me, Sierra," he muttered.

She removed her mouth. "Maybe I should stop. Wouldn't want a dead body in my bar."

"No, please. Don't stop."

She wrapped her lips around him, dragging her tongue down the length of him. She cupped his sac, kneading his balls gently.

"God that feels so fucking good. Your mouth is hot."

No need for words. She responded by taking him fully in her mouth. Every last inch, until the tip of his head touched the back of her throat. Then slowly she worked her way back, rolling her tongue along the deep throbbing vein.

She balanced herself by holding on to his muscular leg. She'd missed him more than she ever expected. The taste of him in her mouth was more than she could handle. She wanted to bring him to full climax like she had so many other times so long ago.

Thoughts of days when they were carefree and happy haunted her. Days when they would lay on a blanket near the ocean talking for hours, or out riding the Jet Skis, even long walks in the park. This was the man she had loved all her life, the man she was meant to be with, yet she couldn't. Instead she could offer him one night. One night of sex. A night neither would forget.

His fingers massaged her head as she continued lapping at his long, hard penis. He moved his hips creating an easy tempo, rocking in and out of her mouth. She felt him growing rigid, a sign he was nearing climax.

The condom long forgotten, she reveled in the taste of his pre-cum covering her tongue as it licked along the slit of his head.

"Sierra," he groaned.

Yes, she knew. Fisting his penis she bobbed her head up and down, with a renewed sense of urgency. Her lips met her hand, moving in sync. His cock began rippling under her touch as it started to erupt.

He roared out a string of obscenities as he poured his semen into her mouth. She sucked every last drop, swallowing his love.

"Fuck. I can't remember ever feeling so good in all my life," he said, lifting her to a standing position. "You amaze me. I'm so glad I found you again."

She fell into his welcoming arms, cherishing this time together and knowing she pleased him beyond belief. The pounding of his heart lulled her making her feel safe, secure. Was it possible? Could she have the life she dreamed about with Reed? Could she have her fairy tale ending?

"Me too, Reed." Her honesty rocked her to the core. She was genuinely happy Reed had walked back into her life. It was a part of her that was missing for a long time.

"We need to talk about the accident."

Chapter Three
ஐ

She went stiff in his arms. Why was she so against talking about the accident?

He released his hold on her and stepped back. "Sierra, it's the elephant in the room that no one wants to talk about but the fact of the matter is, we were in a horrific car accident together. Both of us have scars," he said, tracing his finger along the faded scar on her cheek. "We've never talked about what happened. We need our closure on this."

She turned away from him, leaving him standing alone and frustrated. She was clamming up on him. Damn her! He wasn't going to let her walk away this time, to ignore the fact that something terrible had happened.

Fuck he felt responsible for her scar. He lived with the fact that he drove the car that disfigured her face on that horrible fateful day. And her turning her back on him only proved she felt the same way. She blamed him too.

"I'm sorry for scarring you. I've never gotten over how much I hurt you. You have to believe I never meant for you to be harmed." He pulled his pants up as he spoke. It was like talking to a wall. She kept her back to him.

"Can't you at least look at me? Scream at me if it makes you feel better. Tell me I'm a monster and I ruined your life. Anything, Sierra. Just don't ignore me." He moved closer and touched her arm lightly.

She cringed and turned on him with a vengeance.

"I've suffered for many years with my scars, Reed. I don't blame you. I blame the asshole who hit us. It's not your fault. We were at a stoplight for Christ's sake. How would you know the idiot barreling up behind us would lose control of his brakes?"

"I—"

"Exactly," she said, venom seeping from each word but not for him. "You wouldn't. You're not the cause of this scar. Or these," she said, lifting her shirt.

He gasped.

Sierra quickly turned away from him, sobs racking her body.

"Sierra, I had no idea." Reed tried to gather her in his arms.

"Don't fucking touch me," she screamed, pushing out of his embrace. "I don't want your sympathy. I didn't want it then and I certainly don't need it now."

"I don't understand. Of course I sympathize with you. I was there. I dealt with the severity of the accident. I just hadn't realized how much scarring it left you with."

"Well now you know and you can leave."

"Leave? Why would I leave?" He stepped closer and she moved further away.

"I don't want you hanging around just because you feel like you owe it to me. To ease the guilt you feel over what happened. You weren't the cause of the accident. We were in the wrong place at the wrong time. So take your guilt somewhere else. I don't need it."

"I'm not leaving. This is ridiculous."

Banging on the front door startled them both.

"Who is it?" Sierra called out.

"Sheriff McCoy. Open the door."

She looked at Reed questioningly.

He shrugged. "Damn if I know what he wants."

Body Shots

He watched as she wiped away her tears, trying to conceal the hurt she felt. She unbolted the lock and opened the door, allowing the sheriff and another officer to enter the bar.

"Sorry to bother you ma'am but I'm here about an assault that took place earlier."

Reed stepped up behind Sierra, offering her support. She was in no way ready to answer the questions the sheriff had for her. And honestly she'd barely witnessed what took place.

"Yes, Sheriff. I'm the bouncer who took care of the incident in question. I'm Reed Walker."

"Well, Mr. Walker, you're under arrest."

"What?" Sierra and Reed said in unison.

"You're under arrest for the assault of Johnny McCoy. You have the right to remain silent..."

Reed tried to argue while the other officer cuffed him. The sheriff continued reading him his rights.

He looked at Sierra helplessly.

"Take him to the office and book him for aggravated assault," the sheriff said.

"Sheriff this is all a misunderstanding," Sierra offered.

"What the fuck do you mean aggravated assault?" Reed protested.

"Resisting arrest?" the sheriff asked, crowding Reed's face.

"No." What the fuck was going on? Was this some kind of joke? He was trying to stop a situation from getting out of hand and this is how he's repaid, by being arrested for assault charges? *Fucking great.*

"Sheriff McCoy, I think there's been some kind of mistake. Reed didn't assault anyone. He was preventing a raucous from going too far."

"I'm sorry about barging in here in the middle of the night, ma'am but we're taking your friend here down to the station. If you want to bail him out that's your business."

"No Sierra!" he demanded. "I'll be fine. Do *not* come bail me out."

Reed shook his head disgustedly. No sense in getting her involved in this stupid situation. He was sure once they got to the station and heard his side of the story it would all be cleared up.

They dragged him out to the waiting car and threw him into the backseat. He wanted to threaten them with an assault charge but knew he was better off if he kept his mouth shut. He didn't need to add any other charges in case this one stuck. As the police cruiser pulled away he spied Sierra staring out the window at him. He cursed himself for the sadness that filled her eyes. There was so much more to say but that opportunity was over. Thanks to some smart-ass punk he was being carted off to jail.

Unfuckingbelieveable.

* * * * *

Sierra paced the length of the bar wondering what had just happened? First they were in a heated discussion over the accident and then next thing she knew the police were here dragging him off to jail. She knew there was the possibility that Sheriff McCoy would be pissed about his son being thrown out of Crimson Nights but she thought his anger would be geared toward her, not Reed. He was only trying to help her and now he was in trouble. She had to go to the station. She had to bail him out. It was the right thing to do seeing as how he saved her bar from becoming ransacked. Yes, she had to bail Reed out, even if he told her no.

Locking the doors she headed to her car and drove in the direction of the station. With any luck she would have him out within the hour. God, she prayed Sheriff McCoy would come to his senses.

Getting Reed released wasn't as easy as she expected. It seemed the sheriff wanted to hold him for questioning in another incident. Sierra knew this was personal. There wasn't another incident. Just someone who stood up to his son. Someone who didn't care that he was the sheriff's son. Someone not afraid of the repercussions from throwing Johnny's sorry ass out on the street. Honestly, Sierra was happy Reed had been there and threw him out. Johnny could be quite the troublemaker when he wanted. Always getting drunk and belligerent. Something she didn't need in her bar. For the most part Crimson Nights was a small quiet bar, where people came to listen to good music, dance, hang out with their friends. It was a relaxing atmosphere. Except when Johnny and his friends came around. He constantly leered at her and frankly it gave her the creeps. But she ignored it because of who he was. Everyone knew if you messed with Johnny you'd be on the sheriff's shit list.

Besides she knew what Johnny was capable of and Sierra didn't do rowdy or fights. She left that for the other bars in the area. Johnny was the exception. She hadn't had the guts to kick him out. She allowed him to do what he pleased for the most part, afraid the sheriff would pull her liquor license if she screwed with his son. And the sheriff proved her point. He would screw with you if you messed with his son. Luckily, he hadn't sought revenge on her but she didn't feel good about him going after Reed.

Reed was the most honest-to-goodness man you could ever meet. He wouldn't cause anyone harm, he protected his own. But she wasn't his. As much as she wished she could be, she wasn't and couldn't.

"Ms. Allen?"

Sierra looked up to see a young officer looking at her questioningly.

"Yes."

"They're ready to release Mr. Walker."

"Oh, thank you." She stood and shook the officer's hand.

"You can meet him right down the hall." He pointed to where she should meet Reed.

"Thank you again." She hurried down the hall to find Reed. She didn't want to spend another minute in this place.

They were uncuffing him when she walked into the room. He was agitated, she could tell by the way green specks flared in his brown eyes. But he remained silent.

"Ready?" she asked.

"Most definitely." He turned to the officer who released his handcuffs. "I'm still free to go, right?"

"Yes but don't leave town."

"Not likely to."

Sierra wondered how he was going to stay in town. He didn't live in her small town. It was a fluke he was here in the first place. He lived two towns over. He had to leave to get home.

They walked to her car in silence. Sierra had a million questions running through her head but afraid to ask any of them. What happened in there was his business and if he wanted to share it with her he would. Until then she'd wait.

"Are you okay?" she asked, once they settled in her car.

"Fine. I wish you hadn't come down and bailed me out." He stared out the window.

"Why? It's the least I could do."

"Yeah. You've suffered enough because of me. You don't need to add this mess to the list."

She reached out and touched his leg. "I'm here because I want to be. No one made me come down here. And no one makes me do anything I don't want to do. You're here because of me."

"I'm here because I chose the wrong person to kick out of your bar." He turned to her. "But you know what? I'd do it again if it prevented a fight from breaking out. What that kid did tonight was wrong. You don't throw your drink at anyone, specially a lady."

A twinge of jealousy coursed through her veins at the mention of the drink incident. Was he interested in Lita? Is that why he picked a fight with Johnny McCoy? She could definitely see why a man would be interested in her. She was beautiful. Flawless. Everything Sierra wasn't.

"Hello, Earth to Sierra."

"What? Oh...sorry. What did you say?"

He intertwined their fingers. "I said, thank you." He kissed the tips of each finger.

She melted under his touch. "You're welcome."

"Can you take me back to my truck and I'll be out of your way, finally."

She put the car in gear and hit the accelerator. He was ready to leave. Would this be their last goodbye? Would she finally have the closure she'd been looking for?

"I thought I heard them say you can't leave town."

He laughed.

"What's so funny?"

"I think the kid watched too many cop shows growing up. I mean seriously. Do you think they can't find me? I'm not that far away. They have all the details from my license, including my home address."

Sierra didn't find this humorous. She was afraid for him. What if they had meant it? What if he left and they brought him back to jail? Then what? She shook the thought from her mind. What was really going on in her head? Was she panicking? Afraid if he left town he'd leave her for good?

That was the way it had to be, wasn't it? Those were the boundaries she set up when she allowed Foul Play to play in her bar. One night. One night for closure. Now he was sitting in the passenger seat of her car and Sierra wasn't so sure she was ready for the closure she thought she was seeking all along.

"Why don't you stay at my house," she suggested.

Her fingers wrapped around the steering wheel tightly waiting for his answer. Had she really offered up her house to him? The idea of having him in her house, in her bed was ludicrous. It was bad enough she'd allowed him to fuck her in the bar. Bringing him home would make it that much more personal. A level she wasn't ready to go to with anyone, not even Reed Walker.

"The sun will be coming up soon and I'd like to get some sleep. Are you sure you don't mind me crashing at your place?"

"Not at all." She let out the breath she hadn't realized she was holding. Reed was coming home. To sleep in her bed.

* * * * *

"Nice place you have here," Reed said, as they entered her apartment over the bar.

"It works for me."

"I'm sure it does." It was small but not too small for one person. And she had the best commute to work. "Do you like living over the bar?"

"You mean because of the noise? I'm in the bar most of the time anyway, so it doesn't bother me. And if I happen to have the night off I deal. It's my bread and butter."

He nodded in agreement.

"Please feel free to sit." She pointed to the couch.

With all her overstuffed decorative pillows, he wondered how she sat on the couch. Being polite he took a seat. She was offering him a place to crash after all.

"If you like you can sleep in my bed and I'll take the couch."

"Oh," he said, surprised. He was hoping to have her wrapped in his arms. Not another room away from him.

"What is it?" she questioned.

"I just thought... I hoped that maybe you would..."

"Would what?"

"Let me hold you," he confessed. He didn't care if they didn't have sex. All he wanted to do was hold her in his arms, close to him. But he could see she was struggling with the idea. Why? Why didn't she want to be close to him?

"Reed, I..." She patted her legs and sprang off the couch. "It's not that I don't find the thought of being in your arms appealing, it's just that I'm tired."

She was lying. He saw the way she averted her eyes when she spoke. It wasn't about being tired.

"I promise I won't take advantage of you. You can keep your clothes on. I just want to hold you." This time he lied. His cock grew stiff just thinking about her being in his arms. He wanted to slide inside her and pump his seed into her over and over until they were both too sore to move. But he would do the gentlemanly thing like he said and just hold her.

"You promise."

Was that a hint of relief in her eyes? A promise to keep her clothes on and she was thinking about his offer?

"I swear."

Her shoulders sagged in obvious relief. She turned and stared out the window.

"I'll be on my best behavior." God, he hoped he could keep his cock under control.

"Okay." She kept her back to him. What was bothering her so much?

He stood and stepped over to where she stood looking out the window. He placed his hand on the small of her back.

"Are you okay?" He didn't want to force her to do something she didn't want to do.

"Yes, I'm fine." She smiled up at him. "Just tired. Ready for bed?"

"Lead the way."

Her bedroom was not how he pictured it. The deep dark colors of the furniture and the bed set were in contrast to the pale colors he'd imagined. The walls were painted a grayish color. Definitely not what he imagined.

"You've got a gothic style going on."

"Yes, I like my room."

He sensed her irritation. He wasn't trying to insult her.

"I like it. I just thought being a woman and all you'd have girly colors."

She laughed.

"What?"

"You're such a guy. Just because I'm a woman I should have pinks, purples or yellows? These colors represent my heart and what it feels most of the time."

Ouch. Did she think she had a bleeding heart? Was her bleeding heart from the years they spent apart?

"I didn't mean to offend you. I'm sorry."

"No worries." He watched her retrieve a pair of panties from the dresser drawer and slip them on. She slipped off her skirt and laid it on the edge of the bed.

"I know I promised you could keep your clothes on but I hate sleeping with anything on. Is that going to be a problem for you?"

"Nope." She scooted under the covers with her shirt and panties still intact. Lifting the covers up to her chin.

Reed shrugged out of his clothes, down to total nakedness and slipped under the blankets next to her. The satin sheets caressed his back and bare ass. He couldn't understand how she could sleep with clothes on in these sheets. It was like heaven.

He reached his arm out offering her a place to rest her head. She accepted and cuddled into the crook of his arm.

"I could stay in your bed forever." He felt her grow stiff in his arms. "These sheets are divine." She relaxed again. What was going on inside her? Did she not want him here? If that was the case why had she offered him a place to sleep?

"I'm glad you approved." She snuggled deeper into his embrace.

She yawned.

"Am I keeping you awake?" he asked. He kissed the top of her head. And before he knew what was happening his cock came alive. Sierra had that effect on him. She stirred emotions he'd long since forgotten existed and that scared the hell out of him.

"No, just thinking."

"About?" Maybe she was thinking about the accident and wanted to finally talk about what happened. That would be an improvement but Reed wasn't so sure he wanted to talk about it right now. Not when he had an impressive hard-on going on. It was a shame to waste a good erection when he had a beautiful woman in his arms.

"This," she said wrapping her hand around his shaft.

"Oh," was all he could muster to say. He was too shocked. He thought his invitation was for sleeping only. He didn't think he was going to get lucky again.

She continued stroking him. He moved his hips with her slow steady strokes. He wanted to be inside her wet pussy, caressing the walls of her cunt. He wanted to feel his balls slapping against her ass cheeks.

He groaned.

"You don't like."

"Oh I like. I like way too much." He pulled her closer, searching for her mouth. In a hurried desperation he captured her lips.

His hand reached out for her breasts. He massaged her breast through the fabric separating his hand and her tender skin. He wanted her naked, beneath him. He moved to lift her shirt up, to touch her skin.

Her hand clasped over his.

"Sierra?" In the darkness he searched her eyes for answers.

"The shirt remains on," she said, through gritted teeth.

Damn, what was going on? He'd seen the scars. So why was she making such a big deal out of this.

"If you insist," he said releasing his hold on her shirt.

"I do." She softened when she realized he wasn't going to push the issue.

But he planned to, just not now. He was too horny and too exhausted to fight her now.

His hand slipped down and he rubbed his finger against her clit.

"Can these come off?"

"If you're a good boy," she teased.

"Oh I can be a good boy." He flipped her on her back and straddled her, pinning her to the bed. "I can be a very good boy."

The streetlight shone in her face, providing Reed with a look of terror. She looked like a deer caught in the headlights.

"Sierra, what's wrong?" he scooped her into his arms. "Please don't be afraid of me. I only want to bring you pleasure."

"I'm not afraid," she said, pushing out of his arms. "I just want to be clear that my shirt remains on."

"I'm not going to do anything you don't want me to. I wasn't going to tear your clothes off. I've never forced myself on a woman and I'm not about to start now."

He rolled off her to his side of the bed and turned his back to her. He was hurt and angry. He would never do anything to betray her trust. Not in a million years.

"Good night, Sierra." He couldn't bear to see the look on her face. That look of fear haunted him, rocking him to the core. He'd seen it once before when they were in the car accident and she looked to her left only to find him not there. But relief came when she looked behind her and found him in the backseat.

She touched his back. "I'm sorry, Reed. I'm not trying to hurt you. I know you would never do anything to hurt me. I panicked."

Her sorrow filled his heart, breaking him inside.

"It's okay," he said softly. "Get some rest. It's been a long night."

She eased away and he sensed she turned away. What the fuck just happened? He only wanted to make love to the woman he'd missed for so long and she freaked. Freaked like he was going to rape her or something. He'd never hurt her. He had to make this right.

He rolled over and spooned her.

"I'm sorry." He kissed her neck.

"Me too."

He held her tightly afraid to let go. He planted tiny kisses over her neck and shoulder.

"Want to start over?" she asked.

"Yes."

Her hand reached behind her and she stroked his manhood for a second time. He didn't wait, his hand sought her pussy. Dipping into her panties, his finger slipped into her folds. She was still nice and wet.

Desire crept up his skin. His balls tightened with each stroke of her soft hand. He wanted to plunge into the depths of her cunt. But he refrained. He would move at her pace, for fear he'd scare her again.

She moaned when his finger entered her channel. She pushed her bottom against his stiff cock. His finger slid in and out coating her lips with her sweet honey. Her folds swelled under his touch.

It was all he could do to not fist his penis and ram it into her waiting pussy.

"Are you sure?"

She moaned again and brushed her finger over his leg.

"Condom," she uttered.

Reed removed his finger and reached for his pants. He still had some left. He pulled out the remaining few, removed one and tossed the others aside. He quickly sheathed himself. He spooned her again when he realized she wasn't going to offer herself any other way.

He nestled his cock at the entrance to her pussy. Brushing his lips across her shoulder he whispered, "Last chance to change your mind."

"Never."

His cock nestled into her hot channel. Her juices coated the condom allowing him to glide in with ease. When he filled her to the brim, she pushed him deeper.

"Fuck me, Reed," she whispered.

Gripping her hip Reed ground his cock further into her canal, her slickness heating his penis. She felt so right.

He guided her left leg up onto his so he could have better access to her clit. As he rocked into her tight walls, his finger rubbed her clit in tiny circles.

"Oh Reed. That feels so incredible."

He picked up the pace, his finger rubbing harder against the nub. She bucked her hips back against him, demanding him to fill her deeper and deeper while he played with her magic button.

Her cries of ecstasy were making him lose his grip on reality. She was so vocal.

"Yes. Yes. Rub harder. Fuck me. That's it."

Reed tried to focus on fucking her and not on her cries of glory.

"I'm going to explode all over your cock, Reed."

He didn't know who this Sierra was but he liked her. He loved the way she demanded what she wanted. How she told him what was going on with her body.

He wanted to reach up and tweak her nipple but knew he couldn't. He had to keep his hands below her waist and nowhere else or he could risk losing her forever.

Increasing his speed, Reed dragged his finger up and down her folds, teasing her clit. His cock drove into her slick pussy with a fierceness Reed didn't know existed.

"Oh. My. God. It's... I'm... Oh, fuck." She grabbed a pillow and clung to it. Muffling the last of her screams.

Reed felt her pussy contracting against his cock. Her body shuddered while she rode through the orgasm. He didn't let up on rubbing her clit. Her body responded by continuing to climax over and over. When her body began to settle Reed wasted no time in starting over again. He wanted to hear her cry out all morning long.

As he pumped into her again he felt the building of his own orgasm. Wanting to hear her lovely voice crying out his name, begging him to make her come harder, he rubbed her swollen clit.

She cried out as he emptied his seed into the condom. They lay both trying to catch their breath. Reed gathered her close. Their sweat mingled together as he kissed her neck.

"Oh Reed. I never knew my body could handle so many orgasms."

"You haven't seen anything yet," he promised. He nibbled on her earlobe. Reed wanted to open her body to new experiences. Show her how much pleasure two people could have.

"Mmm." She ran her fingernail over his leg. "I can't wait for round two."

Reed slipped out of bed and discarded the condom in the bathroom. He returned to snuggle close to her.

She rested her head on his chest as he held her. She felt right in his arms again. Perfect. He wished he could put them in a time capsule and stay like this forever.

Chapter Four

Sierra thought she'd died and gone to heaven when she woke the next day. Until she reached out her hand to pull Reed closer, wanting to hear the steady beating of his heart, only to find his side of the bed empty.

Her pussy ached but she wanted him again. And again. And again. She couldn't get enough of him.

She listened closely for the sound of the shower or the smell of coffee brewing. Nothing. In fact the only thing she was certain of was the dead silence. She felt eerily alone.

Jumping out of bed, panic filled her. She searched every room only to come up empty. She returned to the bedroom ready to cry. He'd left her. This time he turned the tables on her.

Then she spotted it. A note sitting on the nightstand.

Thanks for letting me crash. Had to run. Talk to you soon.

That was it. Short and not so sweet. The only evidence he was ever there was her sore pussy, a few love marks on her neck and a note.

Well that had been two weeks ago and still no word from Reed. She should be thankful he hadn't contacted her. But she wasn't. She was hurt. Empty inside. She longed for him. To see him again. Longed to feel his strong protective arms wrapped around her.

The only good thing that came out of that night was that Johnny hadn't returned to her bar. For whatever reasons he stayed away and that was fine with her. She didn't need trouble in her establishment.

She was on the phone when Reed walked through the door. He strutted over to the bar, as if he'd never walked out of her life.

"Listen Lita, someone's here. I'm sorry you're feeling sick but don't worry about it. I'll figure something out for tonight. You rest and I'll talk to you soon."

She hung up and walked over to him. "What can I get for you?"

"Sounds like you're in need of a band tonight. I know it's short notice but I can pull the guys together to help you out if you'd like."

"I don't think so, Reed. You should just walk back out that door and pretend you never entered my bar in the first place."

"Hey, what's going on?" He reached out to grab her hand but she pulled away.

"I don't need you here messing up my life. I was fine before you showed up." Fine and not heartbroken.

"Did I do something?"

"Ha. It's what you didn't do," she spat.

"What didn't I do?"

"Where should I start? Let's see. You left with barely a note. You haven't called or come by in what? Two weeks? So was I just a booty call?" Why was she getting into this with him? It didn't matter. Because in all honesty he could only be a booty call. She couldn't admit she still felt something for him. She couldn't act on those feelings. She had to push him away and for good this time.

"Sierra. You were never a booty call. I'll be honest. I was a bit worried that I was a booty call when you wouldn't take your shirt off and I don't want to cause you any more pain but you have to trust me when I say I'd never use you. I needed time to think."

"Think about what."

"A way for us to get over all this pain."

"And what brilliant solution did you come up with?" Because she couldn't think of any way for them to get past the pain. It ran too deep for too long.

"I've decided if you don't want to talk about the accident I won't push. I'll wait until you're ready. And when you are, I'll be by your side waiting."

"You'll be waiting a lifetime, because I'm never going to be ready to talk about the accident."

"Do you need me to call the guys and see if they're available tonight?"

So he wanted to change the subject, did he? Fine by her.

Her head told her to say no, to refuse his offer to help but her heart pulled at her to say yes. She needed them tonight. People were expecting a band and if she didn't have one, they would find somewhere else to hang for the night. The thought of potentially losing all that money made her act sensibly.

"Okay. I'd really appreciate that."

"Awesome. Let me call the guys and arrange it."

Maybe she could arrange for Henry to work tonight. Alone. If she took the night off then she wouldn't have to worry about *after* the show. When Reed might linger. Lingering would lead to other things. Things her heart wasn't ready to do again. She already struggled with the demons from their last encounter. She thought having sex with Reed would be therapeutic, healing. Wrong. It only proved how much she still loved him. And she wanted more of him.

Yes, taking the night off would be the smartest plan for tonight.

"They had such a good time last time, they all agreed to fill in."

She smiled. "I'm grateful for the last minute offer. I would have understood if they couldn't." *Probably been relieved too.*

"We can use the exposure and the cash. Besides, I like playing here. We've been playing at a lot of different clubs lately but Crimson Nights is by far the best one."

His compliment touched her. She liked to think she had a decent place and to have him validate it, made her feel warm inside.

"That's nice to hear. Nice to know I'm keeping up with the competition."

"I'd say you're a step above the competition."

"So what brings you here today?" *And how long before you leave again?* Being alone with him was not a good idea. Not one patron was here today, yet.

"Court."

"Oh, how did that go?"

"Good. I had to pay a fine."

"Fine? Does that mean they dropped the charges?"

"Sort of. I don't think I deserved the fine but the alternative is worse, so I paid it. Fucking kid. He causes trouble and I pay the price."

She knew all too well. "Johnny's been like that for as long as I can remember. He uses his father's power for his personal gain. He's trouble with a capital T. I prefer him to not come into my bar but I don't need the headache that comes along with keeping him out."

"I guess," he muttered.

"Can I offer you something to drink?" *Or a taste of my pussy?* Where had that come from? She wanted to stay away from him, not fall back into the sack.

"No, I have to run, especially if we're gonna play tonight. But I'll take a rain check, after the show."

She knew what he was implying and there was no way she was spending the night with him. Even if she was dying to feel his cock filling her pussy to the brim. Or having him do shots off her body.

"Yeah, a rain check." She plastered a false smile on her lips.

"See ya tonight." He tapped the bar then hurried off.

"Tonight," she whispered. "Not if I can help it."

Reed had a swing in his step as he strode out to his truck. He was one lucky dude. Finding Sierra after all this time. She was so beautiful. The scars didn't bother him. It pained him to think he was the cause but it didn't change how much he loved her, then or now. If anything he loved her more. She was a beauty. Strong. Sexy. Sexy wasn't the word. She was drop-dead gorgeous. He couldn't wait to strip her clothes off and enjoy every last inch of that sensual body.

He was going to claim her as his tonight. He let her disappear ten years ago but never again.

He planned to make her Mrs. Reed Walker once and for all.

* * * * *

Reed didn't see the humor in her taking the night off. She was intentionally avoiding him. Why? He thought they were getting along better. Shit, she looked hurt earlier. He thought for sure he was making headway. Was this payback for his silence? He couldn't help it. The fact that she wouldn't let him get a close look at the scars really bothered him. Yes, she flashed them at him and yes in his stupidity, he gasped, but he hadn't realized the extent of her injuries. Maybe he deserved payback for overreacting. He had so many thoughts filling his mind, like the idea she might have a bleeding heart. These were things caused by him. His doing. And the thought of bringing her more pain tore at his heart. So he stayed away. And what a mistake that had been.

He wasn't putting up with her disappearing act. Not again. He knew where she lived. She couldn't hide.

He sang his heart out, knowing she was just above him. Did she hear him belt out the love song he'd written for her? He imagined her upstairs drowning out the sound of his voice. Well she could try to hide but he wasn't having any of it. He was going to show her once and for all they were meant to be together. Whether she liked it or not.

As the crowd died down and the band packed their things for the night, Reed hung around hoping she would come down to close up the bar for the night. He figured he was out of luck and decided to call it a night.

Though he was tempted to go banging on her back door, he knew it was late. Tomorrow was another day. He wasn't letting her off the hook scot-free. She would eventually have to face him.

He neared the door when he heard Henry say hello. "I didn't expect you, Sierra."

Reed froze.

He waited.

"I didn't expect to come down either but I thought the coast would be clear and I would check on you."

Reed cleared his throat and turned.

Her eyes widened at the realization he was still here.

"Sierra?"

"Reed. I didn't think… I thought you—"

"Thought I'd be gone by now. Thought you could avoid me?" Three long strides brought him face to face with her.

"Why are you avoiding me? I thought we had a date for tonight."

"A date? I never agreed to a date."

He watched her face go from shock to distraught. Fear filled her emerald eyes.

He reached out and traced the tip of his finger over her lips.

"Our rain check? I think I'd like that drink now."

She closed her eyes.

"Sierra," he whispered.

She backed away. "Henry I'll finish closing. You can take off."

"You sure?"

Reed watched the exchange between owner and employee. Henry was looking out for Sierra's best interest. Something Reed appreciated. He liked knowing she was safe when Henry was around. A backup for when he couldn't protect her.

"I'll be fine. Reed and I have some business to discuss."

"I paid him," Henry declared.

"I know. We have other things to discuss." Her words were soft, where he was harsh. Henry was leery of Reed and he didn't blame him. Why should he trust a total stranger alone with his boss. Especially a stranger who was making her do things out of her norm.

Yes, they had things to discuss. Like why she was avoiding him.

"You're the boss." Henry grabbed his coat and headed out the door.

Finally Reed had her alone. Time to show her why they were meant to be together.

Sierra's body went into overdrive as Reed approached her. This was the reason she hid upstairs. Her body deceived her whenever he was close. Her head knew they couldn't be together but her heart and body had a mind of their own.

He wrapped his arms around her waist. She felt his bulge against her back. She wanted him inside her. She shook the thoughts from her mind. She had to end this once and for all. She had to make it clear there wasn't going to be a repeat performance of their night together.

She turned, ready to lay her cards on the table.

He captured her lips. His tongue plunging into her mouth, invading. He tasted of tequila, reminding her again of their night together.

She melted into his arms, accepting his kisses.

His hard penis rubbed against her.

She moaned.

Just one more time. One last time and that was it. Because she couldn't continue to do this. But what would it hurt if she had him inside her one more time.

Nothing.

She pushed away. "I have an idea."

She rushed to the bar and picked up a bottle of strawberry schnapps and a shot glass. "Body shots, with *my* favorite liquor."

He rested his lean muscular frame against the pool table. "Strawberry schnapps? That's a sissy drink." His green speckles teased.

"Really. Then I guess you don't want to see what I can do with a bottle of schnapps? I think you'll regret it in the morning."

Their easy banter intrigued her. It was natural, like they'd been together forever. She'd forgotten what it felt like to have an easy rapport with a man. But they weren't a couple. This was sex and only sex. In the morning they would go their separate ways and she'd never ask his band back to her bar. She'd never let him back into her heart. It was way too risky.

"I'm all yours," he said, spreading his arms wide.

At least for the moment. If she was going to do this, she might as well go out with a bang.

She placed the stuff on the pool table.

"I think you have too much clothing on," she said, tugging his shirt from his pants. "I want to see more of this body."

Reed bent his head allowing her to remove the shirt with ease.

She traced her fingers down either side of his ribs, over his tight abs. He was perfect. So fucking perfect.

Unlike me.

She pushed the thoughts out of her head. Tonight she wanted to be with Reed.

Needed him.

The tip of her finger circled his nipple, forming a hardened bud.

Reaching for the bottle she dipped her finger into the contents. She licked it from her finger. "Mmmm."

"Tease."

She smiled sucking on her finger.

He tried pulling her close.

"No. No. No." She pushed against his hard chest. "This is my show."

He let out a deep breath. "If you insist."

Dipping her finger back in, she covered his nipple in the sweet liquid, then licked it off.

He groaned.

She repeated with the other one. She followed the line of hair that led deep into the confines of his pants where his god-like penis waited for her. Waiting to bring her glorious pleasure.

"Lay back, big boy," she instructed.

"Here on the pool table?"

"Why not?"

He shrugged. "Damned if I know."

He hopped onto the table.

"Wait!" She shouldn't do this. This was a bad idea. But she wanted it. Needed it. Fuck it all. She was going for it.

"What?"

"Never mind."

Reed laid his body across the pool table as she requested.

"Why don't you join me?" He slung his arm around her shoulder pulling her down to his level.

His warm breath tickled her ear. "Maybe I will."

He released her.

Regaining her composure she strutted around the table, looking for the best angle to cherish his body. She stopped and poured herself a shot.

"Care for one?" she asked, offering him the shot glass.

"This is your show, remember. I'll just lay here and enjoy." He folded his arms behind his head.

She tossed back the liquid. A small bite at the back of her throat, nothing too harsh. Just the way she liked it.

She poured another. This time she used it to pour into his round belly button.

He squirmed, sending liquid dripping down his side.

Sierra quickly lapped the alcohol off him.

"Now this is what I call a shot." She worked her way up to the rest of the schnapps. Covering the hole with her lips she sucked, dragging the alcohol into her mouth. Taking a step back she swallowed.

Reed was right. Doing body shots was erotic. Sexy. Seductive. Electricity coursed through her veins.

She climbed onto the pool table and straddled him. Heat radiated off his body, sending her libido into overdrive. Her pussy juices soaked her panties. Her oversensitized nipples yearned to feel his mouth wrapped around them, sucking, pinching and biting.

She wanted him but she wanted to taste his skin covered in strawberry schnapps again.

Body Shots

Downing another shot, she smiled wickedly at him. Never had she had a man under her, in her control. Having Reed under her spell was delish.

"You're enjoying yourself aren't you?" He reached up and touched her cheek. "You're beautiful Sierra."

She leaned against his hand.

"Let me make love to you."

She shook her head. No. No making love. Making love required feelings. She wasn't about to admit feelings. This was strictly sex. Sex for the sake of sex.

Filling the shot glass she swallowed back the pain creeping up in her throat, threatening to expose her feelings.

One more.

"Ready to be seduced, Reed?"

Sadness filled his eyes but she ignored it. Pushed any thoughts that she might have hurt him with her rejection right out of her head. She'd concentrate on bringing him pleasure then she'd fuck his brains out.

Reed wasn't sure what was going through her mind but he knew she was struggling with her feelings.

Good. It meant she felt something. He wondered for a moment if she was capable of caring for him. It would kill him if she couldn't. Because he loved her. Loved her with every ounce of his being.

If she wanted to pretend they weren't making love, he'd go along with it. But in the end she'd come to realize it wasn't just sex. It was much much more.

Her finger grazed his nipple as she covered him in the cold liquid again. She drove him mad. He wanted to plunge his cock deep inside her. Feel the walls of her pussy quivering around him.

He ached. His cock ached to be free but he was at her mercy. He had to wait for her set the pace.

He had to admit having her straddled over him doing shots off his stomach was a major turn-on. Her vixen attitude.

When she unbuttoned his jeans and freed his cock he sighed with relief. She inched his pants down over his hips leaving his cock standing at attention, begging to be wrapped in her sweet juices.

Instead of wrapping her pussy lips around his cock she covered him in schnapps, immediately followed by the warmth of her mouth.

"Oh God, Sierra," he muttered.

She teased him with her glorious tongue. Lapping up every last drop. She licked the pre-cum from his slit, sending tremors through his body. He wanted to fill her, erupt inside her.

"I need to be inside you," he whispered.

She took the throbbing head of his cock fully in her mouth, gently sucking.

"Fuck." He'd meant inside her cunt but this would work too.

As she worked her way up the center of his shaft he shuddered. She was killing him. Torturing him. He wanted to pull off her sweatpants and drive his hard cock into her. It took all he had to refrain.

Her head bobbed up and down. Devouring him like a lollipop. When the tip of his cock hit the back of her throat he thought he was done. He thought for sure he'd explode inside her.

She eased her mouth back slowly, lingering.

"I can't hold on much longer," he choked.

Her eyes caught his and sparkled with delight. She resumed her assault on his cock. Lips wrapping around him. Mouth descending, then climbing back up. Her tongue tickling his pulsing vein along the way.

Her hand cupped his balls, massaging. He was going to come. There was no more holding back. No more refraining. He had to let loose and she was urging him with her wet lips.

He pumped his hips, filling her mouth to the hilt. Fucking her mouth felt so good. So right. As his seed poured into her waiting mouth he cried out.

"I love you, Sierra."

If his words registered in her head she didn't let on. She continued draining him until there wasn't a drop of cum left. She crouched over him and opened her mouth to speak.

"Well, well, well. Looky here," a familiar voice said from behind her. "Looks like I caught Sierra in a very compromising position."

Reed swung her off him ready to attack the intruder. "Get the fuck out or I'll lay a beating on you."

"I'd be careful who you're threatening there tough guy." Johnny held a baseball bat in his hand, casually slapping it against his free hand.

"I suggest you leave."

Johnny walked behind the bar and swung the bat across a row of liquor bottles. "I don't see it the way you do. In fact I'm not leaving until I decide I'm leaving."

He swung again, shattering more bottles.

"Please Johnny, just go. Why do you have to wreck my place?"

"Because you called the cops. You had my father's peons come and haul me out of here. For what? This loser?"

"I don't want any trouble, Johnny. He was only trying to keep the peace."

Reed quickly pulled his pants up to his waist as he watched the little fucker destroy the bar. He wanted to wring his scrawny little neck for bringing pain upon Sierra.

"Your beef is with me. Leave her out of it," he insisted.

"Yes, my beef is with you. Who the fuck do you think you are? I told you you'd be sorry for messing with me and I meant it."

Reed covered Sierra as Johnny moved closer.

"You can try to protect her all you want but once I flatten your ass out, I'm going to fuck her. Yup that's right. I'm gonna stick my cock in your woman's pussy and she's going to be begging for more." His evil laugh filled the room.

"You'd like that wouldn't you, Sierra?" He tried moving closer but she scrambled to the end of the pool table. Reed stepped in front of him.

"I said your beef is with me."

Johnny swung the bat, aiming for Reed's head. Reed ducked and lunged tackling him.

Sierra let out an ear-piercing scream.

They wrestled on the floor and the bat went rolling away. Johnny slipped out of Reed's grip and dived for the bat. He grabbed it and came up swinging, hitting Reed on the back of the head, sending him reeling to the ground into a crumbled heap.

"No. Reed!"

Sierra saw the anger in Johnny's black eyes. She searched the bar for an escape. She was trapped. Any way she tried to flee he'd catch her. And with the bat still in his grip she didn't want to end up like Reed. She had to keep her wits about her to save him.

There was no blood spilling from his head, so hopefully that was a good sign.

"So this is the type of guy you long for?" He slammed the bat against the pool table.

She jumped and let out a yelp.

"Is it?"

"What are you talking about, Johnny?" She couldn't understand why he cared what her type was.

"Do you enjoy having his cock fucking you, whore?"

"Johnny, why are you doing this? What did I ever do to you?" Inside she was terrified but she had to try to conceal her fear. It would only please him more to know he frightened her. She had to remain strong if they were going to get out of this in one piece.

"Nothing," he spat. "Nothing at all. You wouldn't even give me the time of day. I could make you happy."

Was he serious? Why would she be interested in someone so much younger than her? And since when was he interested in her? He never showed signs. Yes, he hung around the bar a lot but he never spoke to her. Unless his leers were his way of showing her he was interested. Yuck!

"Johnny, I'm not looking for anyone to make me happy. I'm happy being alone." She tried reasoning with him.

He laughed, an evil cackle.

"Really? Is that why I found you giving him a blowjob?" He spat towards Reed. "Maybe I should whip out my cock and let you have a little sucky?"

She cringed as he reached for the button on his pants.

"Johnny, Reed and I...we have a past. We were looking to see if we had a future."

"And?" He dangled the bat, reminding her he could knock her out cold at any moment.

"And that's it. It's a past, with no hope for the future."

"Good because we deserve a future." He stepped closer to her. With his free hand he grabbed her hair. "You are mine, understood?"

With her head twisted back and his face mere inches from her, Sierra knew she needed to remain calm. There was emptiness, yet hatred in his eyes.

"Yes," she said weakly. She prayed he wouldn't lay a hand on her. But then again maybe if he saw her scars it would scare him away, like other men before.

"Johnny, I don't think you'd want me if you seen the real me."

"Don't go trying to use some psychobabble on me."

"I'm not. My body is scarred. Some say it's scary looking. You don't want someone who's all scarred up do you?" *Please dear god let him just leave.*

"Show me," he said, releasing his hold on her hair.

She rubbed her head.

"I said show me. Now." He cracked the bat once more against the pool table.

She flinched.

"Sierra!"

She lifted her shirt, revealing her scars.

She watched him wince but he continued to stare. Almost fascinated. He reached out and touched her.

"Did he do this to you?" he demanded.

"Who, Reed? No. This was an accident. It was no one's fault."

The bat dropped to the floor with a thump. Johnny pushed himself on her sending her backwards on the pool table. He clawed at her sweatpants trying to get them off. His other hand groping her.

She wanted to cry out from his touch, his rough hands scratching at her skin. But she remained silent, knowing if she uttered the wrong word she'd be in trouble.

"Johnny, please," she begged. "Don't do something you'll regret."

"I'd never regret fucking you." His words dripped like venom in her ear.

"Please," she said, quietly.

His fingers wrapped around her breast, kneading it painfully. She closed her eyes silently praying he'd get off her and leave. She prayed he didn't rape her.

"Johnny!" an unfamiliar voice shouted. "Get off her immediately."

Sierra opened her eyes to see Sheriff McCoy standing over her, alongside him Henry. Dear God, her prayers were answered.

"Dad, leave me alone. This is between me and Sierra."

"No, son. This is between you and me. You can't push yourself on a woman. And look at the damage you've caused."

Relief washed over Sierra as Johnny pushed off her. She thought he was going to surrender to his father but was sadly mistaken. He bent over reaching for the bat. He lunged forward swinging at his father and Henry. Both moved quickly before he could make contact. Out of the corner of her eye, Sierra saw Reed sitting up, rubbing the back of his head.

"Oh. Dear. God." She swallowed back the fear that crept into her throat. *Don't let him hurt Reed again.*

Sheriff McCoy and Henry tackled Johnny. Henry ripped the bat from his hands and tossed it aside, while the sheriff handcuffed his son.

"Dad, why the fuck are you doing this to me? You can't arrest your son."

"I can and I am, son. You've thought you're above the law for too long and it's time someone showed you you're not." He lifted his son off the floor and held him by the handcuffs.

He turned to Sierra.

"I'm terribly sorry for what my son has done. We'll pay for all the damages he's caused and it's likely you won't be seeing him for a long time."

Reed stood and staggered over to Sierra.

"Are you okay?" she cried.

"I think so but my head is pounding."

She wrapped her arms around him. "I was afraid he killed you."

"Nothing is going to keep me from you."

"You plan on pressing charges?" the sheriff asked Reed.

He nodded. "I sure do."

"We'll see you at the station then."

"Yes, you will."

The sheriff dragged Johnny out. He cursed and threatened until they couldn't hear them anymore.

Sierra turned to Henry.

"What were you doing with Sheriff McCoy?"

"When I was leaving I saw Johnny's car parked down the road. So I circled back and waited to see what he was up to. When I saw him heading for the back of the bar with a baseball bat, I called the sheriff and told him to get here immediately. I was afraid of what Johnny would do."

"I don't know what would have happened if you hadn't seen his car." The thought of him possibly raping her sent a chill down her spine. "I owe you my life and Reed's."

"Don't think anything of it. I'm just glad the two of you are okay. We have some cleaning up to do but all that stuff is replaceable. You aren't."

"I second that," Reed said. "I don't know what I would have done if I lost you."

"We should get you to the hospital," Sierra said, feeling the lump on the back of his head.

"I'll be fine," Reed insisted.

"I'll start cleaning up around here. You two run off to the hospital and get that bump checked out."

"No one is cleaning up right now. You go home and get some rest," she chastised Henry. "And you. I'm taking you to the hospital for an exam."

Both men looked at her sheepishly.

"Fine," Reed said, humbly.

"You're the boss."

"That's right I am. And it's about damn time you got that through your thick skulls."

Together they locked up the bar, before heading off in separate directions.

Chapter Five

"I'm so glad you didn't have a concussion," Sierra said, as she gazed up into his eyes.

They'd been lying in her bed for an hour since they returned from pressing charges at the police station, after their trip to the hospital, where Reed was diagnosed with having a nasty bump. All the tests came back normal.

"You have a thick head," she teased.

"I know someone with a thicker head."

"Oh yeah."

"Yeah and very stubborn."

"I'm not stubborn." She pouted.

"No?" He eased himself onto his elbow. "Why are you still wearing this t-shirt? Why won't you let me take it off?"

She lowered her eyes afraid to see the pain written all over his face. Yes, when it came to getting fully naked, she was stubborn. She didn't like her body or the reactions it caused.

"Sierra, look at me." He lifted her chin.

"Reed, you've seen the scars. And I've seen how they affected you. Why do we have to torture ourselves by the constant reminder?" She could spend the rest of her life being in his arms, having sex with him, as long as she could keep a shirt on.

"Sierra, I want to cherish every inch of your body, including your stomach. Do you think it's fair to cheat me out of loving you completely?"

She knew he was right but that didn't change the way she felt. She couldn't and wouldn't allow him to see her stomach.

"I understand what you're saying but..."

"But nothing. I want to show you how much you mean to me and that includes having you in my arms naked. Nothing between us." He pulled at her shirt trying to remove it from her stranglehold.

"Reed." She attempted to roll away but he forced her to look at him.

His stern look gave her pause. Would he leave her if she didn't comply? But what would he think when he got an up close and personal look at her scars?

"Did you bring up the strawberry schnapps?"

"Yes and the tequila." What? Did he need to do a few shots before looking at her stomach?

"Sierra! I know what's going through your mind and you can just forget those thoughts. I said I want to cherish your body and that means doing body shots on every inch."

She struggled with his words. Was he being sincere? She wanted to believe him. She wanted to believe he wanted her and that he wasn't looking to atone for his sins. Sins he felt deep inside. She didn't blame him for the accident. She never had and never would. It was just a stupid twist of fate. But she didn't want him to suffer with someone deformed, because in all honesty that's what she was, deformed. From the scar on her face, to the ones riddling her stomach. No one could change her appearance and no one should be subjected to it, unless necessary. And she didn't think it was necessary for Reed to be stuck with her or her deformities.

"Please let me love you." He looked at her with such admiration, she wanted to cry. She didn't deserve him and he didn't deserve being stuck with someone scarred like her. He should be with someone like Lita, the singer from Rebel Yell. She was gorgeous. A goddess.

She pushed the thoughts to the back of her mind. She wanted this with Reed. She wanted to experience all she possibly could before it all slipped away again.

She nodded. "Okay. I'll get the tequila."

"Bring the schnapps too," he called.

Her bare feet padded across the room to the kitchen counter where she'd left the alcohol earlier. Her heart pounded in her chest. She was going to remove her shirt, bare all for Reed. The only man she ever loved and she was going to show him just how much.

Butterflies filled her stomach as she walked back into the room. He sat propped up in the middle of her bed, with only a huge grin on. It seemed like she'd waited for this moment forever. Now he was in her bed, naked. Ready to make all her dreams and wishes come true.

Placing the bottles, salt and bowl of lemon wedges on the table, she smiled down on him.

"Ready?" she asked. More for herself than him. Because he claimed he was more than ready but she was nervous.

"Please," he urged.

The shirt came off with ease, then she removed her bra leaving her completely naked and very vulnerable.

"Come." He patted the bed next to him.

She fell into his strong, welcoming arms where she felt secure. Pressing her body against his, she attempted to hide the scars.

He shook his head. "Not this time. No hiding."

"This isn't easy for me, Reed." Admitting her weakness was the first step in moving forward, right?

"I know, sweetie. But I'm not going to hurt you. I'm only going to love you."

She bit her lower lip. Taking a deep breath she did something she never thought possible. Something she'd never dared with any other man in her life.

She rolled on her back. The sunlight streamed through the cracked blinds glistening on her skin, exposing the reality of her scars.

Body Shots

Pain covered Reed's face. "I can't tell you how sorry I am this happened. I wish it was me with the scars." He bent, kissing each scar, his soft lips lingering after each touch.

"No, Reed. I don't wish this on anyone."

"It's not fair you had to deal with the pain all these years. If only I could have taken it away. I would have."

"I never blamed you. You have to know that." She lifted his hand to her mouth, kissing his palm. "It wasn't your fault. You couldn't have known." Neither could have known what fate had in store for them that day.

"Then why did you take off? Leave me when I loved you more than anything?"

He deserved the truth. He deserved to know it was *for* him not *because of* him that she left. She could see how the thought of it was killing him. She knew if there were never an accident they would probably be married with a family by now. The realization cut her to the bone.

"Reed, I was ashamed of who I became. Look at me. I look like a monster." Monster was the only word she could find to wrap it neatly in a bow for him. She wasn't normal after the accident. Far from it. Christ, the scar on her cheek, though faint, was still a constant reminder of that day.

She snuggled back into the safety of his arms, afraid to look him in the eyes. She worried her lower lip, biting back the tears that threatened to flow. She didn't want him to think her hideous.

"Honey, I don't see a monster. I see a beautiful woman who may have a few scars but that doesn't change how I see you. You're perfect in every way. You're perfect to me."

How long had she wanted to hear those words from his lips? Never in her wildest dreams had she believed he'd utter them, let alone be in her bed ready to make love to her. As she lay naked in his arms she began to believe they had a chance at a future.

"Lay back, please." He looked down into her eyes and all she saw was softness. Reed wanted to cherish her body. He didn't see the hideous monster she saw when she looked in the mirror.

She hesitated.

"Please?" he cooed.

Sierra slid her body down.

Reed's hand skimmed over her skin, resting on her breast. He rubbed his thumb over the nipple until it became firm under his touch. He bent, taking the other nipple between his lips.

"I've waited a lifetime for this," he murmured.

Sierra let out a small cry as his mouth moved down to her stomach. He nudged her legs apart with his hand. Spreading her legs, she welcomed his finger, as he entered her pussy.

He dragged the digit up her folds, coating her with her juices. His finger lingered over her clit, teasing.

His tongue circled her bellybutton. Flames licked her skin with every new touch of his warm tongue. Juices soaked her opening. She wanted to come. She wanted to feel him inside her loving her.

"Reed," she cried.

"Not yet sweetie but soon." He removed his finger leaving her empty, aching for his touch. He climbed over her and grabbed the schnapps.

"Time for me to show you how much I love this body."

"With a girly girl drink?" she teased, trying to make light of the situation. Her feelings for him were scaring the hell out of her and she didn't want to admit what she was feeling.

He chuckled. "Even with a girly girl drink."

She tried relaxing as he gazed upon her body, taking in every imperfection.

Tipping the bottle he dripped the cold liquid into her navel. She fought against the cold wanting to wiggle it out.

Reed placed his hands on either side of her stomach, settling her. His hot breath close, warming her skin, while loose strands of his hair tickled.

Lips wrapped around her navel, creating suction he pulled the schnapps into his mouth. Jolts of electricity ran straight to her core.

"Holy shit," she cried.

"I told you."

Yes, he'd told her, but he'd failed to say he could make her climax without touching her pussy. She was so close she could taste it. Another shot and he could send her reeling into a full-fledged climax.

As he poured another shot into her navel she forgot about her scars or fears and enjoyed the sparks coming from his body, charging hers. Her skin tingled with every touch. Her pussy lips began to quiver as an orgasm rippled through her body. Reed's mouth sucked the liquid from her navel once more, sending her careening over the edge and just when she thought she couldn't take it anymore, he slid two fingers into her contracting channel. She arched her hips accepting them, wanting more.

His mouth moved down to her clit enveloping the tiny bud between his lips, sparking a new sensation, one she felt down to her toes. He finger-fucked her, licking her clit while she rode out the last of the mind-numbing orgasm.

Bathing in the aftermath of such intense feelings, Sierra smiled.

"You like?" Reed asked, hovering over her frame.

"No, I love." She reached out and touched his face. The face that haunted her every waking dream since the day she walked away from him. The face she'd loved since she was barely an adult.

He looked at her questioningly.

"I'm sorry I ever left you. I'm sorry we lost so much time together. I love you, Reed."

A grin formed and he bent capturing her mouth hungrily. "I love you too, Sierra."

SHAKEN AND STIRRED
M.A. Ellis

Trademarks Acknowledgement

The author acknowledges the trademarked status and trademark owners of the following wordmarks mentioned in this work of fiction:

Brooks Brothers: Retail Brand Alliance, Inc.

Deere (John Deere): Deere & Company Corporation

FFA: Future Farmers of America Corporation

GQ: Advance Magazine Publishers Inc.

Gentleman Jack Rare Tennessee Whiskey: Jack Daniel's Properties, Inc.

Jack (Jack Daniel's): Jack Daniel's Properties, Inc.

Ketel One: Double Eagle Brands, NV L.L.C.

Lamborghini: Same Deutz-Fahr S.p.A

Lipizzaner Stallions: White Stallion Productions, Inc.

Louboutin: Christian Louboutin

Mercedes: Daimler Chrysler AG Corporation

Old No. 7: Jack Daniel's Properties, Inc.

Porsche: Dr. Ing. h. c. f. Porsche Aktiengesellschaft Corporation

Resistol: RHE Hatco, Inc.

Sapphire (Bombay Sapphire Distilled London Dry Gin): Bombay Spirits Company Limited

Stetson: John B. Stetson Company

Whitestrips: Proctor & Gamble Company

The Lone Ranger: Classic Media Inc.

The Wild, Wild West: CBS Broadcasting Inc.

Chapter One

ଈଓ

"Alrighty...let's recap, shall we?"

Susanne Webb swirled the thin black straw, forming a mini whirlpool in her cocktail as she listened to her new friend.

"I'm focusing on the Rocky Mountain High toothpaste maven and you're looking at that West Palm 'you're fired' piece of work."

"I think we can call them by their names," Susanne laughed. "We're not knee-deep in espionage, Gia."

"Are you crazy?" the built-like-a-brick-house brunette said in a loud voice before quickly lowering her tone. "You've gotta be crafty, woman. Competition has officially turned brutal. This morning one of the chefs in my sector lost an entire eight-quart bowl of the best white chocolate in the free world when a sous-chef from the entrée division 'accidentally' tripped and upended his bottle of water into the bowl. Allegiances are being formed and then realigned at rates that make a woman's head spin."

"Well, we're not so cutthroat here on the mixology side of things," Susanne said, taking a sip of her no-frills vodka and cranberry juice. She'd spent the last four days creating cutting-edge cocktails for celebrity judges and icons of the restaurant world. She had no time for alliances and no need for anything at the moment other than two simple ingredients and a wedge of lime. The producers of the competition had them sequestered in a high-end oceanfront hotel. There were no phones or internet or hotel menus that they might glean some great pairings from—something that would give them just the edge they needed to blow their fellow contestants out of the water. She'd stick with the basics all the way around. They hadn't let her down thus far.

"Not cutthroat, huh? I can guarantee the Dynamic Douche Bags are plotting your demise as we speak." Gia nodded her head toward the corner and Susanne spun slowly around on the tall barstool to take a look.

The two men had staked their claim on the farthest corner of the lounge, which was just fine with Susanne. The duo of overly confident, undeniably pampered, highly inebriated bartenders-turned-managers should have been cut off an hour ago. But the man and woman behind the huge, brushed metal bar were extending some professional courtesy to their brethren. Susanne understood their willingness to allow the drinks to flow. It was no different from people living vicariously through the successes of their children or favorite sports teams. Rooting for the people you share a commonality with was second nature. Bartenders were no different from any other working stiffs who inhabited the planet. When one of their own grasped a handful of fame, pride surged in all.

And tomorrow when the competition was over, Susanne intended to be the victor. The thirty-thousand-dollar cash prize was a decent payday but it was the contacts that would be made that Susanne found ten times more rewarding. There was no way she was letting anything deter her from bettering her livelihood.

It was fortuitous that the members of the National Consortium of Restaurateurs had chosen South Beach for this year's event. High five for home-field advantage! Knowing where to find the best local ingredients, a fact that was paramount to winning any creative culinary competition no matter what the subgenre, had given her a leg up. She had been nearly giddy when the previous elimination challenge required the use of at least one fresh Chinese fruit. She owed her ex's grandmother a debt of gratitude for smuggling in a fragile sapling when she had emigrated from southern China seventy years ago. Susanne's lychee martini had sent two contestants home and propelled her into one of the three final spots in the spirits division.

She watched her male competitors each wrap an arm around the other's shoulder in a show of mock solidarity. There was no way in hell they were having a true "I love you, man" moment.

"Don't waste your time worrying about them. You've kicked their collective asses with your arsenal of creative concoctions and they know it."

Susanne looked at Gia and smiled. She had met her ally in the hotel's registration line less than a week before. Somewhere between the "Enter Here" sign and a heavily tanned customer service associate asking them "Who's next?" they had struck up a friendship—both heaving sighs of relief when they established that they weren't competing against each other.

"Right back at you, queen of the coconut crème brûlée," Susanne said.

"You're too kind," Gia said, offering Susanne a regal nod. "And I'm sure as shit not going to get an executive pastry chef position with Ms. Whitestrips with something that mundane. The gods of superfine sugar and fire were apparently watching over me yesterday. The last thing I want tomorrow is another win by default."

"You did not win by default."

"Right. Three desserts over-caramelized, three chefs who needed to be eliminated. Mere coincidence? No freakin' way. Change of subject—word on the boulevard is they're bringing in entertainment to help alleviate the night-before-finale jitters."

"Really?" Susanne had learned by the end of the first day that for some reason the pastry folks were the gatherers of the gossip. "They've got plenty to choose from this weekend. There's some huge world championship bull-riding thing at the arena. The Lipizzaner Stallions are somewhere in The

Gables and I think my aunt said one of the larger circuses is setting up outside the stadium."

"Holy shit," Gia said, taking a sip of her club soda and lime. "None of those sound overly diverting. I doubt a bunch of bowlegged chuck-wagon-food lovers are going to be rubbing elbows with eight of the nation's leading restaurant gods. And I hope to hell they keep the equines safe from that dude Ken, who is tops in the appetizer division. He was telling everyone, the other day, how wonderfully tasty horsemeat can be if marinated properly. What a psycho."

Susanne joined Gia in a shiver of disgust before commenting. "Then it's probably going to be clowns and sword swallowers."

"Hah! That might just give you the edge you need. I'm pretty sure those two pretty boys you're up against aren't strangers to sheathing a dagger or two in places not mentionable in mixed company. Something long and strong that subliminally represents a fourteen-inch cock will throw them into a tizzy, ensuring that you, the always-focused Mistress of Mixology, shall blend her way to victory."

Susanne smiled and shook her head. "They're not gay."

"You sure?"

"Pretty sure...but then again, I was wrong about you."

"Most are," Gia said with a wink. "God played a cruel joke on the male populace when he gave me huge boobs and a giant ass. I seem to be every guy's wet-yet-unattainable dream."

Susanne nodded and took a sip of her drink. She knew from experience how the bulk of male minds processed a woman's worth. Giving consideration to what was above shoulder level was generally an afterthought for most men. She'd seen it time and again in the food and beverage industry. In the case of women like herself—women who weren't "mammary gifted" as her grandmother liked to say—men tended to automatically consider her a little more intelligent than her counterparts. It hadn't helped her sex life all that much, and it sure as hell had lost her tip money over the years, but it had certainly proven beneficial to her progressing to a level way beyond that of flair bartender.

She had been executive bar manager for over five years, working hard to reach for a piece of pie that most would consider highly elusive to a woman with few business connections. She was ready for the move to the upper echelon. She would still implement her management skills but a win would guarantee she could have the pick of positions in the private sector of her choice. Those jobs came with excellent benefits and starting salaries that could never be equaled in the public arena. If she were fortunate enough to be hired for an estate position she could add all meals and lodging to the benefit package and that would put her just shy of six figures.

"Holy dick-on-a-stick! Speaking of wet dreams! The Pony Express has apparently arrived."

Susanne followed Gia's wide-eyed stare to the columned entrance of the lounge. Murmurs drifted through the crowded room as, one by one, the patrons noticed the denim-clad group of men who suddenly dominated the space. Some were large and bulky, others were not, but they all exuded an air of pure masculinity.

"Are you, or are you not gay?" Susanne asked offhandedly as one drop-dead-gorgeous man after another started to break away from the pack. Several headed straight for the bar while others ambled slowly over to the huge wall of windows that offered a panoramic view of the wave-cresting Atlantic Ocean.

"I wasn't always a lover of the boxed lunch, babe. I'm more than capable of appreciating a perfectly chiseled body, be it male or female. These guys are gorgeous. Look at that one at the end of the line. Something that yummy puts a whole new meaning to 'bringing up the rear'."

Susanne had already noticed the man who towered over the rest of the entourage. The contrast between his camel-colored hat against the dark browns and blacks of the other men in front of him caught her attention.

"Think he's the good guy?" Susanne asked softly before glancing back at Gia. "The Lone Ranger of the rodeo world perhaps?"

"Are you kidding? The way those jeans hug all the right places? I think he's probably a *very* good guy. Excellent eye, Suze. You feeling lucky enough to take part in a little game of Five-Card-Studly?"

Susanne was unable to keep her gaze from drifting back to the spot where his tall form seemed rooted in place. "I'm not here for diversions."

"No matter how tasty they might be?" Gia asked.

"Absolutely not."

"Well, maybe you should be. Loosen up a little and see what the night brings. You've got zero prep work—nothing to brainstorm or devise. Until they give you the final drink challenge, your time is yours. Make the most of it, for god's sake. I'm thinking you should let your last night as a contender go out with a bang. Literally."

"You're ridiculous," Susanne said and laughed in a not-so-convincing manner. She'd made the dreaded mistake of telling Gia just how nonexistent her sex life had become.

Now that the band of cowboys had dispersed, the relaxed stance of the man's lean body set him apart from the other men in the room. While there was a nervous energy surrounding them, this man looked totally at ease with the activity surrounding him. Susanne took a moment to soak in every shred of his gorgeousness, forced to start with his firm jawline since the brim of his hat was obscuring the upper portion of his face. His dark facial hair was closely trimmed into a goatee and disconnected mustache that Susanne had seen on a thousand men, a thousand times before. For some ungodly reason, she had the urge to walk over and rub her thumb over the little vertical patch of hair between his full bottom lip and that strong chin.

"Holy crap," she whispered, clearing her suddenly dry throat before focusing on something other than the fact that she wanted to kiss him. She looked into her drink, wondering if the barmaid had given her a gratis double of Ketel One.

"If there were a *GQ* for ranch hands, that man would be cover worthy," Gia said.

Just like that, Susanne looked back in his direction, picking up her perusal. He wore a white shirt. No western designs or cording or pearl-type snaps, which were worn by some of his associates. Just pure, crisp cotton that accentuated the sun-kissed hue of his face and the tempting view of the small triangle of his chest that leaving the top two buttons undone afforded anyone who cared to look. And a great number of the female contestants who were crowded into the lounge were definitely looking.

The cut of the shirt accentuated the delicious fact that his broad shoulders tapered to a lean waist. He wore a dark leather belt with some sort of silver buckle but nothing as large and gaudy as some of his peers. His jeans were a medium shade of denim that was neither tight nor loose and Susanne watched him lean back against a pillar and cross one booted foot over the other. The simple action forced her to admit that Gia had been spot on. He possessed an enticingly impressive cradle of male flesh that would no doubt warrant him very good indeed.

Susanne shook her head, trying to clear the illicit images that were starting to swirl. She focused instead on how he should have seemed out of place in a room filled with sleek furnishings and polished-chrome designs but he didn't. Due in part to his palpable confidence. Having been surrounded all week by men who were constantly on edge and rethinking their every decision made him all the more attractive.

"Oh my god. Look," Gia whispered conspiratorially.

Susanne reluctantly pulled her gaze from the cowboy and tried to see who had caught her friend's attention. Gia was already on her feet, smoothing the creases from her black dress pants.

"I might have to reevaluate my opinion of campfires and baked beans," she said. Susanne watched her square her shoulders as if preparing for battle.

"She's just my type. Look at those legs. My god, they go on forever. Wish me luck, woman."

"Good luck," Susanne finally said, but Gia was already halfway across the room, making a beeline for a woman wearing gray ostrich-skin boots, a short, black denim skirt and silky, silver tank top.

Her friend's movement caught the attention of every man in the room, including the one still lazing in the entryway. He lifted his head and Susanne got an unobstructed view of his face. His nose was long but not quite straight, as if it had been broken at one point and not quite properly set. She had no earthly idea why she found it totally sexy. Her taste in men tended to run more toward the Brooks Brothers set.

Your taste in men has sucked so far.

At least the executive types offered her something more conversational than local sports and fishing tournaments.

Right. They talk about their jobs and their cars and the next big business acquisition. But surprise of all surprises, they seem to forget to talk about their wives or girlfriends. Imagine that!

She watched him glance toward his left, in the general vicinity of Gia's intended hook-up. His lips curved upward into an amused grin as he pushed away from the column and took a few steps toward the cowgirl and Susanne immediately assumed he and the beauty were a couple. The woman hadn't missed his approach either and shot him a dangerous look. One that clearly said "keep the hell away".

Interesting.

He stopped abruptly, as if he'd hit some invisible force, and crossed his arms over his chest. Susanne watched him watch Gia and the cowgirl, studying his profile until he suddenly whipped his head around and pinned her with his dark gaze.

The air rushed from her lungs. He studied her face for what seemed like forever before dropping his gaze slowly down her body. Susanne swallowed, steeling herself for the inevitable reaction of him quickly looking away when he realized the voluptuousness that men obviously loved was nowhere to be found.

But he didn't look away. He perused her body with a scrutiny that had her cheeks flushing and the junction of her thighs starting an erotic little throb. His gaze lingered on her feet and she doubted that he recognized a pair of discounted Louboutin slingbacks when he saw them. It was more probably that he secretly harbored a red-toenail fetish.

Now wouldn't that be grand!

Susanne's field of vision turned foggy as she imagined him undoing her sandal and tossing it haphazardly to the floor, which in the real world would undoubtedly have her issuing a cautious warning. She honestly believed it should be a federal offense to manhandle fine footwear but in her daydream it would be a moot point. He'd run one calloused palm along the outside of her leg before snaking over her hip and a second later she'd forget about four-hundred-dollar shoes and focus solely on his palm gliding over the curve of her ass. Back and forth, he would tease before gently sliding a finger along the leg edge of her panties until she—slut of the dream realm—would helpfully shift her hips to allow him better access.

Susanne caught herself before her legs actually opened and blinked away all erotic thoughts. She took a steadying breath before spinning around on the stool to face the bar. She wasn't looking for some down-and-dirty-farm-boy fantasy. She shouldn't care that he might possess six-pack abs and a cock that was so mountable she was likely to offer up a rousing "hi-ho, Silver" when she straddled it. She needed to get a grip.

Yeah! A grip on any part of him that might be over six inches in length.

She also needed to grow up and lose the schoolgirl fantasies.

They say eight seconds is a legal ride, Susie.

Susanne mentally chastised herself. She wasn't supposed to be thinking about anything strong and straight up unless it had an alcohol base and could be easily topped with edible garnish.

She focused on the shelves holding the bottles of liquor, happy they weren't backed with mirrors. She didn't need to keep tabs on Cowboy Sexy. She needed to finish her drink and head back to her room — call it an early night. She needed to concentrate on all the roadblocks and challenges the judges could throw into her finely honed repertoire of possible award-winning cocktails. She did *not* need to focus on —

"Excuse me, darlin'. Is anyone sitting here?"

A low Southern drawl that had the tiny hairs along her arms rising. Her pulse raced and her previous intent to avoid him evaporated into thin air.

His voice was way smooth-as-silk sexy and as he shifted a little closer, Susanne could actually feel the heat rolling off his body. From the recesses of her mind Gia's bold advice taunted Susanne, daring her to consider the possibility that mindless intercourse might actually be the perfect distraction. But she'd never done the one-night-stand thing. It wasn't her style. She had never been a wild child, and the way her heart was threatening to beat right out of her chest, she never would be. Besides, it was pretty arrogant to think he was even interested. Maybe the poor guy just wanted to sit down.

With an imaginary "poof" Susanne's erotic fantasy dissipated and she turned and offered him a polite smile.

"My friend just left for a minute—"

"Don't fib, sugar. Your girlfriend is on a mission. It was written all over her face when she sashayed over and blindsided Chrissy. I don't think we'll have to worry about those two for quite some time. They headed for the dance floor, hand in hand."

Susanne looked over her shoulder, trying very hard not to glance downward as he took a seat and hooked one boot heel over the rung of the stool. She focused her attention on the dance floor, craning her neck until she saw the flash of silver fabric and Gia's long, dark hair swaying to and fro.

"Interesting," she said softly.

"Understatement," he chuckled.

He shifted and his knee brushed her leg, sending an unfamiliar jolt of electricity up her body.

Susanne suddenly remembered the way the cowboy had reacted when he saw Gia approaching Chrissy.

"Jealous?" she asked. The last thing she needed was to be part of some payback plan.

"Hell no." His laugh was low and deep. Genuine. "And I apologize for throwing a kink into the one-word answer game we were playing. I'm thinking you'd have come out the winner, sugar."

"I'm not a game player," Susanne said, looking into his eyes. Now that he was less than two feet away, she realized they were a deep gunmetal color.

"Not a player...just a competitor? What division?"

Susanne arched a brow and he offered her a benign look.

"Surprised to find out we're not here by chance, that a bunch of plowboys were actually invited to the hottest ticket in town? It's true. And let me tell you, it was hell on the valet trying to find parking spots for all our horses."

In the land of Porsche and Mercedes and Lamborghini the picture he painted was totally ludicrous and Susanne was unable to keep a straight face.

"What's your name, cowboy?"

He tilted his head back a little and looked down his crooked nose at her, doing his best to offer her a you-have-got-to-be-shitting-me look.

"Sorry. I've always wanted to say that," Susanne defended.

"Never had the chance before?"

"Not in Miami."

"So the men 'round these parts aren't much into throwing on a pair of boots and their best hat and waltzing on up to a beautiful woman sitting at a bar? Hoping for nothing less than the possibility that she just might be considering a little cowpoke role-playing? 'Poke' being the operative word, of course."

Susanne looked into his twinkling eyes and fought to keep her breathing normal and the conversation carefree.

"Oh, there's more than a little role-play going on in this town but I don't think it involves steers and sagebrush. At least, I hope it doesn't. I've been a loyal supporter of the Holstein for many years."

"Well, well. A city girl who knows her breeds. I'm impressed," he said, offering her a quick wink. "Where've you been hidin', darlin'?"

It had been ages since Susanne had actually returned a bar-side flirtation. She was starting to enjoy herself.

"I spent thirteen years in southwestern Missouri. But I don't remember rural role-playing being a sanctioned FFA event. I'm not sure what that fantasy involves," she said.

"Where I'm from, it usually consists of a stable with some fresh-cut hay, a horse blanket and a squeeze bottle of Tupelo honey."

"A barn and some honey? That's it? No green and yellow tractor? No hundred-degree afternoon with the sun beating down and a swimming hole just waiting to cool a person off? I would have thought a picnic lunch and a quart of sweet tea at a bare minimum."

"Not since high school, sugar. I generally don't need some stretched-out scenario to get me to the main event. But if you have a pair of cutoffs and a little white tank top in your suitcase, then we can go back in time. I'm imaging how hot you'd look carrying that basket across a field of alfalfa, your hair all sun kissed and blowing in the warm summer breeze."

She stared at him long and hard, wondering how his voice could have the dual power of lulling part of her into a relaxed state while setting every sexual fiber in her being on edge. He leaned forward and brought his mouth close her ear, as if he had the biggest of secrets to share with her.

"Can you see it?" he whispered, his breath sending a wave of shivers down her spine. "Me crawlin' down from the cab of that Deere. Wantin' nothing more than to dribble that sweet tea all over your hot body and lick every drop away."

Susanne sat stock still and tried to get her heartbeat under control, praying he couldn't hear the rapid drumming. Flirtation was one thing. The way her body was reacting was something altogether different. Just that quick, his words were making her burn. It was a far cry from the aloof no-strings, country-lovin' attitude she thought she might actually be able to adopt for the evening.

"All I can see," she said, forcing herself to lean away and not into him, "is a woman who thought she could be totally spontaneous. I kick major ass at the impromptu drink making, but this? Sorry, Tex, I can't pull it off."

"Can't you?" he asked, lowering his eyes. He pursed his lips into a thoroughly dejected pout. "Well, that's a damn fine state of affairs."

"I'm sorry. Please, don't think I'm some sort of barfly tease." She gnawed at her lower lip, effectively halting any further explanation.

His gaze lifted and settled on her mouth and her lips began to throb.

"Let me get you a drink," she offered.

"A drink?" His blinding smile returned as quickly as it had disappeared. "If they have some specialty that's guaranteed to work as well as a cold shower then order away 'cause that's what I need, sugar. You've got the most kissable mouth I've ever had the pleasure of seeing."

His words stunned her. She didn't believe him. But part of her wished she could.

"You can stop. Really. You're handsome as hell and I'm sure this works with most women but you need to realize that I'm not going to sleep with you." She turned around and tried to get the bartender's attention.

"Whoa now. There's a helluva lot that happens between kissing and consummating. It would definitely still involve my mouth—probably my teeth now and again. A finger or two."

He placed his forearms on the bar and made a great show of studying his large hands. His fingers were long and roughened but his nails were nicely kept. He drummed them slowly against the metal and she realized that precision tapping was for her benefit—a sign that he had all the time in the world. That he'd go slowly. Keep his promise that there was a "helluva lot" between the lip locks and the sex.

What more could you want?

Susanne motioned for the bartender a second time, annoyance flaring. She wanted to buy him a drink to apologize for her come-and-get-me attitude and then she wanted to leave.

Leave? Or escape?

"What'll it be, handsome?" the woman purred.

Susanne's mouth actually dropped open when the blonde planted her elbows on the smooth surface and offered the cowboy an enticing smile and a healthy glimpse of bosom. It was the most blatant, inappropriate display Susanne had ever witnessed and she'd seen a lot in her years behind a bar.

"What I'd like from you, miss, is a Jack on the rocks." His voice dripped with amusement.

Susanne snapped her head around, surprised to find him staring at her and not the huge expanse of cleavage that was offered up.

He reached forward, shocking her further when he rubbed one long, roughened finger along her jawline from ear to chin before pushing her mouth closed. The light movement caused a slow heat to creep down her neck and across her collarbone. A sheen of moisture broke out along the swell of her breasts a second before her nipples tightened and she barely managed to stifle her gasp.

"And what I need from you is even simpler." He spoke in a husky tone as he gently cradled her chin in his palm and pulled her face closer to his. A delicious little flutter teased her belly as he rubbed his thumb against her skin.

"I want you to step back into that fantasy land we were discussing. Give me a chance to answer one of your life's burning questions."

Susanne stared at him, no longer certain she truly wanted whatever diversion they were about to take part in.

"C'mon, sugar. Ask me my name again. In that same sweet voice that could have me doing anything your little heart desires."

Unable to draw her eyes away from his penetrating stare, Susanne gnawed at her bottom lip and tried to think of any sane reason to refuse his request but her rationale seemed to have disappeared in a cloud of dust.

"Do you know how bad I want to nibble that soft skin at the corner of your mouth?"

His grip tightened and Susanne squirmed in her chair, desire slamming into her with a vengeance.

"We need to get the introductions out of the way so I can kiss you properly. Ask me, darlin'."

Her heart shifted into double time, its erratic thrumming jolting through her body as she faced the utterly insane truth. She wanted that kiss. And a great deal more.

"What's your name, cowboy?" Her voice wavered.

"L. Treyton Ryder." His eyes gleamed teasingly as he touched the tip of his hat with his free hand and the fluttering that had burst forth in Susanne's stomach began to migrate lower. "But you can call me Trey, darlin'."

Who knew that all those "darlin'" and "sugars" could have a woman's panties ready to incinerate.

"What's the 'L' stand for?" Susanne asked, searching for a neutral topic that might divert her from climbing into his lap and seeing if his kisses were as good as his game.

"You don't really want to know." He chuckled, offering her another sexy smile.

"Tell me anyway," she demanded.

"Lucifer."

Lucifer?

Second after second ticked away.

"Of course it is," she finally said, feigning nonchalance.

His lips parted on a wide, white, totally devilish grin.

"And you are?"

Susanne met his teasing gaze, hoping her eyes weren't crossing from the rush of want that coursed through her.

"Screwed," she snorted.

He tilted his head back and gave her an amused look before leaning forward and sending another wave of shivers down her spine as he brushed his lips against the sensitive skin along the curve of her ear.

"Not yet, sugar. But it sure as hell would be my pleasure to oblige," Trey whispered. She had delivered that line with such matter-of-factness that he wasn't sure how he'd managed to rein in his laughter. It had been so damn long since he'd sat next to a woman and shared even a small fraction of the honest-to-goodness barstool banter very few women could offer. He had forgotten how much he missed it.

Trey boldly dipped his head, planting a quick kiss on the side of her neck before pulling away. It wouldn't do to start full-out necking with her in public even if he was correct in his impression that her proper exterior hid something totally naughty underneath. While that behavior was one hundred percent acceptable at most of the other bars he frequented on the few occasions he accompanied his trainers on the circuit, tonight it was one hundred percent impermissible. His uncle had a plan and Trey had every intention of following through with the edict the old man had set forth.

But good intentions had flown right out the proverbial window the minute he saw her spin around and study the group of bull riders who had sauntered into the rooftop bar. He'd assumed he could walk over and have a simple conversation without the needs of his long-neglected dick overriding his common sense or the mission he had been handed.

You lying turd. It's got jack shit to do with not getting laid and everything to do with that deadly blend of innocence and sultriness. That dark auburn hair. That lithe build. Those fuck-me-ten-ways-to-Sunday shoes. You fall for it every time.

Trey would like to curse the fact that the voice of reason sounded suspiciously like that of his brother. He couldn't deny he was sitting across from a woman who had his blood burning from simply looking at him with the greenest eyes he'd ever seen. He preferred his women to have long hair. He loved the sensation of wrapping the length around his hand at just the right moment. But the thought of the ends of her bobbed auburn hair brushing his skin as she kissed her way down his stomach had his sac tightening with desire. She was staring at him with an intensity that forced him to get his libido under control and backtrack to remember the last thing she had said.

"Would that be *Ms.* or *Mrs.* Screwed?" he asked, not missing the way her skirt rode a little higher when she shifted on her stool and re-crossed her legs. *Damn, son!*

He prided himself in being a man who missed very few details when encountering a new opportunity, be it professional or personal. Tonight he had allowed the boys to run interference for him and it had given him those few extra moments of being able to covertly study the woman his uncle wanted disqualified.

"Or is that a nickname?" he asked when she failed to answer. He could see she was wary. *Time to change tack.* There was no doubt in his mind he could ease her back into the flirty attitude she had abandoned just moments before.

"So maybe we switch to a standard cowboy fantasy. How 'bout that?" He watched her breasts rise and fall as she took measured breaths and then exhaled slowly. He knew all about inner battles. And the beauty across from his was seriously fighting one of her own.

"Is that where I have to dress up in a sheep costume and call you Daaaaaa-deeee?" she asked.

Trey shook his head and smiled at her ability to battle her apprehension with a dose of humor.

"That one's as old as the hills, sugar. Try another fantasy."

"I don't know," she said. "Sexy schoolmarm?"

"Hmmm." He gave her suggestion mock consideration. "That has merit...but not tonight. I'm thinking something a little more contemporary."

"Contemporary, huh?"

He saw a flash of unease in her eyes a moment before she turned back around and focused all her attention on her drink.

"Well, I don't have the body for that Texan-cheerleader costume you probably keep in your saddlebag for occasions such as these."

"You're right about that."

She snapped her head around, eyes flashing with anger and just a tiny bit of hurt. He was pleased he had her undivided attention, that her emerald eyes focused solely on him.

"Your body's perfect for me, sugar. I like my women like my horses—long sturdy legs, great teeth and willing to let me ride them 'til they drop."

Her eyes darkened and he knew he had once again mastered saying the right thing. In this case, it was the god's honest truth.

"Gee, Satan. I bet you say that to all the girls."

He reached out and covered her hand with his, forcing her to meet his gaze.

"Actually, Susanne, I don't."

Chapter Two

"Yeeee-haaaaw!"

Susanne jumped, the boisterous call that sounded directly behind her startling her to the point that she pulled her hand from Trey's grasp.

"Trey. Miss," the cowboy said, nodding at each of them as he continued to spin a large lasso in front of him. He reached down and pulled a length of twine from the large ring attached to his belt loop and gave it to Susanne. "We're goin' to be teaching y'all how to tie 'em right after the performance. So you'll have mini-lassos as souvenirs."

Susanne watched him effortlessly move the spinning rope up and down, to the front and then to the back of his body. Cheers erupted from across the room and Susanne glanced in that direction to see another rope worker jumping inside and back out of the lasso he brandished. The man beside them took a few steps away from the bar and mirrored the other man's efforts, adding a little more flair of his own.

"Can you do that?" Susanne asked.

"Absolutely," Trey said in a firm tone.

"Just as good?"

"Better."

"Reeeeally?"

"Really."

"Now who's playing the one-word answer game?" Susanne shot him a sideways glance and frowned when she met his gaze. "You're not even watching him."

"I don't have to," he replied in a confident tone. "I'm a rope master. You'd be surprised how proficient I am. I've got knots for every occasion."

He took her hand and traced a tiny circle around the tip of her thumb, the single motion sending a jolt of lust coiling through her body.

"Some are basic. Slip knots. Square knots. Others are designed to tighten with opposing force, which is what you use for calves."

He pulled the twine from her grasp and she watched his long fingers move with slow precision as he worked with the cord.

"When anything is flipped onto its back and its limbs are bound, it's going to struggle," he said, voice dropping to a husky whisper. "At least at first."

Susanne looked up, directly into his intense gaze, and the breath she'd been holding escaped in a rush. The tiny throb at the juncture of her thighs began to pound in earnest. She could tell his hands were moving but she couldn't draw her gaze away from his face.

"Of course there's other rope work that allows for easy release." He looped the rope over her wrists and drew it snug before Susanne realized what was happening. He guided her hands upward until they were at chest level and offered her a slow, sexy smile. "See this little half moon?"

Susanne looked down to where he was wiggling a piece of cord back and forth with his little finger. He traced the twine over and over and over and Susanne shifted in her seat. The whole series of events was beginning to be a bit much. Heat flooded her body as he hooked his finger through the loop.

"Freedom is only a little tug away." He gave a quick yank and the knot slid loose and the length of cord fell into her lap.

She stared at it as the seconds ticked by and the pounding in her ears intensified.

This is not good, Susie. The voice in her head was sorely lacking in conviction. Intuition told her that sex with him would be remarkably good. Thoroughly satisfying. Terribly wrong for a woman intent on focusing on the prize at hand.

Which prize are we talking about because I'm thinking he's pretty trophy worthy?

His gaze drifted to her lips and then slowly lowered to her chest. With any other man she'd have been incensed at the blatant public perusal. With any other man her nipples wouldn't have hardened into aching little nubs.

"Come to my room, sugar."

The realization that she wanted to go with him was shocking, that she wanted him to do illicit things to her body was frightening. He wrapped his warm hands around her trembling fingers and squeezed gently.

"I'll be a gentleman. I swear. No nude, post-lovemaking photos or texting the other guys," he teased. "You have my word."

"Maybe I don't want a gentleman," she blurted.

His gaze raked her features, studying her for a long time before he stood up so quickly the stool rocked on two legs. He pulled his wallet out of his back pocket with an urgency that had Susanne's desire fanning and quickly tossed a twenty on the bar.

"I can do that too, sugar. Whatever you want. Just come with me," he said, throwing back the remainder of his drink. "Now."

Susanne slid her feet to the floor and slowly stood, making sure her shaking legs would actually hold her upright. She was about to embark on a journey she had never taken. Sex with a total stranger. The idea made her mind and her body a little unsteady. She slid her purse over her shoulder and prayed her voice wouldn't waver.

"No," she said loudly, pleased when she caught the attention of more than a few of the people surrounding them.

She waited for the look of consternation to crease his brow and then whispered. "Give me ten minutes, Tex. Then you come to me."

* * * * *

Real smooth. Just sashay out of the bar like I'm a pro of the one-night fling. Susanne sat on the arm of the couch, sexual frustration vying with utter embarrassment as she chastised herself.

"So much for 'you come to me', dumbass!"

Less than fifteen minutes prior, as she made her exit she had felt a surge of womanly confidence like nothing she had ever known, secure in the fact that the most attractive man in the room wanted her. She had smiled the entire elevator ride to the penthouse level. She had found herself whistling *Happy Trails* while quickly freshening up. It wasn't until she was squatting in front of the bar to see what offerings might be found that she realized her colossal blunder.

She glanced at the phone, wondering if she should call the operator and ask for his room since she had totally neglected to tell him her suite number.

Maybe I can get Robert to call for me.

The suite's butler had been a godsend more than once over the past days. Tonight, just as every other, the man had asked her if there was any further assistance he could provide before she retired. She had asked for a bucket of ice.

He'd be back any second. She was a little uncomfortable with the whole "you rang" principle but she was seriously considering adding a second nighttime request. The light chiming of the doorbell echoed through the room and she hurried to let the butler in.

Ask him to make the call.

Susanne made her way across the marble foyer and quickly opened the door.

"Thanks so much, Robert, but I have one more favor—"

"Who the hell is Robert?"

Susanne's heart kicked into double time when she saw her cowboy standing before her. He held a fifth of Jack in one hand and a bowl of whipped-cream-topped blackberries in the other.

She stared at him, her astonishment quickly turning into pure feminine anticipation.

"You found me," she said in a surprised voice.

"Yes, ma'am," he replied with an amused grin, moving his body forward, forcing her to take a few steps backward so he could enter her room.

"But I forgot to give you my room number."

"Darlin', I can find a missing longhorn in a three-hundred-acre pasture. What would have you thinking I couldn't find you?"

"Well, I didn't leave a trail of trampled grass and fresh cow poop."

He pushed the bowl of fruit in her direction and offered another of his hearty laughs.

"True. I had something more noticeable and a lot less odiferous to follow—the floor the elevator stopped at and the distinct triangle and dot pattern those sexy heels left in that thick carpet. I hope to hell you're not planning on taking those off anytime soon."

She took the crystal container from his hand, doing a double take as something slid from his shoulder into the crook of his arm. "Is that a—"

"Drapery cord. Didn't want to waste time heading back to my room for some real rope, which would be too rough and abrasive for your sweet skin anyhow."

Before she could comment, he wrapped his free hand around her waist and pulled her against his body, covering her mouth with his for a series of slow, lingering kisses that left her dizzy.

"Watch the berries. We're gonna need those later," he warned.

She quickly set the bowl on the foyer table.

"We are?" she asked, taking the bottle from his hand and setting it beside the fruit. "Are you going to serve them to me, wearing nothing but your Stetson and boots?"

"It's not a Stetson, it's a Resistol, and if that's what turns you on, sugar, absolutely." He ran his hands down her back and firmly grabbed her ass cheeks, massaging the full globes as he nestled his hips between her thighs.

She gasped as the bulge of firm, denim-clad flesh rubbed against her triangle of aching flesh. "You're already hard!"

"I've been this way since you let me lasso your wrists downstairs."

Susanne shifted against him, all but purring at the delicious sensation. It had been so long since she had been wrapped in a pair of strong arms. "You're lying. There's no way you walked through that lounge with a raging hard-on."

"I sure did. Why do you think we wear these big-ass hats? It's not just to protect us from the sun, sugar. They come in handy when totally hot women all but beg us to hogtie them and have our way with them."

"I never said that."

"So, I went to the trouble of ruining the window treatments at each end of the hallway for nothing?" He slid his palms lower and slowly hiked up the hem of her skirt until he could skim the back of her thighs with his work-worn palms.

"I never said that either."

"Well, what are you saying?" he asked, reaching over and snagging a plump blackberry, dragging it through the whipped cream before popping it into his mouth.

Susanne stared at the tiny drop of cream that clung to his mustache.

"You're not some psycho hayseed, are you?" She leaned forward and kissed the cream away. "Because I've really never done anything like this before."

"No, Susanne. I'm not a psycho. And you haven't done anything like what? Kissed a man with such sweetness that his dick is threatening to go off before he can make you scream with delight?"

"Oh my god, Lu—"

"Trey, sugar. Call me Trey. Yelling 'oh god' one moment and 'oh Lucifer' the next might be a bit confusing for the powers that be."

He dipped another berry and brought it to her mouth, rubbing along the crease of her lips until she opened her mouth and took the plump fruit from his fingers.

"Trey," she said after she swallowed.

"I like that, sugar." He pulled the bottom of her silky tank top from the waistband of her skirt with a smoothness that confirmed it might be her first X-rated rodeo but it wasn't his. She lifted her arms and he pulled the fabric upward and over her head. "Say it again."

"Trey." She whispered the word as his mouth claimed hers once again and this time it wasn't a gentle caress. It was rough. He teased the sensitive skin on the underside of her lower lip before gently thrusting the tip of his tongue between her teeth. Over and over. A little deeper each time until he was caressing the roof of her mouth in unison with the rocking of his hips against her throbbing pussy.

He shifted his knee to the inside of her thigh and pushed her leg open as his hands continued to caress her ass in concentric circles, each swipe bringing his fingers closer to the center of her drenched panties.

"You're so hot," he whispered, pressing forward to reach her fully.

His fingertips skimmed each side of her engorged vulva and a little whimper escaped her lips.

"Shhhh. Easy now. We've got all night."

"Not really. Security checks at midnight. No sleepovers allowed."

He rubbed her a little more firmly, tracing her fabric-covered slit from clit to anus, never quite reaching either. She thought she had picked up on his tempo and shifted quickly, forcing his finger against her aching nub. Unabashedly, she rotated her hips, working herself closer to orgasm, the fact that it wasn't her own hand bringing her to the peak making the sensation all the hotter.

"Screw security," he rasped, turning sideways to work his belt buckle open one-handedly. "The way you respond, I'm staying all night. That's it, sugar. Work those hips for me. I want you to come all over my fingers."

Susanne closed her eyes and concentrated on his words instead of her own wantonness. She'd never been adept at dropping her inhibitions. Until now. She heard the sound of his zipper being lowered and tried not to peek. His chest vibrated against her arm, an indication she hadn't been even remotely covert.

"Go ahead and look, Susanne. See how hard you've made me."

She opened her eyes fully and gazed at his cock—above average in length and thickness. The head was broad and flushed. She watched him work his hand up and down the shaft, the erotic sight forcing her to move faster.

"That's it, baby. The sooner you come, the sooner I can bury myself in your sweet pussy."

Susanne suddenly didn't want to wait to feel him. She was on the brink of exploding but she wanted to go with him.

"I want you now," she moaned, halting the movement of her hips.

"Don't you stop," he ordered in a tight voice, his breath tickling her ear. "You're first, sugar. That's the way it works."

"Not in my world." She tried to laugh but he chose that moment to shift his hand so his palm was cupping her mound, purposely not touching her clit.

"Move," he ordered.

"No. I want you inside me."

His hand disappeared and she thought he was about to capitulate. With one spin she found her palms and breasts pressed against the wall and her hips pulled backward, the heels of her shoes pressed against the blunted tips of his boots.

"You *are* going to come, Miss Susanne. Right now."

He yanked her panties to one side, the sound of rent fabric spurring her desire. His fingers brushed her clit and she bit her lip to keep from moaning. His strength should have been frightening but she found his power aphrodisiacal.

"I can smell how excited you are," he said before nipping at her earlobe. "How're you going to taste?"

His other hand returned to her mons, holding her throbbing flesh for endless seconds before he slid a solitary finger into her wetness and then out again. Using her own arousal for lube, he touched her clit once more and Susanne rocked back against his thighs.

He circled her sensitive nub with a slightly increasing pressure that rocketed her back to the edge.

"Was it better over the panties?"

He couldn't actually expect her to answer, could he? All the moisture seemed to have left her mouth. Her lips were dry, her throat suddenly parched from her rapid open-mouthed breathing.

"Tell me," he ordered, thrusting his rigid cock against the fullness of her ass.

"U-under," she panted.

"So you like it just like this?"

He was asking her what she liked. What she wanted. No one had ever asked. They had fumbled and blundered but never inquired.

Tell him how you want it.

"Faster," she cried.

He ignored her plea and pulled his finger a hairsbreadth away.

"So the next time we make love and I want you to come first, you're not going to argue?"

Next time? She heard him suck his finger into his mouth and hurried to answer. "No. I won't argue."

"Promise?"

"Yes. I promise." She shifted her hips, cursing when his stance held her legs apart. She wanted the throbbing to stop. She wanted to come so badly. "Please. It aches."

"I know, sugar." He brought his hand back to her swollen nub and used his thumb to buff it with a precision that had her gritting her teeth as her body started to shake.

"You ready for me to make all that aching go away?" he asked in a voice that sounded far, far away.

"Yes," she cried out as the first wave washed over her. "Yes, yes, yes."

Trey wanted to give her more than a few seconds to regain her senses but the wetness seeping out of her pussy and the tiny little moans that were still coming from her mouth were his undoing. Three steps and he could have her holding on to the hallway table, her skirt pulled up over her lush ass and his dick buried deep inside her. But this first time, he'd let her choose.

"I always want to hear 'yes' from you, Susanne. No more 'nos'." He leaned into her, covering her more fully. "I want you, sugar. Right now."

He gently ran his fingers through her pubic hair, amazed at the amount of wetness that clung to her curls, and gave a little tug.

"Okay," she said, her ragged breathing beginning to slow.

She pushed her back against his chest and he stood but didn't let her go until she forced her hands between their bodies and quickly unzipped her skirt. He moved one foot, so she could bring her legs together. She shimmied her hips from side to side and he curled his fingers to keep from touching her smooth skin. He watched the fabric hit the floor. Her panties followed and then all sound seemed to cease as she stepped forward and braced herself straight-armed against the wall. It was a pose he knew he wasn't likely to forget. Not anytime soon. It screamed "take me".

She shifted her feet, the globes of her heart-shaped ass rocking from side to side as if she'd somehow been able to read his previous thoughts. Or maybe she knew how much of as ass man he truly was. A set of full breasts were nice but they didn't compare to the wonders of smooth, taut butt cheeks.

"Shit, woman. Which way to the bedroom?"

"I thought you wanted me now?" Her tone was all innocence but when she looked over her shoulder, her eyes told a totally different story. They were glowing with desire.

A gentleman would ask her if she was certain but the lure of her lush ass was a distraction he couldn't combat. He reached out and ran his hands along the outer curves of her hips, giving her toned flesh a firm squeeze before moving upward over her rib cage. He skimmed the undersides of her breasts and she leaned forward quickly.

He pulled his hands away and worked his jeans off his hips as he bent and placed a kiss along her shoulder blade.

"You can have your way now," he said against her soft skin. "But you know I'm going to see all of you soon."

The mere thought of all the things he wanted to do with her caused his cock to twitch and he took a handful of his turgid flesh and allowed himself one selfish downward stroke before pulling his wallet from his back pocket and quickly retrieving a condom. Stepping forward, he ran his engorged cock head against Susanne's drenched flesh before ripping the foil packet open and sheathing his shaft. He bent his knees to allow for the perfect alignment and took a deep breath.

He innately knew her pussy was going to be tight. One of his favorite sensations in life came from working himself into a woman's heat. Nothing compared to the feel of lubing his cock with pussy juice and slowly pushing his way inside. He ran one finger along her slit, unable to stop himself from a tiny bit of insertion to test her tautness. She gave a little moan and he shook his head.

"So fucking snug, sugar." He removed his finger and ran his cock head up and down her drenched slit before pressing just the tip of his cock between her inner lips. He gritted his teeth and pushed inside, stopping when the rim of his cock cleared her tight opening.

"I'll beg forgiveness now, in case I go off after a dozen or so strokes."

"Oh shit," she moaned. "You're too big."

Trey snorted and wrapped his hands around her hips. He sensed that she was about to wiggle and held her still.

"The words every man wants to hear the first time he breaches his woman's pussy. Mercy, don't move. I'm going to try to do this with a little finesse, even though my balls are all but ready to explode."

"I don't care," she said, the muscles in her ass tensing under has hands. He pressed a fraction of an inch forward and felt her quiver.

"I want you to fuck me. Now," she ordered boldly.

She tried to move and he tightened his grip, praying she wasn't going to be bruised come morning. Her words sent a jolt of lust spiraling through his body, and despite all good intentions, he began to rock his hips in a short motion that afforded him the opportunity to brush against her G-spot.

"Oh my *god*!"

"Is that really all you're looking for? A quick fuck?" Part of him wanted her to say "no" so he'd be forced to take things slowly but another part—a more primal one—hoped she'd say "yes" so he could drop his restraint. The urge to pound hard and fast into her welcoming warmth was overwhelming.

His gaze drifted up the smooth planes of her back while he waited for her reply. All he received in response was another low moan and the sight of her dropping her chin toward her chest. The little movement parted her long hair, exposing the base of her neck. Like a stud to a prize mare, he had the urge to cover her, to seat himself fully while he nipped the little patch of skin and claim her for his own.

It was an overwhelming feeling—completely foreign—and he forced himself to look away, focusing instead on his cock sliding in and out, her juices slicking his latex-covered shaft with an erotic shine. He slowed his tempo to a near stop and her curse barely registered. He pulled completely out and then pushed back inside, slowly burying inch after inch until his balls were flush against her skin. The feeling was pure heaven.

"Oh god please," she whimpered, dropping her palms and upper body a little lower on the wall. The angle forced her body to tighten around his shaft and he quickly slid an arm around her waist for support, his vision momentarily blurring.

"Are you trying to drive me insane, woman?"

"No."

He pulled free again, taking his shaft in hand as he shifted his feet and rubbed his slicked cock head over her clit. He tapped randomly against the swollen flesh, nearly coming from the duality of her soft folds and engorged flesh. He'd never felt a clit so pronounced. So hard. He couldn't wait to see it up close. To suck the little nub into his mouth.

"What'd I say about you and the word 'no'?" Her body quivered and he switched to a steady tempo that had her moving one hand from the wall. She reached down and grabbed the hand covering her hip.

"Please," she moaned, squeezing his fingers.

"I like 'please'. And I like *to* please." He shifted and plunged into her hot pussy once again, thrusting with a steady rhythm that broke a fine sheen of perspiration along his spine.

"Can I please you, Susanne?"

"Yes," she cried, catching his pace and perfectly offering an alternate thrust that had him moaning as well.

"You feel so fucking good. Like you were made just for me."

"I was," she gasped. "I was."

Trey felt the familiar gripping that heralded his oncoming orgasm and he thrust faster, the front of his jeans-clad thighs loudly slapping the backs of her legs. He knew his body well. He probably had less than a dozen strokes left before he came and he pulled her upper body toward him, nuzzling her neck as he brought their bodies tightly together.

"I'm not going to last much longer," he said with a mildly disheartened snort.

"Then come," she panted harshly, turning her head so he could place a quick, intimate kiss on her parted mouth.

"After you," he said, sucking the patch of skin he had found so tempting into his mouth. She writhed against him and he bit down gently.

Her orgasmic cry echoed through the room. He lasted two more strokes before he pulled out and jerked the condom off, tossing it toward the trash can. With a harsh groan, Trey closed his eyes and shot his hot seed over her lower back. He milked his cock until all that remained was a solitary drop of cum dangling from the tip. He watched it fall, his heartbeat backing down from its frantic tempo as he slowly forced himself back to earth.

"You didn't need to pull out," she said softly, walking her hands up the wall for better support. Her voice sounded a hell of a lot more alert than he felt.

"I'm one hundred percent clean, darlin', and I'm willing to bet you are too, but I'm not much of a gamblin' man...even with a condom," he said, unable to help wondering if there was something else he could have done to make her totally incoherent. She continued to shift her hips as if tiny aftershocks might be rolling through her body and a trail of pussy juice was sliding down the inside of one of her thighs. "Where're the tissues?"

"Just use my panties, I think they're probably ruined anyway," she sighed and he could hear the smile in her voice.

He bent and snagged her torn underwear, carefully wiping her clean. His knuckles brushed her over-sensitized labia and she sucked in her breath.

"I'm on the Pill."

Her succinct announcement had his balls curling inward and his cock offering one quick flex.

"That'll be good to know for next time," he admitted with a surprised smile.

She flipped her dark hair over her shoulders and stood up straight. Despite the confident pose, her voice held a chord of apprehension. "When do you see this happening again?"

Her skin was like alabaster and he ran one hand from her neck to the base of her spine, enjoying the contrast of his dark skin to her paleness. He hooked his finger around the fabric of her racerback bra and pulled her upper body away from the wall.

"In about twenty minutes." He turned her toward him and kissed her softly, not questioning why having her secure in his embrace seemed like the most important thing in the world. He scooped her into his arms and headed toward the living area.

"That quick, huh?"

She heaved a heavy sigh and tilted her head backward against his shoulder. He looked down, saw her half-closed eyes and satiated smile and stopped dead. He staggered as a sharp pain in the vicinity of his heart struck him.

That's not good, son. You're supposed to be detached, remember? Could just be an irregular heartbeat. An unknown medical condition would be preferable to feeling guilty over fulfilling his promise to his uncle. And there was no way he was ready to consider that she had somehow touched a part of his soul that had been buried for a very long time.

He sure as fuck didn't want to head down that trail now but with his brother's recent engagement Trey had come to the realization that they had possibly wasted a good number of their prime years—years that should have been focused on fidelity-based relationships rather than various forms of taboo delights. In their minds, they always assumed fate would offer them the perfect woman who could share in the ménage lifestyle they oftentimes enjoyed. Their dreams had never included Trey being alone or their brotherly bond nearly severed.

Susanne reached up and cradled his jaw in her small hand before slowing tracing the lines of his mustache and goatee with one slender finger. He turned his face into her palm and nipped at her skin. He needed a distraction and he needed one quickly.

"Country boys are resilient...when we need to be," he finally said, offering her a wink. "Grab the Jack and tell me which bedroom is yours?"

"To the left," she said, unscrewing the bottle and taking a healthy sip.

"Easy now. I've got plans for you, missy."

"Do you now?" she teased, nuzzling his chest.

He couldn't wait to get his shirt and her bra off so they could be skin to skin. He'd never had such a strong desire to show a woman exactly how good of a man he could be. He'd always been a considerate lover but with Susanne he had the overwhelming urge to pull out every sexual trick he had learned and every technique he'd perfected over the past twenty years, just in case that's what it would take.

Take? For what, son?

More than a night or two of random loving? More than being a man who was willing to share his chosen woman? That had worked out nicely until his sibling had met the love of his life and turned suddenly possessive. Trey had been pissed at first. Pissed and hurt. But now he couldn't blame Gabe. Not one bit. While the sharing over the past four years had been fun, it wasn't realistic from a let's-settle-down-and-raise-a-family standpoint. And with the Ryder clan, it always came back to family. And wasn't that a kick in the ass?

"Why are you smiling?" Susanne asked as they walked through the doorway to her room. "You looked really far away for a second but now you just look diabolical."

He lowered her feet to the floor and took the bottle from her fingers.

"Speaking of diabolical—I forgot the berries. And the cola. We keep swiggin' this straight and no one's going to remember what happened, come morning."

"Would that be a bad thing?" she asked in a demure voice that didn't remotely go with the image she presented.

Trey tossed her the silky cord that had been looped around his wrist the entire time they'd been making love and took a step backward to study her half-naked body.

"You look totally hot, standing there with your upper half covered and your pussy bare. You're runnin' that rope through your fingers like you can't wait to feel its soft restraint."

She quickly tossed the rope on the bed and set the bottle on the nightstand before reaching for the front clasp of her bra.

"No, no, no. I want to strip you the rest of the way. Just stand there until I get back."

"Is that an order? One that will be punishable if I disobey?"

"Yes...and yes," he said, swallowing hard. He was more than adept at all manners of discipline but doubted she knew what she was hinting at. "Are you up for the punishment?"

"If it feels as good as it did a little bit ago? Maybe. As long as it's not to the point that I'm crying in pain."

Her gaze darted to the rope that lay on top of the comforter and Trey felt his sac give a slow, lazy roll that set his teeth on edge.

Trey snorted, unable to stand not touching her when she was so damn appealing. He wrapped his arms low around her waist and pulled her roughly against his body, marveling at the little jump his dick gave.

"Oh, there'll be cries. And there'll be pain of a certain sort," he said, taking her face in his hands and kissing her deep and slow, not stopping until her little mewl of pleasure echoed through his mouth. He pulled back and ran his hands up the sides of her body until he was cupping her breasts.

"Your pussy is going to be throbbing, each little pulsation of desire begging for my touch. And these..." He brushed over the center of her lace-covered breasts, back and forth until her nipples hardened. "You're going to offer me the world to make the ache in these tight little buds go away."

"Am I going to need a safeword?"

"Safeword?" He looked down and studied her eyes. They were filled with a combination of curiosity and desire and he offered her a throaty chuckle before he forced himself to back up. "Trust me. You'll never use it."

"You don't know that," she replied, reaching for him as he stepped away.

"I do, for a fact. When it's all said and done, sugar, you're going to be pleading with me *not* to stop."

Chapter Three
୫୨

Overbearing men did nothing for Susanne. Egotistical statements and invisible me-Tarzan-you-Jane chest thumping normally sent her into complete ice-princess mode.

So why am I letting Cowboy Sexy slide?

Maybe it was the utterly confident tone of his voice. Maybe it was the way he looked down, eyes twinkling with promise as he held her loosely in his arms. Maybe it was the way his unzipped jeans rode low on his hips as he turned and walked out the bedroom door. Maybe it was none of those things. Maybe it was as simple as her being a totally horny woman looking for a night of possibly the best sex ever.

Too late...that just happened in the hallway. Yeah. Braced up against a wall, half undressed. *What sad testimony to my recent sexual encounters.*

She'd had men make her pussy tingle before. But not like Trey, aka Lucifer. She hadn't drunk so much that she imagined, through all the thrusting and moaning and slapping of flesh against denim, that level of respectfulness he exuded. There was no doubt in her mind that the man was pure authenticity. A gentleman.

He'd thrown the sexual ball into her court. He gave her the opportunity to obey or disobey – one way or another – so there would be no mixed signals. She took one last glance at the small coil of silky rope and her pulse spiked. She didn't want to overanalyze why she inexplicably trusted him. All she wanted to do was simply embrace the moment and *feel*. She heard him walking toward the bedroom and quickly undid her bra and tossed it aside.

He ambled into the room, sexily barefoot, carrying the bowl of berries, a can of cola and a glass of ice.

"You took off your boots," she blurted when she noticed his bare feet.

"And you were a very naughty girl and took off your bra. Even when I asked you not to."

He walked up to her until their bodies were nearly touching and then leaned around her right side to place the bowl on the nightstand. His chin grazed the outer edge of her shoulder and she shuddered. He automatically reached out and slowly ran his palms up and down her arms, barely touching her flesh.

"Cold?" he asked, hands hovering just below her shoulders. His large thumbs drifted to the sensitive crease of skin between her upper arms and the outer curve of her breasts and Susanne shivered once more before a rush of heat rolled through her body.

"No. I'm hot."

"Don't I know *that*?" he barely whispered. His gaze traveled over her exposed skin as if he were memorizing something of great import and Susanne fought the urge to squirm.

She was about to tell him there wasn't anything there worth looking at for that long when he grabbed both her wrists and pushed them behind her back. The quick movement forced her breasts to jut outward.

"What should I do to a woman who can't follow a simple instruction?" His voice was a low, seductive caress that had her nipples beading.

He caught both her wrists in one of his hands and moved to her side. She tested his grip and the pressure slackened just enough that she realized he'd let her go if she wished. He slowly lowered his mouth toward one nipple, his breath leaving a warming trail along her cleavage and she knew what she truly yearned for.

With a wide, open-mouthed caress he covered her nipple, his tongue tracing lazy circles around her areola until her belly coiled and a trail of wetness slid down her inner thigh. She arched her back, trying to silently guide him to the other side but he wouldn't be detoured. He licked and sucked and licked and sucked, his mouth never losing suction. She tried to shift her upper body from side to side but he trapped her distended nipple between his teeth.

"You want a little more?" he asked around the hardened flesh, looking up at her through long lashes.

"Yesss," she hissed, unable to pull her gaze away.

He covered his teeth with his lips and took hold of the turgid peak, biting down with a slow, steady pressure that had her rubbing her thighs together in a futile attempt at stopping the shot of electricity that rocketed straight to her pussy.

"More?"

"Yes," she cried, hips rocking.

He took her other nipple between thumb and forefinger and tweaked the tight peak hard enough that her moan turned desperate.

He pulled his head back and simply stared at her breasts.

"I wanted to take this nice and slow but those little sounds you're making are driving me to distraction. Keep your hands behind your back."

Susanne did as she was told, holding her breath when both his palms covered her nipples, pressing the peaks into her breasts before testing the weight.

"They're a perfect fit," he said, kneading her flesh in a slow, steady rhythm. "Don't you think?"

She didn't answer, just stared as gripping turned into rubbing and rubbing brought him full circle to where he held each of her nipples firmly between thumb and forefinger. He didn't pinch but instead rolled the flesh with a light friction that had her inner muscles mirroring the stimulating motion.

"At some point, we're going to get a pair of nipple clamps. Would you like that, sugar?"

"I don't know," she blurted, closing her eyes against the mini-orgasmic wave that washed over her body. Her breasts swelled and she let out a ragged breath.

He tightened his grip with a slow, steady pressure, not stopping until she moaned.

"Ah, darlin', it's so good to find a woman who's not afraid to tell me what she wants. Promise me you won't hold anything back."

"Promise," she said, breathless from the way he was teasingly squeezing and releasing her nipples. A long spasm rolled through her abdomen and Susanne straightened abruptly. She heard the harshness of her breath and pulled backward, the self-inflicted tug taking her another step closer to orgasm.

"Mmmm. Brought you close, huh, sugar?"

He straightened and she actually whimpered when he let go of her nipples. He drifted his fingers up the slope of her neck before threading them through her hair and pulling her close, kissing her to a point of senselessness, where she felt as if she were falling.

A second later she was airborne, her eyes opening in shock as she bounced once before landing fully supine on the bed. With mind-numbing speed he unbuttoned his cuffs and had his shirt over his head and was on the bed and straddled her.

His torso was ripped and tanned, proof of a lifestyle that included manual, outdoor labor. At some point she'd find out exactly what her cowboy did for a living. A fine line of dark hair ran down the center of his stomach and disappeared into the vee of his unbuttoned jeans and she suddenly felt overexposed. While he was gorgeous in his semi-clad state, she suddenly wanted to see every inch of his hard body.

"Are you going to get naked?"

"In a bit." The way his lips turned upward in a sexy grin made her heart race. Him reaching down and picking up the length of cord had the same beat echoing in her head...her stomach...her pussy.

"Give me a leg," he ordered. The timbre of his voice left no room for argument.

He rose onto his knees and Susanne felt a surge of trepidation. Part of her considered telling him to forget about playing the game. She'd never been bound before. It always sounded titillating when she read about it in her magazines or when the patrons on ladies' night would discuss such things over five-dollar dirty martinis. But faced with the reality of the situation, she paused.

"I won't hurt you, Susanne."

His intuitiveness soothed her uneasiness.

"Just don't say 'no' unless you really mean it. Do you trust me?"

Do you trust me? Surprisingly, she did trust him—a man she had known only a few hours—more than all her other partners combined. Swallowing the last bit of nervousness, Susanne bent her knee and slid her foot along the bed and through his spread legs. She ran the toe of her shoe up his inner thigh, gently brushing the growing bulge of his erection before moving higher and placing her foot flat against his chest.

"You are a tease, aren't you, Miss Susanne?"

"Not usually," she said, gasping when he grabbed her foot and planted a hot kiss on her ankle.

"Fine time to change," he chuckled. "These heels are so hot. I know they have to come off eventually but not yet." He placed the sole of her foot against the comforter and trailed his fingers up her leg, resting his wrist on her knee. "Give me your hand."

Susanne did as requested, watching carefully as he tied her ankle and wrist together. He looped and twisted the cord so quickly that she lost track of what he was doing, but when he was done a long single strand lay loose and off to her side.

"That's your safety loop. Just like I showed you downstairs." His voice had become so husky that Susanne dragged her gaze from her bound extremities to his face. She watched his nostrils flare ever so slightly before the angle of his jaw shifted. He stared at her pussy and she self-consciously moved her other hand to cover her exposed flesh.

"No." He moved his leg to the inside of her knee and yanked her hand away. "Don't you dare hide that from me. I want to see every glistening fold...taste every drop of your sweet essence."

He brought her hand to his mouth and licked her palm with long, bold strokes that made her think of how wonderfully he'd lick other places on her body. Places that were flushed and swollen and orally neglected.

"I want you to taste me." The words slipped easily from her mouth.

He picked up the rope and pulled it underneath her bottom, quickly securing her other hand to her ankle, leaving another free length of cord. She stared down her body, shocked yet thrilled at the way her limbs were placed. She was open, the core of her womanhood available for whatever he desired. The position ratcheted her anticipation to the point of physical discomfort and she wiggled her hips. She was hot. Wanting. Her body feeling so full of itself that she felt as if her nether regions might burst.

"Easy now. We have to make this perfect in every way so for just a minute, quit thinking about what I'm going to do to you and listen."

He put a piece of rope in each of her palms and curled her fingers over it. "All you need do is rotate your wrists outward and the loop will pull free. Simple but on a hair trigger so hold the rope a little looser if you don't want to have premature freedom."

"Trey?" A solitary question had been swirling through her mind. One she felt compelled to ask. "Do you do this a lot?"

"No, Susanne," he said unflinchingly, looking up from his handiwork to meet her eyes. "It's not a daily occurrence. A little rope play now and again but it's not essential to me when I make love. It's been quite a while since I've actually had the opportunity so don't think it's some sort of fetish either."

"So this is kind of like a treat?" She didn't like the contemplative sound of her own voice one bit.

"A treat? No, this isn't a treat," he chuckled, sitting back on his haunches. He ran the back of each of his middle fingers up the fronts of her legs, over her kneecaps and then down the inside of her thighs. His darkened gaze followed the electrifying trail.

"Peanut butter pie is a treat, sugar. This is way more special than an after-dinner favorite. Your pussy's beautiful."

He rotated his wrists and placed his palms on the smooth flesh of her inner thighs. Gently, he pushed her legs open until her knees were nearly touching the bed. Susanne swallowed, not sure how to answer. A simple "thank you" didn't seem right. The way he was staring at her—she didn't even know if she could speak.

"Just the way I imagined. Pink in some places, plump in others." He brushed the tip of one finger across her vulva and Susanne's thighs twitched at the jolt that shot to her core. "Still skittish. Not used to being stroked like this?"

He moved his finger to the other side and leisurely rubbed the full flesh, over and over until a trickle of wetness rolled from her folds. His finger stilled and she watched him watch the trail of her desire. The tiny drop teased the skin between her pussy and her anus and she was about to shift against the erotic discomfort when he blocked the liquid's progression with his thumb.

Susanne held her breath as he lubed his thumb with her juices and began to trace tiny circles against the sensitive strip of skin. He worked upward toward her pussy and she wantonly spread her legs as far open as they would go. He met her gaze, held it as he drew away from the place she longed for him to stroke and started a teasing trail toward her rim. She tensed.

"Don't," she said quickly.

He gave her a little smile and immediately stopped.

"Because you don't like it? Or have you never tried?"

"I've tried. Just not with a real—penis."

His eyes darkened and she immediately regretted her words.

"Did you like it?" he asked in a deep whisper.

"Yes," she admitted. Just the two of them talking about her asshole being stroked was enough to have her insides trembling.

"Maybe later we can try the real thing?"

She offered him a little negative shake of her head and he winked as he circled back toward her throbbing cunt.

"We'll see," he said in an offhand manner that was anything but. His self-assuredness would have set Susanne off if she weren't in the beginning throes of a slow-building orgasm. They were her favorite kind. The ones she never had enough willpower to bring about when it was just her and her toys. The kind you fanned and then banked. The kind that went on and on until you finally exploded.

"I swear to god, I've never wanted to roll my tongue around a clit more than I do this second."

His admission skyrocketed her need and when he ran the tip of his thumb against the little cap of skin covering the top of her clit her long moan echoed through the room.

"Shit," he muttered. A look of pain creased his forehead as he reached inside his jeans and shifted his erection.

Susanne tilted her hips toward him, hoping he'd give in and offer them both a little relief. "I'm ready."

"Your glistening pussy is proof of that but I haven't had a chance to even taste you. Really taste you."

"You have tasted me," she said, urgent for him to plunge into her hot sheath and show her how a man truly rides the woman he desires.

"Licking your juice off my finger and feasting on a fine set of nipples doesn't come close to what I want to do," he said, leaning forward to place a kiss against the center of her breastbone.

"I want you inside me again. Don't you want that?" Susanne watched as he slowly kissed his way downward. He traced a circle around her bellybutton with the tip of his nose, the stubble on his chin brushing just above her mound, the combination of sensations doubly teasing. He placed a series of light kisses over her abdomen before delving lower and she automatically tensed.

"Don't be nervous, sugar."

"I'm not," she lied. Sophisticated women who were used to having oral sex lavished on them at every turn wouldn't be nervous. They'd be lying back, waiting for the experience to begin.

"Before I became a breeder, I worked as a prep cook at a five-star restaurant in Dallas."

Susanne stared at him, body thrumming.

What the hell does that have to do with the price of corn in Kansas?

"It's where I learned the intrinsic worth of a stiff whipped cream."

He picked up a plumb blackberry and she swallowed against the dryness in her throat.

"Don't move," he ordered in a deep voice, his gaze skittering over her body.

Anticipation drew her muscles taut. She didn't know what he was going to do with the berry but her mind was far from at a loss as to the many places it could go. His hand drifted toward her breast and she shut her eyes, not sure if she was ready for "fun with fruit".

She felt a cool wetness in the center of her chest and peeked through her lashes. One by one he systematically placed a trail of berries down the center of her body, using the whipped cream to hold them stationary. He reached her bellybutton and added one on each side before moving lower and placing two more on her lower stomach.

She watched him survey his work, a huge grin brightening his gorgeous face.

"What's so funny, Tex?"

"Not as noticeable as a row of runway lights but they do lead to the prettiest landing strip I've ever seen."

Susanne jerked when he traced the outer edge of her neatly trimmed pubic hair. Up and down in tiny increments, his fingers coming closer to her throbbing opening with each progressing downward stroke. The tiny lull of desire brought on by their playful banter flared instantly to life. She shifted her hips, trying to deflect his fingers but all she received for her effort was the dislodging of two berries.

She looked at him, gasping as he took her outer labia between thumb and forefinger and slowly pinched the engorged flesh until she was biting her lip.

"I asked you not to move. When I find the ones that rolled away I'm going to do torturous things to you with them."

Oh my god. What can he do with a single berry? And what could be more torturous than the way he was currently capturing her flesh? Susanne shivered. Knowing she definitely wanted to find out.

He released her labia and Susanne moaned loudly as a rush of pleasure-pain washed over her lower body. Methodically, he sucked each berry from her skin, laving the creamy remains with his hot tongue until every drop had disappeared. He worked from bottom to top, nibbling at her flesh at unpredictable intervals that had her nerves tightening.

She watched it all through half-closed eyelids, her anticipation nearing the breaking point as he slowly devoured the final berry. "Tasty," he said, reaching over to scoop up a bit more whipped cream from the bowl. He sucked half of the dollop into his mouth as he pushed back onto his knees.

"What if I put some here?"

He smeared the remainder along each side of her engorged clitoris, the erotic contact rocking her enough that she felt the rope she held in her right hand give a little. She immediately stilled, not wanting to be free from his sweet confines.

"That was to make up for the berry that slipped down your right side." His fingers prodded the area of the bed where her body met the comforter until he found the renegade berry. He tossed it onto the nightstand and began a quick search on her left side for the other berry, finding it closer to her hip.

"Now this one looks salvageable," he said, balancing the huge berry between his thumb and index finger. "Let's see if you do better this time at keeping it where it needs to be."

Susanne watched as he dipped the flatter end into the whipped cream and lowered the fruit between her spread legs.

"Oh no," she whispered.

"Oh yes," he said, gently placing the treat directly over her clit before sliding slowly off the end of the bed.

She might have been mortified if he hadn't distracted her by slowly lowering his zipper the rest of the way and dropping his jeans to the floor. It was clear that nothing came between her cowboy and his Levi's and Susanne licked her lips at the godlike picture he presented.

That perfect cock looked a whole lot bigger when it wasn't surrounded by half-dropped denim. Fully erect, it brushed against his lower abs and Susanne dropped her knees as far as possible.

"Do you think I need all that room?" he asked with the sexiest of grins before he crawled back between her thighs. "You did a great job of keeping this in place, sugar. That deserves a reward, don't you think?"

He looked at her face and she nodded quickly.

He plucked the berry away and sucked at the cream, turning it in his hand until the pointed end was facing downward.

"Remember that game we played as kids? The one where someone would use their finger and write a word on your back and you had to guess what they wrote?"

He glanced intently at her pussy and Susanne shivered.

"I'm up for a more adult version. How 'bout you?" He swirled the berry against her aching nub in a half dozen strokes. Susanne closed her eyes and focused on breathing normally, which was terribly hard with him stroking the berry along the side of her vulva. She shifted her knees and the cord pulled a little tighter against her wrists.

"Sugar," he said. "I spelled 'sugar'. You didn't get that one. Close your eyes and concentrate. I'm sure you'll figure out the next one."

The torturous feel of the knobby fruit against her swollen clit had her toes curling in her shoes. This time there were more strokes. They varied in pressure. Some firm and sure as he pressed hard against her while others barely brushed her nub. Part of her doubted he was actually spelling a word. Another part wished he wouldn't stop. Her body began tightening inward and she knew if he'd just pick one tempo and stick with it she'd reach her peak quickly.

"What was that?" he asked, pulling the berry away once again.

"I don't know," she groaned. "I don't care."

"That's not nice." There was a wicked tone to his chuckle and Susanne thought she might actually be dealing with the real devil. "I was spelling your name. Wanna try once more?"

"I don't," she said quickly, arching her back when he settled on a steady back-and-forth motion. He'd found the spot—the perfect rhythm.

"No more games." She sobbed as her core tightened. "Please."

"Spoilsport. I was going to do 'sweetness' next. From the way your thighs are quivering, I'm not sure I would have made it to crossing that 't' before you exploded."

"Oh, *fuuuuuck*." The tiny spasms rocked her and she flung herself against the mattress. He diligently kept the pace, stroking with a precision that rocked her right over the edge. Had her eyes been open, she was fairly certain she'd have seen stars dancing across the ceiling.

"Jesus, sugar. You are a sight to behold when you come. I don't know if there are enough hours in the night for me to show you how many ways I can make you explode. How many times I can watch the pleasure cross your gorgeous face."

Susanne loved his accent and even if the words he was speaking were total crap, she didn't care. Her body was in that pleasant stage of post-orgasmic floatation but for some reason it differed from the ordinary. She seemed to be staying adrift longer than normal, mentally crediting it to the fact he'd had her on the brink for so long that when release finally came, it overshadowed the results of even her best vibrator.

"Mmmm." She started to scratch her nose and the realization that she was still tied slammed into her. It was followed by her pussy clenching at the thought.

Look at you. Satisfied like never before and still wanting more!

Only because she knew the man kneeling before her probably never ever broke his word. She found that as attractive as his chiseled body and rugged face. Maybe more so.

"Has anyone ever told you you're egotistical?" She sighed, wiggling her fingers to find the lengths of cord that would set her free. "And you shouldn't make promises you can't deliver on."

"Has anyone ever told you they wanted to lick your pussy until you screamed their name?" He reached over and lifted the cords up and away from her searching fingers. "And you shouldn't goad a man if you're not willing to suffer the consequences."

His eyes glimmered, the deep gray irises turning darker.

"Give me the rope." Her tone held conviction.

"Consequences, sugar." He flicked his wrists and the cords began to sway to and fro. "If this were real—if you were truly my sex slave for the night—it wouldn't matter that you're uncomfortable. Your goal would be to do whatever I ordered, just to please me."

"Lucky this isn't real then." Her eyes followed the swing of the cord. "I want the loops, Trey. I want free."

"No you don't. You don't want that at all. And until you can be honest with yourself, we'll just have to go with what I want. And right now..."

He let go of the cord and she squealed as he gripped her upper arms and pulled her quickly to her knees.

"I want your pussy against my mouth."

He picked her up and slid her legs along the comforter until she was at the edge of the bed.

"That's a real sexy pose, me just able to see the shadow of those sweet lips. But I'm way past the teasin' stage. Open your legs," he ordered in a firm voice that had every nerve ending in her body coming to attention. Her heart thundered and she quickly obeyed, sitting back on her heels for her own comfort.

"Wider."

Susanne spread her knees as far as they would go, dropping her butt lower to accommodate her bonds. She looked down at him, hoping to gauge his reaction, but his eyes focused on her pussy.

He leaned in, his breath teasing her thighs as he whispered. "That's the way."

She wrapped her hands around her ankles as an erotic shiver stole through her body. She dug her nails in a second later when she heard him blow out and a cool stream of air drifted over her hot slit. He buried his nose against her mons and she jerked upright at the first hot pass of his tongue against her clit.

"I like that better," he said, slowly sucking the little nub into his mouth then releasing it with a little "pop" before sitting back on his haunches.

Susanne lowered her butt back to her heels, shocked at how one single caress could have her cunt throbbing once again.

"Do you like when I lick you?"

"Yes," she answered quickly, hoping he'd see her rapid response as part of the game and not the desperation that was building inside.

"And you want more?"

"Yes." *God yes!*

He backed away from her until his stomach was resting against the mattress and locked gazes. Susanne waited, knowing a demand would be made.

"Bring that honey to me." He opened his mouth and ran his tongue over his bottom lip.

Susanne rose to her knees as far as the cord would allow, unable to bring her aching flesh close enough to the relief his lips promised. She arched her back, still nowhere near as close as she needed to be.

"C'mon, sugar. Just a little farther."

He swooped down and left a trail of kisses along her lower stomach and Susanne thrust her hips forward with total wantonness.

"Just like that." It was the last thing he said before sticking out his tongue and running it down one side of her bare labia and up the other. He tilted his head and placed a long kiss against her slit. She felt just the tip of his tongue trace the edges of her opening and she placed her index and middle fingers tightly together, using them to balance herself against her heels, waiting for the little jolt of pleasure that was sure to rock through her when he touched her clit.

The front of her thighs burned but there was no way to take the pressure from them without losing contact with his talented lips and tongue. She chose not to move, knowing the reward for her patience would be worth the slight discomfort.

He worked his way around, up and down, side to side, never fully touching the little kernel that seemed to tighten more with each open-mouthed caress. She clenched the cheeks of her ass and pushed her muscles to their limits as she tilted her pelvis toward him.

"That feels so good," she whispered, closing her eyes and letting her head fall back. It helped alleviate the pressure on her spine but did nothing for the full-body ache his tongue work caused.

"Mmmhmmm."

His response vibrated through her and Susanne groaned aloud. "Oh god. Do that again."

He ignored her plea and licked the juice from her slit with one long, solitary stroke that brought the tip of his tongue flush against her clitoris. He flicked the little nub once and she flinched. Twice more and she growled his name.

"This is never goin' to be enough," he said, starting a slow, circular rotation that had her exhaling the breath she hadn't realized she'd been holding. His calloused hands slid up her outer thighs, leaving a trail of tingling warmth in their wake. His tongue circled and circled along the smooth lower edge of her clitoris and then over the looser skin of the hood, over and over, with a steady pressure that had her gritting her teeth.

"More." She barely heard her own whispered plea but his hands suddenly grabbed her ass and forced her closer. She gasped as the firmer pressure forced the budding of another orgasm. The fact that she might never get enough of *him* flashed across her mind.

"I need to taste you," she moaned.

"You will." The slight pause had no effect on his working her toward the brink of orgasm.

She wanted to do to him what he was doing to her. She wanted to lick his body until she had committed every manly inch to memory. Her legs were starting to shake and she knew there wouldn't be much time.

"I want to suck your cock," she said desperately.

"Later."

"Now."

"Later."

"No!" she yelled, louder than she'd intended. Forcing a modicum of space between her hips and his lips took monumental internal strength.

"Bring that back up here."

"Untie me."

"I'm not done yet."

"I need to touch you."

"After you—"

"Now." She sobbed her frustration, falling sideways on the bed. The long end of one of her bindings struck her thigh and she wiggled frantically, trying to catch hold of it.

A part of her realized he'd shot to his feet.

"Sugar! Easy." She felt the firm tug of the cord and her right arm and leg were suddenly free. She stared upward into his startled eyes before sitting up and reaching for the other cord. She grabbed it and yanked but it wouldn't come free.

"Susanne. Let me."

Her heart was drumming in her ears but the knot finally pulled loose and in one smooth move she scooted off the bed, landing on her knees as she wrapped both hands around his cock. She looked up at him with desire-filled eyes.

"Don't ever make me wait again."

She tightened her grip and watched a glistening drop of pre-cum form at the tip. She bent her head and ran her tongue around the head of his cock in the same teasingly circular motion he had used on her until she heard his low rumble of delight. Satisfaction surged and she lightly raked him with her teeth. He buried a hand in her hair and Susanne could feel his battle for restraint.

She waited to see what he was going to do. His fingers flexed. Once. Twice. And then relaxed.

"Are you just going to play with it?" he asked in a strained voice. "Or are you goin' to suck it proper?"

His words proved he truly was a master of deceptive control.

Susanne hid her smile, and with a little restraint of her own, swallowed him slowly.

He'd lost the upper hand.

Who gives a fuck?

It was his place to set the standards.

According to whom?

First nights were just that. Firsts. Women kept those memories in a little mental compartment for all of eternity and they pulled them out of storage when they needed to serve a specific purpose. They never forgot those memories were there.

Guess what you're never going to forget? How hot Susanne looks right now – on her knees with her hair a mess. Or how she moans when you run your tongue around the left side of her clit. Or the way she can deep throat your cock better than any other woman on the planet.

Trey shook his head and tried to think of something other than the fact he wanted to let her and masterful cock-sucking skills take him right over the edge. No, that was his inner horn dog in him talking. He wanted to hold out. He wanted to bury himself in her again. At the very least, once more. But damn. The woman was making it more difficult by the second for him to consider that an achievable goal.

He loved the way she made him feel and not just when her lips were doing things that made his blood boil. Something strange had touched him when he'd taken her in that hallway.

Up against a wall? True horn-dog moment, son.

She looked up at him, her gaze all innocence one second and pure seduction the next. She stopped mid-swallow and hesitantly squeezed his balls. He couldn't decide if he wanted to fuck her right there on the floor or wrap her in his arms and protect her for all eternity.

She's going to be hurt either way, come morning. Why change your ways now? I say, go for the poundin'.

There were times he hated that motherfucking voice but Susanne chose that moment to go down on him in earnest and Trey pushed everything except the need to pleasure them both from his mind.

"Get up here, darlin'. You've tasted enough," he said, threading his fingers through her silky hair.

"I haven't tasted *everything*," she said in a steamy tone that made his dick surge. "See, even *it* wants me to keep going."

"I don't give a shit what *it* wants," Trey said. He pulled her from her knees to her feet and then quickly hooked her leg high on his hip before bouncing her into his arms. She wrapped her legs around his waist, the heat from her pussy scorching his stomach.

"I want you so bad," he whispered hoarsely. It was the truth. He could find pussy anywhere. He wanted *her*. He burned for Susanne.

"I want you too," she replied.

She gripped his shoulders and he took a deep breath before picking her up and then lowering her onto his cock. *Jesus god.* There'd never been anything like this. The heat. The softness. The perfect fit. He started as slow as his aching balls would permit, working her up and down his shaft as sweat broke out along the center of his back. She gave the occasional wiggle against him but he knew that after her break for the blowjob she wasn't as close as he'd like her.

"How 'bout we try something a little more traditional?" he asked, not giving her a chance to answer as he took a few steps toward the bed. He carefully lowered her, keeping their bodies joined as he positioned her heels on the sideboards.

With a leisurely ease he was far from feeling, he thrust in and out, watching her face closely to ensure he'd know when he hit the perfect depth. He pushed a half inch farther and her eyes widened. He looked down at his dick and pulled nearly all the way out. When he thrust again and stopped, a little moan escaped her mouth.

He wanted to be so much deeper in her heat but he wouldn't rush. Not with Susanne. Not this time. And if someone forgave him for his transgressions and granted him another chance to be in her arms again, not then either. He flexed and released his hips, his cock rubbing the spot on the front of her vagina with every movement.

"It's heaven. Don't you think?"

"Heaven," she agreed, and he stroked a little quicker, relieved when he felt her pussy clamp down.

"Or hell," she panted, covering her stomach with her hand. "I'm on fire."

"Me too, sugar."

"Ohmigod, I mean it. This doesn't feel right. I'm so hot."

"Shhh. You're fine. Trust me. You'll see." He covered her hand with his and gave it an encouraging squeeze before pushing it to the side and replacing it with his palm. He pressed firmly down against her abdomen, silently praying that he'd be able to last.

"Shit!" She picked her head up and looked at his hand and then into his eyes, desire and fear and confusion swirling. "Stop. This doesn't usually happen."

"It does with me."

"How?" She was watching his cock go in and out.

"Don't you know, darlin'? It's the curve."

"Oh fuck." She threw her head backward and covered her eyes with the backs of her hands. He felt the roll of tension that snaked through her body, knowing she was struggling against the feeling.

"Don't fight it. Breathe and let me take you a little higher."

"No!" He watched her breasts rise and fall, all the while holding back his release as he pumped harder.

"Come with me, sugar. I know you're close." Gripping spasms were milking his shaft and he felt the jolt of electricity that heralded his impending release.

"For me, Susanne. Come for me." It was part order, part plea.

She sobbed his name, clutching the sheets as she finally gave in and allowed the orgasm to envelop her.

For the first time in years, he felt the glorious sensation of unencumbered release. No spilling himself into a condom or on a belly or over some shapely ass. His hips kept pumping, delirious to be seated inside a woman's warmth. *His* woman's warmth.

The thrumming in his temples lessened to the point that it no longer competed with his wildly beating heart. He looked down at Susanne's limp body, waiting until their breathing had slowed before he spoke.

"How was that?"

"Awful," she lied, listening to her heartbeat resonate through her head. There was a second where she'd thought it might actually burst from the frenetic activity. She pushed herself fully onto the bed. "That was not traditional."

He slid up beside her and propped his head on one hand, offering her a pleased grin as he brushed her hair out of her eyes. "The crazy shit's over. I promise."

She couldn't move. Couldn't.

"That's too bad. I was starting to like that crazy shit," she finally said.

He wrapped an arm around her waist and pulled her against his body, pushing at her hips until she was forced to roll onto her side. His heat enveloped her from shoulders to toes as he molded his large frame to her. His hand drifted to her breast, his thumb tracing a lazy figure eight just below her heart.

"How 'bout I amend that to 'the crazy shit's over for now'?"

She knew he was smiling and it brought on a lazy grin of her own.

"Perfect," she said softly, feeling the lethargy begin to take hold. She wiggled her hips to get more comfy.

"You're not going to fall asleep on me, are you?"

"I've had a hard day, cowboy."

"Keep doin' that, sugar, and you're going to have a hard night as well."

Susanne closed her eyes and sighed as pure contentment washed over her. She hadn't felt this relaxed and secure in a very long time. The voice of reason should have been warning her but for once it was nowhere to be found. Maybe it was basking in the afterglow of great sex too. If that were the case, she needed to do this more often. That voice was damn annoying most of the time and she appreciated the silence.

"I was really looking forward to you riding me, Susanne. Watching you get one of those long legs up and straddle me. Slide down my cock nice and slow before reversin' around so I could get a good view of your ass. Lord, sugar. That would be heaven."

He eased his hips back a bit and she felt his cock jump.

"Mmmmm. Tempting, Tex. Very tempting." Susanne mustered enough energy to roll toward him and push him to his back. She slid her arm around his waist and threaded her leg between his thighs.

"Is this all part of some devil's plan?" she asked, laying a kiss on his nipple before resting her head on his chest. His body tensed but she didn't give the reaction a second thought.

"What plan?"

"The one where you make love to me so often that I can't get out of bed in the morning."

"Because you're too sore?" he asked, a hint of worry evident in his tone.

"No, Mr. I'm-so-full-of-myself-because-I-have-a-rockin'-penis."

Susanne felt the rumble of his silent laughter.

"Then why?"

"Because I doubt I'll have the strength left to move."

"Trust me, Susie Q. You've left me shaken too."

Susanne laughed and shifted against him. "And I was definitely stirred."

He was quiet for a moment and then his chest rumbled. "I got it now. Shaken *and* stirred. That's cute, sugar."

She lay there, listening to the rapid thud of his heart as she slid further into slumber. "You're an awesome lover. But you already know that."

"Never hurts to hear it again." He slid his arm around her back and gave her butt a tiny squeeze before resting his hand on her hip. "And a man's only as good as the woman who'll let him love her. Thank you for that, sugar."

He wrapped his other arm around her back and hugged her tight.

"You're welcome, Tex. Very, very welcome."

Chapter Four

"I'm not going to do it." Trey stared across the balcony table at his uncle, the sound of his heart echoing in his ears, drowning out the crash of the surf twelve stories below. In all his years he'd never disobeyed. Not an order. Not a request.

"Don't be a fool, son. Of course you're going to do it. That was the plan." His uncle, the man who had raised him and Chrissy and Gabe, took a healthy bite of his western omelet and offered a dismissive nod.

Trey saw his sister bristle and shot her a quick look, hoping she wouldn't interject anything and make matters worse. The girl wasn't known for her even temper, especially where her lovers were concerned. And there was no doubt that last evening, after he'd carried Susanne to her room and made love to her in every way imaginable, Chrissy and Susanne's friend had been exactly that. When he'd departed early that morning, he hadn't really needed to trace Chrissy's trail of discarded clothing to the suite's other bedroom. He'd seen the telltale package of cherry pull-apart licorice on the hallway table and known his sister was there. He had no idea how his sibling felt about being part of their uncle's scheme, and for once he didn't care. There was only one thought on his mind.

"I'm not ruining her chance of winning just so you can have first crack at her."

"I don't believe I was the first one to have a 'crack' at her." The old man chuckled wickedly and Trey shot to his feet.

"Pick one of the others," Trey ground out, his body tensing.

"Sit the hell down, boy. No need to be fannin' those feathers like a banty rooster. I'm not lookin' to tap your woman—just her mind."

"She's not my anything," Trey admitted. The sickening realization of that statement knotted his insides. He wanted her now as desperately as he had when she was lying naked before him.

"All the more reason to make sure she comes to me," the old man said smugly. "What better way to keep track of the woman than to have her at arm's length at all times? How are you going to woo her if she's a thousand miles away doing the biding of that comb-over shithead she seems to think holds the keys to her future?"

In that moment, Trey realized he'd been played. He knew his siblings had shared their concerns about his loneliness, his unhappiness. It should have occurred to him they wouldn't be able to keep their mouths shut. Hell, if one of them had been as down as he'd been, Trey would have beaten down his uncle's door with the news. They all knew their uncle wouldn't sit idly by and let them wallow in hurt or depression.

They also knew Walter Ryder was a master at killing two birds with one stone. The man had made a lucrative living by concocting deals that were mutually beneficial to all parties involved. Trey suddenly realized he had been part of one of those deals.

"You old bastard."

"Guilty as charged. But you have to admit this is going to be useful to us both."

Trey didn't want to admit the possible truth in his uncle's statement. And he didn't want to admit the old man could have expended so little effort and found the perfect woman for both of them.

"I can't let you tarnish her reputation just to ensure she ends up in San Antonio. Hell, her goal was to move an hour north of here, not halfway across the country."

"Won't know that until she's forced to decide, will we? Hell, she might even pull herself from the competition when she sees you're part of the judging team. Women, I've learned, have unbelievably strong codes of honor," Walt said.

"Maybe you could take a few lessons," his sister sarcastically suggested.

"You hush with that freshness, Missy. You were to help Trey divert Miss Webb from the proverbial herd, not look for a filly of your own. Why you couldn't have just married that Winn boy is beyond me," Walter muttered, but he and Chrissy clearly heard his words.

"Besides the fact that I don't do *dick*, Uncle Walt, Jimmy Winn had no personality. None whatsoever."

"Heir to the largest stud farm in west Texas? Damn girl, we could have bought him a personality."

Trey watched his sister push out of her chair, unexpectedly pleased that she offered their uncle a temporary distraction. He needed a moment or two to think.

"Couldn't you just pretend it was one of those swirling rubber dongs and not a real penis?" his uncle asked with all seriousness.

Chrissy shook her head and with a disgusted growl turned toward the suite, yelling over her shoulder as she disappeared through the doorway, "He was hung like a fucking rabbit, Walt!"

Silence enshrouded the balcony as her words lingered in the air.

"Well, shit. No help for that, now is there?" His uncle's resigned tone somehow broke through the previously serious mood and both men laughed.

"No, sir," Trey said, with a smile. He owed his sister a small debt of gratitude. Once again, she had defused a situation that was heading south fast.

"Any chance that last night you showed Miss Susanne that most of the time everything *is* bigger in Texas? Did you cut the mustard enough to have her wanting to see you again? To take my offer if she doesn't win?"

Trey laughed. "She's going to win, old man. There's no doubt in my mind."

"So that's a 'no' to you making the Ryder men proud where mounting is concerned."

"Chrissy might feel fine talking to you about her love life but I'm not going there, you old pervert."

"Fine by me. Just so you know what you need to do when we take our place at the judges' box."

The anxiety Trey felt over his uncle's request slowly dissipated. He did indeed know what he needed to do and suddenly he couldn't wait until the moment he and Susanne came face-to-face once again.

* * * * *

After his under-the-cover-of-darkness departure, Susanne really hadn't expected to see him again. But there he was. Undeniably handsome. Impeccably dressed. Standing in the last place on the planet she would have ever imagined seeing him. The last place she'd ever want Trey to be.

The bright track lighting made his hair seem much lighter but the stubble along his chiseled jaw was a testament to the true color. Wearing a pair of khaki slacks, a white polo shirt and a navy blazer, he looked as if he'd left his horse at home and was ready to step foot on any one of the massive yachts docked at the marina. He looked as if he absolutely belonged in the Tejas International judges' box. The thought made Susanne's already jittery stomach turn a double somersault.

She had worked very hard over the past six hours to hide her abject disappointment from earlier that morning. All it had taken was one roll to the other side of her empty bed to realize two very important things—one-night stands totally sucked and she had somehow lost a decent portion of her heart to him. Trey Ryder—masterful lover, easygoing jokester, devil incarnate.

Yeah. Not only had she pushed each and every one of her sexual boundaries, she'd done it with one of the judges. She rubbed the area below her breastbone in an attempt to stop the reflux of churning stomach acid.

It's the Jack. You shouldn't have drunk it.

Susanne gave a disheartened laugh that caught the attention of the men flanking her. She wished she could blame her distress on something as mundane as a few glasses of fine whiskey. Which she would never be able to drink again because just the thought of the smoky blend sparked images of Trey.

She knew she was fucked. Fucked with a capital F. It was only a matter of time before someone commented on the fact she'd been talking to him in the bar—that they'd left within minutes of each other. One of the staff was probably watching the security tapes right now. From there it would be a call to the production manager and then she'd be disqualified. After everything. Booted out over a booty call. A five-hour booty call. The only five-hour booty call in her existence. The best five-hour—

Stop it! Focus, for shit's sake. No one's saying a word.

That seemed true enough but she was getting furtive glances from the elderly man Trey was conversing with as well as his sister. She'd met Chrissy when the woman strolled buck-naked from Gia's room that morning, retrieving each piece of her forgotten clothing as she went. They had had a pleasant conversation as Trey's sister stood in the living room and dressed. Susanne wondered if the woman had also neglected to mention to Gia that she had a bright yellow judge's pass just waiting to be used. Her friend was going to hit the roof. The pastry division might just get an eyeful of a pure unadulterated catfight when Gia took the stage.

There was no way coincidence was even a passing possibility. The thought sent a surge of anger rocketing through Susanne. It was very clear that the previous evening had been some sort of game to them. His sister had played Gia and he'd played her. All those endearments delivered in that hot Southern drawl? The little let-me-get-to-know-you talks between the mind-blowing bouts of lovemaking.

Making love? Hah! Apparently a man could be focused and masterful and coitally courteous but when the night was done and he rode off into the sunrise, none of that really mattered because he, like ever other guy she'd fallen for, was full of shit. In his case, it happened to be *bull*shit and she'd been dumb enough to step right into it. With both feet. God, she was totally pitiful.

He had asked question upon question and she had dutifully answered them. Everything from the childhood she had mentioned to exactly why she was here and who she had targeted for her dream job. She should have had a clue that he somehow had an inside track to the entire event when she didn't have to explain the pros of going private as opposed to targeting a Vegas venue. *You should have had a clue when you realized you never told him your name but he called you "Susanne" in that sexy drawl and you crumbled.*

He had brushed her hair out of her eyes and told her he had every confidence that she would win but pointed out that if she didn't, he had names of a few estate managers who might love to have her join their team. She looked toward their judging box and shook her head.

And at what point did I decide I might actually be falling in love with the asshole?

Yesterday she would have considered the thought completely ludicrous. Yesterday love wasn't an option as far as Susanne was concerned. Now, even in light of the fact that he had obviously deceived her, it was a point she couldn't argue.

She could still try to convince herself it was all about the sex. That's what Gia would suggest. But somewhere between that fourth and fifth orgasms she had decided there was something a little more meaningful than mere fornication happening. No, that wasn't at all when it happened. It was when he took her face in his hands and said he'd never before made perfect love to anyone, ever in his life. When she had seen the regret and pain that etched his face when he had opened up about his previous sexually adventurous lifestyle. When right before dawn he'd pushed them over the edge together, calling her name over and over on the way down. That was the moment she realized all the talk about "the one" might not be so far out of the realm of believability. It was when she realized Trey Ryder just might be the man she'd been waiting for.

"Fifteen minutes, folks." The loud voice of the assistant producer echoed through the room and Susanne's heart beat a little faster.

This was it. Spirits were always first. They would have ten minutes to create a drink to go with the final theme, another twenty to mass produce it for the judges' boxes. She took a few deep breaths and did a quick count to determine how many drinks she would have to make. Eight for the main judges. Seventeen if she took care of the secondary attendees. Easy. Definitely doable if she kept it straightforward. And if she totally avoided eye contact with a certain judge's box.

She turned and checked her station for the umpteenth time. Everything was in order.

"A moment of your time, Miss Webb, if you please?"

Susanne spun around to find the executive producer standing in front of her station.

"May I introduce Walter Ryder, chief operating officer of Tejas International. He'd like a quick word."

She looked at the man and didn't say anything. It was more than clear where Trey got his rugged good looks. And his unique eye color.

"Miss Susanne. A pleasure to meet you. I've heard a great deal about you."

"Is that so, Mr. Ryder?" She couldn't mask the anger in her voice.

"It is. And I did so like what I heard." He offered her a wide grin.

She felt like screaming.

"How can I help you?"

"All business, huh? I can appreciate that." He crossed his arms over his chest and nodded. "And I can understand your pissiness."

Susanne's eyes widened and she opened her mouth to speak.

"Don't go off on me now," he interjected. "There'll be time enough for it later, and quite frankly, I've spent what should have been a beautiful morning being berated by my niece and my nephew, so I don't need your two cents' worth."

Susanne clasped her hands in front of her and squeezed tightly. She had no other choice than to smile blandly and let him have his say. There was no doubt that more than a few people in the room were watching them.

"I just wanted to get a leg up on that pompous ass a few boxes down. I know you think he's the golden carrot you've been lookin' for but let me tell you somethin', missy. His net worth has just dropped considerably, due to a Brazilian casino deal gone bad, and rumor has it that he's one fiscal period away from declaring bankruptcy on all his Malaysian pre-constructs. You'd be well advised to look for an employer who's a little more solvent. One who has equally attractive properties. One who treats his people like family."

"And that would be you?" she asked, trying to ignore the fact that he and his nephew possessed the same crooked, self-assured grin.

"Only an egomaniac has prospective employees run the gantlet to prove their worthiness. Those of us at Tejas know there are better ways of ensuring we get the top talent."

"Do they involve forcing your family members to put those possible employees into compromising positions?" she asked in a caustically soft voice. She'd seen enough behind-the-scenes business subterfuge to realize the easiest way to achieve a goal was simple blackmail.

"First of all, no one forces any member of my family to do anything they don't want to do."

Susanne pressed her fists against the ache in her stomach, praying she wasn't about to throw up.

"Five minutes!" This time the announcement was delivered over the speaker system and Susanne looked at the makeshift production booth in the corner of the room. No one seemed to be paying a bit of attention to her and Walt Ryder.

"I won't lie. My initial intent was to have you disqualified. Easiest means to an end. I've done my research well. I can use a woman with your practical experience and creativity. I want signature creations. Something Tejas can call its own. I'm a businessman, darlin'. I take the path of least resistance when I see something I need.

"If Trey had listened and just let security see him when they came 'round, we wouldn't be standing here."

"No," Susanne spat, unable to keep quiet any longer. "My ass would have been tossed out, my reputation in shambles. For all I know, it might still be. No one likes a cheater, Mr. Ryder. And no one forgets."

"Call me Walt, darlin'."

"Oooooooh." Susanne growled her frustration.

"You're safe. No one's going to say a damn thing and do you know why?"

She heard the sharp edge to his voice and looked into his eyes. They were steely. Serious.

"My nephew is a man of integrity. Where was he when security did their sweep? Not sitting in the middle of your living room like I suggested. Or lying spread-eagle, naked as the day he was born, in the middle of your bed, which would have really brought my plan to fruition. Don't worry, he didn't kiss and tell. I raised my sister's boy to be a perfect gentleman. I'm seventy, sugar, but I'm not dead. I sure as hell know what I'd be doing holed up for six hours in a beautiful woman's suite."

Susanne felt heat creep into her cheeks. Dear god, things were really sad if an old man could make her blush. She looked away, mistakenly in the direction of his box, and met Trey's penetrating but somewhat worried gaze.

"He went against my express wishes for one reason and one reason only."

She forced herself to look at him, trying not to let her heart override her mind.

"For you, Miss Susanne. He did it for you."

* * * * *

"What the hell did you say to her?" Trey demanded the moment his uncle stepped back into their box.

"Take it easy, son. All is well."

"That'd be a first where your 'interventions' are involved," his sister huffily said, stacking her arms over her breasts.

"You calm down too. I'll speak to your friend as well, when the time comes."

"Great! Thanks for nothing! Here's a news flash—Yente, the Matchmaker you're not. I don't even want to be here," she said, starting to get to her feet.

"You sit your fanny down, Christina. Right now."

His uncle took on the no-argument tone they had learned to obey and his sister did as she was told.

"We're going into this united. Just as planned."

"So you didn't offer her a job?"

"I threw the bait out there but for some reason, she didn't bite."

Trey raised his chin and looked his uncle square in the eye. "I told you before, I'm not exposing her. And neither are you."

"Agreed."

The speed with which his uncle capitulated was suspicious.

"As long as you make sure, when this day is done, that woman is on the payroll."

"And how the hell am I supposed to do that? I'm pretty certain, if she didn't hate my guts before, she does now. You did tell her exactly what you were up to, didn't you?"

Trey secretly hoped his uncle had come up with some last-minute Hail Mary play that would have her running straight into his arms when the day was over.

"I did."

"Fuck," Trey swore softly.

"Look on the bright side," his uncle said and laughed. "At least now she's not looking at you like she wants to cut your balls off."

Trey looked up to find Susanne studying him, her expression not quite as dark as it had been but still not anything that could be misconstrued as remotely friendly. He heaved a heavy sigh and took a seat next to his uncle, telling himself he should be happy for small favors.

"Yeah, you old coot. There is that."

* * * * *

"Congratulations to the three of you. Over the past five days you've proven your creativity and tenacity and today, you'll need those skills and more to walk away with the honor of being proclaimed Master Mixologist. In addition to the cash prize, the winner will have the opportunity to chat with each of the eight celebrity restaurateurs as well as our four guest judges, each of whom have culinary sectors in each of their business empires."

Susanne tuned out the rest of the host's words, knowing the introductions were for the benefit of the cameras. Every contestant knew the skinny on who was there, what specific opportunities and areas of specialization each man and woman held.

Wouldn't it have been great if those dossiers had included the names of extended family members who might happen to show up in a bar and unceremoniously proceed to rock a woman's semi-mundane world?

"So, contestants, your final challenge is quite simple. Last evening, we provided you all with various diversions throughout the night. Let's take a look."

The host paused but held his spot on the stage. Footage of the evening's events would undoubtedly be inserted during the final editing process. The host began talking again, thanking all those who participated in making the night a grand success.

"Your challenge is to take a moment from your final evening here in Miami and build a drink that encompasses the essence of that moment. You can use anything in the kitchen. Anything you would have had access to last night. Good luck. Your time starts now."

Susanne's mind raced and she turned quickly and surveyed her choice of glasses. She stole a quick glance at her competitors and saw neither had gone for a martini glass and she made her choice, trying not to second-guess her decision. Her previous win had been with a martini. The judges might find it redundant but her intuition was telling her to go for it. She filled the glasses with crushed ice and rushed to put them in the freezer before facing the wall of liquors.

Take a moment from your final evening here in Miami.

There was no logical path for her thoughts to traverse, other than directly back to Trey. A man had never been her inspiration for a drink and she hoped like hell that when she won, she'd be able to concoct some feasible explanation for her creation other than the fact that she was going for something that reminded her of his lovemaking. Something that made you burn but in the sweetest of ways.

Not vodka. *Overdone.*

Not gin. *Not even Sapphire?*

No way. Rum could work. *Too sweet.*

She closed her eyes, remembering the feel of his hands, the soft insistence of his lips, his tongue snaking between her teeth as he stroked the recesses of her mouth, demanding she give something in return. She recalled the way she had swirled her tongue around his. How he had moaned and plundered deeper.

Susanne's eyes shot open. She knew what she needed. She searched the shelves, praying she'd find a bottle of top-shelf blackberry brandy. It was the exact taste she thought of when she thought of Trey. Blackberries. And a subtle hint of Jack.

"Yes," she hissed loudly when she found two bottles of the liquor, one domestic, and one imported from the Netherlands. She opened both and poured a sample of each into shot glasses. She opted for the import with its fuller flavor and headed toward her lineup of cocktail shakers. With any luck, she'd get the ratio close the first go-round. She snagged the bottle of Old No. 7 and tried not to think too far ahead.

She measured, shook, strained and tasted. Her first try was a little too heavy, the whiskey too unrefined to balance the essence of the fruit. She needed a mellower blend.

I raised my sister's boy to be a perfect gentleman.

Susanne looked up, directly into Walt Ryder's eyes as inspiration assailed her. She rushed to the liquor shelves and grabbed a different bottle. By the third attempt, she had her creation exactly where she wanted it. To make certain she couldn't improve further, she made one more martini, not adding the brandy until after the drink was strained into the glass, instinctively knowing the blackberry would shine through a little more. She brought the glass to her lips, tasting perfection as her mind ran a little wild.

You're gonna need a kickass garnish. Something with a little more impact than wedges or twists or licorice straws.

Susanne stopped mid-sip as an idea hit her.

"Can we use things from our rooms? Everything in there was accessible last night," she yelled to the host, setting the glass down as she ran to the bar fridge to see what berries were inside. Blueberries. Raspberries—red and hybrid yellow. No blackberries.

Dammit!

She looked up just as the producer gave their host the thumbs-up sign.

"Am I allowed to leave the room or do I need to have it brought here?" She aimed her question directly toward him.

The producer talked rapidly into his head set and Susanne saw a flurry of movement to her right before the crack of the speakers sounded and the entire assemblage heard his decisive, "You can go."

She ran out of the ballroom and down the corridor toward the lobby, the jingle, jingle, jingle of the cameraman's huge key ring offering a distraction from the sound of her heart beating in her ears. She knew she must look like a maniac but she didn't have much time to pull this off. A mad dash all in the name of garnish. One that would be the perfect accompaniment to the drink. One that totally represented the man who inspired her.

They rushed the elevator and guests scattered. The camera lent an air of credibility, she guessed. She yanked her key out of her back pocket, inserted it the slot and pressed her floor number while opening the emergency phone panel and dialing the hotel operator.

"Room 2112. It's an emergency." The cameraman peered around his screen at her and she gave him a stern look as she waited. "Robert! Listen. I need you to meet me at the elevator in thirty seconds with the following items."

* * * * *

Trey watched a triumphant grin break out upon Susanne's face as she raced around the makeshift bar and headed toward the door, a cameraman suddenly flanking her.

"She's got something good up her sleeve," his uncle whispered with a chuckle, rubbing his weathered palms together with glee.

Trey wished he felt as happy.

"I think those two guys she's up against just shit their pants," Chrissy said loudly.

From the next booth the king of culinary throwdowns shot them all a displeased glance and Trey smiled an apology, while mentally agreeing with his sibling.

Trey thought Susanne looked as if the hounds of hell were snapping at her heels when she rushed from the room and he couldn't figure out what could possibly be upstairs that might ensure her win. He watched the two men continue their own flurry of activity while the minutes ticked away. From his vantage point in the judges' booth he hadn't been able to see the actual mixing Susanne had done but he'd seen her grab martini glasses, a bottle of some dark liquor and the Jack. That's when the little gut-kick sensation had hit.

She had myriad spirits to choose from, yet she'd picked his brand of preference. Which meant she was thinking of him. Maybe he'd made enough of an impression that she hadn't totally written him off.

Or maybe that's just wishful male thinking, son.

He looked at his uncle to make sure those words hadn't come out of his mouth. The old man focused on the action in front of them, a pleasant grin plastered on his face.

At the moment, he didn't share his uncle's merriment. His emotions kept swinging from one end of the spectrum to the other. He needed to talk to Susanne. Explain his side of the story. He was certain his uncle had done a less than admirable job of that. Walt tended to offer explanations on a need-to-know basis and Trey was certain there were plenty of things Susanne needed to know, staring with why he had felt compelled to sneak away in the dead of night like an old tomcat.

He would love to have had her wake up in his arms. He still would. Admitting that fact lifted a little of the weight off his chest but the chances of her forgiving him were fairly nil. Even if Walt somehow worked his magic and she ended up coming to Tejas he wasn't sure he'd get a second chance to charm her. To woo her, as Walt said. She could easily choose to be headquartered at any one of his uncle's domestic estate offices. She had no reason to pick a ranch in Texas over the villa in Boca or the chalet in Tahoe. He doubted the fishing lodge in Minnesota would be at the top of her list, which left Phoenix and Kansas City.

He was about to weigh the merits of each city and how often he might be able to leave his job to be with her when the door swung open and she hurried back into the room, a bowl of blackberries in one hand and a plastic grocery bag swinging from the other.

She went for the blackberries, son. Now that's gotta mean somethin'.

Trey hoped like hell that, for once, the familiar voice in his head was right.

Chapter Five

Susanne began working her way down the boxes of judges, carefully placing a cocktail in front of each one as she spoke. She couldn't have been happier that they had drawn numbers and her offering was to be served last. One of the not-so-dynamic duo had imploded when he had failed to taste the strawberries he had used for garnish. Two of the judges had actually gagged when they tasted the mealy fruit. Her remaining nemesis was so convinced his *Cubano* mango mojito was prize worthy that he had already adopted a victorious air that more than a few of the judges had obviously found annoying. Neither men had used the same muse as Susanne and she turned up the wattage on her smile. Anyone in her industry knew that skill could take you to the top of the ladder. Personality was key to being permitted to jump in the pool.

"The inspiration for my drink came from the talented men from the National Rodeo Association who, each in their own way, thoroughly entertained us on our last evening here in Miami. I see some of them are here today." She inclined her head toward the left side of the stage, smiling at the collective nervous shuffling of cowboy boots. "I think a round of applause is in order for their stellar performance."

She moved down the line of judges as clapping broke out, happy she hadn't been standing anywhere near Trey when those words had left her mouth.

"Until last night, I didn't know that much about cowboys other than what I had seen on television or in the movies. But let me tell you something, reruns of *The Wild, Wild West* don't do these men justice. Obviously, they're not lacking in courage and strength. They haul themselves up on fifteen-hundred-pound animals whose sole purpose in life is bucking them off their backs and trying to trample them into the ground. I've heard it's similar to an Anthony Bourdain critique—but a little less fearful."

A round of light laughter erupted, including an indulgent smile from the man himself and Susanne didn't stop.

"I learned they're strong as can be but there's an innate sweetness there as well. I found out that oftentimes it's right there at the surface and other times it's hidden a little deeper."

Susanne stopped in front of the country's top Southern female chef and carefully handed her a drink. "Either way, it's a heady blend. All that ruggedness and sly smiles. One that's so hard to resist with all those 'yes, ma'ams' and 'it'd be my pleasures'."

"I like the sound of that, darlin'," the silver-haired beauty interrupted. Her deep, contagious laugh carried through the room and Susanne couldn't help but grin. "Keep on talkin' but if it's a-goin' to get any hotter in here, someone needs to grab me a fan!"

Susanne waited for another round of laughter to die down.

"With all that in mind, I've created the Devil-tini. What I was striving for with this drink was a layering of strong and sweet. I chose whiskey and blackberry brandy as the key components. The whiskey offers the potency but through distillation it's been mellowed enough to ensure sipability. And because those cowboys are the epitome of courtesy, I went with Gentleman Jack Rare Tennessee Whiskey. The most mellow of Lynchburg's offerings, it contains a hint of fruit, which allows a smooth transition between the higher alcohol content and the brandy."

Susanne made it to the Tejas box, priding herself on the fact that she was able to hand them their drinks without a single spill. Her palms were clammy and she didn't want to think about what might be going through Trey's mind as she offered her explanation. The look on his face was borderline disbelief.

She backed up so she could address the entire group of judges, forcing herself to forget about him until her explanation was complete.

"If you're a fan of initial sweetness, then by all means go for the actual blackberry before your first sip. For those who like their sweetness at the end, I waited until after straining and slowly added the blackberry brandy. This gives the drink that deep coloring at the bottom of the glass and offers a fruity finish. Enjoy."

Susanne looked at each and every one of them as they tried her drink. No grimacing. More than a few head nods. One big smacking of lips. Susanne smiled in the woman's direction and received another wink.

"Great creativity with the garnish," a heavily French-accented voice offered.

"Thank you, Chef Torres," she replied, her chest swelling with pride as she secretly agreed. They never need know the true impetus of the cherry licorice lasso or the plump blackberry it held suspended at mid-drink level.

"Is that licorice tied in an authentic roper's knot?" the host asked.

"I'm not sure," Susanne replied with a short laugh, her stomach twisting. "I was just trying to find a way to make the berry look like it had been lassoed and not fall to the bottom of the drink."

"I think it might be." Susanne heard the older man's voice and miraculously kept the smile plastered on her face as she turned her head in Walt's direction. He looked at Susanne and raised one white brow. "I'm no expert but my nephew is. What's the verdict, son? Does the lady know what she's doing?"

Trey's dark eyes bore into Susanne's and she felt her mask of neutrality begin to crumble. His gaze raked her from head to toe and back again and she prayed like hell the cameras weren't able to capture the heated look.

"No doubt about it, sir. The lady definitely knows her knots. It's the sort of skill that would make any cowboy stand up and take notice. I'm thinking she might have learned from the best."

Susanne broke out in a cold sweat as she watched him slide his chair back and actually stand up.

Dear god in heaven. What's he doing?

"Could just be dumb luck on her part," the old man said in a voice that conveyed a high level of doubt that had the other judges shifting in their seats, giving him their full attention.

What do you think, Susie? When this is over, I say we kill the old bastard.

Susanne's heart drummed in her chest as Trey ignored the frantic waving of the stagehand. His long strides and determined walk had a flush of heat shooting through her.

Please, please, please. Someone make him stop. Don't let him come closer.

She'd had every intention of hating him...until his crazy uncle had made her reconsider motives and culpability. She wanted this win so much but she was horribly afraid that she wanted him more.

He didn't stop until they were standing toe to toe and she was staring at his chest.

"And I hate to prove you wrong, old man, but there isn't a dumb bone anywhere in that beautiful body."

She heard the gasps of the production staff, the murmurs from the judges' boxes. A lone "Go for it, Ryder" from the general vicinity of where the other cowboys were sitting.

Her eyes began to burn and she bit her lip.

"Look at me." His warm breath tickled her nose, his words barely audible.

"No," she whispered on a ragged breath. This was it. The end to all her hard work. Any second now the producer would be yelling "cut" and her dreams would be over.

Maybe not all of them.

He gripped her chin and slowly eased her head backward, forcing her to meet his eyes.

"I thought we had an agreement, you and I. About that word 'no'."

"That was before you disappeared," she replied a little louder than was necessary. She didn't care. Until she saw a flash of hurt cross his eyes.

"I'm sorry about that. I truly am. But I'm here now. Exactly where I want to be. Where I was meant to be. With you in my arms."

"I'm not in your arms," she said, silently cursing when her vision became watery.

"Is that good or bad?" he asked, brushing the wetness away just as the tear began to fall. He cradled her face between his large hands and waited for an answer.

"Bad," she finally replied.

"As bad as me kissing you in front of half a million people."

Once again, he was letting her decide what was to come. She could tell him to go. Turn him away and pray the producers would think he was insane. Too much sun, maybe. One fall too many from a bucking bull.

He stood before her, the brim of his hat blocking the light from above. She hadn't really noticed until that moment that his headgear was solid black. Today, he had bad boy potential. She liked that part of him and doubted she could ever live without it.

"Don't worry. The producers will edit all this out," she said, offering him a slow, teasing smile as she wrapped her arms around his neck.

He pulled her tight against his body and kissed her with an intensity she'd never known. It was thrilling. Frightening. And when she tried to pull away it was Trey who clung to her.

"You realize that I can't let you go, don't you, Susanne. Not for some grand finale. Not for some other man, though you've convinced yourself he can offer you everything you want. There's only one man who can do that, sugar. And he's standing right here before you with his heart on his sleeve, a helluva lot better head of hair, and a Texas-sized hard-on."

She smiled up into his face and traced the sexy contours of his goatee before smoothing her fingers over his mustache.

"Ah, Tex. Those are the words every woman wants to hear when she realizes she's finally roped her man."

He tossed his head back and laughed before hugging her close and whispering against her ear. "And all it took was my favorite brand of whiskey and a package of pull-apart licorice."

"And blackberries, darlin'," she said with a smile. "Don't forget the blackberries."

Devil-tini

This is my take on the drink Susanne created in *Shaken and Stirred*. While she did not use vodka in her winning libation, I simply cannot partake of anything shaken or stirred without it. Using vodka with a hint of vanilla really mellows the sharpness of the whiskey. And speaking of whiskey, you could probably use your blend of preference, but I'm sticking with the Jack. *Viva* **Lynchburg!**

1 ½ oz. Gentleman Jack whiskey
1 oz. vanilla vodka
2 oz. blackberry brandy
3 oz. very cold cola

Using crushed ice, chill your martini glasses.

Mix the Gentleman Jack, your favorite vanilla vodka and the blackberry brandy in a large cocktail shaker with crushed ice. Shake until your hand appears to be completely frozen.

Discard the ice used for chilling and pour the ingredients of the shaker into the glass. Add the cola and garnish.

*Note for the daring: if you'd like to take a chance at feeling the true power of carbonation, add the cola before you begin shaking the drink. It will make your martini ice-ice-baby-cold but please divert the lid away from the glasses or anything else fragile. Without a firm hold, your shaker cap might channel a great blue whale and suddenly BLOW.

Susanne's Lasso Garnish

Cherry-flavored, pull-apart licorice
Blackberries

Like any first attempt at bondage, this could take a few tries to get it right. If you master it the first time around, it might be time to investigate your kinky side!

Cut one length of licorice in half. Gently make a loop nearly the size of your berry of choice and tie a simple double knot. Ease the berry into the loop and lower it into your martini, allowing the long length of licorice to hang over the side of the glass.

SLOW AND WET
Helen Hardt

Chapter One

"Slow and wet, darlin', slow and wet. You know just what I like."

Jillian grinned against the steel of Dale's gorgeous cock. Oh yeah, she knew what her man liked. And she liked it too. That was her naughty secret to giving the fantastic head Dale adored. Concentrate on what felt good to her tongue and lips, and his pleasure would follow.

Right now, licking every inch of his erection felt sweet as honey-lemonade on a hot summer day.

Jill swirled her tongue along his length, up over his cock head, and tormented him with long, wet strokes. When she reached the base, she circled around his sac, savoring every moan, every sigh from his firm, full lips as she cupped him and sucked each ball into her mouth.

"You're killin' me," Dale said, his voice low and husky.

Jill smiled again and twirled her tongue around his sac then licked up the long shaft to tease him underneath. She flicked her tongue over his cock head and sucked it between her lips.

He moaned. "Damn, Jill. You give great head."

Flexing her tongue into a point, she fucked his tiny slit. Once. Twice. Three times. He grabbed her cheeks, fisted his hands into her auburn tresses, and pulled her forward, forcing her to take his entire length.

She devoured him, his salty manliness an enticing flavor. But only for a few seconds. Jill liked to be in control when she sucked Dale, so she eased back and twirled her tongue over the sensitive head of his penis. She resisted the urge to take him in her hands, to curl her fingers around his steely hardness.

Instead, she rained tiny kisses along his length. With each of his trembles, her pulse quickened. Nothing turned her on more than turning him on.

Taking his cock head into her mouth again, she let it rest against her bottom lip while she flicked her tongue over the top.

Slowly, she crept forward, her lips molding around his hot cock. She increased her suction just a little, then stopped and backed off every now and again, teasing him.

When he grabbed her head again, the muscles in his forearms taut with tension, she took pity on him and took another rigid inch into her mouth.

"Just a little farther, darlin'. God, that's good, the way you suck me."

Each time he tried to pull her forward, she retaliated by taking an inch away. Smiling against his hardness, a tiny giggle escaped her throat. The vibration must have tickled him because he shuddered and growled out a low curse.

She gave in and took another inch. His cock felt hot and moist in her mouth, and she loved it. Loved him, though she hadn't told him. Dale Cross was her cowboy. Her lover. Her Prince Charming.

Her destiny.

He just didn't know it yet.

Her hips undulated in rhythm with her soft thrusts on his cock, and with each forward motion, she imagined him sinking that rock-hard length into her moist pussy. She was already wet. Had been since he'd greeted her with a kiss when she showed up at his place to surprise him. She'd been out of town on business for a week and hadn't been able to wait a minute longer to see her man.

And now she couldn't wait a minute longer to fuck him. She wanted his hardness inside her, stretching her.

She took his entire shaft into her mouth one last time, letting the knob of his cock head graze the back of her throat.

He groaned, shivering against her, his dark nest of curls tickling her lips and chin. Her pulse raced with the urge to finish him this way, to let him erupt in her mouth so she could taste his salty cum as it slid down her throat.

But no.

She wanted to fuck.

Now.

Though sorry to let it go, she removed her lips from his hard length. It stood erect in all its glory, shiny from her saliva, its golden color marbled with two veins meandering around its thickness.

Dale Cross had the most beautiful cock Jill had ever seen.

She pushed him onto his back and started to climb on top of him for a ride, but suddenly found herself on her own back, her cowboy staring down at her with mischief in his eyes.

"Hey, Dale. I wanted to fuck."

"Darlin'," his brown eyes gleamed at her, "I promise you the fuck of the century. Later. Right now I want to taste that sweet pussy."

Jill sighed and relented. As much as she loved fucking Dale and sucking his cock, having him lick her pussy was right up there on the feel-good scale too.

Dale smiled between her legs, pulled each thigh over his shoulders, and buried his face in her wetness. He sucked pussy the way he did everything—with a singular purpose and motivation to be the best.

From his bronc busting, to babysitting his niece and nephew, to helping his grandmother run the ranch that would be his someday. He tackled each job that came his way with effort and finesse.

Goose bumps formed on Jill's body and her nipples stiffened when his silky tongue slid over her slick pussy lips.

He nibbled at her clit, bringing her almost to the precipice, and then backed off, teasing her.

"Please, Dale. Let me come."

"You'll get what's comin' to you, darlin'," he said. "You drove me insane with your cock suckin'." His lopsided grin, lips shiny with her juices, tantalized her from between her thighs.

She met his smoldering gaze. "That's not fair, Dale."

"Not fair?" He chuckled and nipped her thigh. "I'll show you not fair. I'm gonna kiss your hot pussy 'til you scream, lady. How's that for not fair?"

He dove back into her cunt, licking and nibbling. Jill cupped her breasts, squeezed them, and plucked her hard nipples. The sensation traveled at light speed and landed between her legs, adding to the torment Dale was inflicting on her.

He sucked at her, and the smacking of his tongue and lips made her tingle.

"Damn, you sure are wet," he said against her folds. "So wet for me. So juicy. I guess you missed me, huh?"

"Y-yes. I missed you more than I can say. Now please let me come."

He shook his head, and his wavy dark curls tickled her inner thighs. "I missed you too, Jill. I missed your hot kisses, your tasty nipples, your sweet pussy." He flicked his tongue over her clit and then dragged it downward through her folds, all the way to her anus, where he swirled it in lazy circles.

She shivered.

"Mmm," he said. "When are you gonna give me your ass, darlin'?"

"I...I don't know." She couldn't think about that now. All she could think about was coming. She feared she might explode into a million pieces if he didn't let her release.

His laugh rumbled against her ass cheeks as he fingered her tight hole. "I got it nice and lubed up right now. Let me just..."

Jill gasped as he penetrated her.

"Just a finger. Relax."

She loved this man, and she wanted to please him. She loosened, and found she liked the feeling of his thick finger sliding in and out of her ass.

"You're so pretty, darlin'," he said. "So pink and puckered. I'm gonna fuck your pussy today. And someday," he sighed, his voice a heady rumble, "you're gonna let me sink my cock into your virgin ass, and we're both going to love every second of it."

"Sure, Dale, sure." Jill was pretty certain she'd agree to anything right now, if he'd just let her come.

"Promise, darlin'? Promise you'll let me fuck your ass someday?"

"Dale..."

"It doesn't have to be today. But I want you so much. I want to claim every part of you."

"Yes, Dale. Fine. Just. Please. Let. Me. Come."

The hot breath from his laugh tickled her clit. "You've been a good girl. You deserve a reward."

His finger still penetrating her ass, he lowered his mouth to her pussy and sucked the whole swollen fruit into his mouth while he tongued her clit.

She exploded and her womb convulsed. The spasms radiated outward, until every nerve ending in her body sizzled. Still he fingered her ass, and the intense pressure added to her blazing climax. She soared as the ripples surged through her body.

"Dale!" she cried. "That feels so good. So fucking good!"

He licked her folds, and she floated downward, her body sinking into the softness of his bed. His finger left her ass and he tongued her once, twice more, before he crawled upward and crushed his mouth to hers in a searing kiss.

He tasted of the crisp honey-lemonade they had shared, spiced with her female musk. Intoxicating.

Their tongues dueled and tangled, their breaths mingled, until he ripped his lips from hers, panting.

"Condom," he said, and extended his arm and fumbled in his nightstand drawer. A few seconds later, sheathed, he plunged into her hot, willing cunt.

Jill let out a soft sigh as her walls clamped around him. Good. So damn good. Like he was born to fill her. A perfect fit.

"Darlin', you're so tight right after you come. So hot."

His voice, deep and hoarse, swirled around her like a smoky bourbon. So fucking sexy. He pulled out and thrust into her again, his hardness sliding along the swollen nub of her clit. She squeezed her legs together and hugged his hips as he drove his cock harder and harder into her. Each time he pulled out, she whimpered until he drove back in.

"So tight, Jill. So fuckin' tight."

With each thrust, she longed to cry out her true feelings of love for him. Was it too soon? They'd only been seeing each other a couple months. But with each kiss of his lips, each stroke of his long, hard cock, Jill knew, without a doubt, that she was in love with Dale Cross.

The way he worshiped her body, made love to her soul, he had to feel the same way. Didn't he?

She grabbed the firm cheeks of his bottom, and he groaned.

"Yeah, Jill. I love when you play with my ass."

She squeezed him and pushed downward, forcing him farther into her heat. "Dale," she panted, as her climax ascended, "Dale, I—"

"Jillian, I can't hold on any longer," he rasped. "I'm sorry, darlin', I wanted you to come again… God!" He thrust into her one last time, releasing.

Her orgasm hit her as his hot cum shot into the condom. She spasmed around him.

"Yeah, yeah," he said. "You're coming too. I'm glad. So glad…" His voice trailed off and he kissed her neck with firm, moist lips. "Damn, I've missed you."

Jill's whole body quivered from her climax, from his sweet kiss, but mostly from his admission that he'd missed her. She'd missed him so much she'd gotten a speeding ticket getting back home to see him. The job offer she'd received—complete with significant pay increase—to relocate back to Denver paled in comparison to life here with Dale. She'd say no first thing tomorrow.

"Give me a few minutes, darlin'," he said, "and I'll be good to go again. I'll last longer next time, I promise."

He slid off her slick body onto his back and reached for her. She snuggled into his arms and inhaled his intoxicating blend of cinnamon, cedarwood and male musk. Dale never wore cologne. Jill breathed in the spicy aroma again. Mmm. If he could bottle his own fragrance, he'd make a fortune.

She lifted her head and took in his sculpted chest, the dark hairs curling over his nipples, matted with the sheen of his sweat. He looked good enough to eat. Again.

He tilted his head toward her. "You want some more lemonade, darlin'?"

She nodded and stretched her arms over her head. "I've got a thirst to quench, that's for sure, cowboy."

The adorable dimple in his right cheek twinkled at her when he smiled. "Sit tight. I'll be right back with a cool drink."

Jill watched his lean backside as he strode out of the bedroom. He was so handsome, with a face and body like a god. She could look into his beautiful bronze eyes forever and never tire of their piercing fire.

She stretched again and let her body sink into the cool cotton sheets covering Dale's king-sized bed. A bed she hoped to occupy for a long, long time.

Her fingers wandered to her nipples and she stroked them, bringing each to a tight bud. Mmm. So good. She plucked at them lazily, imagining Dale's talented lips sucking each one. She let one hand drop and graze her swollen clit. Her pussy was still soaked, and she rubbed the smooth folds between her fingers. Within minutes, she was close to climax again.

But where was Dale?

How long did it take to pour two glasses of honey-lemonade, anyway?

"Dale?"

She sat up, her pussy still pulsing with the need to come. But why go at it alone? She'd just as soon bring herself to orgasm with Dale's hard cock in her mouth. And this time she'd swallow him whole and feel his hot cum trickle across her tongue.

She stood and ambled out the door. "Cowboy, I'm still horny, and it's going to take more than your famous honey-lemonade to cool me off—"

She stopped abruptly in Dale's kitchen, her words dangling in midair.

Dale stood at the counter, his back to her, wearing green cotton boxers. When had he put them on?

But her boyfriend's attire was the least of Jill's concerns. At the table sat another cowboy nearly as hot as Dale himself.

And not a thread of clothing covered her.

The blond cowboy's lips curved into a grin as he ran his long fingers through his tousled hair. Lapis lazuli eyes raked over Jill's nude body.

"Seems I've been gone too long, Dale," he said. "The scenery's definitely changed around here," he arched a nutmeg eyebrow, "for the better."

Jill's skin heated and she crossed her arms over her puckering nipples. She couldn't help staring at the broad chest clothed in a black western shirt. The first few snaps were open, and several golden chest hairs peeked out.

Dale turned around and his jaw dropped. "Jill!" He rushed toward her, pulled her into his arms, and shielded her private parts from the other cowboy's view.

"We used to share everything, Dale," the blond said with a husky laugh.

"Go get something on," Dale whispered in her ear.

"I heard that," the man said, still smiling, "and I've already seen her gorgeous tits and her pretty red nipples." He cleared his throat. "And what's down below. Why not introduce us?"

"Be happy to," Dale said, "once she's properly covered."

The other cowboy ignored Dale and stood, offering his hand. His denims hugged hips as lean as Dale's. If he turned around, she'd no doubt see an ass just as fine too. He was almost as tall as Dale, which made him six-two, at least.

"I'm Travis Logan…" His voice was slightly deeper than Dale's, with a little more of a cowboy twang. "Dale's best friend since we were kids, and you're the prettiest thing I've seen in a month of Sundays."

The bold words sashayed around Jill's heated body, and her already hard nipples stiffened further and poked into Dale's golden chest. Dale's cock came to life inside his boxers and brushed against her tummy. An icy tingle raced through her. Amazing, how Dale could affect her so.

Or was it Travis?

Couldn't be.

"Trav, don't you have any shame?"

"You've known me almost my whole life, so you know the answer to that question." Travis grinned. His full pink lips were nearly as luscious as Dale's.

"Yeah, I guess I do," Dale said. "Trav, this is my girl, Jillian Reynolds."

A rush of warmth coursed through Jill at the words "my girl".

"Mighty pleased to make your acquaintance, ma'am." Travis squeezed her hand, and a flare of heat skittered over her skin. "Seems Dale has all the luck. Beautiful women have always flocked to him."

Jill leaned farther into Dale's chest, but Travis continued to hold her hand, rubbing his thumb into her palm. His touch felt nice. Which wasn't good. She whisked her hand away.

"Remember the good old days?" He spoke to Dale, but he stared at Jill, dropping his gaze to her breasts, which were still crushed against cowboy number one. "When we did everything together?"

Dale cleared his throat. "I remember."

"We were team ropers," Travis said to Jill. "Champions. Started when we were kids. Couple years ago, though, I went solo in ropin', and Dale here switched to bustin' broncs. I've been away since then, tourin' the circuit."

"And you, Dale?" Jill raised her gaze to his brown eyes.

"You know where I've been, darlin'. Here, helpin' my grandma run this place. Doin' the local rodeos."

"But didn't you ever want to tour?"

"Heck, no. I'm a homebody. I'm happy here, runnin' the ranch," he smiled, "hangin' out with you." He turned to Travis. "Jill's from Denver."

"I took you for a big-city gal," Travis said. "What are you doin' in a little cow-town like Sweetwater Junction, Wyoming?"

"I'm in computer sales. A few months ago, an opportunity came up to relocate here, and I jumped at it. I wanted to get away from the hustle and bustle."

Travis chuckled and shook his head. "If only I'd come home sooner, I might have seen you first." He winked. "'Course that didn't always matter."

"Trav..."

Jill's heart raced beneath her chest. Why? From being held in Dale's strong arms, no doubt. Or was something else going on?

Naked.

Shit, she was still naked. "Uh, Dale? I need to—"

"Yeah, you sure do, darlin'." He grabbed her rump and lifted her, and she wrapped her legs around his waist. "We'll be back in a minute, Trav. Fully clothed."

"Damn," Travis said. "Can't say I've seen enough of the beauty of my hometown just yet."

"Yeah, you have," Dale said, walking back to the bedroom. He looked over his shoulder. "You've seen all of Jill you're gonna see, pal."

"Don't be so sure about that, buddy."

Had Jill imagined the words? Or had they actually come from the gorgeous blond cowboy?

She tightened her thighs around Dale's sexy waist. Didn't matter anyway. She needed to get dressed and then douse herself with about a gallon of Dale's honey-lemonade.

Then maybe go jump into Sweetwater Lake.

And she wasn't even sure that would cool her off today.

* * * * *

"It wouldn't hurt to ask her, you know."

Dale sprinkled seasoned salt on the three sirloin cuts, flipped them carefully, and poked Jill's to make sure it wasn't too done. His girl liked her steak oozing.

He turned to Travis and tried to look nonchalant despite the hairs on the back of his neck standing tall.

"She's a nice girl, Trav. She wouldn't be into that."

"Lorna was a nice girl too. Remember? She was my girl, Dale, but you took many turns with her, and it was fun for all of us."

"That was years ago."

"Four years, buddy. We had some good times. We were a team."

"We were team ropers, Travis. Not team fuckers."

Travis tossed his head back and let out a guffaw. "I seem to recall we did pretty well in the team fuckin' department too. Lorna never had any complaints, and neither did any of the others."

"This is different."

"How so?"

"She's…" Dale hedged. Words he couldn't form stuck in the back of his throat.

"I can tell she's special to you."

"Yeah." He cleared his throat and poked at a steak that really didn't need poking. "Aw hell, I don't know."

Travis took a long sip of his honey-lemonade and shook his head. "I never thought I'd see the day."

"See what day?"

"Nothin'. Never mind." He arched one eyebrow. "This is your chance to give her a hell of a gift, bud. Two huge cocks for the price of one."

"I'm all the cock she needs. Besides, haven't we outgrown all that?"

"Outgrown the desire to give a woman the ultimate pleasure? Heck, I sure haven't. Why not let her make the decision?"

Dale shrugged. He couldn't deny he'd been aroused at the way Travis had raked his gaze over Jill's nude body. His sex had stiffened in his drawers and pushed into Jill's soft flesh. Watching his friend fuck his woman appealed to him on a primal level. But what really turned him on was the thought of offering her something purely physical, purely hedonistic. Purely for her ultimate pleasure, as Travis had said.

Would Jill want something like this? Lorna had wanted them both, and Travis had allowed it.

He poked the steaks once more then transferred them to a platter. He looked over his head to see Jill push open the sliding glass door.

"The salad and veggies are ready whenever you two are." Her smile lit up her gorgeous face, and her auburn hair fell in ringlets around her creamy shoulders.

"We're comin' now, darlin'," Dale said, glancing sideways at Travis.

But Travis didn't catch Dale's eye. His gaze was settled on Jill.

Chapter Two

Both Travis and Dale had stared at her all through dinner. Now, her back turned as she loaded the dishwasher, the heat of their dual gazes still penetrated her like the Wyoming sun on a cloudless summer day.

"Jill?"

She turned at Dale's voice. "Yeah?"

"Trav has a few things to take care of."

"Oh, of course." She cleared her throat and advanced toward the two men, her arm extended to Travis. "It was great to meet you. I'm sure I'll see you again soon."

Travis' husky chuckle eased over her as his large, calloused hand enclosed hers. "Soon, yes, I hope. I'll be back later tonight, if all goes well."

He pulled her toward him and gave her a chaste kiss on the cheek, shook Dale's hand, and then headed out the front door of the ranch house.

Jill stared into Dale's bronze eyes, puzzled. "What did he mean, 'if all goes well'?"

Dale took her hand. "Come on. Mabel'll be here in the morning to clean the kitchen. You know you don't need to do this."

"But I don't mind—"

"I do," he said, and led her into the living room. He sat down on his rustic leather couch and patted the soft cushion next to him.

She sat, and he gathered her into his arms and kissed her neck.

"You didn't answer my question. Is Travis staying with you tonight?" Jill's muscles tensed, she wasn't sure why, as she waited for his answer. Did she want Travis to stay?

Dale let out a short cough. "No. Not the whole night, anyway. He, uh, has a place not far from here where he hangs his hat when he's in town."

"Oh. Well, maybe we'll see him tomorrow."

"Nope. While we were grillin' the steaks, he told me he was leavin' come sunup for another rodeo gig."

Jill swallowed, a strange sense of loss nagging at her. She quickly batted it away. So she wouldn't see Travis again. Dale was the man she loved. He was inside her, a part of her. She breathed in, catching his masculine scent. She'd do anything for Dale Cross.

"Thing is, darlin'," Dale continued, "Travis was wonderin'..."

"Wondering what?" Why would Travis wonder anything that mattered to her and Dale? A chill slithered across the back of her neck, and her sex responded. Strange.

Dale stood abruptly. "I'll be right back."

"Well...okay." She watched his gorgeous denim-clad ass as he walked back to the kitchen. Magnificent. He returned a few minutes later with two glasses of lemonade and handed one to her.

"I put a shot of bourbon in, the way you like it."

Jill took a sip of the crisp beverage. "Thanks. Now what's going on?"

Dale took a long, slow drink of his lemonade. "There's something I want you to know about me, Jill. Something I want to share with you."

"Okay." Nervous ripples skittered across her skin. The thought that Dale had hidden something from her agitated her. She loved him. Would marry him if he asked. And now? She inhaled, bracing herself.

"Travis and I...well..." He stood again and paced to the end of the room and back.

"Dale, for God's sake, what the hell is going on?"

He gazed into her eyes, his own burning with fire. His strong hands cupped her cheeks and he leaned down and pressed his lips to hers in a gentle kiss. Jill's heart leaped into overdrive. She opened to him, let his smooth tongue entwine around hers. What started as gentle soon became passionate and lusty.

Dale ripped his mouth away. "Damn, I can't even kiss you without losing my mind."

Her nerves settled — a bit — and she let out a laugh. "And that's a bad thing?"

"No. No, not at all." He sat back down next to her and took her hand, massaging each finger. "I want to give you everything, darlin'. You're so damn special to me. And there's somethin' I can give you that... Well, I don't know if you want it."

"I'd love anything you gave me, Dale." *Especially if it's circular in shape and symbolizes forever.*

He smiled, his eyes crinkling, and Jill's heart jumped. "Travis is attracted to you, darlin', and the two of us, well... We'd like to make love to you, if you're willin'."

Ice prickled Jill's skin, even as her pussy warmed. She was taken aback, but also turned on. Two men? Two hot men? But she was in love with Dale. Why would he want this? And was it wrong for the idea to intrigue her? Make her hot?

Because it did indeed make her hot, despite her feelings for Dale, and Dale alone.

"You would share me?"

He lifted her hand and gently slid his lips across her palm. Her tummy fluttered. "It's not sharing you, not really. It's giving you a night of pleasure. Pure, unadulterated pleasure. Something I can't give you alone. Two mouths to kiss you. Two cocks to fuck you, darlin'. But if you don't want it, that's okay."

"And you've...you've done this before?"

"Yes."

"And enjoyed it?"

"Yes. I've enjoyed giving a woman that amount of pleasure. And the woman has always been extremely satisfied."

A knife of jealousy stabbed her. She didn't like thinking of Dale with other women. But heck, she was no virgin herself. Of course he'd had other women before her. She nervously swiped at the beads of condensation on her glass of lemonade. "And you and Travis don't...with each other?"

He smiled, and a chuckle escaped. "No, darlin'. That's not what this is about. We both love givin' a woman the ultimate sexual experience. It's for you, not for us." He let out a shaky laugh. "Well, a little for us, I guess. I'd love seein' you like that, Jill. I'd love to be able to give it to you."

Naked between two beautiful men? The idea had merit. Ménages had starred in her fantasies on more than one occasion. But with Dale? The man she loved?

He looked at it as a gift. Something he wanted to give her. And though she wanted to accept—oh yeah, she really wanted to accept—would it change his opinion of her? Would he look at her the same way afterward? Would he ever fall in love with her, feel about her the way she did about him?

Jill gulped the rest of her drink and handed the glass to Dale. "No more. At least not laced."

"Okay, Jill." Dale's tone reeked of resignation. "I understand."

"I'm not sure you do," she said, as she feathered her fingers over his forearms, his sinewy muscle tripping her pulse. She was wet. She wanted this. An experience she'd never forget. A precious gift from the man she loved.

And if he couldn't love her back? She'd relish this night. And tomorrow she'd pick herself up, dust herself off, and take that job offer.

"I don't want to be drunk tonight, Dale. I want to feel every slide of those four hands, every pucker of those two mouths, every thrust of those two big cocks."

He smiled. "I promise you, darlin', this'll be a night you'll never forget."

* * * * *

"Any ground rules?" Travis asked, as four strong and capable hands gently peeled the clothes from Jill's body. A soft summer breeze cooled the Wyoming summer night, and the moon veiled the threesome in delicate light. Dale's backyard was enclosed, private, and carpeted with soft grass. The men had laid a king-sized cotton throw on the ground.

When Dale didn't answer right away, Jill's flesh heated. Ground rules? What were they talking about?

"You can do whatever she wants you to do," Dale said. "But her ass is mine."

"Understood."

As her naked body was exposed, determination overcame her shyness. Heck, Travis had already seen her naked. She wouldn't think. She'd just feel, and she'd top any previous ménage these two cowboys had orchestrated.

She fingered the snaps on Dale's shirt and ripped them open, letting her fingers wander over the dark hair dusting his sculpted chest. She bent and flicked her tongue over one copper nipple, and her pussy jerked as the nub hardened under her lips. She tugged on it, Dale's groans fueling her desire, as she unbuckled his belt and unzipped his jeans. She pushed them down his strong thighs, and he stepped out of them. Looking over her shoulder, she saw that Travis had also undressed. Light golden hair covered his muscular chest and well-formed legs. His cock, slightly longer than Dale's but not quite as thick, jutted from a bush of dark blond curls. Moisture trickled down her thigh.

She turned back to Dale and he took her mouth in a searing kiss. As their tongues tangled, hard flesh pressed against her back, and a second pair of lips trailed tiny, moist kisses over her shoulder. She shuddered and her skin tingled. Dale's hard cock pressed into the soft flesh of her tummy, while Travis' nudged her back. Dale's hands cupped her breasts and squeezed them, and he eased her down to her knees. His mouth still clamped to hers, he pressed his cock against her, as Travis did the same from behind.

When Dale finally broke the kiss, panting, Travis nudged her shoulder and pressed her onto her back, then leaned over her and took her mouth. His kiss tasted of passion and fire, while Dale's had tasted of intensity and emotion. His tongue had a rougher texture than Dale's, and Jill found she enjoyed the different sensation. He used less tongue than Dale, but his kiss was no less intoxicating. Dale's lips trailed along her neck, up to her earlobe, where he nipped her. She shuddered. But just as she deepened her assault on Travis' mouth, her lips locking his, Dale yanked her away by the shoulder. The suction of the kiss broke with a loud smack.

"New ground rule," Dale said huskily. "You don't kiss her."

Jill didn't hear Travis' response, if there was one, because Dale crushed his mouth to hers in a kiss so passionate and possessive it erased all memory of Travis' lips. Dale's tongue tasted of honey, of spice, of sweet love, and Jill drowned in the pleasure of his kisses.

When he finally ripped his mouth from hers, Travis sat over her with a pitcher of honey-lemonade.

"Dale told me this is your favorite drink, sweetheart," he said, a glint in his bright blue eyes. "We thought you might enjoy a little tonight."

"I'd love some." Jill smiled and looked around. "Looks like you forgot the glasses, though."

"Who needs glasses?" Dale said, his tone teasing. "Go ahead, Trav."

Travis tipped the pitcher, and the liquid trickled onto Jill's hot body. She squealed, and her nipples puckered into tight buds. The cool beverage flowed over her breasts, her belly, her thighs, easing between her legs and into her wet folds.

"Now I guess we'll have to clean you up, darlin'," Dale drawled.

"It'll be a pleasure," Travis said. He cupped the breast on his side and thumbed a hard nipple. "She sure has pretty tits. The nicest I've seen in some time."

"Mmm-hmm." Dale bent to taste one. "Sweet and red and hard as pearls." He licked the tip of her nipple, and Jill moaned, shuddering. "Two mouths, darlin'." Dale's breath vibrated against her flesh. "Two pairs of lips to kiss you. Two tongues to lick all that syrupy lemonade off your hot body."

Travis' firm lips latched onto the other tight bud. His touch was lighter than Dale's. He licked where Dale sucked. And Jill found she loved each sensation. Warmth spread through her breasts and flashed to her pussy, which pulsed between her thighs. Dale tugged, and Travis kissed, and Jill thought she'd implode with want.

After lingering moments of vivid stimulation that trickled to her sex, she needed more. The nipple Travis licked wanted to be bitten, and the one Dale nipped wanted to be licked. "Could you guys switch places? Each suck the other nipple?"

"Anything you want," Dale said, his voice hoarse. "This is for you."

They quickly switched, and Jill sighed and sank farther into the moist cotton, her nipples tight with anticipation. The smacks and slurps of the two luscious masculine mouths sent shivers across her skin.

"Mmm, gorgeous." Travis' deep voice rumbled against her sensitive flesh. "The tart lemon mixed with your sweet flesh."

"Yeah, delicious. And beautiful," Dale agreed, and tugged harder with his teeth. The pleasure shot to her cunt with lightning intensity.

"Such pretty red nipples, so tangy from the lemonade," Travis said, "and I bet that's not all that's pretty and red."

"And tangy," Dale added.

Cream oozed from her pussy. She knew she was wet and swollen and ripe for the plucking.

Dale released her nipple with a soft pop, leaned forward, and thrust his tongue into her mouth for a scorching kiss. The fresh citrus taste of the lemonade he'd sucked exploded in a candied bouquet.

He trailed moist kisses over her cheek, then down the hill of her breast to her tummy. He swirled his tongue into her navel while Travis continued to lick her other nipple. Her body heated, then chilled, then heated again. She writhed under the expert hands and mouths.

When Dale reached her patch of russet curls, he spread her legs and groaned. "You're swollen and red. So pretty. Will you show Travis your pussy, darlin'? Let him lick you?"

Dale's eyes smoked a deep umber, and Jill's body ached for a cock. Any cock. Travis' cock. "I want Travis to lick me. To take me."

Travis released Jill's nipple and smiled against her fleshy breast. "It'll be my pleasure." He moved to join Dale.

Her legs spread wide, Jill watched the two heads—one dark, one blond—eye her pussy with rapt attention.

"She's delicious, Trav." Dale swiped his tongue over her clit, and a zing of heat slid up her spine. "Taste her."

Travis bent down and slithered his rough tongue over her clit. Again, she noted the different textures of their two tongues. Both drove her crazy with lust.

Dale slid his fingers up and down her slick labia, squeezing them together, while Travis continued to nip at her clit.

"Gorgeous, darlin'," Dale said. "Just gorgeous. You've got the prettiest pussy I've ever seen. How does it feel, Jill? How does it feel to have me play with your lips while Trav licks your clit?"

Feel? How could she put it into words? Amazing wouldn't begin to describe it.

"Mmm," she said. "Dale, I can hardly breathe it feels so fantastic."

His chuckle rumbled against her thigh, sticky from the lemonade and her own cream. He nipped her there and continued to slide his fingers over her slick folds. She writhed, searching for her release, but Travis' lips denied it. Every time she was about to come, he released her clit and kissed her belly.

"Dale," she panted. "I want…I need…"

Two of Dale's thick fingers thrust inside her pussy, and she shattered, clenching around him in sweet convulsions. "Dale!" she cried. "That's so good!"

"Come for me, darlin'," he said. "Just like that. Milk it. Cream all over my fingers."

Once her spasms slowed, Dale removed his fingers and shoved his hot tongue into her willing flesh. "I'm suckin' the honey out of you, darlin'," he said against her wet pussy. "Every last drop."

Travis moved forward, took a hard nipple into his mouth, and licked gently. "You've got one sweet pussy, Jill," he said against her breast. "Dale's a lucky man."

"Mmm. I sure know it." Dale swiped his tongue through her labia once more and then nipped her clit, sending an aftershock shuddering through her.

"Get a condom, Trav," he said. "I want you to take her first. She's so fuckin' tight right after she comes. You're gonna love it." He looked up at Jill, his eyes burning into her. "That okay with you, darlin'?"

God yes. "Please. Take me, Travis."

Travis released Jill's nipple. "Don't have to twist my arm."

A minute later, Travis knelt between her legs, sheathed and ready to plunge into her.

"You sure, bud?" He nodded at Dale, who was kneeling behind Jill's head, his cock dangling in front of her lips.

"I'm sure," Dale said, "if it's what Jill wants."

Jill panted, and her eyes blurred. She wanted that cock, wanted those dark blond curls to tickle her labia as he drove into her. "Yes." Jill puffed against Dale's engorged shaft. "Fill me up. Now."

"You got it, sweetheart." Travis entered her in one smooth thrust.

"Ah yes." Jill's walls clenched onto Travis' hardness. Different than Dale. But big, and hard, and hot. The feelings were different too. More primal, more urgent, completely focused on pleasure for pleasure's sake.

"Let him fuck you, darlin'," Dale said. "Concentrate on the physical. I want you to feel good."

"Mmm, I do, Dale." She reveled in the raw joy of being taken. Travis' skillful pounding held her body in thrall. But Dale's words, his deep timbre, his concern for her enjoyment, bewitched her and filled her heart with unimaginable sensation.

"Would you suck me while he fucks you?" Dale's cock nudged her lips. "Would you let me fuck your sweet mouth while Travis fucks your pussy?"

"Cowboy, you know I'll always suck you," Jill said, and she twirled her tongue over his head. She licked off the bead of pre-cum and savored the saltiness. "Mmm. I love how you taste."

"I bet I'm not near as tasty as you are," he said. "Yeah, that's it. Suck me. Suck my cock."

Jill craned her neck to take more of his manhood between her lips. He knelt above her, and she licked the underside of his swollen length. She inhaled the muskiness of his balls then lapped at them, tonguing every peak and valley of his sac.

"You drive me crazy," Dale said, panting.

She lowered her head back to the soft blanket and licked his cock head some more. "I love your cock, Dale. I love to suck it."

All the while Travis pumped into her, and her pussy creamed over him as she neared the precipice again.

"You're getting close, sweetheart," Travis said. "You're pussy's clenching. Damn, you feel good. Such a sweet fuck."

"Do you want to come all over Trav's big cock, darlin'?"

Jill released the tip of Dale's length. "Yeah, Dale—" Jill paused, unable to form words. She wanted Travis. Wanted him to pound into her. Wanted to clench around his thickness. "I-I want to come."

"Go for it, Trav."

Travis' calloused fingers grazed her clit, and she burst, soaring higher than the first climax. Travis continued to thrust, and Dale soothed her with sexy words, how hot she was, how beautiful, how hard she made him. She absorbed it all in a heady rush.

When her release subsided, Travis pulled out of her, his cock still rock-hard, and disposed of his condom.

"Your turn, bud," he said to Dale. "And my turn to feel those gorgeous pink lips around my cock."

"Do you want that?" Dale asked Jill. "Do you want me to fuck you while you blow Travis?"

"Mmm, yes." More than anything, she wanted Dale's cock inside her. She wanted to force every last drop of cum out of him. And sucking Travis didn't sound too bad, either.

Dale leaned down and kissed her, slowly and passionately, then flipped her over onto her tummy. "On your hands and knees, darlin'. I'm takin' you from behind."

Dale fumbled with a condom, and soon his length teased the cheeks of her ass.

Travis knelt in front of her, his cock weeping with precum. She grabbed his taut butt for support and licked the salty drops from him.

Meanwhile, Dale kissed her thighs, nipping and licking, then tongued her pussy. "Mmm. You taste so good, Jill. Just like honeyed cream." He slid his tongue over her labia, then up over her anus. Her tight hole puckered, and she shivered. Would he take her ass tonight?

Would she let him?

Chapter Three

Travis reached for the pitcher of lemonade and poured some over his cock. "I want it to taste good for you, sweetheart."

His beautiful sex tasted just fine to Jill, but the lemonade added an extra zest that she had to admit made it even better. She teased his cock head, licking around the sensitive rim and underside, then took him a little farther. She slurped every drop of that mouthwatering beverage from him. And she enjoyed every minute.

"She gives great head, Trav," Dale said as he inserted a thick finger into her cunt. Her walls pulsed around him. "So tight, darlin'," he said. "I need to fuck you right now."

He thrust into her wet channel, and his balls slapped against her clit, making her shudder. He plunged deep once, twice, then once more, and Jill was on the verge of another breath-stealing climax. She grabbed Travis' ass and took his cock into her mouth again.

She sucked him deep into her throat, his moans igniting her to take him even farther.

"Sweetheart, that's amazing," Travis said. "Absolutely amazing."

"Told you, Trav," Dale said, his words breathless. "Damn, you're tight, Jill. So tight and sweet. I love fuckin' you."

Jill wanted to answer, to tell Dale she loved fucking him too, but her mouth was full of cock. She moaned, grinding back against Dale's thrusts. She felt so full, so well pleasured, and neither Travis nor Dale had released yet. The night was still young.

Slow and Wet

Dale continued to pound into her as she blew Travis. When the pad of his finger pushed against her anus, she trembled.

"Okay?" Dale rasped.

She released Travis' cock to answer. "Yeah, cowboy. Go ahead."

The cool sensation of lubricant, coupled with the heat of Dale's fingers, melted against Jill's tender flesh. He massaged her tight rim, then inserted his wet finger slowly, stretching her. The feeling was so invasive, so intense, but she relaxed into it, and found pleasure in having Dale fill her so thoroughly. Travis' cock still dangled in front of her, but she leaned back into Dale's body and quivered as he added another finger and fucked her in two places at once.

The climax took her by surprise. He hadn't even been touching her clit, but she shattered, and tiny sparks erupted on her flesh. She soared higher and higher, and her only regret was that Dale wasn't coming with her. She cried his name, her voice not quite her own.

"That's right, darlin'," he said. "Come. Come for me. Only for me."

Only for me.

Had Dale forgotten Travis was there?

Once her pussy relaxed, Dale removed his cock and pulled her against his chest in a tight embrace.

"That was phenomenal, Jill," he said. "Like nothing I've ever felt before."

"But you didn't—"

"No, not yet." He cupped her cheeks and pressed his lips softly to hers. "What was phenomenal was making you come like that. I loved it."

"But I want you to come. So far, this night's been all about me."

He chuckled against her lips. "All about you? I've had a rippin' good time. And so has Trav. Haven't you?"

"Hell, yeah. Watching you, and being a part of it, boggles my mind."

"You want to come some more, darlin'?" Dale kissed her cheek.

"I...I..."

"I'll take that as a yes." Dale's husky laugh vibrated against her neck. "Let's get you cleaned off. The hot tub's all fired up." He stood and lifted Jill, and she wrapped her legs around his waist. Amazing, how their two bodies fit together, as though they'd been created for each other. Skin-to-skin with Dale was the most erotic, delicious and sweet sensation she'd ever felt.

"Come on, Trav," he said.

* * * * *

Dale kept his hot tub lukewarm. That's how he and Jill preferred it. They could stay in as long as they wanted without getting overheated. Still, to prevent dehydration, he kept plenty of water handy.

And another pitcher of honey-lemonade.

The warm water swished around his body, tickling him. His erection still raged. He could have come. He would have gotten hard again right away. Jill had that effect on him. He could fuck her every night for the rest of his life and not get tired of her beautiful body, her tight pussy, her amazing selfless heart.

God, he loved her.

The words he'd never said to a woman didn't particularly surprise him. Even though he hadn't formed them until now, they saturated his mind, as if they'd always been there and always would be.

He loved Jill.

She sat on the edge of the hot tub, her legs spread, Travis' blond head bobbing between them. Her eyes were closed, and her body glistened with shiny perspiration in the moonlight. Sexy little moans escaped her throat. She was beautiful. So fucking beautiful. And now, as he watched his best friend eat his woman's pussy, he knew, without a doubt, he'd spend the rest of his life with her.

Tonight was a gift. A gift she deserved, and he was glad to have given it. An experience she wouldn't soon forget.

But it wouldn't happen again.

Jillian Reynolds would be his, and his alone, for eternity.

He tapped Travis' shoulder impatiently. "My turn."

Travis lifted his head, his chin gleaming with Jill's sweet cream. "Sure, bud." He moved to the other side of the tub.

Dale buried his face between the legs of the woman he loved. She smelled like peaches. Peaches, lemons, honey and Jill. An inebriating combination, and one he wouldn't tire of any time soon. Slowly, he licked her slick folds, like silk against his tongue.

"Ah, Dale." She sighed. "I love when you lick me."

He groaned into her, taking her swollen labia between his teeth and tugging. She squealed. God, he loved sucking her, making her feel good. He knew just what she liked, and he lived for her moans, her sweet cries of ecstasy.

Between his legs, his cock throbbed. He'd been close to release several times already, but he held off for her. He wanted to give her everything tonight. The ultimate pleasure.

He sank his tongue into her moist slit. Nectar drenched his mouth and chin. He lapped her thoroughly, tensing his tongue and fucking her as deeply as he could. Then he pushed her thighs up toward her chest, careful so she wouldn't lose her balance on the edge, and licked her puckered anus.

"Dale!" she cried.

"Mmm. Good, darlin'?"

"The best."

He released her thighs and nipped the inside of one. "I'm gonna take you there tonight."

"Mmm. I know." She inhaled, her beautiful breasts bobbing lightly against her chest. "I know."

"First, I want you to come again, though," he said, and then tongued her clit. "I want you to come. Then I want you to let Travis fuck your tight pussy again. Would you like that?"

"Mmm. Anything for you, Dale."

"It's all for you, darlin'. Only if it's what you want."

"It's…it's what I want."

"Then come," he rasped, his tone commanding, "come for me, Jill."

Dale thrust two fingers into her wet channel and sucked her clit hard. She shattered, her walls clenching around him as he massaged her G-spot and fresh cream drizzled over his hand. When her spasms slowed, he removed his fingers and pulled her into the warm water.

He sat down on the bench, the water coming midway up his chest, and pulled Jill onto his lap. "I want you to slide your clit up and down my hard cock, darlin', while Trav fucks you. Would you like that?"

"God, yes," she said.

Dale watched as Travis, condom already in place, moved behind Jill. His lady didn't know it yet, but this was the last time she'd fuck another man. One last gift to her, to be sandwiched between two men, the object of both their desires. A jolt of jealousy speared into him and shattered his resolve for a moment. But he inhaled, gripped Jill's slippery body, and willed to give her this satisfaction one last time.

She sighed, soft and feathery against his neck, when Travis entered her.

"You have the tightest little pussy," Travis said, his face twisted into a grimace.

Slow and Wet

"Yeah, she sure does," Dale agreed. "Enjoy it." *For the last time.*

Jill slithered up and down Dale's shaft as Travis fucked her from behind. Dale was so hard he thought he'd explode if he didn't get to come soon. She was so beautiful. Her auburn ringlets, moist from the exertion and the steam from the tub, framed her pretty round face. Tiny beads of water dripped from the strands. A delectable strawberry hue flushed her cheeks, and her lips—those soft, sweet lips—were as red as a ruby. Dale cupped her silky pink cheeks and drew her mouth to his for a kiss.

A searing kiss that thundered through him. Jill's mouth was sweet as cherry wine. He thrust his tongue inside, sweeping it in the satiny warmth, branding her. It was a possessive kiss. A kiss that said, *You're mine. Another man may be fucking you, but you're mine. Now and forever.*

Jill's delicate sighs echoed with a soft vibration into Dale's mouth. Her clit sliding up and down his cock was sweet torture. Behind her, Travis grunted, his face flushed.

"Dale," he gasped. "I can't hold off any longer. I have to come."

A ribbon of possessive lust knifed through Dale at his friend's words. This was Travis. His buddy. He loved him like a brother. Loved him enough to let him pleasure his woman. But it was over now.

He ripped his mouth away from Jill's and inhaled a much needed breath.

"No."

"No?" Travis groaned as he pounded into Jill's pussy. "What do you mean?"

"I mean no. You don't come inside her."

"It's okay, bud. You know I'm wearing a raincoat."

"It's not okay. I don't want you to come inside her. Pull out and finish yourself off."

Travis' gaze met his, and Dale knew his friend understood. He withdrew, pulled off the condom and tossed it on the edge of the tub, then squeezed his eyes shut as he gripped his cock. Thick streams of cream spurted into his other hand. When he was finished, he wiped his hands on a towel sitting on the edge of the tub, then plunked down onto the lounge seat with a heavy sigh and a splash. He closed his eyes.

Jill's face was buried in Dale's neck, her moist body clamped to his. She hadn't watched Travis get off, which intrigued Dale.

"Darlin'?"

"Hmm?" Her voice hummed against Dale's earlobe.

"Are you ready?"

"Yes, Dale."

"You know what I'm talkin' about, don't you?"

"Yeah." The soft flutter of her lips against his neck as she smiled warmed him. "I know. And I'm ready."

She lifted her head and her flushed face had never looked more beautiful. He stood and helped her up. Without any prompting, she turned her back to him and braced her arms on the edge of the tub.

So beautiful. Tiny droplets of moisture meandered down the swell of her round cheeks.

So trusting, to give herself to him like this, and in front of his friend. At that moment, he loved her with an intensity he hadn't known existed.

"Jill." His own voice had deepened.

"Yes?"

"This is something I only want to share with you."

She nodded and wiggled her bottom against his erection.

Did she understand what he meant? He wasn't sure. His original plan had been to initiate her ass while Travis fucked her pussy. To let her be filled in the ultimate way. Previously, when he and Travis had pleasured women in this manner,

Dale had always taken the pussy. Now, as he readied to make love to his woman in a new and exciting way, he yearned for oneness with her, and only her. Travis could watch, but the act was for Dale and Jill alone. He cleared his throat.

She twisted her neck around and met his gaze with her emerald eyes. "What is it?"

"I know you're a virgin here."

She nodded.

"What I mean is...I am too. I've never had anal sex. This is something I've saved for someone special. And I want that someone special to be you."

"Oh, Dale. Thank you." Her smile dazzled him, and he bent to press a chaste kiss to her lips.

He pushed the head of his cock into the soft valley between her butt cheeks and slid it up and down. Her little moans excited him. He looked over his shoulder. Travis was gone.

Dale smiled. His friend had decided to give them some privacy. He was the ultimate good guy.

He let his dick rest against the soft flesh of Jill's cheek as he reached for a tube of lubricant he had set next to the tub earlier. He squeezed a generous amount into his palm and smeared it over her anus. He worked one finger in, then another, relishing the firmness of her muscles. Damn, this was going to feel good. With his free hand, he reached around the front of her and teased her clit. When he'd added a third finger, and a gush of nectar from her pussy coated his other hand, he knew the time had come to make her his.

Jill undulated against Dale's invading fingers. The invasive pain morphed into pleasure, and she found herself both desiring and fearing his cock. But the warmth from his confession—that he'd never shared this with another—gave her courage. Though she'd given up her vaginal virginity long ago, she could give this virginity to the man she loved.

The man she hoped to spend the rest of her life with. Hope speared through her. She'd know soon enough whether she'd be turning down that new job.

He pressed moist kisses to her dripping neck. "Darlin'."

"Yes?"

"I think you're ready."

She nodded. As ready as she could ever be. Ready for her man to take her.

"Don't worry, I'll go slow."

She nodded again, and the rip of a condom packet zinged in her ears. Cool lubricant coated her, and a few seconds later, the head of his cock nudged her anus. He pushed in, stretching her, and she winced at the sharpness.

"Easy, darlin'," he rasped against her neck. "I don't want to hurt you. You tell me if I need to stop."

No. She'd give him this gift. She wanted it as much as he did. And after what he'd given her tonight—the joy of being pleasured by two hot men—she wanted to give him something equally precious. Within a few seconds, she adjusted. "Go ahead, Dale. I want this."

"Ah, Jill." He inched in a little farther. Not so bad this time. When his fingers found her clit, she relaxed and backed into him, taking him deeper.

"Darlin', that's nice," he said, his voice deep and husky.

She backed into him again, taking more of his enormous cock, and found that the fullness completed her in a primal yet soul-wrenching, way.

"That's it, take all of me." Dale thrust into her ass, and when his balls slapped against her pussy, she knew he was part of her.

And that he would be forever.

"Darlin', I want you so much," he said. "Tell me when you're ready."

So sweet to think of her, when he no doubt wanted to pound into her with a vengeance. They'd been going at it for hours, and he hadn't come yet.

She wiggled against him, the intrusion of his cock in her tight tunnel a shocking, surprising pleasure. No longer uncomfortable, she found the fullness exciting. Was it pleasure because it felt good? Or was it pleasure because it was Dale inside her? In a place he'd never been with another woman, and she'd never been with another man?

Warmth exploded through her veins. Her blood boiled beneath her flesh. At that moment, she'd never wanted a man more.

"I'm ready, Dale."

He pulled out and thrust in, and shivers rippled through her pussy. A soft sigh left her throat.

"Okay?" he asked.

"Mmm. Better than okay. Take me, cowboy. Take me to where neither of us has ever been. I want to go. With you."

"My sweet Jill."

He plunged into her again. Waves of joy sparked between her legs and threaded outward to every cell in her body. She met him thrust for thrust, taking all he gave her, and relishing the carnal baseness of it. So good.

Dale's fingers worked her clit as he penetrated her, and moisture drizzled down her inner thighs. Swirls of steam surrounded them, and beads of sweat trickled down her cheeks and neck. Dale's other hand found a breast and cupped it, squeezed it, and then plucked at her hard nipple. The sensation—the amazing sensation—rainbowed over her flesh, through her blood, all the way to her heart.

And she exploded into the most earth-shattering climax she'd ever known. Icy-hot spasms shook the walls of her pussy and ribboned through the rest of her body, culminating in sweet chills that rippled across her tingling skin.

So intense was this joining, that for one glorious moment, their bodies and hearts seemed fused as one.

"That's right, darlin'," Dale's voice cut through the fog of her desire as her climax slowed, "come for me. Only for me."

Only for me.

He gripped her hips and thrust one last time into her, his slick body covering hers as he released. His cock pulsed into her tightness, and she backed into him again, wanting to give him everything she had.

Everything she was.

Vibrant images and half-formed thoughts jumbled inside her head, a mass of feelings she couldn't quite string together in any coherent way. But three words forced their way to the top of the heap.

I love you.

How she longed to utter them. And to hear Dale say them back. Maybe sometime soon.

Dale was still buried deep within her.

"Ah, Jill." He panted against her neck. "This meant so much to me."

"Me too." Truer words had never left her lips. Tears stung the corners of her eyes.

He slid out of her and she turned to face his deep, dark eyes. So gorgeous. His handsome face was shiny with perspiration, threads of nearly black hair stuck to his cheeks. Droplets trickled along the chiseled angles of his cheeks, nose and chin. His night beard had surfaced and caught drips of moisture.

He'd never looked better.

She pressed her body against his in a fierce hug. She slid her slick breasts against his dampened chest hair, and her nipples pebbled.

She'd never get enough of this man.

Oh, to be alone with the one she loved…

Alone? She jerked away. Where had Travis gone?

"Dale?"

"Hmm?"

"Where's Travis?"

He pulled her back into his embrace and chuckled against her cheek. "He must've gone inside. Probably wanted to give us a little privacy. And I don't know about you, but I appreciated it."

She smiled against his beefy shoulder. "Me too."

Dale lifted her, easing his hands under her slick bottom, and set her on the edge of the hot tub. He quickly disposed of the condom. "You thirsty, darlin'?"

She was. Ravenously so. "After that? You bet."

He reached for the lemonade and handed it to her. She took a long drink straight from the pitcher. The crisp citrus flavor flowed down her throat like nectar from the gods.

After a couple more swills, she handed the pitcher back to Dale. "Here, you must be thirsty too." She grinned. "Have I ever told you how much I love your homemade honey-lemonade?"

His lazy grin lit up his handsome face. "A few times." He downed several swallows of the beverage. Still holding the pitcher, he helped her to her feet. "You want to go inside?"

Inside? Travis would be there. And though she liked the other man, she kind of wanted to be alone with Dale for the rest of the night. But they couldn't be rude to his guest.

"Sure. Let's go on in."

Dale wrapped her wet body in a fluffy towel and led her across the redwood deck to the sliding glass doors. The house was dark, and Dale flipped the light switch in the kitchen.

"Trav?" he called out.

No response.

"Maybe he had to leave," Jill said.

"Hmm. That's not like him to just up and disappear."

Jill walked around the kitchen and turned on another light. Her gaze darted to the counter and landed on a folded piece of paper addressed to Dale and her. She picked it up and ran her wrinkled fingers along the crease. "Dale? I think he left us a note."

Dale came up behind her. "Go ahead and read it, darlin'."

"I wouldn't feel right. He's your friend."

"I think you're as close to him as I am now." He smiled and chucked her under the chin.

"Still—" She handed the paper to Dale.

"Okay." He unfolded and glanced over it, and Jill's skin chilled a little. She wasn't sure why.

"What is it?"

He grinned. "Nothing. Here," he handed her the letter, "you can read it."

Jill took the crisp white paper and read the words.

Dale and Jill,

Thank you for tonight. I've never experienced anything quite so intense, and I won't forget it. You two have something really special together. Don't let it get away.

Hope to see you both again soon. I'll call you when I'm back in town, Dale.

And Jill, it was a true pleasure to make love to you, one I know Dale won't grant me again. Don't ask me how I know. He'll tell you when he's ready.

Fondly,
Travis

Jill's pulse raced like a hummingbird's wings. Her skin heated. "Dale?"

"Hmm?"

"Is that true? You won't let him make love to me again?"

He cupped her cheek, and the wrinkled pads of his calloused fingers felt rough, but she loved it. "Oh yeah, darlin'. That is so fuckin' true."

"Why?" Jill's heart thudded. "I thought you and Travis liked to give a woman the pleasure of two men."

"Yes, I can't deny that. But it's past tense for me now."

"Oh?"

He smiled. "God, I hope you feel the same way."

"Well sure. I enjoyed tonight, but if you don't want to do it again, I'm okay with that."

"Good." He fingered her moist curls. "You're so beautiful."

Emotion tugged at her tummy. "Thank you."

"I wanted to give you tonight. It was for you. An experience you deserved to have. And it was your only chance to have it."

"It was?"

"Sure as hell was, if I have anything to say about it." His bronze eyes burned into hers. "Do I, Jill?"

Desire swept through her, laced with a touch of confusion. What exactly was he saying? "Do you what?"

"Have anything to say about it."

"If you have something to say, Dale, I sure wish you'd just say it."

"Okay." He cleared his throat and seared her with his smoldering eyes. "I won't share you again. I want you to be mine, and only mine."

She launched herself into his arms. Happiness—pure, unadulterated joy—surged through her. "I'm yours," she said. "I'm yours, Dale. I didn't need tonight."

"You mean you didn't enjoy it?"

"Oh, I enjoyed it. It was a pure physical pleasure. But with you, Dale, I get more. We came together tonight on a level that was way more than physical."

"Ah God." He rained kisses across her cheeks before clamping his mouth to hers. The kiss spoke of passion. Of possession.

Of love.

When he released her, he cupped her face and gazed into her eyes. "I love you. Do you know that?"

She nodded, and a lone tear trickled down her cheek. "I love you too, Dale. I have for a while now."

He brushed the tear away. "Don't cry, darlin'." Then a grin split his face from ear to ear. "Damn, woman, why didn't you tell me?"

"Why didn't you tell me?"

"Because I'm an idiot." He laughed. "It took ol' Trav." He sighed.

"I suppose he knew what he was doing."

"Hell, he might have had an inkling, but he also wanted to get in your pants. And I can't say as I blame him. I'm thinkin' the same thing right about now."

"Yeah?" Her body responded with chilled skin, a heated pussy. Moisture dribbled between her legs. Mere words from Dale could turn her on. "After the night we just had, you're ready for more?"

"With you? Always." He seared her lips with his. Her hands crept over his muscled chest. She fingered his hard nipples, and then rested her hand over his heart. It beat in synchrony with her own.

When he broke the kiss, he wrenched the towel from her body. His fingers slid into her slick folds. "Mmm. So wet for me. Already so wet."

She quivered at his touch, and then removed the terry towel from around his waist. His cock stood at attention—

hard, long and magnificent. She dropped to her knees and flicked her tongue over the salty head.

"Wet," she echoed. "That's exactly how I'm going to give it to you, cowboy. The way you like it. Slow and wet."

SET ME UP
Kat Alexis

Dedication

For my family. Every time you have cereal for dinner, every time I put off the laundry for one more day, all the time you give me to work on my books — I appreciate the sacrifices you make! I love you more than you know!

— Eve

For Naomi, my favorite wonder-in-law. Thanks for splitting deserts every holiday, always suggesting paper plates and never being afraid to add a little bit more drama to life.

— Allie

Trademarks Acknowledgement

The author acknowledges the trademarked status and trademark owners of the following wordmarks mentioned in this work of fiction:

Batboy: DC Comics, Warner Communications, Inc.
Diet Coke: The Coca-Cola Company
Lucky Charms: General Mills, Inc.

Chapter One
When in Ireland…

Freedom.

Independence.

Blessedly alone, finally.

No one needed her. No one asking her for assistance or help. Not a single person on the planet depending on her for anything. She didn't have to put on a brave smiling face and pretend everything was fine.

It was over.

Indigo Larsen exhaled a final breath, letting go all the tension, anger and grief that had weighed her down for the past three years. Caring for her dying father had taken everything out of her and left nothing for her draw on.

With the house sold and her father's law partner buying out her share of the practice, Indigo had nothing left to do and no one to care for. People advised her to keep the house, find a man and settle down.

"Hell no." She shuddered at the thought. She wanted her life attached to no one, much less a demanding and domineering male. Thirty-two years of living with her father had taught her exactly what she didn't want. Although Indigo knew her father had loved her, he'd never felt the need to say the words aloud. As an only child, whose mother had been lost to a car accident thirty years before, Indigo felt adrift without knowing why.

Her father had put the idea in her head. Toward the end of his life, Edward Larsen turned reflective and less sober.

"Indie," he'd whispered. His once booming lawyer's voice now reduced to scratchy murmurs. "Indie, my love, don't settle here after I'm gone. Don't waste your time waiting for your life to start. After I'm gone sell the house, the practice and everything else you can't carry on your back. Then get the hell out of this place. You deserve so much better than what I ever gave you." A withered hand clasped Indigo's with surprising strength. "Grab every opportunity life throws you. Don't turn your back on adventure because you're afraid. Don't let fear guide you. If something makes you want to back away run to it."

Indigo patted his wrinkled hand and wondered what had come over this once taciturn man. "Dad, it's okay. Don't worry about me. My job at the bank is still waiting. I can—"

"No," Edward cut in. "Listen to me, Indie. Sell everything. Every stick of furniture, every dish and plate, sell them. Use the money to live your dreams. Don't die with regrets in your heart. When your time comes I want you to be able to look back on your life and smile in satisfaction not frown in disappointment."

So she'd come to Ireland, the home of her mother's people. The heritage responsible for her midnight hair and deep-blue eyes along with a temper she'd tried, sometimes unsuccessfully, to control.

A land of magic and myths, Ireland called to her in a way nothing had before. Standing here inhaling the fresh scent of the sea and land, Indie's body came awake with a jolt.

Long hair flew in her face obscuring her vision for the moment. With an impatient hand, Indigo brushed the strands back. She wanted nothing to interfere with her first solitary view of Ireland.

Green as far as the eye could see, soothed her weary soul. Small white dots in the distance moved. Sheep, she guessed. Hills rolled gently into valleys, small huts puffed cheery white smoke from stone chimneys. The smell of flowers and grass tickled her nose.

All around her life carried on in beautiful harmony. Death tainted nothing here. Everything felt fresh, clean and alive. Everything she wanted to be. Renewed.

Could she find herself in a strange country while not knowing a single person there? It didn't matter, not anymore. Indigo would be damned before she let life pass her by again. She'd made a promise to her father and nothing would stop her from keeping it.

Thanks to her father's planning and generosity Indigo had more than enough money to wander the world for years. To explore everything she'd only dreamed of to her heart's content.

"Thanks, Dad." The wind gently tugged the words from her lips and drifted them into the perfect blue sky.

She would savor new experiences. Dance on the edge of danger. A small smile curved her lips at the thought. "Maybe not danger exactly but daring and different." The words pleased her. She could be daring and different. What a better place to discover who she was than the wilds of Ireland?

Pleased with herself and the world in general, Indigo strolled back to the miniscule rental car and drove into the tiny village that waited below.

* * * * *

"Slide me another, lad."

Aedan Ciaran smoothly lifted the glass and drew the perfect pint. With a flick of his wrist he sent the beer down the dark oak bar.

Old Paddy caught it with a wink and turned his attention back to the TV anchored above the bar.

"Seems to me," Morgan Kelister spoke to no one in particular, "changes need to be made here."

Aedan snarled. Morgan always wanted to change something in their village but Cearnaigh would always be perfect in Aedan's eyes. He loved his small piece of heaven on earth and wouldn't change places for all the wealth in the world.

"You be wanting to change things that need no change." He growled while his hands automatically cleaned dirty dishes. "You want change so bad, take yourself off to America or Australia. I hear tell they love things constantly different. We're Irishmen. Change isn't in our blood."

A loud round of agreements and applause greeted his comment. Morgan grumbled under his breath before pushing away from the bar. "Mark my words, Aedan Ciaran, change will come soon enough for you. And you'll end up ass over elbows before it's all said and done."

Before Aedan could respond Morgan stalked out of the pub. Weary eyes looked his way and Aedan could do nothing but shrug his wide denim-covered shoulders and laugh off his childhood friend's prediction as shivers crept up his spine.

"The boy's determined to set us up as the next great tourist destination in Ireland. Can you see it, Aedan, the Village of Cearnaigh, in all those fancy travel magazines?"

"We've got the right of it now, as we are. No crime, other than the O'Banyon cousins getting into their cups and beating one another up. A quiet place where we don't have to watch the children every second. Aye, I say we've got near perfection as we are. Why change something that isn't broken?" Aedan spoke from the heart while wiping down the bar.

This place, Ciaran's Pub, had been in his family for well over two hundred years. The bar wasn't fancy but it was solid. Good strong oak floors that held up years of hard-walking and hard-drinking men. Finely polished pine tables and booths filled most of the space until only a small dance square was left.

On Friday and Saturday nights Aedan had musicians play and locals would come to eat, drink and relax after a hard but honest, week's work.

And if you asked him, which no one ever did, that's all a man could and should ask for in life. An honest day's work for an honest day's wage.

"Ho, Aedan my boy, you have some of our Irish finest hidden behind that big bar of yours?" Jamie O'Neil called out.

Aedan wanted to say no but the men knew better. Aedan's family had been charged with guarding the *Teanga Fírinne*, which loosely translated to *Tongue of Truth*, for generations. He didn't question where the bottle had originally come from. Irish blood ran through his veins, there was no reason to question the unexplainable. But like his ancestors before him, Aedan knew with any power there held responsibility as well. He couldn't and wouldn't hand out the drink easily. His ancestors found out the hard way the damage too much *Tongue of Truth* could cause.

"You'll not be getting your hands on it, Jamie." He returned with a quick smile to take the bite out of his words. "You get one drink to celebrate the momentous events of your lifetime. This being a Friday in April doesn't seem to count as a life altering event."

The rest of the men and women laughed along with Jamie. Each person had grown up with the stories and rumors and knew the rules. They would never break them but like good Irish men and women they were, they would always try to bend them.

"Aedan, I heard tell there's an American lass staying at the Purlies. Have you seen her yet?" Colleen Pagents asked around her husband's pint of beer.

"Nay, she's not set foot in here but she will. They always do," he responded without giving the new tourist too much thought.

"I suspect you're right. Be nice to this one," Colleen warned him.

Green eyes clashed with green eyes.

"Colleen, my love, when have I ever not been nice to the tourists?" he queried with an innocent expression on his too handsome face.

"You're polite all right but a body could get frostbite with your niceness. This is just a young lass. She's seems right sweet. Pretty little thing truth be told but there's something sad in her eyes."

"Sad is she? And you said she's a pretty thing to boot? Well," Aedan smiled knowing it bared his teeth in more of a predatory snarl. "Maybe I should find the wee one and give her the Ciaran's personal welcome to Cearnaigh. Show her a hospitable time, offer her a wee taste of the Irish."

"Behave, you cur, she's an American and not likely to put up with your nonsense. I only said she looks sad. Maybe I should have spoken to Morgan. He'll look after her right and proper." Colleen nodded her red head in clear decision.

"I'm wounded you don't trust me, Colleen, love. I promise on the *Tongue of Truth* I'll not insult the skinny, demanding American no matter what a bitch she turns out to be," he promised humor twinkling in his bright green eyes.

"Too late." A husky feminine voice came from the open door he'd failed to notice. "The demanding bitchy American has been insulted. What now, Irish?"

The pub fell silent as all eyes shifted from the stranger in the door to where Aedan stood shocked.

An angel stood in his pub doorway black silky hair tumbling around her shoulders. Indigo blue eyes stared back him, daring him to continue insulting her. She crossed her arms and tucked dainty hands under the most luscious breasts Aedan had ever laid eyes on. Everything about the American screamed sex from the top of her tangled hair, to the generous curves of her waist all the way down to the sexy tips of her toes.

His cock hardened and his brain scrambled. There had to be a way to undo his mistake. The Irish were famed for their charm, so where the bloody hell was his when he needed it.

Quickly he untangled his tongue. "It's a mistake I've made insulting a woman such as yourself without even having laid eyes upon you. My deepest and sincerest apologies, love. Anything I have is yours." He swept his arms out to encompass the bar along with his oh-so-humble body.

Blue eyes danced over him and the bar then rejected them both. "I don't believe you have anything I'm interested in," she coolly informed him, dismissal all but dripping from her tone. "Thanks for the offer but I'd better head back to the inn."

Damn and blast it, Aedan didn't want to let the woman go. She was the first stranger to interest him in many a year. Since he didn't know how long she planned to stay in his village, he had to act quickly.

"Aedan, didn't you swear on the *Tongue of Truth* to not insult the lass?" Colleen asked from her perch in front of the bar. "Seems to me, you need to learn about keeping your foot from between those sexy lips of yours. You offended the lass after swearing you would not do so. It's up to you to make up for it.

He squinted at the woman he'd known his entire life. What was she getting at? Everyone knew they didn't share the beverage with strangers or outsiders. Maybe Colleen had sensed a kindred in her. Either that or his friend had finally tumbled too deep in her pot of gold.

"Yes, Aedan, you'd best be keeping your promise or you're no Irishman at all." Jamie called out in agreement. "Don't be giving us a bad name."

Damn them, they'd forced his hand. Fine, with any luck the American would refuse. He'd charm her then fuck her before sending her on her way.

"And so I did. Please," Aedan waved his hand to an empty barstool beside Colleen. He gave the American a wide smile filled with too many teeth. A smile he knew didn't reach his eyes, "Have a seat and I'll fix you right up."

Say no.

Say no.

Tell me to go to hell. Aedan pleaded in his mind. Instead the contrary and willful American crossed the room, pulled out the stool and sat her luscious self down. "Thanks. I'll take you up on that. One *Tongue of Truth* please."

Chapter Two
Did anyone get the number of that bus?

☙

A rough hand slid to the back of Indigo's neck and held her tighter. His other arm glided up her side. Tingles trailed his touch.

If this was a dream, she never wanted to wake. The man beneath her stroked her like a kitten. She'd be purring in no time. His body was hard and firm. Her curves fit perfectly into his hollows. A hard cock pulsed inside her.

She speared her fingers through the man's long hair and rose up to kiss him. Plunging her tongue into his mouth, she mimicked the thrusting of her hips on the thick cock already filling her. Indie had never been so bold in her life.

Grabbing hold of his biceps, Indie leaned further into him. The muscles flexed under her touch. He was strong, warm and safe.

His body was incredible beneath her. Breast to chest, thighs to thighs and everything in between.

His erection grew inside her channel. Harder, longer. The bulbous cock head scraped all the lovely nerve endings already on fire.

Indie moaned. "More."

She grazed her nails down his muscled chest. He groaned. A deep rumbling sound she felt against her naked breasts.

"You're magnificent, woman," he whispered against her lips, his hot breath tickling her. The melody of Ireland wove through his words seducing her all the more.

Should she be worried that her dream man felt more real with every hard push of his hips?

When a warm tongue lashed her nipple, Indie choose not to care where her reality was parked. She wanted to come and more than anything she wanted this man to get her there.

She plunged her tongue into his mouth again, taking charge.

He thrust his penis harder inside her. His balls were tight up against her body and felt velvety and wonderful.

His hands went around her waist guiding her rhythm.

"Oh no. This is my show." Indie moved his hands to her breasts and held them there.

He pinched her wet pebbled nipples as she moved up and down on his hard cock. She eased up slowly, enjoying the sensation of his uncircumcised erection rubbing against her sensitive walls then with a quick slam of her hips she thrust down fast.

"Yes, me darlin'. Just like that. Ride me." His hands curled around her breasts and he roughly kneaded the plump flesh.

She gasped and clenched her muscles in response. The pleasure-pain felt incredible.

His eyes glowed an unearthly green. Actually glowed as though lit from within by candles. They were beautiful and mesmerizing, filled with power and pleasure.

What the hell?

He pulled her to him and kissed her thoroughly. His tongue stroking her lips, his teeth nipping at her.

His eyes no longer mattered.

"Oh God. More," she panted, rising faster on his pulsing cock.

Heat coursed from her breasts to her pussy and back. Her skin burned. She moved faster.

Up and down.

Faster and harder.

Bracing her hands on his pecs, Indie dug her nails into the firm muscles and rode him hard. With every rise of her body, she squeezed him tight, then plunged down grinding her pelvis against his.

She reached behind her and grasped his balls. They were tight against his body as she massaged them, tickling the sensitive skin underneath.

He gasped and rose up sharply. "Careful, darlin'. Don't want the fireworks to come too quickly."

"Oh God. I'm coming," she moaned. "More. I want more."

Before she knew it, he'd swung her around until her back pressed against the chair they'd been doing their best to test the warranty of and was thrusting. Hard. Fast. Furious.

His hands held her legs on his shoulders. The angle forced his penis deeper with every heavy thrust. His beautiful face filled with ecstasy as he fucked her. His chest heaved as he pushed his cock deeper into her wet body and his body glimmered.

It glimmered gold.

Sparks of light shone from his flesh and gold dust rose from him with every push of his body into hers. He smelled of fresh green clover and warm spring nights.

Waves of pleasure started in her clit, heat spreading in pulses through her body. Every muscle tightened. Her vagina clamped down on his penis as the climax hit her with a force she'd never known.

Indie clutched his straining biceps. Her nails bit his flesh as he rammed into her, keeping the climax going until a second wave washed over her, drowning her.

Nothing had ever felt this good.

His movement never faltered instead picked up speed as he raced to his own pleasure. Once. Twice. On the third heavy thrust he erupted inside her with a shout. Beams of gold shot from his skin and bathed them in a molten glow. His eyes glowed hotter as hot jets of his semen filled the condom she only now realized separated them. His chest heaved as he collapsed on top of her. The strong solid weight felt good against her breasts.

Shivers coursed through her as she stared at her lover. His eyes were back to the beautiful emerald green and his flesh while tanned was no longer glowing.

Wow. Dream sex is fucking awesome!

He disposed of the condom, cleaned them both off with a cloth then gathered her to sit across him in the chair, pulling her close into the crook of his shoulder. He lazily stroked his hand over her shoulder and down her arm.

Wanting even more, Indie kissed his shoulder and slid her way down his body. Her hard nipples grazed his ripped abs. They were focal points for lightning bolts of sensation firing straight to her vagina.

"Now where are ya off to, darlin'?" His voice sounded both pleased and puzzled. As if he couldn't understand why she'd leave the comfort of his arms or where her energy to do so came from.

"Not far." She kissed her way down his chest. Inhaling the clean musky scent of male flesh with pleasure. He no longer smelled of clover but of strong male.

Sitting on the floor, she was at eye level with his cock. His very large cock. The veined organ pulsed and bobbed toward her. She licked her lips and ran her tongue from his balls to the weeping tip.

He groaned harshly and grabbed the chair arms.

The dark salty flavor teased her tongue.

Indie wrapped one hand around the base of his cock, enjoying the silken feel of the hot skin over hard flesh and stroked. She scraped her teeth along the sensitive underside of the flared head and taking him all the way into her throat hummed around the thick shaft.

"For the saints, woman. You're a menace to a man. But don't stop," his voice growled above her as his breath sped up.

She smiled around his thick cock.

Her nipples pebbled and her pussy, already soaking from earlier, wept.

She hummed deep in her throat again. The sound joined his moan of pleasure. She withdrew and stroked him softly. Teasing, she asked, "Do you like that?"

"For sure, I do." He looked at her with green eyes alight with pleasure and desire. They were glowing again.

Bending down to suck him in, she tightened her grip on his flesh, stroking up and down, harder and faster.

"Heaven help me. I'm gonna come." His voice was strangled with need.

Indie released his cock from her mouth. "I want to see it. I want to see you come." She licked around his balls and nuzzled his soft sac breathing deeply. The clover scent was back and his skin so beautiful and firm had gone molten again.

What was he? It didn't matter. This was her dream and he was everything she wanted.

Indie gripped his cock firmly and stroked. Her other hand massaged his balls with a careful but firm touch.

His eyes closed tight and his cock hardened to marble. He was close.

With one last stroke and a guttural shout from him, warm creamy semen shot from his cock onto her breasts. It was beautiful. Rich golden-pearly drops coated her skin. Indie massaged the fluid into her flesh.

"Saints be praised, I'm a lucky bastard," he choked out.

Indie laughed along with him. Her body flushed and hot with desire. "And you're about to get even luckier," she whispered while pressing wet kisses along his golden neck and shoulders.

Strong arms wrapped tightly around her. "Hmm," he murmured and rubbed his hardening penis against her slick opening. "Something ya need there, lass?"

Indie met her lover's glowing clover-green eyes as she sheathed his cock with another condom and spread her thighs on either side of his strong hips. "I'm just going to borrow this for a minute or two," she told him while one hand braced her body and the other slid and slipped his throbbing cock head along her dripping slit.

"I'd been of a mind to take a wee nap," he teased her while desire flushed his cheeks red.

"Go ahead," she panted as her body opened to accept every hard inch of him. "Don't mind me. I promise to put it back where I found it after I'm done."

He laughed. A deep, rich, comforting sound that shot straight from her heart to her vagina where her grip tightened.

"Ahh, love, right there now. Show me how you ride," he said before bringing his dark head up to lave her breasts with his tongue, teeth and lips. "Take me. Take all of me. That's a girl."

And proceeded to show her that Irishmen had a natural affinity for rhythm and drive.

After they both started to breathe normally, Indie lay across his lap with his semihard penis lazily thrusting inside her.

"You're on your own for this one, Lucky Charms. I've got nothing left." A yawn accompanied her statement.

He chuckled and it warmed her inside as she dozed to the rhythm of his strong heartbeat pulsing beneath her cheek and in the depths of her body.

* * * * *

Oh. My. God.

Indigo awoke to a man beneath her and a hard cock inside her.

What in the hell happened?

Where was she?

She tried to pick up the lead weight of her head but incessant buzzing and flickering stars in front of her eyes made it impossible.

She cracked one eye. A cautious look around revealed the deep cherry wood of dressers and a four-poster bed.

The bed they weren't in.

Oh dear lord.

She was currently impaled, there was no other word for it, on a thick cock while the man attached to said cock sprawled in the chair beneath her.

A leather recliner to be exact.

Well, hell.

How had she gotten here? A one-night stand, while she'd never done that, would've been okay. She could've snuck out and headed back to the inn.

So much for that plan. With the penis currently growing inside her, heavily muscled arms pinned her to an equally muscular chest, Indigo's chance of silently crawling away in embarrassment grew to nil. The walk of shame after what appeared to be an incredible night of sex was going to be pretty fucking long. Because this wasn't the cute little B&B she'd checked into yesterday.

After stowing her luggage she'd wandered around the village and into the local pub where a gorgeous man insulted her and then…

A drink. That's what started it.

Something about redeeming himself and Indie needing the *Tongue of Truth*. Whatever that was.

Strong fingers teased her nipples into peaks. Her flesh was firm and heavy. The hands of an artist, long fingered and elegant, plucked and pulled her nipples to aching points of painful arousal.

The bartender had poured two shots of dark red liquid into cut crystal glasses. The deep crimson color resembled blood. Actually it resembled the scratches marring his muscle-defined chest. Scratches she'd clawed into his skin as he kissed his way down her eager body and back up again.

Heavy breathing saturated the air. Softly whispered words she didn't understand filled her head. His lips firm and full, perfect for kissing. The warm thrust of his tongue in her mouth stroking her, mimicking the thrust of his cock against her jeans-clad pussy.

The steady rise and fall of his chest ruffled her feathers. How could he sleep so peacefully? She shifted to try to escape.

His breathing changed.

He was awake. "Hello, love."

"Um. Yeah. Hi."

His artist's fingers caressed up her side bringing goose bumps to the surface. He palmed the curve of her ass. The calloused flesh scraped her and sent a shiver through her.

"How are you, this fine day?"

Confused. Angry.

Hot. Melting.

And really, really horny...

"I'm fine." There went that spectacular wit, she thought with dismay. Would she forever be cursed to polite answers around this man? Her brain shuddered to a stop at the thought. Why would she even assume she'd see this man again? This would be her first and last one-night stand.

"You are at that."

Indie inhaled and finally looked up into the face of the man she lay on.

"More. Fuck me harder." Thrusting hips pounded her from behind. She was bent over a wooden counter. The bar? A table? Both?

A glint of gold caught her eye. She blinked to clear her eyes and focused on her hand. A beautiful Celtic ring gleamed in the late morning light through the lace curtains.

"Where did this come from?" A nervous squishy feeling took over her stomach.

The man she lay on smiled. "All married women in my family wear the eternal heart for a wedding band."

Her stomach dropped to the floor. "Huh?"

Her eloquence should astound him.

"We're married, darlin'. You and me, two souls intertwined for eternity."

Indie scrambled off him, ignored her nudity and his to glare down at his muscle riddled body. "Married? What the hell do you mean married?"

Chapter Three
Never mix alcohol and sex!

ഇ

Aedan thought about getting insulted by his new wife's threats and promises. But how could any male listen to their mate's words when her body spoke so much, so eloquently.

Puckered pink nipples poked out against their confinement in one of his flannel shirts. Long lean runner's legs, made for grabbing and holding a man tight while he pounded them both to mindless pleasure, swung back and forth in front of the dresser on which Indigo sat perched.

"Whatever you put in that drink will get you arrested." Indie coolly informed him while desperately trying to pull his ring off her finger.

"It won't come off, love." He tried to tell her for the tenth time but as with the previous nine other times his wife ignored his advice.

"I don't trust you. I don't know you and you say we're married. Why don't I remember it? Where's the paperwork to prove it? Besides, I'm an American citizen. There should be years of paperwork to get through for a foreigner to marry a local. Nothing is this easy." Suspicion clouded her dark blue eyes.

Aedan wanted to fall to his knees in surrender at Indigo's next action.

When pulling, tugging and yanking on her poor finger hadn't helped matters, his mate popped said finger into the warmth of her mouth and sucked. Hard.

His knees began to buckle as memories of having his cock balls-deep within the hot depths of her lips crashed in him.

With a flailing arm, he sank to the side of the bed and tried to control the harshness of his breathing.

In and out.

In and out her finger went. Wet and slippery from its time spent in that hot piece of heaven his cock had only known once.

"Hey." Indie snapped her fingers. "You still with me, Lucky Charms?"

Even the damn nickname she stuck him with sounded amusing instead of insulting. "We're married. Father Patrick performed the ceremony himself. The paperwork's behind the bar, locked up tight in my safe."

With a last ball-squeezing lick, Indigo pulled her finger away from her lips. "What man of the cloth would marry two obviously drunk people? Where can we find this holy man? I need to have the marriage annulled and get the hell out of this village before I lose the rest of my mind." She hopped from the dresser and paced.

He'd known it would come. Knew Indigo didn't want him as a permanent part of her life. But still when the words came they pierced him deep and hard. It wasn't his fault they were mates. Blame the fates, the sugar-sniffing bitches. They made the choice to bind two souls together.

"Father Patrick, is gone for the day. Even if he were still here, the good father would do nothing to ease the way of an annulment," he admitted to her.

Indigo stopped her pacing long enough to glare at him. "Why wouldn't he? The two of us weren't exactly in our right minds. This should be an open-and-shut case."

Well now here came the bitch at the bottom. The one really big thing he'd been dreading telling her.

"See now, lass, there's being in your right mind and being in your *right* mind. The good father knew we were both in the right. He performed the ceremony according to custom and he'll not be letting either of us out of this marriage."

Beaded nipples rose and fell with each deep breath Indigo took. Aedan licked his lips remembering the taste and texture of those sharp little nubs under his lips, between his teeth and hardening under his tongue.

"We'll go over his head. There has to be a supervisor or something. I'll tell them what I remember. You tell them what you remember. Before you know it our marriage will have never existed and we'll be free to resume our lives." Indie's deep blue eyes glowed with anticipated victory over the church and him. She rushed around the bedroom grabbing her clothes from the floor. Quickly she dressed sans underwear because earlier they'd been found ripped to pieces and covered in gold.

An ache pounded in his head had Aedan reaching up to try to massage the pain away. "I will tell them what I remember. I remember vowing to love, honor and cherish you. To stand beside you through everything life offers. I remember bringing you to my bed and making love to you as my wife. I am your mate, your husband."

"You aren't my anything." Panic flooded those memorizing violet eyes before she turned away from him. "It was a mistake. One I intend to correct as soon as possible."

He ignored her sharp outburst and continued before losing the courage to continue. "According to not only the laws of the Church but also the laws of fate and leprechauns you are the one chosen to be with me through all time."

Her beautiful face lost all color. One dainty hand came up, palm out to warn him way. "Stay back, Aedan. I don't know what's gotten into you but I want you to stay very, very far away from me."

"Not possible, my mate." He took no joy in taunting her with the truth. No male wanted to be rejected by the one fated for him. But Aedan would be damned if he just let his only chance at true love walk away from him.

"Oh, it is *so* possible, whackjob. I'm going to the nearest American consulate and pleading for protection. Then I'll get on a nice big plane and fly the hell away from you and your crazy country. Then I'll get my annulment with or without your help."

Then she went off. Ranting about things he didn't bother to understand. Aedan only knew her words pierced his heart in a way nothing ever had before.

Temper flared through him. Wasn't good enough for her, was he? He, Aedan Patrick Rory Ciaran, direct descendant of the last great Fae king, wasn't good enough for a mere short-lived clumsy mortal? Ha, if only she knew what a great honor he bestowed upon her.

In another time, Aedan would have done his best to soothe and calm but Indigo hit his every hot spot without trying. She'd insulted his family, village, country and he even thought he caught an insulting reference to four-leaf clover in her rant.

"That's enough, Indigo," he said softly when she stopped to breathe between bouts of hysteria. "It's time to let it go. You'll not be getting your separation, no matter how hard you try. The good father knows I'm bonded to you until death. Considering I'm damn near immortal that's really saying something."

Anger-flushed cheeks drained of color, those long graceful legs capable of locking a man to her wobbled then gave away as his words sank completely in and she sagged against the bureau.

With wide fear-filled blue eyes Indigo asked the one question he knew had been coming. The one question that could possibly drive them apart forever.

"What are you, Aedan?"

He drew a deep breath, wanting this conversation over and wishing it never had to happen. "I'm a leprechaun, lass.

Born and raised in the mists of Ireland and here's where I'll be staying."

"You can't be," she whispered. One hand supported her leaning weight while the other covered her soft lips an expression of delayed horror filling her features. "There's no such thing as leprechauns. It's only a myth. Not real, just silly bedtime stories for kids." She inhaled sharply and gathered herself. "Stop lying to me, Aedan. I don't know what type of joke you're playing but it isn't funny and I want you to stop it."

He didn't let his heart go soft at her wounded expression. He kept a leash on his temper and compassion. If he let one go the other would follow soon after and he didn't know if human mates could survive a rampaging leprechaun.

Not that he'd ever intentionally hurt his chosen female but accidents had a way of happening when one of his kind lost their temper. Which is why he was holding on to his with every bit of strength he possessed.

"You seek proof?" he queried in a soft voice. Flexing his fingers to ready the magic already jumping and eager in his veins. "You saw my eyes when we made love. They glow with the fae magic in my veins. You saw the gold dust as I came inside your body. Not enough proof of my claim?" He cocked his head as an idea occurred. "If I give you proof beyond human explanation what will you give in return?"

Wet black lashes blinked up at him. "I don't know what you mean." Hesitant and unsure where as last night they'd been filled with passion and fire. It made his stomach ache to see her lack of acceptance.

Harsh laugher escaped him. Did he really have anything to lose at this point? Frustrated, Aedan raked his hand through his already messed up hair. He was a leprechaun. Leprechauns were not cowards to hide behind their pots. He gathered his courage and wished for a bit of his own luck before turning to face his none too pleased mate.

Indigo took two steps back for every forward one of his. Maybe facing her doubt and fear head-on would work better than easing her slowly. "If I prove to you I have magic. I can command and control magic what do you promise me in return for the show of my power?"

A wet pink tongue darted out to lick petal-soft lips. Aedan wanted to groan as his should-be-paralyzed cock stirred to life. "I don't believe any of this."

"Good then you've nothing to lose in placing a small wager." He taunted back, eager for her to agree, desperate to feel her body come to life once more beneath his. The mating heat rode Aedan hard. His body flushed at the erotic ideas flooding his brain.

"If I win, I get to leave here, the marriage annulled with no questions asked." The tension eased from her shoulders as Indie fought a way her way through the tangled conversation.

"Aye."

Small white teeth bit into her lower lip. "And if in some weird alternate reality you actually are telling the truth then what do you want from me?" She stalled a bit before continuing. "I'm guessing money means little to one of *your kind*."

He jumped on her hesitation, ignoring the small stab of hurt. "If I prove myself and my claims to you, you must promise in return that you will stay by my side for a week. No trying to run from me or our bond. You'll not deny who and what I am to you. You will do everything in your amazing ability to get to know the person I am. The one you allowed to fuck you all night last night. And this morning," he added with a wry smile.

Bright pink embarrassment or passion rose in her cheeks. Indigo straightened to her feet, head high, shoulders back. "If, and that's a big if, you can prove to me you are what you say you are and that magic is real and not just some trick of the light, then okay. I'll agree to stay with you for one week. Getting to know who you are besides a great lay and a big pair of balls."

Shock held him silent. Who the hell was this woman with her changing mood and personalities? One minute a fierce fighter, ready to battle to the death, in the next she looked like a lost child, unsure of herself and her place in the world. Then she opened her mouth only to sound like a cocktail-swilling, designer-shoe-wearing man-eater.

"Maybe," he said slowly never letting his eyes leave hers, "we can both take the time to understand each other. Because I swear, Indie, I feel like there are more women in your head then in the village houses combined."

At his comment, she smiled. Granted it was a small smile but it came from the heart. So he took it into his own.

He quickly dressed in jeans, boots and another flannel shirt. Indie had kept his favorite one when she'd dressed ready to bolt earlier.

"Ready to see some magic?" he asked, his mood light and steps almost jaunty with renewed enthusiasm. He opened the door of his apartment with a flourish. He knew just where to take his stubborn mate.

A place filled with the enchantment of Ireland and with the sensuality of his forbearers.

"Yeah, Lucky Charms, take me to see your magic."

"Your wish is my command." Aedan grasped her hand firmly in his and held her against his chest while ignoring her childish nickname for a cartoon charcater. "Hold tight, me darlin'."

Rainbows shimmered around them as a feeling of weightlessness coursed through Indie. The colors were vibrant and Aedan's beautiful smile was the last thing she saw before they disappeared from existence.

Chapter Four
Under and over the rainbow!

ಐ

They materialized in a field stretching as far as her eyes could see. The soft afternoon sunlight shone down on them setting fire to Aedan's golden skin. His eyes were the same color as the soft thick clover surrounding her bare feet.

"Where are we?" she asked, not wanting to believe he'd transported them there with a mere thought. Even though the evidence stared her in the face.

"We're behind the veil. In the fae world. My kind live quite peacefully among the humans but since you wanted proof of us, I thought to bring you here. To the center of our powers." He released her hand and took her chin in his rough palm. "Indigo."

She turned to him and looked up into his eyes.

The beautiful green glowed bright with desire. His hands stroked up her sides to palm her heavy breasts and squeeze them. Hot sweet breath caressed her face as he stared at her. "Indie." His deep voice was seductive and filled with promises in the afternoon sun.

Her breasts throbbed under his firm hand, an answering ache pounded in her pussy as moisture wept from her core. Indie squeezed her thighs together but the contact just made her more aware of the heat flooding her body. Her clit tingled as he leaned forward and devoured her with a kiss.

His lips pressed against hers and he moaned into her mouth when their tongues met and danced together. The man could kiss. No question. Soft bites on her lips, then soothing caresses of his tongue. His hand tangled into her long hair, holding her closer for his taking. His pleasure.

Not to be outdone, she pressed her body tighter against his. The hard planes of his chest abraded her nipples through her shirt. She gave as good as she got. Indie loved kissing and doing so with Aedan was pure sensation and heat. Pure pleasure.

Touching. Tasting. Teasing.

The strong column of his cock rose against her stomach as she wrapped her arms around his neck and kissed him deeply stroking her tongue against his.

They were floating. Indie looked down and squealed, grabbing tighter to Aedan as they rose off the ground. A rainbow surrounded them.

Holy shit. They were actually in the rainbow. "What's happening?" she asked, breathless with fear and a little excitement.

"I'm going to make love to you, wife. Here on the rainbow. Let go now, you won't fall. I promise. My magic will care for us both."

She shook her head vehemently. "Oh no. I'm not letting go of anything until my feet are safely on the ground where I belong."

He chuckled. "Indie, me darlin'. You're a part of me now. My powers extend to you. You can walk on rainbows if you so choose. Let go. You won't fall. I won't let any harm come to you. Trust me."

Aedan gave her one last kiss and let go.

"Hey!"

Indie floated next to him. Surrounded by shimmering colors and raindrops. It was incredible. Rainbows were always beautiful to her and now that she was actually in one, she was at a loss for words to describe it.

She ran her hand through the orange and red bands. They shimmered and vibrated.

"Oh my God. This is incredible."

Aedan smiled. "Aye, it is that. And it's going to get better."

She gasped as he gripped her ass and tugged her back against him, the glimmering colors not affecting the molten gold his skin had turned. It felt good to be in his arms again. Nothing else mattered but being with him. Feeling his kiss.

Riding his cock.

A growl erupted from his chest as she took his bottom lip between her teeth and bit softly.

Pulse beats pounded in her ears as everything was blocked out but him. Wanting to feel him, Indie slid her hand down and reached for his heavy cock.

Aedan's glittering eyes were so hot they seared her. She sizzled from her lips to her pussy. "I'm going to make love to you."

His words thrilled her. "Oh." Indie's shirt clung to the moisture coating her breasts. The anticipation of being with Aedan again had her heart beating so fast it was a wonder she didn't have a stroke. The scent of her arousal mingled with the afternoon breeze and his enticing fresh scent.

I wish he was naked.

His clothing vanished.

"What the hell? Did I say that out loud?"

"No, love. Did you wish it?"

She swallowed hard. "Yes."

He threw his head back and laughed. "Delighted as I am you wish to see me naked does it help in convincing you?"

"It's pretty hard to dispute with your cock staring me in the face," she said wryly.

Her hand stroked his erection. The hard shaft fitted perfectly against her palm.

"Let me return the favor."

Her clothes disappeared a moment later.

"Hey!" But her protest turned into a moan as Aedan's strong hands stroked up her stomach and aimed for her eager aching breasts.

The rainbow shimmered around them as a hot look passed over his angular features.

As though time had stopped, Aedan slowly leaned over her and kissed her. Warm firm lips pressed into hers as the weight of his body covered her. The rainbow felt as soft as cotton beneath her. When his calloused hands slid between them, she whispered her encouragement. His kiss grew more passionate as he molded her heavy breasts in his palms. He flicked her tight nipples then pulled on them with his fingers, softly twisting.

Indie moaned into his mouth, twined her tongue with his and nibbled his lips.

She sighed when he trailed his hand further down and cupped the heat of her pussy.

Her head snapped back as his strong, thick fingers slid between her wet folds. "More. Oh Aedan. More."

She sighed when his mouth latched onto an aching nipple. His lips closed around it, drawing hard. "Me darlin'," he muttered, then gripped the bud between his teeth, giving it a soft bite. Her eyelids popped open and the passion of being with this man in his world hit her in her soul.

The rainbow surrounded them, he surrounded her. Then he was inside her. His thick cock parted her flesh and thrust home. Balls-deep inside her body, he held her. They held each other. Floating in the miasma of colors and brightness of the rainbow, they came together. She wrapped her legs around his waist and crossed her ankles together at the small of his firm muscular back. The rounded muscles of his ass bunched and clenched as he thrust into her pussy with the rhythm of the seas she could barely hear over the pulse pounding in her head.

She kissed her way up his neck, peppering small love bites all along the corded muscles in his neck. Arriving at his ear, she licked the shell and nibbled the lobe. Aedan thrust harder and faster into her pussy, their combined juices easing his way into the core of her body.

Words, both English and Gaelic, floated through the air with them. "More. God, more, Aedan. Harder. You're right on my clit. That feels so good."

Her words sent him into overdrive and he removed her arms from his neck. "Lie back, love."

Trusting him completely, she lay back as he continued to fuck her. Indie had never felt more open or freer. She threw her arms out wide, knowing she couldn't fall through the veil of the rainbow. That he wouldn't let her fall.

His penis touched her deep inside. All the way to her heart. She was starting to feel things she didn't want to feel. Especially not for a man she barely knew.

"Me darlin', you're so beautiful in your pleasure. As lovely as the Isle of Eire. Lovelier than the sunset."

Speaking of which, she noticed the sun was going down and sending fiery flames through the already shimmering rainbow. Everything went gold, including this man she was dangerously close to falling for.

He thrust harder and brought his hand between them, flicking his thumb over her too sensitive clit. She clenched around him and cried out. That was all it took. Shaking and crying out, she came with a force that sent power and pleasure coursing through her veins.

Aedan kept up his rhythm and brought her to orgasm twice more. Each more powerful than the last.

His green eyes glowed as he looked down at her and the gold dust emanating from his body diffused into the spectrum surrounding them.

"You're mine, woman. We're fated for eternity." With one last thrust he emptied himself in her. The molten semen burned her inside and the heat from his body warmed her outside.

Before she could blink, they were no longer in the rainbow but a cave. The sun was setting beyond the mouth and the interior glittered as gold as Aedan's skin. They were still joined and the heat from their bodies created a wonderful cocoon for them.

"Where are we now?" she asked, curious at the intensity of the golden cave.

"We're in my cavern. The one place on the earth that only I know about. And now you as well, my love. For lack of a better term, this is my pot of gold," he said around her nipple as he lowered her to the floor.

Indie expected it to be cold and harsh but it wasn't. Like the man on top of her, it was firm and warm. She didn't think she'd ever be cold again. Good thing because she hated the cold. Aedan would keep her warm though. From the inside out.

He kissed her with an intensity that surprised her. Biting, nipping, laving and stroking her tongue and mouth. "This is the seat of my power. If anyone else but my mate were to find it, they could control me, control my powers. You are my true mate, Indigo. I trust you to know this place and not use it for ill."

"Well, that'll be easy since I've no idea where we are or how to get there. Does the train or bus come by?" Her joke fell flat. His glowing green eyes intensified as he stared at her.

"You're able to wish yourself here. Just like you did with my clothing."

Indie didn't want to talk about powers and wishes. It was all too much too soon. But she felt she at least owed him the assurance she'd never use this place against him. "I promise, Aedan, I will never reveal your secr—"

His lips covered hers effectively cutting her off.

Passion rose again between them. Not that it had gone far anyway.

His cock, still inside her from their last bout of lovemaking, grew inside her pussy. They made love slowly this time. Each taking the time to worship the other's body. The golden cave echoed with their cries of passion.

Aedan was lit from within as he brought her to peak after peak of orgasm. His molten skin branded her with heat everywhere they touched. There wasn't an inch of her body, he didn't know intimately. He'd explored her thoroughly and tenderly.

As the last orgasm hit, they shimmered back to the clover field. The sun was already touching the horizon and bathed the area in a riot of color and beauty. Nothing was more beautiful than the man who lay next to her on the bed of clover.

They were no longer joined but the hard erection rubbing against her thigh told her that wouldn't be the case for long.

Indie's thighs fell open while he nibbled his way across her chest from one nipple to the other. She moaned and ran her fingers through his long dark hair when the pressure of his tongue lashing her areola sent lightning sparking through her already overheated body.

Aedan trailed kisses down her stomach allowing her a taste of the feast he was going to make of her.

Already wet and pulsing, she sighed as he slid his hand down and thrust two fingers inside her pussy. He pumped his fingers in and out while his tongue found the sensitive nub of her clit and caressed it.

She lay there writhing as he licked and stroked her clit with his tongue. She threw her head back and dug her heels into his shoulders to move her hips in time with his movements, begging him not to stop.

"Oh God," she cried on a shuddering breath.

Soft laughter vibrated against her making the kernel of her clit harder.

"Aedan" she whimpered.

Indie bit her lower lip and tried not to thrash her head with the pleasure assaulting her senses.

Burning pressure pulsed through her body as he fingered her scorching pussy and he set up a rhythm between his fingers in her pussy and the hard sucking motion of his lips on her clit. Her whole body shook, her pussy squeezed harder on his fingers, her thighs quivered.

"Not yet, you don't, woman. I want to be inside you as you come." He licked her clit one last time before he rose over her, shielding her body from the encroaching night as the sun slowly descended to the horizon.

When he pressed his chest against hers, a thin cry broke from her lungs.

It was too much. The contact overwhelmed her. Her nipples scraped across his chest, shooting darts of electricity straight to her pussy.

"So lovely, me darlin'. Magic pales in comparison," he breathed. His hands grasped her hips and held her still.

The thick, blunt tip of his cock nudged against her dripping entrance and Indie reached up to grip his shoulders as he slowly slid his cock inside her.

They both moaned as she stretched to accommodate him and their combined juices wept from her to ease his way.

Inside her to the hilt, he ground himself against her clit and sent heat pulsing over her. With each thrust her breathing grew harsher and more strained.

Their actions were having the same effect on him. His chest heaved and stars lit his glowing eyes. She trailed her nails across his golden shoulders, digging in as he kept up his relentless pace.

He groaned as her fingers trailed down his arms and tightened on his muscles.

"My woman. Mine." He withdrew again and slid back in, harsher, stronger. "I don't have much control left, me darlin'."

Aedan pulled out slowly, agonizingly, then stroked back inside her. Hard and fierce.

"Just fuck me," she begged, her muscles pulsing and contracting again. She wrapped her legs around him and held on for dear life. Squeezing him with her thighs, the flutter of orgasm started in her clit and traveled out to the rest of her body.

He pulled back slowly, his cock dragging at her sheath. "You drive me mad, woman. Beyond all control," he said, slamming into her pussy with his hips. "Can't stop."

Indie couldn't believe how good his cock felt. Thick, heavy and pulsing. Her channel contracted and gripped him in a vise. A scream of pleasure escaped her throat and mingled with his grunts as he fucked her.

Feral growls raged from his chest as he pounded faster.

Indie welcomed the heat building inside her.

Groaning harshly from his movements, he thrust harder and reached between them to pinch her clit.

Her breath stopped, her stomach clenched, then she exploded. A scream tore through her.

"*A grha!*" Aedan shouted with one last stroke as he came in a rush of heat. Gold dust exploded from his skin.

He'd invaded every crevice of her being. There was nothing of Indigo, Aedan did not possess. Indie's breathing slowed as they collapsed on the bed of clover.

She was well and truly fucked.

Chapter Five
Why me?

ಏ

Indie's lungs gasped for air. Her body thrummed with delicious pleasure and soreness. When she'd challenged Aedan to show her his magic, she'd had no idea what the man or leprechaun would do.

Now she did. Making love on top of a rainbow, in a vast pot of gold, in a field full of four-leaf clover and so many otherworldly locations Indie had lost count of the places and her orgasms.

"So how do you like me now?" A wicked grin stretched across Aedan's lips as he lay next to her. One arm held his head while the other trailed gentle fingers across her bare stomach.

"I...whew," she stumbled for the words. The magic had been amazing and mind exploding but she had a feeling that even without it Aedan would have had her seeing stars anyway. "Amazing," she finally managed to get out. "I'll never look at a rainbow the same way again."

His soft husky laughter tickled her ear where his tongue gently traced its sensitive shape. "You're believing in the magic now, are ya not?"

After everything he'd shown her and they'd done the man still had to ask? "Yes, Aedan, I believe everything you've said."

The tightness of his shoulders eased with her words. Had he really worried that she would still doubt him? Silly man — er leprechaun — he'd given his word and now it was time to live up to hers. But first she had to know.

"Aedan, how did you become a leprechaun?" Since she'd never done research on them Indie had no clue as to what they were or the sum of their powers. At his confused look, she rushed to explain. "I mean you didn't get bitten or drink someone else's blood? Radioactive waves didn't hit you from a passing meteor?"

Booming laughter started the birds into flight over their heads. The damn man—er, leprechaun—laughed until tears rolled down his beautiful sculpted cheeks. "Indie, my love, you've got the imagination of an Irish woman and that's high praise indeed." Calloused fingers wiped away the remaining moisture from his clover green eyes. "I be born to what I am. There's no blood or biting involved." He shuddered as though the thought of either scenario made him sick. "Nay, lass, I am not a hairy dog to run on all fours and bay at the moon. Nor do I seek my rest in a wooden box and drink from the necks of mortals."

"Well, that's good. I won't have to worry about keeping the lid on the toilet down." Her eyes hungrily ran over his naked body. Her mouth watered at all that luscious tanned skin just waiting to be explored by her tongue. But tongue mapping Aedan's body would have to wait at least a few more minutes. There were a few more questions rolling around her head. "How do you control the magic? Were you born knowing how? Did you have to go to school? Are there any evil leprechauns? And why the hell do all the books claim your people are short and covered with hair?" Somebody had really dropped the research ball on that one.

Aedan's chest had a light sprinkle of hair but other than that, his groin, head and eyebrows, the man's body didn't have a strand of hair. He smiled slightly as his finger twined a strand of her hair around his finger.

"So many questions, my *liaria* but I will answer because it seems I cannot deny you anything." He leaned over to plant a quick kiss on her lips. "I'll start from the top. Leprechauns are born with the magic and knowledge inside them. We do have to take lessons of sorts to learn control and expand our powers but that's mostly taken care of by one's kin. Just as every human is born different so is it true for my people. Evil lies in the soul not the shape of a being. We have the para-police who track and punish those who break our laws." He gave her a wide grin full of charm and mischief. "As for the why of the stories, well, it seems we leprechauns are not known for our romantic sides. We are a practical people. But there was one of us who had a penchant for trouble. He became the Seelie queen's lover for a time. When he left her bed, he didn't look back and the queen became furious because no one left her until she was tired of them. The queen knew she couldn't curse him. Leprechauns hold the universe's luck within their bodies. Instead she turned to the mortal realm and caused us to become the joke of the veil. Now we are portrayed as short stubby men with long beards, pointed ears and some sort of foot covering that jingles when we walk."

"All that because of one woman's pride?" Seemed a bit over the top to Indie.

"Nay, all this because of a Seelie queen's pride. 'Tis a totally different matter when one insults a queen with such power." Aedan explained while his hand drifted from her neck to gently cup her breasts.

"I guess that makes sense." Her hand reached up to lovingly stroke the strength of his jaw. "So you've got me for a week. What's the plan?" she asked in a lazy voice. Currently with her body lying naked in the setting sun, Indigo didn't feel the need to move for at least another eight or ten hours. The man had loved her so well and often her body felt comatose.

Until Aedan cleared his throat and drew her attention back to him and his incredible body. Her eyes drifted from his sensuous lips, to his tight flat nipples across the rock hard abs of his stomach and down to…

Holy green jelly, batman!

"There is no way you could want to...or even by able to..." her voice drifted off as his semi-erect penis grew longer beneath her gaze.

"You were saying?" His talented lips drifted along her neck causing shivers to race down her spine and wetness to pool between her thighs.

Twisting her head to give him better access, Indigo hummed in pleasure. "I guess there are some benefits to being with an immortal," she murmured, caught up in the sexual spell Aedan easily weaved around her. "Besides the endless orgasms and hulking pot of gold I mean." She teased him while wrapping her arms tightly around his neck.

Strong fingers tightened briefly around her shoulders before releasing her. He pulled her arms from around him. With a grunt of surprise Indie found herself lying alone on the ground while Aedan strolled away fully dressed.

"Hey!" She sat up wincing at the cold air blowing against her body. Until Aedan had stopped touching her, Indie hadn't noticed the drop in temperature.

"What happened? Where are you going?"

"I'll be seeing you in a bit, love. Might be a good idea to cover all your naughty and non-naughty spots. The weather is going to get nippy tonight," he answered over his shoulder and strolled away. Well-worn jeans cupped his tight ass in a way that made Indie want to beg him to stay just so she could explore more of his body. She wanted to push him on his stomach, straddle those leans hips and drag her tongue from the base of his neck to the bottom of his sexy feet.

When his lust-inducing body disappeared from view, Indigo shook the desire from her mind or tried to.

"What the hell is happening to me?" she wondered aloud. She'd never been the sort of woman to let herself get caught up in a man. Independence ruled her world and she'd never wanted to change it.

Now a man she'd barely known for twenty-four hours, who'd given her more orgasms in that short time period than she'd had her entire life, had calmly waved a hand and walked out of her life.

And she wanted to cry. To scream out in anger and plead with him to come back. What exactly had happened to make him leave? How could they go from loving each other completely to him walking away without a backward glance?

She looked around the once peaceful and sensual field to see if something had changed but everything remained as it had been. A carpet of ankle-deep green clover spread out as far as the eye could see. The sea crashed against a distant shore somewhere to her right and the sun rode low in the sky.

If their surroundings hadn't changed him then it must have been her. But what had she done? They'd been talking, laughing and screwing each other's brains out for most of the day. It's not like she could insult him with her mouth stuffed full of his cock.

With a groan from her body's previously unused muscles, Indigo slowly rose and dressed. Wondering all the while what had changed the man from playful lover to disinterested ex in a matter of seconds.

Throughout the long walk back to the village and her B&B Indie's mind wandered back over the day. Nothing came to her, not one single thing had marred the beauty of their time spent together.

Except the belief creeping into her mind the *Tongue of Truth* was the real reason for their excellent day. She'd never experienced anything like this. Lust at first sight was common enough. But there was definitely more here and it was scaring her to death. How could any real relationship — if that's what they were having — start with a night of drinking? She should've been taking her walk of shame, not a walk through the clover.

Oh God. What have I gotten myself into?

"Well, be looking what the cat dragged in." A cheerful voice interrupted Indigo's mental loop-de-loop.

She looked up to see the happy face of the inn's owner, Molly O'Banyon. "Sorry, did you say something?"

Molly, a thirty-something woman with silver blonde hair, blue eyes and lush curves, laughed at the startled expression on Indigo's face. "Oh well now, I can see our Aedan has ya well and truly befuddled. Did he come with you or will you be meeting himself later?"

Indie knew the other woman's questions were purely sisterly nosiness. Everyone in the village seemed related to one another in some fashion. But she'd been raised in a big city where personal questions were asked for personal reasons. A flare of jealously reared up at the thought of *her* Aedan anywhere near the blonde's generous curves.

Unfortunately it didn't seem like Aedan had the same problem. He'd just up and left her after the sex was done. So much for thinking forever.

"I don't think so, Molly. I'm sure he's at the pub." Her voice came out listless and whatever interest she'd had in dinner disappeared under the weight of Aedan's disappearance. "He won't be coming here for me." She fought the tears fighting to break free at the thought of Aedan's desertion.

"Now, what man in his right mind would leave a lovely lass like you alone, much less his own wife?" Molly shot back, anger building in her lovely peaches-and-cream complexion.

Indie's head flew up at the tone in the innkeeper's voice. How dare the woman judge her? Why she didn't know a thing about Indigo? Pompous, self-righteous—

"That blathering idiot should know better. Leaving a poor wee one like yourself alone on the second night of what's supposed to be your honeymoon. Wait 'til I get me hands on that thick neck of his. He won't know a pint from a pence when I'm through with him. Just see if he won't."

Molly was angry on Indigo's behalf? The thought floored her and insults died on her tongue.

No one had ever defended her. Her mother had died too young and her father remained buried beneath his court cases. Tears prickled the back of her eyes and Indie had to press the heels of her hands to her lids to stop the water from flowing free.

A warm hand clasped her shoulder. "Come with me, Indigo, I'll be showing you all Irish are not cut of the same cloth. That sheep-brained man should know better. We'll get you fixed up nice and tight with a cuppa tea and a dash of Ireland's finest. Just you follow me now."

With her shoulder a prisoner of Molly's gentle but firm grip, Indigo had no choice but to follow the other woman. She'd accept the tea, chat for a moment or two then escape to her room. She could be packed and ready to leave in under ten minutes. Unfortunately Indie knew there wouldn't be a train or bus leaving the village until tomorrow morning at the earliest.

Still it wouldn't hurt to gather her things, get a good night's sleep and get the hell out of the village before Aedan ever knew she was gone. As if the man would bother to notice at all.

With a firm plan in mind Indigo allowed herself to be pulled into the warm, cheery, soft-yellow kitchen.

Four hours later Indie felt on top of the world. Whatever Molly had put in her tea made the worries ease off her shoulders and fanned the flames of hope in her chest. It also made her fifteen feet tall and bulletproof, at least for the moment.

"Who the hell does he think he is anyway?" she asked while trying not to stumble around the pretty kitchen. "I'll tell you who he is. He's Mr. Fuck-'Em and Leave-'Em."

"And so you've the right of, Indie." Molly agreed from her supine perch on the kitchen counter. Baggy jeans covered her hips and an old dark blue fishermen's sweater clung to her generous top. Monkey socks beat to a melody only she could hear and every once in a while her blonde head would bobble and wobble to the same rhythm. "Men are good for one thing only and most of the time you don't even need 'em for that."

"Amen, sishter," Indie slurred and slid down the cabinet closest to her new best friend. "Yous tell it." She tried again to untangle her tongue from the roof of her mouth.

"I went to the city one time about two years ago. Went in search of..." Molly stopped, squished her face up then let it relax. "Can't remember now why I went but I was there. While I was there I passed the most interesting shop."

She paused and it took Indigo a moment to figure out why. Then she jumped in with the expected question.

"What did you find, Molly, my sister from an Irish mother." The last she tacked on as an afterthought but found it hilariously funny.

Molly must have felt the same because when Indigo tilted her head up, she could see the B&B owner rolling back and forth on the short width of the counter clutching her stomach.

"Oh that's good, sister from an Irish mother. I like it. I like it very much. I'll have to start telling the others." A belly laugh rolled out of her and proceeded to carry her off the counter and down to the floor where she landed face-first almost in Indie's lap.

"Shhhh, you don't want to wake them up," Indie cautioned trying to press a finger to Molly's lips but unable to get her hand to cooperate. Instead she ended up smacking herself on the face and both women burst into laughter again.

"Wake who up?" The blonde asked around muffled laughter. "There's no one staying here but yourself."

Startled Indigo looked around. Huh, there really were no other people in the kitchen with them. "Must be those voices in my head again." She joked and the two women keeled over laughing again.

Before Indigo had a chance to recover, Molly started speaking again. "I found a sex shop, if you can believe it. They sold *everything*." Her voice lowered on the last word. "I didn't think I'd be able to force myself inside but I did." Pride rang through her lovely drunken Irish voice at the information. "You wouldn't believe how clean it was. The clerks were ever so helpful, not scary and scummy like I thought. Very professional as if they were selling clothing or makeup. One girl told me about her B.O.B." The last was said in a conspiratorial whisper.

"Bob?" Indigo felt lost in the conversation. "Who's Bob?"

Molly leaned closer, her voice low or at least Indie thought Molly tried to speak softly. Instead she ended up almost shouting the words in her ear.

"B.O.B.'s a Battery Operated Boyfriend. Runs on batteries or plugs into the outlet. He never says he's too tired. Never tips a pint too many. Always ready and always able. Never wants a night out with his mates. Will never be caught checking out other women. And most important, he always leaves you satisfied."

"I wanna B.O.B.," Indie wailed in sudden depression. She wanted a battery operated boyfriend that wouldn't cheat on her, leave when things got to serious or walk away when he'd gotten what he wanted. "I need a B.O.B.!" she shouted. "I want a plug-in boyfriend."

"I've got me one," Molly announced proudly. "It's a purple dragon with a snout, tail, ears and everything. I *love* my dragon." She said the last with a happy dreamy sigh.

"I'd love your dragon too." Then because Molly's pleasure dragon made her think of dragons in general she started to sing the old children's song about a dragon that lived by the sea.

She had a really nice loud rhythm going when a man's voice blasted through the kitchen.

"What the bloody hell have you done to my wife?" The enraged male voice cut through the whiskey and B.O.B.-induced female bonding.

"Go to hell." Indigo shouted at her supposed husband. "I don't need you anymore," she told him proudly while trying to figure out why the floor kept moving without her permission as she tried to stand. Wasn't that nice of Molly to have her head in the perfect place for Indie to heave herself up. "I'm getting me a R.O.B."

"It's B.O.B.," Molly corrected from her now-supine position on the floor. "And we'll go into the city tomorrow to get you one. Never need a man again."

Black spots danced around Indigo's eyes and the floor bucked and swayed beneath her unsteady feet as she rose to face Aedan. "R.O.B. and I don't need you anymore. He'll never leave me in the middle of a freakin' clover field unsatisfied. And if he pisses me off I can always unplug him and stick him under the bed. R.O.B. is the new love of my life and I'm through...I'm throu—"

Before the words could form everything in Indigo's world spun around in a bright circle then went black.

* * * * *

Dragons, Whiskey and Leprechauns...oh no!

His *liaria* slept deeply beneath the covers of his bed, her lips parted with a slight, cute snore escaping them.

Yesterday afternoon Aedan would never have thought to see this woman in his bed again. Yet here they both were. If his friend Kaden were to be believed then talking about his feelings and the reason he stormed off yesterday would help resolve their differences.

He'd gone behind the veil to get away from his unfamiliar emotions. After meandering around in a mental fog, Aedan found himself in front of the Nugget, one of the veil's few neutral gathering spots. Most immortals choose to stay within their own kind but a few of each species would get curious and so safe places like the Nugget were born.

Seeing Kaden in the bar had shocked him. Since his mating, Kaden spent most of his time with his mate on the other side of the veil.

But as the night waned and whiskey was drunk, Kaden revealed how he made mistakes in claiming his *liaria*, whom he first spotted in a water vision—the visions brought on solely by someone's desire and a coin in a well. He let past mistakes and regrets choose his actions and almost lost the love of his immortal life.

Kaden had told him the only reason his *liaria*, Lyra had taken a chance on him was because Kaden had been completely honest with her. Honest about his past, the mistakes he had made. The other leprechaun had laid everything on the line for his female.

Pride, Kaden advised, had no place between mates. "Be as honest with her as you'd want her to be with you," was his friend's last piece of wisdom before disappearing through the veil and to his Lyra who waited on the other side.

Yeah, right. Aedan hadn't wanted to listen to a word his old friend said. After all, until his own *liaria* showed up, Kaden had never spent much time on the mortal side of the veil. But the man had a happy mate to go home to which is more than Aedan could claim.

A soft pain-filled moan reached his ears as Indigo's eyes fluttered open. "Stop them," she whispered in a ragged voice. "Oh for the love of coffee..."

He closed the distance between them. His bare feet made no noise on the rug-strewn floor. "Indie, my love, what's the matter?" he asked, but had a pretty good idea of the drumming and pounding going on inside her head.

In a slow agonized move, Indie rolled to her stomach and shoved the pillow over her head.

Gingerly, Aedan pulled one end of the white case up. "If you can manage to swallow a few sips, I've got a cure for you."

This earned him a one-eyed, suspicious stare. "What kind of cure?" she rasped, not easing her hold on the pillow.

"Hair of the dog, if you will. Something we Irish hold sacred to our hearts," he told her, careful to keep his voice low and his touch light.

The pillow shuffled away and two bleary blue eyes peered suspiciously at him. "Why would you want to help me? You made your feelings abundantly clear yesterday afternoon."

The hurt and confusion layering her voice caught him in the heart. He'd caused his mate pain. By the seven hells, he'd caused them both pain because of his pride. Time to put an end to the pain, confusion and doubt once and for all. But first he had to get Indigo over her whiskey hangover.

"We be needin' to talk, I think. There's a lot I've not told you and even more that needs to be said." With steady hands he reached for the glass resting on the nightstand. Its purple, gold and green colors gave him hope.

Aye, it was good to be Irish and even better to be a leprechaun with the possibility of endless love to look forward to.

He used his free arm to wrap around her waist and pull her upright. "Take a slow sip, love. There's a girl." He murmured his praise gently in her ear as she swallowed the *Tongue of Truth*.

Once he deemed she'd had enough of the mystical potion, Aedan set the glass down on the table beside the bed and turned to face his mate. "There's a world of words that need to be said between us, Indigo. First I need to say how sorry I am for walking away yesterday. My pride got in the way of my heart and I couldn't see the truth behind my ego."

Warm color flushed her cheeks red as Indie sat up within the shelter of his arms. "What did I say? I need to know so I can never say it again." Her blue eyes shone with honesty and compassion.

Aye, he was a lucky bastard to be given a second chance.

"You were but teasing me about the benefits of being with an immortal. Somehow my pride twisted the words. The words I heard meant the only reason you'd be with me is because I can perform on cue. Like a stud machine, just drop a coin and there I whirl." The thought still sent a pang of nausea through his gut but the desire for total acceptance forced him on. "There have been matings based solely on the sex each partner can provide the other. Given the fact that once a leprechaun finds and binds his mate, they can be with no other, it makes it awkward when the rosy glow of lust wears off. I didn't...don't want that for us."

Aedan opened his heart and let all the confusion, desire and love pour out while he kept his eyes firmly on the ceiling, not yet ready to see his mate's reaction. "I want what our union is meant to be. A joining of hearts, souls, bodies and minds. I want to give you everything. Your heart's every desire. If you need, I provide. I want to be the one you turn to on a bad day when things go wrong. When the news is good and bursting to spill from your lips, I want to be the first person you think of to tell. You are my center, my soul, the very reason for my existence. Without you I'd have no reason to live. You are my one true love." The last words came out as a whisper. His heart beat heavily in desperate anticipation of Indigo's reaction.

"How can you say these things? We don't even know each other. It's the drink talking. That *Tongue of Truth* is some powerful elixir."

"Nay. The liquor is the device through which the heart speaks. It's formed from powerful fae magic. It only reveals what's truly in the heart of those who imbibe. It never would have had the effect on us that it did without the fates meaning for it to be so. I swear on my life, *liaria*. It is so."

Silence settled over the room. Only the sound of their joined breathing could be heard. Aedan wanted to shout or throw something. Do anything to break the quiet that threatened to strangle him.

"Do you have a coffeepot?" she finally asked, her voice devoid of emotion.

A bloody coffeepot? The woman was out to make him daft. Reining in his temper, Aedan made sure his tone reflected nothing but calm. "Aye, there's one down in the pub. I keep it on hand for when Yanks come in."

"Cool," she said and snuggled into his arms. "So long as you keep me supplied with coffee and Diet Coke I think we can work things out."

He captured her chin, forcing their eyes to meet. "Are you having me on? What's this all about? Please, *liaria*, my heart can't stand the suspense."

Her blue eyes softened as her hand caressed the spot above his heart. "You broke my heart yesterday when you walked away. You left without even looking back. I wanted to die. Instead I got really drunk with Molly. Now I've woken up in your bed. You're telling me everything I want to hear. No matter how crazy it is. And it is crazy. How can I not love you too?"

In one fluid motion Indie rolled them until he lay on his back. She sat astride his hips. Her bare lips rubbed her moist desire along his body.

Aedan's muscles jerked at the contact but he had to finish talking before his libido took over. "You love me?" If she heard the desperate hope in his voice, Aedan didn't care. Pride, he learned, had no place between mates.

Blue eyes glowed as though lit from within. His powers were flowing through her. Filled with love, desire and something deeper that connected to his own soul, Aedan reached up and gently pulled her head down to capture her lips. The shared kiss connected them deeper than flesh and spirit. They bonded in mind as well as spirit. Their love binding and their joining complete.

"Now, mate, let me show you how a fully bonded male leprechaun claims his mate." He gave Indigo an evil grin filled with desire, love and a little bit of naughty intentions. After all, you couldn't expect a leprechaun to change his rainbow overnight.

Indigo sat up, her breasts high and luscious looking. "See if you can keep up," she dared and rubbed her heated desire against Aedan's throbbing erection.

SEXPRESSO NIGHT
Kelly Jamieson

Chapter One

How long was he going to just lie there?

Not that she minded being on top, but dammit, she just wanted him to take charge for once!

Chris looked up at her, his mouth curving into a lazy smile. "What?"

The softness of his touch, his erection brushing her hip, his gentle smile, made her want to weep with longing for more—forceful hands, demanding kisses, the weight of a hard body pressing her down. She closed her eyes against the dark hunger rising inside her, the craving to be pushed, taken to the edge.

And he had no clue. She searched for the words to tell him how she felt. Her eyes fell on the silk neck tie he'd discarded earlier, draped over the night table. She reached across him for it.

The cool silk slid through her fingers as she held it up. "Here."

He blinked. "Huh?"

"Tie me up. Do whatever you want."

His body jerked so hard she actually tumbled off him. He sat up, his eyebrows pinched together, mouth a tight line. "What the hell? *Tie you up?*"

She swallowed and pushed her hair off her face. And laughed. "I'm joking. A joke."

He subsided back onto the pillows. "Oh." Not laughing. Not even smiling. Well, that had been a genius move.

Cheeks scorching, stomach tight, she flopped to her back and stared at the ceiling.

*****

"She's in a hurry to see her hot barista guy."

"I am not!" Danya slowed her pace and slanted a look at her friend Jenny walking beside her, her dark hair glinting in the sunlight, a mischievous smile curving her lips. "I'm just...thirsty."

"Mmm. Sure. Me too." Marina, on her other side, smiled too, her pale blonde hair and skin a contrast to Jenny's exotic darkness. "It's okay, Danya. We won't tell Chris."

"We're just friends." Even as Danya said the words, a tiny stab of guilt pierced her. She knew she looked forward to Sunday afternoon coffees with the girls way too much — because of Carter, the barista at Karma Coffee. In fact, sometimes she went early so she could sit and talk to him.

And yes, a friendship of sorts had grown between them. Sparks of mutual attraction had ignited the flirtation, but they'd both known it wasn't something they were ever going to let grow into full-blown flames, and now an easy rapport had developed — okay, an easy, *sexy* rapport with a naughty edge.

The three friends strolled along the sidewalk of Cabrillo Boulevard in Santa Barbara. The sun had burned away the early morning fog over the Pacific Ocean and now shone warm and bright. Palm trees lining the boulevard swayed in the gentle offshore breeze.

Seagulls soared in the azure sky and sandpipers hopped over the sand. There weren't many people on the beach yet but it would soon be packed with sun worshipers. On the horizon, the Channel Islands shimmered like a distant mirage in the hazy remnants of the fog.

Danya pulled open the door of the small coffee shop and stepped in, breathed in the air rich with the scent of roasted coffee beans and warm with steam. The hiss of the espresso maker, the clink of spoons against cups and the chatter of patrons mingled with some jazzy background music.

As they found a table in the sunny window, her eyes were already searching for Carter. And yes, there he was, behind the counter, wearing a white apron over a black t-shirt and nicely worn jeans that sat low on his hips. The apron emphasized his broad shoulders and rounded biceps, and when he turned around and said something to one of the girls working there, Danya could see how the jeans showed off a really awesome ass.

She sighed and smiled with pleasure. Then he turned back and caught her eye, just as she was ogling his butt. Her face heated. God, she was probably turning ten shades of pink. He grinned and lifted a hand. She gave him a weak smile and looked up at the menu even though she knew it by heart and knew what she was going to order.

"I'll save the table," Jenny said. "Get me a double tall Americano."

As she waited in line, Danya's eyes kept flicking to Carter, serving people at the counter, laughing and joking with them. His dark hair was a bit long and messy on top, short on the sides. Neat sideburns dipped into a perpetual five o'clock shadow that made him look a little wicked, his chin square, cheekbones high, his eyes espresso-dark.

And he kept looking at her too, eyes crinkling a little at the corners, lips curving into a sexy smile.

"So, what did you and Chris do last night?" Marina asked as they waited to place their order.

"Nothing," Danya said. "He worked all day and he was too tired to go out."

"You have got to be kidding me."

Danya looked at her friend and grimaced. "I know. I went over to his place for a while, but we just sat and watched a movie." Then they'd had sex, and she wasn't even going to tell her friend about *that* humiliating experience. Her body tightened at the memory and she nibbled her bottom lip.

When it was her turn to order, she requested Jenny's Americano and her own skinny vanilla latte.

"Vanilla again?" Carter asked.

Danya's head snapped up and their eyes locked. A smile tipped up the corners of his mouth.

"Yes. Please." Her tummy quivered.

"You should try something different, Danya. Something more exotic."

"Um. Thanks but... a skinny vanilla latte is good."

"How are you today?" he asked.

"I'm great." She watched him as he pulled espresso shots, his movements quick, efficient, graceful. It was like watching a choreographed dance. An artist at work. His long fingers on the pot as he tipped foam onto her drink were so sexy. A warm tingling started deep inside her.

"You always come on Sunday afternoon," he said to her. "You know, you should come Saturday nights. Saturday nights are adult night."

Adult night? In a coffee shop?

"I'll uh...keep that in mind."

"Sounds better than what you were doing last night." He set her coffee on the high counter and paused, both hands resting there as he met her gaze. His voice was so sexy—as rich and smooth as *café au lait*—he could have been telling her he wanted to strip her naked by the way her body reacted. She quivered, even as she hated that he'd overheard her discussing her relationship with Chris. They'd always made a point of never talking about their significant others, as if their flirtation could exist in a separate world from reality. "Is that why the long face today?"

Heat washed up into her cheeks. "Long face?" She forced another smile.

"Yeah." He wiped his hands on his apron, still looking at her intently. "You don't seem your usual cheerful self today."

"Oh. Well." She searched for words, not sure how to respond to that. Had he really paid that much attention to her? "I'm fine."

"Okay. Good." He winked at her and turned to Marina to take her order.

Danya escaped back to the table with the two coffees, cheeks burning, body suffused with heat. He'd winked at her. Holy crap, that was sexy.

"What's wrong?" Jenny accepted her drink from Danya with two hands and set it on the table.

"Nothing."

Jenny rolled her eyes. "You were flirting with him again, weren't you?"

Danya sipped her coffee and glanced over at Carter, now talking with another co-worker. She was probably close to sixty years old, with dyed black hair and heavy eyeliner, and was giggling—giggling!—and blushing like a girl. She gave him a playful swat as she went through the doors into the back.

"He likes you, Dan," Marina said, taking her seat at the table.

Danya shook her head, looked down at her coffee, a small knot of emotions tangled inside her. A harmless flirtation was fun, but a low yearning way down deep inside her for something more than that took hold. She didn't even know what she wanted. Sizzle. Burn. Steam. More than she had.

A *whoosh* of hot foamed milk behind the counter brought her head up. She firmed her lips and directed her attention to her friends. They talked about work, school, homework, evil professors, bosses and their respective boyfriends while they sipped their coffees, laughing, venting, unloading.

When they left, Danya couldn't help but look over at Carter and sure enough, their gazes collided in that weird thing that sometimes happens when two people pick the exact same moment to check each other out. But instead of quickly looking away, he smiled.

"Bye, gorgeous," he called out. "See you next weekend?"

She nodded and lifted a hand in a quick wave.

When the door closed behind them, Marina said, "Oh Dan, he is so hot for you."

"Don't be crazy. I hardly know him." She slid her sunglasses onto her nose.

"What does that matter?"

"I have a boyfriend."

"I just wonder," Marina said as they walked. "What's an old guy like him doing, working as a barista, for heavens' sake?"

Danya was ashamed to admit she'd had a similar thought. The question had been on the tip of her tongue a number of times when they'd talked. But hey, being a barista was honest, respectable work.

"How old do you think he is?" she asked.

"I think he's about thirty-two," Marina said, tapping her chin.

"Thirty," Jenny said.

"That's not old." It was perfect.

What the hell was she thinking? She had a *boyfriend*!

"Okay, just stop it." She held up both hands. "I'm already seeing someone. Sure, Carter is nice to look at, and he seems like a great guy, but it doesn't matter how old he is."

That silenced her friends, who shared a glance.

"What?" she demanded.

Their pace slowed as they dodged and wove around tourists and Santa Barbara residents out biking, roller-blading, jogging and walking.

"About you and Chris," Jenny said hesitantly. "You really don't seem very happy lately."

"I'm happy," Danya said, a bit defensively. "Chris is a nice guy."

"I call bullshit," Marina said.

"Yeah," Jenny added. "You're obviously not happy. What's wrong?"

Danya pressed her lips together. She took a deep breath and let it out slowly. "It's hard to explain," she finally said.

"Chris *is* a nice guy," Marina said. "I like him."

Yeah, he was nice. Last night his solicitous, gentle touch had almost driven her out of her mind, out of her skin with frustration. Any time she tried to show him what she needed, he ignored her. And when she'd suggested using his tie, he'd drawn back as sharply as if she'd kneed him in the balls. She'd laughed it off as a naughty joke, but the rest of the evening had been excruciating, and not a in a good way.

But how could she expect Chris to know what she wanted when she wasn't even sure herself?

After what she'd been through with Evan two years ago, she'd sworn she would never let a man control her, would never let someone do the things he'd done to her. She'd thought Evan was the one, the one who would help her explore that other side of her, to find what had been missing in her life. Big mistake. Huge. Okay, it had been a disaster the magnitude of a California earthquake.

As if she knew Danya was thinking about him, Jenny said hesitantly, "You're over Evan, aren't you?"

"Yes!" Danya's head jerked around to stare at her. "Of course I'm over him." They were the ones who had picked up the pieces when Evan's domination had crossed into brutal sadism. After that she'd known she never again wanted to be with anyone who was into that BDSM lifestyle. And yet Chris' complete lack of interest in anything more kinky than her being on top wasn't doing it for her either.

Chris was a sweet guy. Wrapped up in his career, yes, but considerate, undemanding and laid-back. Exactly what she wanted now.

At State Street the three friends crossed Cabrillo without consulting each other, heading out onto Stearns Wharf. They wandered to the railing and looked out over the ocean, the crisp salty breeze tugging the hair back from their faces. Danya inhaled deeply, loving the tangy, fishy smell, the warm sun on her face.

It was eating away at her inside, the conflict between her head's plan to be in control of all things and her heart's longing to let go of it. Chris was easygoing, let her make the plans, deferred to her on every decision, exactly what she'd been looking for, and she didn't understand why she was so miserable.

She and Chris had to talk. Yeah. Next weekend, they'd make plans and they'd talk and then Chris would drag her into the bedroom and —

And maybe the tide wouldn't come in tomorrow.

* * * * *

Carter Jarvis watched Danya leave Karma Coffee with her two friends. Damn, she was sweet. Every time she came in, a deep, visceral hunger spiked inside him. And those times she came in without her friends and they'd talked, he'd felt a connection that had startled him.

It wasn't just her looks. Yeah, she was gorgeous. Her long glossy caramel and honey-streaked hair, smooth golden skin and big green eyes created an enticing outer package. But intelligence and humor gleamed in those liquid green eyes and the way they fastened on his intently when they talked made him sense something deep down inside her that she kept hidden — maybe even from herself.

"Oh, quit mooning over her," Maria said, snapping a towel at him. He jerked out of his reverie.

"Huh?" he said, playing dumb. "Mooning over who?"

She grinned, cracked her gum, her darkly lined eyes narrowing. "You know damn well who. Why don't you just ask her out?"

"She has a boyfriend." He frowned.

"How do you know that?"

He shrugged. "I hear her talking about him all the time." He grabbed a plastic bin and went to clear tables. With no customers lining up at the counter at the moment, he didn't hesitate to do any jobs that needed to be done.

Too bad that damn boyfriend was in the picture. What was his name? Chris.

Dammit.

"Carter." Juliet approached him. "I need next Saturday off."

"But it's our busiest night."

"I know. I'm sorry." She bit her lip. "I asked Samantha if she'd work for me and she said she would."

Samantha wearing the skimpy little outfit that Juliet normally wore on Saturday nights might not be such a good thing. But he hesitated to say it. He struggled enough with worries that he was exploiting his female staff by making them dress like that, even though they did seem to enjoy it. "Oh."

"I'm really sorry, but my ex says he can't take Jake that weekend and I haven't been able to find a babysitter." The corners of her mouth turned down. "The asshole. It's his weekend."

"It's okay, Juliet. Don't worry. If Samantha can take your shift, that's fine."

Staff problems were never ending. He considered himself fortunate that he had a relatively stable team working for him, experienced and loyal, not to mention some top quality baristas, but the reality of his business was that many of them were students, working a couple of part-time jobs to put themselves through school, much like he had years ago, and often other things in their lives took priority over work. Like parties. Fun. Games.

Much like him years ago. A smile tugged at his lips.

Juliet was a single mom working on a degree in communications. She worked hard and rarely asked for time off, so he didn't hesitate to agree, even though it messed up his scheduling.

"Thanks, Carter. You're the best."

He patted her shoulder. "No problem."

And really, that was the least of his worries. This recession was hitting everyone hard. Competition was fierce. Even fast food restaurants were serving specialty coffees now, dammit.

Of course they couldn't compete with a coffee geek like him. Everyone who appreciated fine coffee—the best beans from around the world, perfectly roasted, combined into his own secret blend and brewed or steamed to perfection—would rather come and spend a little more money at Karma Coffee than at a drive-through burger joint. And he'd come up with some unique promotional ideas, like his Saturday "Sexpresso Night", which was bringing in good revenues.

But still, business was tough these days and he had some difficult decisions to make about his other stores and whether his next buying trip to Matagalpa in South America was worth the expense. He loved that part of the business—meeting with the growers, building those relationships, finding incredible new coffees—but it was costly.

But thoughts of a sexy little honey-blonde temptress pushed aside his worries as he returned to work behind the counter.

* * * * *

"Danya. Is it five o'clock already?" Chris stood in the doorway of his apartment, late Saturday afternoon, shirt rumpled and hair sticking up all over the place.

She swallowed her sigh and moved into his arms. He gave her a tiny hug then stepped back, ran a hand through his hair.

"Yeah."

"Damn. I got busy."

"Do you still want to go out for dinner?"

"Sure. If you do."

She paused. They could stay in..."What do you want to do?"

He glanced behind him. "Whatever you want."

Her body slumped a little. *Whatever you want.* The words that should make her happy only sent her mood plunging to her toes. "Actually, I was thinking we should stay in tonight. I think we need to talk."

"Oh Jesus."

She frowned. "What?"

"That's never a good thing to hear." He forced a smile. "Come in. Here, let me move some things." He gathered up a stack of papers from the couch and moved his laptop to the coffee table.

"What are you doing?"

"Working," he said with a what-else-would-I-be-doing frown.

"Chris, all you do is work."

He still looked distracted. "I know, but I'm trying to get this business going...it takes a lot of work. And it's really important to me."

"Yes," she said quietly. "I know." She sucked in a long slow breath. She closed the distance between them again and pressed herself to his body. He had a great body, for a techy computer nerd. She took his face in her hands and kissed him. He kissed her back, but then moved way.

"Uh...what did you want to talk about?"

She drew back. Maybe instead of talking she could show him... She kissed him again and this time felt more response from him, his mouth moving against hers, his body hardening. This was good...

Inspired, she sank to her knees in front of him and began to undo his jeans.

"What the—"

"Sssh. Let me do this. I want to."

His erection surged beneath the denim and she drew down the zipper.

"Not here. Not like this," he said, hands on her shoulders. "Christ, Danya."

She sat back on her heels and looked up at him, the sting of rejection not as sharp as she would have thought. She blew out a breath. Bah. Who was she kidding? She didn't really want to do that anyway. Not for him.

She sucked on her bottom lip for a moment then climbed to her feet.

"This isn't working. You and me."

His eyebrows pinched together and he stared at her. "You want to give me a blowjob? Fine. Let's just go into the bedroom."

"No." She swallowed painfully. "I want you to want it. I want you to..." She hesitated, unsure of how to even put it into words. Dark images swirled in her head—hands in her hair, being shoved up against a wall, pushed to her knees. She closed her eyes briefly.

"What is it then? Jesus, Danya, I don't get you."

"I know." She touched her fingertips to his mouth. "I don't think I'm the right girl for you."

"Yes, you are! You're beautiful and smart and fun..."

He thought she was fun? "I think your idea of fun and my idea of fun are a little different," she said carefully. "We're just different, that's all. I need...something more."

"More? What do you mean more? Just tell me what you want me to do."

And there was the problem. Could you make someone dominate you?

"I don't think so." She shook her head regretfully, reluctant to tell him the things she needed. If he'd been shocked by a little light bondage and hadn't liked her going down on her knees in front of him, he'd be horrified to know the dark desires pushing their way up inside her. "I'm sorry, Chris."

She left his apartment, heaviness weighing down her body, legs feeling like she had weights on her ankles, wishing with all her heart that things could have worked out between them.

She walked slowly to her car. She'd drive to the beach. The ocean always soothed her with its infinite and rhythmic back-and-forth rush of water.

There, she kicked off her flip-flops, and warm sand shifted beneath her feet as she trudged to the water's edge. The ocean curled cold, foamy fingers over her feet and around her ankles. A spirited beach volleyball game went on behind her, even now in the evening, and a few last sun worshipers stretched out on towels and beach chairs.

After that last mudslide of a relationship with Evan, the one thing she thought she knew for sure was that *she* was going to be in control. So she'd dated guys who let her call the shots. Wasn't that what every woman wanted? A man who deferred to her, who let her have her way in everything? Just like Chris.

But once again here she was, struggling to know who she was and what she really wanted. Fighting against the things she longed for deep down inside her. Those dark desires had gotten her in so much trouble. Maybe she just wasn't destined to have a completely satisfying relationship. Maybe she would never be happy with anything.

She had no desire to go home to her empty apartment, so she strolled onto Stearns Wharf and bought some clam chowder at the little seafood place, sat and ate it. Surrounded by laughing couples and chattering groups of friends, her aloneness settled over her like a heavy blanket. But she wasn't alone in the world. She had a full, busy life. She had her friends. She'd see them tomorrow afternoon for their usual Sunday afternoon coffee.

As she walked off the Wharf, the thought of meeting her friends at Karma Coffee reminded her of seeing Carter again. He'd noticed her unhappiness last weekend, and something soft and warm unfurled a little inside her at that.

It was Saturday night. He'd said she should come.

She still wasn't sure what adult night was at a coffee shop, but hey, it was right down the street from her. She paused—should she turn left down Cabrillo toward Karma Coffee, or turn right toward the parking lot where she'd left her car?

She turned left.

Chapter Two

Danya paused outside the door of Karma Coffee, hand on the pull.

What was she doing? She was walking in here all alone, looking pathetic and needy, no doubt. Maybe Carter wouldn't even be there. At least then she wouldn't feel so self-conscious and humiliated sitting at a table all by herself sipping a lonely coffee.

What was that joke she'd read, about how coffee was better than sex? Oh yeah—drinking coffee on your own doesn't make you a sad loser, but having sex on your own does.

She wasn't so sure that was true, but she yanked on the door and stepped inside.

The ambience at night was completely different than during the day, although the rich scent and sounds were familiar. Instead of sunlight streaming in the big windows, little white lights strung around the room created a soft illumination among the dark wood furnishings and paneling on the lower half of the walls. Small lamps on low tables gave off a golden glow. And the music, instead of an upbeat jazz, was a low, sultry saxophone.

Danya gazed around and blinked. The place was packed! Not only was every table occupied, people stood in small groups, holding their coffees, talking and laughing. Women dressed to the nines and a lot of hot guys.

Danya looked down at her denim skirt, layered tank tops and sandy flip-flops. Not exactly what the other women were wearing, but—oh well.

Shit. Where was she going to sit? Then her eyes fell on a couple of tall chairs at the narrow counter lining one long window. Okay, she could sit there.

She got in line for her coffee, trying not to look for Carter but unable to help herself. But she didn't see him, dammit.

What she did see had her eyes widening.

The girls working behind the counter were not wearing their usual black pants and white shirts. Danya blinked as a young girl in tiny black shorts and a boob-propping bustier pulled an espresso. Danya's eyes moved to another girl, wearing white thigh-high stockings with bows, a tiny pink flutter skirt that didn't even hide the white boy shorts beneath. The white shirt tied beneath her breasts revealed a taut midriff.

Adult night. All righty.

Okay, now she knew why there were so many guys there, lounging at tables, drinking coffee. But hey, almost as many women filled the place.

The girl who took her order wore a black bikini with a short mesh sarong tied low on her hips, stunning, really, her wide smile totally unselfconscious.

"Welcome to Sexpresso Night," she said. "There are three specials tonight. The Flogger, the Hair Puller and Hot Handcuffs."

Danya could only blink, a slow liquefaction occurring inside her at the names of the drinks. "Um...what's in a Hair Puller?"

Jesus. Just saying the words sent a slide of sexual longing through her veins.

"It's caramel combined with our special house blend coffee and milk, blended with ice and topped with whipped cream and caramel sauce."

Oh lord, nothing like her usual skinny vanilla latte, but damn, caramel was a major weakness. Not to mention hair pulling. *Don't go there.* "Okay, I'll have that."

This was kind of fun!

As she took her iced coffee drink and strolled toward one of the few empty chairs at the counter, she felt the eyes of countless interested males on her. Yikes. Hotter than a pickup bar, this place was.

What was she doing there?

She climbed onto a stool in front of the now-dark window, the tiny white lights reflected in the glass, doubling their sparkle. What was with the names of the drinks? And the slutty outfits the baristas wore?

And where was Carter?

* * * * *

Not only had Samantha not shown up to take Juliet's shift, but Jason had called in sick. Dammit.

Carter was running his balls off trying to keep things going. Why, on a Saturday night, did he have to be down two staff? He heaved a bag of beans up the stairs from the basement where he roasted them.

Sexpresso Night had proved so popular he usually had *extra* staff on. He dragged a hand across his sweaty forehead as he paused behind the counter. The place was full. Which was good. Humming and hissing and clinking dishes filled the air. He loved it. He just wouldn't mind a chance to sit for five minutes before they started the cupping.

But first he had to get things set up in the back room. He blew out a long breath. Usually he liked to have that all done ahead of time, but tonight had just been too busy.

He pushed away from the counter and moved around the glass display case full of pastries, and his eyes fell on her.

Danya.

Sitting there at the window counter, all by herself for a change.

His heart stuttered and his feet stopped moving as if suddenly he'd stepped into thick mud.

She sat with her legs crossed, long bare legs, a tiny denim skirt riding high on her thighs, and a pink sequined flip-flop dangling from the top foot. Her chin rested on her hand, her elbow on the counter, and she stared at the dark window.

He blinked, straightened his shoulders and strode across the room toward her, his cupping preparations forgotten.

"Hey." He stopped beside her and she gave a little start. Her big green eyes flew up to his.

"Oh. Hi!"

The instant smile told him there was something there on her side of things too, and he warmed inside.

"Where are your friends tonight?"

"I have no idea." Her smile faded just a bit. "I was just out walking and remembered that you'd said to uh…come on Saturday night. So I thought I'd check it out."

"Awesome. Glad you did."

They eyed each other and heat built between them as if they were standing next to his micro roaster.

"You okay?" Once again, she wasn't her usually breezy, sunny self.

She nodded. "Yeah. I'm okay. I'm great, actually." One corner of her mouth deepened. "I just broke up with my boyfriend."

He knew he should say he was sorry, that was the right thing to say to that kind of news, any kind of bad news, but the truth was, he wasn't in the least sorry. In fact he kind of felt like cheering. Pumping a fist. Grinning.

The smile pulled at his mouth and he tried to push the words out but what came out instead was, "I'm glad to hear that."

She blinked at him. "You are?"

Idiot. But what the hell. He leaned closer. "He obviously wasn't making you happy."

"How do you know that?"

He waved a hand. "We baristas hear a lot."

Her slender, dark-gold eyebrows slanted down. "You eavesdrop on customers?"

He gave her a look. "You were standing at the counter talking about how unhappy you were with him last Sunday. Everyone could hear."

"Oh yeah." She made a face.

"Plus, you've said things that have made me wonder."

Her smile relaxed. "I guess I have."

"So. It's for the best, right? And you picked a good night to come. In about..." He tipped his left wrist to glance at his watch. "Damn. In about half an hour we're doing a cupping."

"A what?"

Did she know there was another meaning to that word? Was that why the spark flared in those witchy-green eyes?

"Cupping. We're going to taste different coffees and learn all about them. Like a wine tasting."

Now her eyebrows winged up. "Really."

"Yeah. It'll be fun. But unfortunately I have to go get things set up. We're kind of short staffed tonight."

"Oh of course, go on. You're working. Wouldn't want to get you in trouble with the boss."

He grinned. "Hell no, that guy's a tyrant."

She shooed her hands at him, but as he turned away regretfully, she spoke up. "Carter?"

"Yeah?"

"Do you need some help? I'm uh...just sitting here."

He tipped his head. She was offering to help him. Damn, that was a rush. "Yeah. Sure. That'd be great." He held out a hand to her again to help her down off the high stool, and had to work to keep his eyes in his head as her short tight skirt rode even higher, giving a glimpse of the crotch of—holy hell—pink panties. He instantly went hard. Dammit.

He turned and led the way through the shop to the French doors at the very back. *Down, boy, not now, not now,* he directed Big Dick. She followed him through them into a small room.

He'd started doing tastings a while ago, another effort to increase business and differentiate himself from all the other coffee chains and fast food restaurants, and had renovated this space specifically for cuppings.

A large round table centered the room, no chairs, and equipment and cups and dishes sat on the counter running along one side of the room. Soft lighting and the ambient jazz music created a warm intimate feel.

He turned to Danya and watched her take in everything. "Interesting."

"Do you know much about coffee?"

"I know nothing about coffee. Except that I like it."

"Good. This will be a great time to learn then."

She shrugged. "What can I do?"

"We need to set out these bowls and cups," he said, moving to the counter. "I'm going to put beans into the bowls and we'll grind them just before we use them."

"Can't get any fresher than that."

He showed her how to arrange things and they moved around the table, the hard dark coffee beans clinking gently as he poured them into small bowls. When everything was arranged to his satisfaction he checked his watch again.

"Perfect." He met her gaze. Damn she was pretty. Thick glossy hair fell over her shoulders and he itched to sink his hands into it, twist it up and tug...just a little...

He was getting waaaay ahead of himself here. But he had a feeling about her, the way she'd listened to his instructions, carried out exactly what he told her to do, the smile of pleasure when he'd praised her. His body tightened again.

He called in anyone who was interested in the cupping and about a dozen people crowded into the small room.

"You do this yourself?" she asked him, standing beside him at the round table.

"Yeah." Funny. She seemed to think he just worked there."Okay," he said, putting his hands together. "Thanks for joining me, everyone. My name is Carter Jarvis and I'm a certified coffee roaster, master taster and three-time winner of the Western Regional Barista Competition."

He glanced at Danya and, with amusement and pride, noted her widened eyes.

"And I'm the owner of Karma Coffee. Welcome to our cupping tonight." Her eyes met his and he grinned at her. "Tonight we have six kinds of coffee to try." He named the coffees and where they were from as he ground the beans.

"For a cupping, we just add hot water to the grounds in the cup." He poured water into the cups from a stainless steel thermal pitcher. "We wait three or four minutes, and then the first thing we do is check the fragrance. First, I break the crust." He picked up a spoon, bent low over one cup and punctured the thick layer sitting atop the liquid. Closing his eyes, he inhaled deeply. He rose and met Danya's eyes, locked on him. "Aromatics are a large part of the taste of coffee." He demonstrated again, then invited everyone to work their way around the table, sniffing and inhaling the dark delicious scent.

"We need to move quickly here so everyone can get a good sniff. Really pay attention when you do this," he instructed as everyone bent low and dipped spoons into the coffees. "This is so important when the volatiles are released." He stopped behind Danya, close enough to feel the warmth of her body, and as she bent over the cup her very spankable ass pushed back and he longed to crowd right up against her.

She lifted her head to look at him, her face raptly focused on him and Christ, that made him hard all over again. *Focus, man.* "This is a very intense aromatic experience," he managed to say. Intense. He wanted an intense experience with her. Oh yeah.

He swallowed hard.

"Now for the tasting. By now the coffees have cooled off a little, which is good for tasting. I'm going to clear off the remaining crust." He picked up two cupping spoons, placed them into the cup near the back. He dragged them forward around the edges to meet again at the front of the cup then scooped up just the grounds. "Now, what we want to do is take some of the coffee with our spoon..." He did so. "And then slurp it...like this." And with a long, loud slurp he drew the coffee deeply into his mouth. Then spit it out into a convenient container. "You don't have to spit it out," he continued. "You should swallow some to evaluate aftertastes, but I drink so much coffee all day I'd be awake for the next year if I swallowed all the ones I taste." They all laughed and he caught Danya's dancing eyes.

"Why do you slurp it like that?" she asked.

"Sounds rude, huh?" He grinned. "It's not just 'cause I'm a guy. There are flavor receptors all through our mouths, right at the back, right up in to our olfactories, so to get the full experience, all the nuances, we want to make sure to aerate the coffee and expose even the back of our mouth to it." He watched her pupils dilate at his words and smiled. "You try it. Be sure to rinse your spoon in the water between tastes, and also your mouth." He indicated the pitchers of water and glasses on the table.

They all picked up spoons and noisy slurping sounds filled the room with earthy, almost sexual sounds. Kind of like an enthusiastic orgy.

Mind out of the gutter, Jarvis.

"Let's talk about some of the characteristics of coffee," he said. "Acidity could be described as the brightness or sharpness of the coffee. Acidity can be intense or mild, soft or edgy, subdued or wild — like sex." That got some laughs.

"Body is sometimes called mouthfeel. It's the weight or heaviness of the coffee in your mouth. Think about thickness when you taste, the physical feel of the coffee in your mouth."

Christ, he couldn't stop making sexual comparisons tonight, and as he caught Danya's eyes he knew she was thinking the same thing.

"Then we have sweetness. Sweetness eases the acidity of a coffee. You need the balance of the two to appreciate both. Just like the balance between pleasure and pain." He caught another wide-eyed look from Danya and grinned. "And finally, there's finish. As I mentioned, there's an aftertaste that lingers and it should be clean and sweet.

"Make mental notes as you taste," he encouraged, walking behind his guests. "Really think about what you're tasting. Which one do you find sweeter?"

Most of the people made a face of uncertainty. Danya pointed to the Columbian. "This one."

He nodded approvingly and she beamed. "Yes, that one is sweeter. What else did you notice about it?"

She took another delicate slurp, making him smile, then said, "Um...chocolate?"

"Very good! I also think there are hints of caramel in it. You might perceive it as burnt sugar. But it's not burnt."

She nodded, hanging on his every word. Sexy as fucking hell.

"This Ethiopian coffee has a nice fruity cup." He indicated which one. "And the Costa Rican is full bodied and spicy — you might taste hints of cinnamon and cloves. The Sumatra is intense, earthy and aromatic." He inhaled deeply over the cup, eyes closed to deepen the sensory experience. When he rose and opened his eye to see Danya staring at him, cheeks flushed, lips parted, heat sizzled through his veins.

"This Arabian bean is wild and exotic. And our French roast, which is our darkest roast, is smoky and intense." He clamped down on the arousal that was threatening to derail his cupping. "All of these coffees are available as beans or we'll custom grind them for you, so if you find one you like, be sure to pick some up."

His sales pitch. Well, that was what it was all about. Sort of. He loved tasting coffee and teaching others about it too. But yeah, if he didn't sell the stuff, he wouldn't be in business.

When everyone had finished and the room had cleared out, except for Danya, he started cleaning up. Happily she stayed to help again.

"That was fascinating," she said, eyes sparkling. "I never realized there was so much to know about coffee. And," she met his gaze, "I didn't realize you're the owner of this shop."

"And three others," he said modestly.

"How did you get to this?" She stacked cups and carried them to the counter where he'd installed a dishwasher just for this room. Together they loaded it up.

"I started serving coffee at a chain coffee shop. Took some courses. Got pretty good at building the specialty coffees. Entered some competitions. The roasting part of it interested me too. I experimented with some pretty arcane roasting methods."

"Like what?" She shot him a puzzled look as she dropped a handful of spoons into the dishwasher.

He grinned. "The best is a Westbend popcorn popper."

Her pretty mouth fell open. "You roast coffee beans in a popcorn popper?"

"Well, not anymore. Not all the time anyway. It's still fun to play around with. You have to listen until you hear the beans crack once. Then a few minutes later they crack and sizzle again. It's fun getting them just to the right darkness."

She shook her head. "That is unbelievable."

"Go ahead, tell me I'm a total coffee geek."

She laughed and they both straightened. He closed the dishwasher door, which was all that separated them, and moved toward her. Their eyes met and held. And held. Then he dropped his gaze to her mouth, her lush, pretty mouth, and he longed to taste it.

"I...um...guess I should go."

"Stay." He didn't hesitate for a second to give the order.

She didn't hesitate for a second to agree. "Okay."

"Come on. Let's go sit down and talk some more. I'll buy you a coffee."

"I think I've had enough coffee. Speaking of not sleeping..."

"Sleeping is overrated." He gave her meaningful look. "There are much better things to do at night. In bed."

Pink bloomed in her cheeks and that made him happy. And made him think of pink blooming on other cheeks at the firm touch of his hand. And that made him horny.

"How about decaf?"

"Okay."

He got them drinks and she waited at a small table that had cleared out. Another long line waited at the counter but to hell with it, he was sitting with Danya. They'd just have to work harder back there.

It wasn't like him to not step in and help out with anything that needed doing, but Danya was here and she'd just broken up with her boyfriend and she was all raptly interested in pretty damn much everything he had to say, so no way was he blowing this chance.

"Here you go."

He pulled his chair up close to hers so their arms brushed against each other. Perfect.

"So what would you think about a cupping party that you had to pay to get into?" he asked, stirring his decaf latte. "I'm thinking of doing that on Friday nights. Maybe twenty-five bucks a person, and you'd get more detailed tasting information, a half pound of coffee to take home, maybe even I'd do wine and cheese before the cupping."

"Wow. That sounds amazing. Before tonight I wouldn't have even dreamed of something like that."

He nodded, lifted his cup to his mouth. "I guess I could try it and see if there's enough interest."

She studied him and the warm interest in her eyes was so flattering, heat shot straight to his groin.

"It's a very sensual experience," she said slowly. "The tasting, the smelling."

"The mouthfeel," he added, holding her gaze, knowing both of them were thinking of other sensual experiences. Other things a mouth could feel.

"Mouthfeel. Um. Yes."

They stared at each other. Her small tongue came out and licked across her upper lip. His blood sizzled.

"Tell me about you," he said, almost groaning at his lack of originality. "I know you're taking courses at UCSB, but what do you do besides that?"

She was sipping her drink and when she lowered the cup, a smudge of creamy froth stayed on her upper lip. He couldn't help it. He had to.

He leaned toward her and brushed his index finger across her mouth.

"You had some froth…"

She blinked at him then lowered her eyes. "Oh."

"You were saying…"

"Um. I got my bachelor's degree in environmental studies a few years ago. I went into the Peace Corps while I figured out what to do with that. I decided environmental law was where I wanted to go, so now I'm just finishing up my law degree."

"Wow."

"And I work as a research assistant with one of the faculty of environmental studies. My boss just got a big grant to start a new project, and he wants me to work on it too."

"What's the project?"

She started telling him about the project to protect the endangered steelhead trout. She was talking about goddamn *trout* and he was fucking fascinated. "It's a fish passage improvement project along Carpinteria Creek and Mission Creek. The projects will involve removing or modifying barriers to fish migration, and removal of non-native vegetation and habitat restoration. Restoring waterways requires a holistic approach that looks at the health and function of the entire ecosystem around a creek."

"You're into saving fish." He lifted one brow.

She laughed. "Well, of course I care about the fish," she said. "But I'm interested in it from the legal perspective — environmental protection laws and what can be done. Anyway, it will be an interesting project to work on."

"Where did you go with the Peace Corps?"

"I spent a year in Guatemala and two years in Matagalpa."

"No way."

"Yes way." She tipped her head to one side. "Why?"

"I've been to both those places, many times. On coffee buying trips. I love Matagalpa."

She gave a little laugh. "I can't believe that. Nobody I talk to even knows where it is."

"Believe it, baby. It's a sign." Carter leaned closer and stroked a fingertip up her forearm, then down, and she shivered.

"Come back to my place," he said, voice low. "For coffee."

Chapter Three

"Coffee." She sat back in her chair, although not far enough away that he could no longer touch her arm. Now all four fingertips slid up and down in a gentle, mesmerizing rhythm. "Haven't we had enough coffee tonight?"

His lips quirked, his touch continued. "That's a euphemism. If I invited you for 'a cup of coffee' that would mean coffee. But when I invite you 'for coffee' it means...something else."

"What else?" She couldn't take her eyes off him.

"What do you think?"

"I think I don't even know you."

"Yes. You do." His fingers stopped on the inside of her wrist, where her pulse fluttered wildly against his fingertips.

With his gaze fastened on hers, she could only nod her agreement. Yes. She did know him. In some kind of elemental, instinctive way, she knew him. And liked him. A lot.

He pushed back his chair and stood. Held out a hand to her.

What was she doing?

She wanted this man. And why not?

So she stood too, picked up her purse and slid her hand into his.

"Let me just tell someone I'm leaving," he said.

The shop was nearly empty now, five minutes after closing time, and Carter went over to speak to the barista in the black bustier while Danya waited near the counter.

"Come out the back way," he said when he returned, again taking her hand in his warm, solid clasp. "I'm parked behind the shop."

They exited into the alley behind the building, dark and shadowy, and with his remote access control he flicked the door locks of his car, the headlights flashing light against the old brick of the building.

He held the door while she slid into the passenger seat. She approved of his car—a fuel-efficient hybrid. "My car is in the parking lot at the beach," she murmured. He glanced at her as he slung one arm over the seat to reverse into the lane.

"Do you want to get it?"

"Will you take me back there later to get it?"

"Of course."

"Then leave it."

She could very possibly have lost her mind. It was all kinds of crazy, going home with a near-stranger. Much as she'd explored the thrill of danger, the excitement of edge play in the past, at that moment she only felt...safe. Excited, yes. Thrilled—you bet. But completely, totally safe.

Carter's small cottage-style bungalow just off State Street was only a few minutes' drive away through dark streets. "Your house is nice," she said, looking around as she walked in. Hardwood floors gleamed beneath their feet. Through an arched door on their right the living room, nearly empty save for a black leather sectional and a big-screen television, sat dark.

"Thanks."

He took her purse from her and set it on a small table.

"This is crazy," she whispered as he settled his hands on her shoulders.

"Why?" He bent his head and nuzzled the hair above her ear. He smelled delicious—warm spicy male and, of course, coffee. Dark and rich and exotic. Her eyes fell closed and she reached for him, set her hands on his waist, solid and warm beneath his white button-down shirt. "I've been watching you for months, coming in to the store. You're so hot and sweet."

Her body went liquid.

"I love your hair," he continued. "It's like caramel and honey. Thick. Smooth."

He stroked a gentle hand over it and she tingled everywhere, a small moan escaping her. More. She needed more.

She opened her eyes to look up at him. What did he see there? Something, because his fingers speared into her hair and he held the back of her head as he kissed her.

His mouth slanted over hers in a long, searing kiss, and she melted into him, clutching his waist with both hands. It was a hard kiss, demanding and devouring, and it should have scared her since she didn't know him at all, but instead it sent fire streaking through her senses.

His fingers tightened on her head then twisted in her hair, and she gasped against his mouth. He drew back and looked down at her searchingly. She held his gaze, her body throbbing against his.

When he tugged again, his gaze focused intently on hers, a barrage of sparks shot from her scalp over her entire body. His eyes, already espresso-dark, went black as he watched her and he groaned. "You like that."

She didn't want to answer. It was crazy to enjoy having her scalp tugged on, but pleasure torched her body at the rough touch. He kissed her, tongue sliding into her mouth again and again. She strained against him, up on her toes, and when he sharply drew on her hair again, pulling her head far back, she moaned. His mouth slid over her jaw with a tiny nip, then to her throat and the pulse that beat there, and he gently sucked on her flesh.

Every nerve ending in her body jumped and danced. She ached between her legs, a ferocious hunger she hadn't felt for a long, long time. Her breasts swelled, her nipples tingled, and when Carter's other hand slid down to the curve of her ass and brought her up even harder against him, another low noise tore from her throat.

"I don't want to scare you," he muttered against her neck. "But I'm going out of my fucking mind here." He backed her up against the wall of his small foyer and pressed into her.

"You're not scaring me." Her hands fisted in his shirt, her head thunked against the wall. She *loved* it. Loved the feel of his big, hard body shoving her up against the wall, her aching breasts press against his chest, the bulge at his crotch pushing insistently into her belly.

His body pressed against hers, the hard wall behind her. Breathless, edgy, excited, her heart surged into a rapid rhythm. Her thighs quivered and thick liquid heat converged between her legs in a needy ache.

He kissed her again and again, their mouths opening and clinging, lifting and then fusing again. For a brief moment, he drew back and pulled her tank tops off over her head. He gazed down at her breasts and she was so glad she'd worn her pink lace bra. His eyes darkened as he admired and he trailed his fingers over the cleavage revealed by the low-cut cups.

"Pretty," he said. Heat swept from his touch up her neck and face, suffusing her in a hot glow. He reached behind her between her back and the wall and found the clasp, flicked it open then tossed the bra aside. As air kissed her bared breasts her nipples tightened and tingled even more, a harsh guttural sound came from Carter's throat. "*Very* pretty." He covered her breasts with both hands and cupped them, squeezed gently, then brushed his palms over her sensitive nipples. Then he kissed her again.

He took hold of her hands and lifted them into the wall above her head, his arms pressing against hers, hard enough that he might leave bruises on the tender flesh just above her elbows. Her tummy fluttered.

A groan tore from his throat when he shifted and thrust one muscled thigh between her legs and she ground against it in a needy cadence, a seeking undulation of her hips.

"I want to fuck you right here," he said, voice thick with arousal.

"Do it."

He released her hands and the slight throb in her upper arms where his bones had pressed against her sent another thrill coursing through her. He reached for his wallet and fumbled for a condom, ripping it open with impressive speed, while she went for the opening of his jeans.

When she pulled him out, her chest ached with the beauty of him, long, thick, heavy veins pulsing. She palmed the velvety texture of his skin, swept her thumb over the crest before he gloved up, and then he rucked her short skirt up to her hips, grabbed her ass and lifted her against him.

The strength it took to lift her and hold her with one arm while he pulled aside her panties and directed his cock to her entrance made her shiver with delight, and then he was pushing into her, big and thick. She wrapped her legs around him.

"You're so wet," he groaned, still holding himself as he eased in. "Dripping wet. So sexy."

He pushed more and more and then pulled his hand out from between them and thrust with his hips to impale her, all the way in, deep and hard. She cried out at the fierce, filling pressure and he slid both his hands under her ass.

"Christ, you feel good," his voice rasped. "So hot, silky hot. I wish I was bare inside you so I could feel you even more."

She trembled at his words. She wanted that too. They moved together, as much as she could in that position, working for her own release by rocking her pelvis against him as he drove up into her. It started low and slow but built fast, rose and twisted inside her, sharp and hot, higher and higher and then sparks exploded behind her eyelids as she came. She couldn't stop the embarrassing noises that flew from her mouth, the pleasure erupting in her. And then with two more hard strokes Carter came too. Through a dark haze she saw his jaw tighten, his eyes close, and his fingers closed on her butt hard enough to leave marks as he surged into her.

They panted together for a moment and then she let her legs slide down from around his waist to the floor. He leaned his forehead on the wall beside her, his heart thudding hard enough for her to feel it, his shirt sweat-dampened, his chest rising and falling with his rapid breaths.

"Sweet Danya," he finally said, and lifted his head. He stroked her hair off her face and kissed her again. When he withdrew from inside her she could have cried. She wanted more. Good as that had been, she hoped there was more.

And there was.

Once again he picked her up, this time carrying her to his bedroom. He laid her down on the bed then moved to flick on the lamp. Light surrounded them in a gentle glow.

She still wore her skirt and panties and he carefully removed them from her body, baring her fully to his eyes. He took her small hands in his and firmly drew them up over her head, then curled her fingers around the iron headboard railings. "Hold on tight," he instructed her. She nodded, eyes huge in her small face as she gazed up at him. The trust he saw there had him so hard he thought his cock would burst.

Arms stretched above her head had her breasts thrusting out, so pretty, her pointy little nipples so suckable. He surveyed her, stretched out on the bed, flat tummy, a sparkly jewel in her bellybutton, smooth limbs, golden skin gleaming in the lamplight, and the surprise of a smoothly bare pussy, the pretty lips pressed together.

"Christ, you're gorgeous."

Carnal hunger swelled inside him, even though he'd just fucked her. His mind raced with all the things he wanted to do to her, and he had a feeling a lifetime wouldn't be enough to do them all.

Jesus, what the hell was he thinking? Yeah, they'd sort of known each other a while, but not like this. He shook his head, trying to clear the fog of lust, but it didn't help.

He'd been jaded for so long. His lifestyle had gotten more and more extreme as he looked harder and harder for pleasure and satisfaction, until one day he realized he wasn't having fun anymore. But now, every ravenous, dominant desire came roaring back.

He reached down to stroke a hand down the length of her pretty body from shoulder to hip bone, and then back up. She shivered, eyes still fixed on him. And she kept her hands fastened around the posts. Good girl.

"Your skin is so soft," he murmured.

Still standing beside the bed, he studied her, tightly puckered nipples that made his mouth water, and those sweet pussy lips pressed together. He wanted to see more there. He covered her mound with his hand, cupping her gently. She pulsed into his palm.

"Open your legs."

She did so, slowly widening her thighs so he could move his hand farther down where she was hotter and wetter. So wet. And he held her there, while his heart thudded out the moments.

He slid his fingers deeper, between the slick folds, then dragged one fingertip over her clit, swollen and so sensitive she jerked on the bed. Her hands came free from the headboard.

"Ah, ah, ah," he said, removing his hand. "I told you to keep them there."

She blinked at him and went to slide her hands back up, but he grabbed them. "You have to be punished now," he whispered, and he flipped her onto her stomach.

Now he could admire that sweet little ass. He wanted to admire it with his hands. He dragged her hands back up to the headboard and once again wrapped her fingers around it. And then he laid his palm on her butt in a heavy caress. Once. She jolted, gasped. Twice. Three times. A warm pink shade bloomed there. "Don't let go again."

He went to his knees beside the bed and kissed the smooth, firm flesh of her butt. Licked. Kissed again. Nipped with his teeth.

"Feel the burn?"

She made a noise of assent.

"You like the burn, don't you?"

Another inarticulate little sound. As if she was trying to say no, but couldn't quite do it.

"Answer me, Danya." He landed his hand on her ass again.

"Yes! Yes, I like it."

She writhed on the bed but kept hold of the iron posts.

"I love your sweet ass. I want to play with it."

"Oh dear lord," she moaned, her face turned into her arm, hair flowing around her shoulders.

And play with it he did, taking his time to explore the curves, the tender place where her ass met her thighs, the backs of her thighs where his touch induced shivers of delight, down to the backs of her knees where he kissed and licked and sucked.

He climbed onto the bed and returned to her bottom. He pushed her legs apart again, this time exploring from behind, lifting her hips a little into the air so he could see. Everything. He could only gaze in fascination at the dip and swell of her labia, her swollen clit and the pretty pucker between her cheeks.

He dragged a finger through the wetness, lifted it to his mouth and sucked. So sweet. He did it again, closing his eyes, using his senses like he did to taste coffee—inhaling the scent, warm and feminine, taking her taste all the way into his mouth to savor it. Rich and exotic and full-bodied.

"So hot," he whispered. "And so sweet."

He dipped his head to inhale even more of it and then he had to taste with a long slow lick. Her body tensed and quivered. "Carter."

"Relax."

She made a little snorting noise that amused him. "As if."

He reached for her waist with both hands and dragged his hands down her sides to her hips, held her as he licked again. And again. His tongue found her clit and teased it, but he didn't want to make her come. Yet.

He lifted his head to make sure she still held onto the bed.

"I want to fuck you from behind," he said, his voice thick with arousal. "I want to fuck you so hard. Do you want that?" She moved her head against her arm, face hidden by hair. He wasn't sure if that was agreement or not, but the way she lifted her ass toward him, he was going to go with hell yeah, she wanted it.

His cock thrust out in front of him, hard again, more than hard, engorged, and his balls drew up painfully tight. He fisted his cock, gave it a couple of hard tugs, sank his teeth into his bottom lip as he fought for control. Control. It was all about control.

With her, it was like the ultimate challenge because all he wanted to do was let go and ravish her like an animal. What was it about her that tested him like that?

Control. Deep breath.

He sat back on his knees, cupped his balls and caressed them for a moment, dragging air into his burning lungs.

After several long breaths, Danya lifted her head and tried to turn to look at him. One hand came off the headboard.

And he laid another firm pat to her bottom.

She cried out and grabbed for the headboard again, but damn if her ass didn't lift again.

"Again." Her tortured cry was muffled by the duvet she had her face pressed into. "Oh God, please, again."

His dick surged painfully. His blood sizzled through his veins, sweat gathered on his forehead and chest and he shuddered as he delivered another heated caress to her rosy ass.

He took care not to hit her too hard. She clearly liked it, and even though he thought he was reading her right, better to err on the side of vanilla than to scare her off.

"Enough." And he shoved her legs wider apart, grabbed another condom and rolled it on, then nudged at her entrance with the throbbing head of his cock.

Danya floated on an erotic haze of pleasure-pain, a high of wicked sensation, a sensual fog. Her ass heated and burned, her nerve endings on fire, body humming. Electric ecstasy sizzled through her veins.

Each fiery caress of Carter's hand sent her higher, spinning out of her body, and as if from a distance she heard herself beg for more. Dear lord.

He was taking ownership of her body, and more than that, he was taking ownership of her soul.

How could she be feeling like this? He'd *hit* her. She should be stopping him. She'd sworn no man would ever hurt her again. But resolve and resistance fought a losing battle inside her as pleasure torched her body, flames licking at her, devouring her. Her pussy ached and dripped. And she lifted into his hand again.

Then she felt him lifting her hips, probing, pushing into her. She couldn't see, face pressed to the bed, could only feel the big blunt head of his cock. She couldn't hear above the roaring in her ears, and then she couldn't even feel the softness of the duvet beneath her, almost as if she were floating above the bed.

This was it. This was what she'd wanted for so long. What she'd needed. He was pushing her to her limits, somehow knowing what those limits were, taking her right to the edge.

"Tight," he muttered behind her. "So fucking tight and hot. Your pussy is pulling me in."

His cock filled her, stretching her, the angle as he took her from behind different, intense, hitting a spot inside her that shot sparks through her body. She couldn't hold back the noises that escaped her, small whimpers and cries of ecstasy as he filled her and withdrew, pumping into her in fast, ferocious strokes.

He kneed her legs farther apart, and a burning ache started in her hips that floated her higher.

"Please," she begged, lifting her head. "I want to let go and touch myself."

He pressed her shoulders back down to the mattress with a hand below her neck and held her there, sending a shock of ecstasy through her. "Yes. Touch yourself. Come for me, Danya."

With a whimper of relief, she let go of the headboard and slid a hand beneath her, wriggling it down until she could reach between her legs. She dipped low, slicked up cream and found her clit, ultrasensitive and swollen. The two sensations—his cock inside her, her fingers on her clit—merged into one intense spiral of heat, a flame, burning hot, flickering high. She fucked him back with each stroke, lifting her ass into him. "Yes," she hissed, her face pressed against the bed. "Oh yes. Yes. Fuck me. Just…like…that." And she cried out as she came, let the pleasure tear through her in violent, consuming waves.

Chapter Four

Danya snuggled against Carter, his arms around her, so utterly at peace, so satisfied, so complete, it almost brought tears to her eyes.

Sunday morning curled up in bed with a man who had just given her everything she wanted was heart-meltingly perfect. Well okay, it wasn't possible to give her *everything* she wanted in one night, but hell, he'd come close.

The softness of his sheets settled over her sensitized skin, his hair-roughened legs rubbed against hers, his hands felt warm and heavy and secure on her body, and she sank into a cocoon of sensual bliss. She listened to his heart thudding beneath her cheek then finally spoke. "Don't you have to go to work?"

"Yeah. Don't you have to meet your friends?"

She lifted her head sharply. "Oh my god! What time is it?"

He laughed and pushed her head back to his chest with a firm touch. "Relax. It's only ten-thirty."

"But what time does your shop open?"

"Eight. Someone else is opening today."

She blew out a breath.

"What time do you meet your friends?"

"Usually around one. I should text Marina…"

He rolled out of bed and strolled naked out of the room. Her eyes followed him, admiring the smooth sweep of muscle over hard-edged bone, the ridges and dips and the strength they contained, the power of his body like a force-field around him. He returned carrying her purse, and the small leather bag in his large masculine hands only emphasized his potent maleness and commanding presence.

With quirked lips, he handed her the purse and she sat up, shoving her hair back. "Thank you." His consideration touched her, and for a moment her hands paused on the purse. Why? Why did this considerate gesture make her feel cared for instead of annoyed? The corners of her eyes tightened.

"What's wrong?"

She looked up at him and blinked. "Nothing." With a small shake of her head, she put that thought away to examine later, and dug into the purse for her cell phone. When she flipped it open there was already a text from Marina, saying they'd meet at one.

She thumbed in her response and sent it off.

"You can come with me," he said, plucking the phone from her hand and stuffing it into the purse, which he then dropped over the side of the bed. "I mean, come to the shop with me."

She laughed.

"And there's lots of time for us to have a shower," he murmured.

Excitement shivered through her. "Oh."

He took hold of her wrists and gently tugged, backing off the bed and pulling her with him.

She didn't resist, drawn by the heat in his eyes, the wicked curve of his mouth. The beard shading his jaw gave him a dangerous, dark edge. The round muscles of his shoulders and arms bulged as he pulled her, his chest wide and smooth, abs ridged and powerful.

She almost choked, her hunger and yearning so great inside her, that she was unable to say a word. When she was on her feet, the rug soft beneath her soles, he stared down at her, still clasping her wrists.

"You're so beautiful," he said, voice raspy-rough.

Liquid heat surged inside her, spilled onto her thighs and she swayed as her knees went soft. He caught her, lifted her, and carried her to the bathroom that adjoined the bedroom.

He set her down near the toilet and turned away to start the water.

"Go ahead and use the toilet if you need to."

What? She stared at his back, gleaming bronze skin over sculpted muscles, and gulped.

No. She couldn't. Not with him there.

He reached into the shower, drawing her eyes to his tight, high ass and how it curved into thickly muscled thighs. His calves flexed as he leaned in to stick a hand beneath the rush of water to test the temperature.

He looked over his shoulder and saw her standing there frozen.

"Danya." His authoritative gaze burned into her.

Biting her lip, her entire body quivering, she lifted the lid of the toilet seat and lowered herself there. It took her a few seconds to relax enough, but then she emptied her bladder, eyes fixed on Carter's back, praying he wouldn't turn around again, but…a faint thrilling possibility that he might sent tingles sizzling over her skin.

It was so intensely intimate, so wickedly personal, and so exciting she actually moaned out loud.

And he did turn around.

She couldn't move, although she'd finished. He held her gaze steadily as she reached for bathroom tissue. Then stood on shaky legs. He held a hand out to her.

"Good girl." He kissed her forehead as he drew her closer. His approval shimmered through her and steam billowed around them in a warm cloud as water rained into the big shower. "Get in."

Her body a mass of hypersensitive nerve endings, she stepped into the shower, into moist heat and sharp, stinging spray. Pleasure cascaded through her and another moan slid from between her lips. Carter followed her into the shower and closed the glass door, shutting them into a misty cell.

He turned her body to face him, cupped her face and kissed her on the mouth, his kiss burning to her very soul. She tipped her face up to him and opened her eyes, sinking into his gaze. At that moment she would have done anything for him. Anything.

She reached for a bottle of body wash sitting on a small shelf and squeezed some into her hand. A spicy masculine scent rose to her nostrils on the steam and she inhaled it. Then she rubbed her hands together and began to wash him, starting at his shoulders and neck. His eyes darkened even more, his mouth a straight line, his jaw tight, but she knew he approved.

She slicked her hands across the slabs of muscles of his chest, down over ripped abs, then square, hard hip bones. His cock jutted between them, thick and flushed, and she stroked her fingers through the dark thatch of curls there, letting the lather froth up even more. He sucked in a tight breath as she took his cock in her hands, stroked up and down in long gliding caresses, over the round head, down beneath to cup the weight of his balls.

"That feels so good, baby."

She washed him carefully, attentive to every inch of skin, every crevice and fold, even up between the cheeks of his tight ass, making him hiss.

His head fell back, his hands on her shoulders, not pushing her down but weighing heavy, and she sank to her knees with a surge of joy and elation. She didn't take him in her mouth, but rather finished washing him, his legs, then lingering on the arch of each long bare foot. He had beautiful feet. She longed to kiss them but hesitated. She felt she knew this man on so many levels, had been intimate in so many ways but kissing his feet would send a clear signal that she wasn't sure she was ready to send.

She tipped her head back, water streaming over her face and down her breasts in warm rivulets, and looked up his body.

"Suck me."

With the greatest of pleasure she leaned toward him, made sure every last soap bubble had rinsed away and then took him in her mouth. Hot and velvet, hard and pulsing, he felt like pure delicious sin. She cupped his balls, held the root of his shaft in the other hand, and tightened her mouth into a ring around him. She took him deep, as deep as she could, and then deeper still, until she had to draw back for breath.

"Oh yeah," he groaned, hands in her wet hair. "Your mouth is a killer, baby. Hot, wet silk. Lick me. Suck me."

She swirled her tongue around, dipped into the small slit and tasted his masculine essence, then sucked him deep again. She tugged on his balls and a ragged noise dragged out of his throat.

"Yeah," he said again. "Oh yeah." So she did it again while taking him deep, almost choking on his thickness. His hands on her head pulled her toward him, filling her mouth, her throat, holding her at the point where she couldn't breathe, just...just...long enough—and then relenting, and she slid off him, gasping, blinking, water raining down over them.

Her heart thudded, lightheaded from the pleasure, the fact the she was giving him so much satisfaction a potent, pussy-melting aphrodisiac, a fierce sweet rush of adrenaline.

"Gonna come," he rasped. "Wanna come in your mouth. Suck me again, Danya."

Her mouth closed over him and pulled him in, tongued him, swallowed him, and she picked up a rapid rhythm, her hand assisting, until his body went tight and still and his hands fisted painfully in her hair.

Pleasure raced through her with fiery heat—pleasure and gratitude and gratification. Almost mindless, drunk with heady bliss, she swallowed everything he gave her with greedy delight, until he finally slipped from her mouth. Holding him with both hands, she licked him clean, his sharp taste lingering on her tongue making her want more. More. More.

"Christ, Danya." He hauled her to her feet and wrapped his arms around her, holding her in a swaying embrace in a tropical rain shower, steam billowing around them scented with spicy shower gel and sex.

She wrapped her arms around him and buried her face in his wet neck, breathing hard, heart racing, body quivering.

"Fuck," he muttered. "I could stay here all day. That was unfuckingbelieveable."

"Mmm." She could not formulate words.

"You should be rewarded for that." He paused. "What would you like your reward to be?"

She lifted her head and peered up at him again through wet lashes. Her heart gave a little bump. Her breath stuck in her throat. Standing on the edge of a mountain, the world stretched beneath her vast and scary, she said, "You tell me."

* * * * *

Danya had to search for her clothes. The tank tops still lay on the floor of the foyer, the denim skirt had made it to the bedroom. She found her bra hanging on the edge of the small foyer table but she couldn't find her panties.

She stood in the bedroom, hands on hips, a small pout on, and peered around the room. They had to be somewhere.

Then Carter walked into the room, her pink panties dangling from one finger.

"There they are!" She crossed the room toward him, hand outstretched to take them from him, the rest of her clothes clutched against her. But as she neared, he lifted his hand so the panties were out of her reach. She paused. Eyed him. "Carter. Give me my panties."

One brow arched and the corners of his mouth deepened. "No."

She blinked at him. "What do you mean, no? I need them."

"You can't wear these panties again," he said, still holding them up in the air. "Not two days in a row." Since he was a good eight inches taller than her, there was no way she could reach them. She frowned.

"Then what am I supposed to do?"

"Get dressed."

The heat in his eyes entranced her, and she hesitated only a couple of heartbeats before she walked over to the bed and dropped her clothes there. Excruciatingly aware of Carter's hot gaze on her, she put on her bra then dragged the crumpled tank tops over her head. She stepped into the skirt and did up the tiny zipper and button low on her hips. She smoothed the cotton shirts to try to get most of the wrinkles out then tugged the skirt as low as she could. It was a short skirt and she'd have to move very carefully if she didn't want the whole world to see her girl parts.

She turned to fully face him, dressed *sans* panties, and bit her lip.

"Very nice," he said and tucked her panties into the pocket of his jeans. Her eyes widened.

"What are you doing?"

"I'll give them back to you," he said. "Later."

Her tummy quivered and heat shimmered over her body at the thought of going out in public without underwear. Lord.

"Let's go," he said, and stood aside so she could precede him out of the bedroom. His gaze scorched her as she walked by him, every nerve alert and jumping.

When they arrived at Karma Coffee, she sat at a table in the window. Her hair was frizzed and wildly wavy, the only makeup she wore was lip gloss, and she still had on the same clothes she'd worn yesterday, other than panties, but she'd never felt prettier or sexier in her life. She couldn't stop smiling and her pussy still throbbed, making her agonizingly aware of how bare she was, the wooden seat of the chair hard and cool beneath her thighs. She tugged the skirt and tried not to squirm.

She propped her chin on her hand and idly stirred her skinny vanilla latte, staring into space. Carter had sat her down at the table, brought her the latte and with a kiss to the top of her head had disappeared into his roasting dungeon or whatever he called it. Her friends should be there any minute.

What had she done last night?

Confusion knotted her insides. She'd let Carter do things to her that hadn't been done to her for a long time. She'd completely let him take over, had unquestioningly done whatever he'd wanted and...she'd loved it.

It terrified her. Why was she falling back into this again? She'd sworn she would always be the one in control.

But look how well that had worked out with Chris. Not.

She sighed, but remembering how she'd felt under Carter's control tugged a smile from her and made her tummy flutter, and her body went soft all over again.

"What's so funny?"

She looked up as Jenny dropped into the chair next to her, still unable to stop the smile tugging her lips. "Nothing."

Jenny eyed her. "Okay. But you seem to be in a very good mood."

"I feel great."

Marina walked in then and joined them at the table. "That's good to hear." She flashed a smile as she pulled her wallet out of her purse. "Things must have gone well last night with Chris."

Danya blinked. "Um. Well. Actually we broke up."

"What!" Both women stared at her.

"Yeah. You were right. I wasn't happy with him." She shrugged.

"And this makes you that happy? My god, things must have been bad."

"I'm not happy because of that." She tried, she really did, but she had to look at Carter, now standing behind the counter talking to one of his staff. Big, tall, frowning a little as he gestured, he had the young man nodding vigorously as he apparently gave him direction.

Marina and Jenny followed her gaze then looked back at her, their mouths open, eyes wide. "Oh dear lord," Marina breathed. "You're going to go after him now, aren't you?"

Danya laughed and sipped her latte. "No."

Carter turned at the sound of her laugh and their eyes met. Joined. Locked. He arched a brow and she squirmed a little in her seat, knowing he was thinking about her bare pussy.

"We uh…went out last night."

"You're kidding. How did that happen?"

Danya smiled. "Why don't you two get your coffees?"

Jenny sat back in her chair and made a noise. "Fine. But you better tell us what's going on when we get back."

Chapter Five

Later, when her friends got up from the table to leave, Danya stood too, slinging her purse over her shoulder. Carter immediately moved out from behind the counter where he'd been leaning, taking a break while there were momentarily no customers.

"Hey," he said. "Where are you going?"

She smiled up at him. "Home."

"Can you wait a few minutes?"

"Sure." She looked at her friends. "I'll talk to you later."

They lifted their brows and shot him a look he found difficult to read—suspicious? Distrustful? Warning?

He liked it that her friends were concerned about her and smiled at them. "No worries, ladies, just want to have a word with Danya."

Their faces relaxed into hesitant smiles. "Okay," the redhead said. "I'll call you later, Dan."

They watched the girls leave then he turned back to her.

"Have fun?"

"Yeah."

"You told them about last night?"

"Some of it."

He held her gaze. Her lips pursed.

"Good."

Her mouth opened and she blinked.

"I like your friends," he said, taking her hand and leading her to the back of the shop to the cupping room.

"You do?"

"Well, from what little I know of them. I like watching you with them. The way you talk to each other, laugh with each other. It's cool."

She stumbled along with him, and he opened the French doors into the cupping room and tugged her in. Then he closed the doors behind them, turned and took her into his arms.

"I just wanted one last thing before you go," he murmured, bending his head for a kiss. A brush of his mouth over hers, velvety soft and lush and sweet. She opened for him immediately and he licked her bottom lip, then inside her mouth, deeper into her sweetness.

The fact that she was bare beneath her little skirt had driven him crazy all afternoon. He'd never worked with a hard-on for so long before. And now, that pretty pussy was his. He slid a hand down her back, over the curve of her ass, then inched the skirt up. Not many inches, it was pretty damn short, but soon the sweet roundness of her ass filled his palm and he squeezed.

She let out a little moan and he deepened the kiss, caressing her cheek first with one hand, then both. "I love your ass," he breathed against her mouth.

"Mmm."

He drew back and looked down at her, flushed cheeks, sparkly eyes, shiny wet lips parted. Wow.

"Come over here." He pulled her over to the round table in the middle of the room, and setting his hands on her waist, he lifted her up onto the table.

She gasped and clutched at his shirt. "Carter! What are you doing?"

"I want to give you your reward. For earlier." And with the skirt up around her waist, he parted her thighs and scooted her forward right to the edge of the table.

"Oh dear lord, you can't do this here! Someone could come in."

He smiled as he studied her pussy, all pink and pretty, the small lips closed up in a girlish, prim way. He parted her with his thumbs and inhaled the scent of her spicy feminine arousal. "Don't worry."

"But...but..." Her words trailed off as he leaned in and licked her.

"So sweet." He licked again. "So wet. Were you wet all afternoon, Danya?"

"Yes." The word came out on a groan. She grabbed his shoulders and held on.

He kissed her folds, soft as flower petals, one side then the other, sucked her into his mouth and gently tugged. She moaned again.

He licked up one side, down the other, pushed his tongue inside her and her body jolted. "Love eating you," he muttered, releasing one thigh to push a finger inside her. Wet heat clutched at his finger, pulled at it. *Fuck.* He kissed her pussy again and again and then finally laid a kiss right over her quivering little clit. "Wanna make you come, Danya. Want you to feel good."

"It does feel good. It feels soooo good." Her voice was a throaty purr.

He tongued her clit, lapped at it then sucked it into his mouth, hard. Her body tightened then convulsed beneath him, and he had to hold her thighs apart with his hands as she came hard against his mouth. She cried out, loud enough for people outside the room to hear, and he wanted to smile.

Her juices flowed onto his tongue, creamy and sweet, and he sucked and licked her until her body stopped trembling. She'd fallen back onto her elbows on the table, her head back, hair dangling down to sweep over the polished wood. He looked up over her belly, her breasts, her exposed throat. His. She was his. She might not know it yet, but she was his.

"There you go," he said, straightening with only a small twinge of protest from his muscles. *Dammit.* He leaned over her and kissed her mouth, his lips still wet from her, and she kissed him back almost as if she were drunk, slow and soft.

"I can't believe you did that," she whispered, trying to push herself up. Her hair was a tousled mess around her head. He helped her sit up, then lifted her off the table to her feet, and tugged the skirt down over her hips.

She leaned into him, as if weak, and yeah, she probably was after that table-shaking orgasm.

She put her fingers to her mouth and gazed up at him. "I was kind of noisy."

He grinned. "You were perfect. Who cares?"

She sucked in her bottom lip. "Do you do this all the time? Bring girls back here and fuck them?"

"I didn't fuck you," he said cheerfully, taking her hand and leading her to the door. Her steps were a bit unsteady. "But no. Not here."

She laughed. "Okay, never mind where you do it."

"Want me to walk you to your car?"

"No. That's okay. It's just a couple of blocks away."

He stood beside her at the door and tipped her chin up. "I want to see you again."

She smiled at him. "Me too."

He pulled out his cell phone. "Give me your number." She gave it to him and he keyed it into his contacts then snapped the phone shut. "I'll call you."

She'd heard those words before, and usually what they meant was "thanks for the fuck, I *won't* call you". And usually that had been fine with her. But she really, really wanted Carter to call her.

She walked to her car in a dreamy haze, still a bit high from the orgasm, oblivious to the Sunday afternoon crowds on the beach and sidewalks. The ache in her thighs and hips was a thrilling reminder of how he'd taken her last night.

Her phone chimed in her purse and she pulled it out. A text.

"*Thanks for coming*," she read, and laughed out loud. "*But I'm still hard.*"

She paused on the sidewalk to thumb the keys. "*I guess that's your problem :-).*"

She kept walking as she waited for his response. Sure enough, another beep. "*Yeah. You'll have to work on that next time.*"

"*My pleasure.*"

An evilly smiling emoticon came back moments later, and she laughed again. She hadn't felt this lighthearted, this freakin' happy in so damn long, it was kind of scary.

It wasn't 'til she went to climb into her car that she remembered he still had her panties.

* * * * *

Reality returned the next day with a job interview. Nearing completion of her law degree, she'd been sending out resumes all over the place. Today she had an interview at one of her top three picks for where she wanted to work.

It took every bit of control she had to push Carter to the back of her mind and focus on the interview questions, and on the questions she asked them.

When she emerged from the office building onto the sunny sidewalk, relief made her feel as if she could float away. She hoped it had gone well. They'd been impressed with her work in South America, at least.

She dug her cell phone out of her purse and turned it on, and it immediately beeped, signaling a text waiting.

"*Where are you?*" Carter. She smiled.

"*Downtown.*"

"Come to the shop and I'll take you for dinner."

Her steps slowed as she walked to her car, looking at the phone in her hand. It was five o'clock. He shouldn't just assume she had no dinner plans like that. She had half a mind to text him back and tell him no.

But why play stupid games like that, when she didn't really have plans, and she really did want to see him again?

"Okay. Be there in five."

She found a parking spot just off Cabrillo, around the corner from Karma Coffee. When she walked into the shop, though, Carter was nowhere to be seen.

"Can I help you?" The barista was young and pretty, with spiky short dark hair and a name tag that read "Juliet".

"Is Carter here?"

"Yes, he is, he's down in his office. Do you want to go down there?"

"Sure." Juliet indicated the door that led to the stairs, which Danya already knew, and she started toward it, but just then, Carter emerged. She loved the broad smile that flashed when he spotted her.

He looked her up and down. "Wow," he said slowly.

She looked down at the ivory suit she wore—slim skirt, fitted jacket buttoned up, pearls at her throat.

"You look different." His eyes fell to her feet. "Love the shoes."

She liked the shoes too, tan stiletto pumps that flattered her legs. She loved heels, though she rarely wore them.

"I had a job interview."

"Really?" He lifted a brow. "Tell me about it over dinner."

"Okay. Where are we going?"

"Well, I thought Amigos, but now seeing you, I think we'll go to Insatiable."

"We'll never get in there."

"Sure we will." He grinned. "I know the owner. They serve Karma Coffee there."

She gave him a slow smile back. "You're quite the entrepreneur, aren't you?"

"I try."

"My car...?" she said as they stepped outside.

"How far do you live from here?" Carter wanted to drive her to the restaurant, not go in separate cars, and he wanted to take her home after.

"Not far. I have an apartment off Upper State."

"I'll follow you there and you can drop your car off."

Now he knew where she lived too, in a small, well-kept apartment building with spilling bougainvillea on the walls and pots of geraniums outside the door.

Over dinner, he said, "So, you're going to be a lawyer."

"That's right. You knew that." She fingered the stem of her wineglass filled with a deep ruby merlot.

"Yeah. But seeing you dressed like that. You look so...professional."

She laughed. "That's good. Right?"

"Oh yeah, it's very hot." And such a contrast between the sweet little submissive she was, it sent a rush of heat to his groin. "I thought lawyers were all arrogant, aggressive sharks."

She made a face. "I don't think you can label all lawyers like that. And I can be aggressive. But I'd rather be assertive. I think you can get what you want without pissing people off. Most of the time."

The two sides of her fascinated him. He wanted her again.

"Tell me about the job interview."

"Bradford, Langton and Smith are one of my top picks. They're huge in the areas of environmental, health and safety requirements and have some really big corporate clients. I like them because they also help companies manage issues of corporate social responsibility and sustainability."

"Awesome. Are they a big company?"

"Yes. All three of my top picks are big. I have another interview Wednesday with Green and Young, and then on Friday I have an interview with a non-profit organization." She made a face. "I'm not sure why I'm wasting my time interviewing with the last one—they're not high on my list."

"You never know."

"I suppose."

They ate dinner amid exchanges of heated, longing glances, touches of hands, laughter and easy talk, and he could see hunger building in her, in the flash of her eyes, the burning awareness that grew between them. Good.

He drove her home, parked on the street and walked her to the door of her garden apartment. She pulled her keys out and looked up at him.

"Would you like to come in? For...coffee?"

Oh hell yeah, he did, but he had a bigger plan in mind, and he was going to have to suffer a little himself.

"I do," he murmured, bending his head to brush a kiss over her cheek. "But not tonight."

"Oh." She blinked, disappointment and maybe even a little hurt clouding her face.

"Believe me, I want to," he said, closing the distance between them so their bodies touched. He pulled her into his arms and kissed her, deep, open-mouthed, tongues sliding, until they were both breathless.

She gazed up at him, wide-eyed and panting.

"I want you to go into your apartment and take off your clothes, and lie down on your bed and masturbate."

Her eyes flew even wider. He could feel her heart pound against him.

"And when you're done, I want you to send me a text message and tell me what it was like."

"Oh dear lord." The words came out breathy and soft.

He pressed one last hard kiss to her mouth then released her and turned her by her shoulders. Her hands shook as she tried to insert the key into the lock, and then she stepped into her apartment. She half-turned back to him, one brow arched, teeth sunk into her lush bottom lip.

"Do it," he said. "Good night, Danya."

His cock was about to burst his zipper he was so goddamn hard, and it took everything he had to leave her there and turn and walk back to his car through the soft evening air. But the thought of her doing what he'd told her to, lying on her bed, bringing herself off, excited him almost unbearably. He knew where he was going to be when he got the text message. His control at being able to leave her both amazed him and made him proud.

And yeah, he was lying naked on his own bed, jerking off with fast hard pulls when his phone buzzed, lying on the bed beside him. He reached for it.

"*i came so hard i hurt,*" he read, and his cock lurched in his hand, lengthening and thickening even more. "*But i wanted you here.*"

His hand went still on his dick as he studied the message. Was she taking a shortcut using the small "i"…or did it mean something more?

And heat built at the base of his spine, sending electric tingles through his body as his own orgasm started and he clenched his jaw and closed his eyes as he spurted semen over his belly in long, wrenching spasms.

* * * * *

Danya could hardly believe what she'd done, but it had been so hot she couldn't *not* do what he'd instructed her to do. And over the next weeks when he gave her more tasks, increasingly sexy, wicked tasks, she did those too.

She was trying hard to keep herself from falling deeper and deeper, but Carter made her feel so accepted, so fulfilled, so good about herself, being with him was like a drug. She also felt what she could only describe as generous—she wanted to give him so much.

"I got two job offers today," she told him, sitting in his kitchen one evening where he was about to teach her how to steam and froth milk. And why that seemed so sexy, she had no idea. "And I don't know what to do."

"Why? Who are they from? I thought you had your choices all listed out in order of preference." He grinned, but she knew he admired her organized approach to her career.

"I do. My first choice is Green and Young. And they offered me a job, at a great salary, lots of benefits—the whole deal. Just what I wanted."

"Then what's the problem?" He poured milk into a stainless steel pitcher.

"Is that skim milk?"

"Christ no." He grinned at her. "You gotta have the fat. For the mouthfeel."

"Oh. Yeah. The mouthfeel." Her tummy fluttered.

"This is a sensory experience, not a deprivation exercise."

The flutter intensified. "Okay." Damn he made it hard to concentrate. What had she been talking about? Oh yeah. "Well, that non-profit organization I interviewed at offered me a job too."

"I thought they weren't even on your short list."

"They weren't, but after the interview I was intrigued by the work they do. The salary is only a little lower. The benefits are pretty good too. It's a small organization and they do a lot of good things. I really liked the people I met and their commitment to the environment. I started to wonder if a lot of the corporate work I would do would actually be helping the environment—or helping the companies who're destroying it."

"Ah." He paused and met her eyes. "I see. Interesting."

"I've been thinking about it a lot, and I just don't know what to do."

"Have you thought about asking Green and Young more questions about their corporate clients and what their philosophy is?"

"I did think of that, and I may do that. There are also more opportunities for advancement with them. I think."

"But you have to be happy with what you're doing."

"Yes." She nibbled her bottom lip.

He set down the pitcher and the milk and walked around the end of the counter to stand beside her stool. He slid a hand under her hair and cupped the nape of her neck, his thumb on her throat. "I don't have the answer," he said, mouth hovering just over hers, his breath a warm, teasing kiss. "But you can use me to bounce ideas off, and whatever you decide, I'll support you."

"Thank you."

Their mouths met in a long, slow kiss. When Carter drew back, he said, "I just have one question."

"What?"

"Will either of them be flexible on start dates?"

"I don't know. Why?"

He went back to his humongous stainless steel espresso machine thing and picked up the milk.

"Because I want you to come to Matagalpa with me."

Her body jolted at that. "Matagalpa?"

"Yeah. I'm planning a buying trip there next month."

"Oh." Her mind spun around uselessly for a few seconds. Was he serious? Could she do that? "I don't have much money," she said slowly, trying to process it all. "My job doesn't pay a whole lot."

"It won't cost that much. I'm looking into some deals on airfare, and that's all you'd have to pay. You can stay with me. I'm going anyway and for me, it's a business expense."

She nodded. She had a little money saved up. It might be crazy to spend it all on something like that, but she was about to start a new job that paid really well and…traveling with Carter made her insides go all warm and gooey. And she loved Matagalpa. The thought of going back there excited her.

"I'd love to come," she said, taking a deep breath. "Wow."

"Great. I'll let you know what I find out about airfares. Okay, so you have to incorporate air into the milk—it improves the taste, sweetens it." He submerged the frother deeply into the pitcher of milk, turned a knob, and waited as it worked. "We want it about a hundred fifty degrees. There we go." He turned it off then pulled two shots of espresso into large cups.

"Macchiato?" she asked.

He slanted her a grin. "Good girl. You got it."

Bending low over the counter like an artist, he carefully poured the foamed milk into the cups, did something fancy with a spoon, then handed her a cup. She gazed down at the gorgeous swirls of ivory in the creamy coffee.

"It's too pretty to drink."

"Thank you." He kissed her nose. "But please, do drink it. That's the best part."

She smiled at him as she lifted the cup to her mouth, not sure if she agreed with him. True, it tasted divine, smooth and rich, but watching him as he'd made it had been so sensual, his movements smooth and assured, his confidence and knowledge and skill a total turn-on.

Sexpresso Night

Oh dear lord, what a sad case she was, turned on by watching a man make coffee.

Chapter Six

"You're going to Matagalpa with him?"

"Yes! Isn't that great?" From the expressions on Jenny's and Marina's faces, Danya judged that they didn't share her joy.

"What's wrong?" she asked, her happiness fizzling out a bit.

"That's kind of fast, isn't it?"

"Well..."

Marina and Jenny exchanged a look. Danya frowned. "Come on, guys. I've found a man I'm really happy with. I thought you'd be happy for me."

"We are. But...we're concerned about you too."

She gazed back at her friends, dismayed by their reaction. "But why? You like Carter, don't you?"

"Well, sure. I mean, as much as we know him." Jenny smiled. "You've only been seeing him a few weeks."

"We just want you to be careful," Marina added.

Danya softened. "Don't worry about me. This feels really...right. I feel like I belong to..." She paused. "I belong with him." She studied her friends. "Despite what you might think, I did learn a hard lesson from Evan."

Jenny's eyes narrowed. "Evan was an asshole. A sadistic monster."

"No kidding." Marina scowled. "I'll never forget that night you showed up at my place...what he did to you..."

Danya winced. "I know." And her friends didn't even know half of what had gone on between her and Evan. That night he'd struck her so hard she'd been bruised and bleeding, they'd seen what he'd done to her on the outside, but the scars inside weren't so visible.

"You know, Danya, that guy was involved in some pretty strange shit." Marina leaned across the table. "Like, he belongs to sex clubs." She lowered her voice. "Fetish clubs."

Danya rolled her lips in. "Yes. I know."

They stared at her. "You knew about that?"

She let a moment go by as she pondered her response to her friends. She'd never told them everything about her relationship with Evan. She took a deep breath. "Yes. I went to those clubs with him."

Their eyebrows shot up.

"It was all a long time ago," she assured them. "I was…experimenting. I'm not into that stuff anymore." They shook their heads slowly. She leaned toward them over the table. "You just need to get to know Carter better. I swear to you, Carter is *nothing* like Evan."

* * * * *

Carter's first wine and cheese/cupping party was a huge success. Danya stayed after to help him clean up even though he had plenty of staff working that night. He'd told her he had something special for her after, and she had been quivering inside with anticipation all evening.

"Well, that's it," he said. The other staff were ready to go, the shop closed for the evening. "Thanks everyone. See you tomorrow."

When they'd gone, Danya turned to him expectantly. "So?"

He grinned and pulled her up against him. "Greedy little girl, aren't you?"

"I'm not greedy! Just curious."

He kissed her and she felt that flutter low in her belly, that sliding warmth between her legs. He was everything she'd ever wanted and she couldn't believe her good fortune at having found him.

"We're going back to my place," he said.

"Oh. Okay."

She'd driven herself to the restaurant and this time followed him to his place. Once inside the house, he said, "First of all, I'm going to give you a task for when you go home tomorrow."

Excitement flared inside her. What was this task going to be?

He picked up a length of rope sitting on the small table in the foyer and her eyes sprang open. "Here," he said, handing it to her. In her hand, she realized it was actually several ropes of different lengths. "Put this in your purse and take it home with you." And he gave her explicit instructions on what he wanted her to do with the ropes, and with another little toy she just happened to have at home.

Her heart thumped in a crazy rhythm as she wordlessly took the ropes from him. They slid through her fingers, soft and silky. She did as he'd said and put them in her purse, unsure if she would actually be able to do what he'd told her.

She knew how to do it. She just didn't know if she could. While the idea of being bound sent sizzles of excitement through her veins, it also raised a shimmering nervousness. Old fears and doubts swirled inside her.

"Now, come with me." He held his hand out to her. She slid hers into his big warm grip and let him lead her down the hall toward his bedroom. Except he walked past his bedroom and stopped in front of a closed door. She slanted him a glance, curiosity humming inside her. What could be in there?

He opened the door and stepped into the darkness and she followed him, eyes searching through the blackness for a hint of what was there. Then Carter flicked a light switch.

Lights recessed into the ceiling illuminated the room with a soft glow. Danya blinked then looked around.

Oh dear lord.

Her stomach clenched, her breath stalled and her skin turned to ice as she surveyed the contents of the room. She immediately recognized everything that was there, every last goddamn hateful thing—the rack, the table, the crops and canes and floggers, the dildos of every size and shape, the butt plugs and the selection of ropes and cuffs.

Insides cold and shivery, she rounded on Carter. "What the hell is this?"

Chapter Seven

Not quite the reaction he'd been expecting.

"My play room," he said, maintaining a reassuring, confident tone. "This is what I wanted to give you tonight."

She stared at him, green eyes flashing sparks, hands clenched into little fists at her sides.

"Are you crazy? Why would you think I'd be interested in something like this?"

He took one mental step back, his mind working. "Danya. This is just one more step, one more limit to push. I know you want to."

"I absolutely, most definitely do not! I don't want anything to do with…shit like this." She waved a jerky hand. "This is just…sick." Her face crumpled. "I can't believe you're into this stuff. I just can't believe it. I thought you were different."

What the hell did that mean? "Sick?" Her reaction confused him. He'd thought she'd be excited…curious…turned-on. Inside, his desire to control and dominate warred with the need to tread carefully here.

He could convince her. If convince was the right word. He was pretty sure this was a soft limit, and if he pushed it, she would like it.

Had he read her that wrong? Usually he was so good at knowing exactly what his sub needed and wanted, what were hard limits and what were I'm-curious-make-me-do-it limits.

Apparently he had, because she whirled around and stalked out of the room, muttering under her breath. He followed her to the door. "Danya. Where are you going?"

"I'm going home," she called back over her shoulder as she strode down the hall, grabbing her purse from near the door. "Don't call me. Don't text me. Don't ever bother me again."

He stood there and watched her cute little ass twitching beneath her snug jeans, shoulders rigid. The door crashed shut behind her. Man, she was pissed.

Apparently he had lost his touch, because he'd been sure the time was right to introduce her to his toys.

Dammit.

* * * * *

Her chest aching, stomach so tight she thought she might vomit, Danya let herself into her apartment and slammed the door shut.

How could she have been so stupid? So blind? She'd thought Carter was different from Evan—in fact, like an idiot, she'd just insisted that to her friends a few days ago—and here it turned out he was exactly the same. A sadistic Dom into perverted stuff like canes and floggers and...

Her eyes burned as she threw herself down on her bed and buried her face in the pillow. The pressure behind her cheekbones made her feel as if her face was going to split open as she tried to hold back tears.

Carter had seemed so perfect. Not wishy-washy like Chris, not a sadistic bully like Evan—just...perfect.

She rolled onto her back and tears leaked from the corners of her eyes and trickled down into her hair. She stared up at the ceiling in the dark, thinking about the things they'd done, the way he'd given her exactly what she wanted. She must have been giving off some powerful submission vibes for him to think she'd want to play in a dungeon.

And then her mind went to all the things she'd seen there, and she shivered. She pictured the crop and her pussy clenched hard. And—she covered her mouth with her hand

and swallowed — would he actually handcuff her, or tie her up and spank her?

She ached between her legs at the thought. He'd made her hold onto the headboard while he spanked her. He hadn't restrained her. Somehow she'd known he was going to take her to her edge, but she also knew he wouldn't push her somewhere she didn't want to go. And the thought of that just melted her insides.

And then...she remembered the ropes in her purse. He'd wanted her to tie herself up. And do things to herself.

A moan leaked from her lips and she closed her eyes against the overwhelming hunger and need that swept over her.

No! She was not going to play his kinky games. It was all fine when she'd thought he was just a strong, dominant man, but now she knew he was a depraved pervert, she wanted to no part of it. She been there, done that, had the souvenir scars inside her to show for it. No scars on the outside, but that was just lucky.

She rolled over again and pressed her hot, wet face against the duvet. She ached, low down inside, and her breasts swelled into the mattress, her nipples as hard as little stones. She tried to breathe through the arousal rising inside her, but after a moment she slid her hand down beneath her, under her tummy, lower between her legs. She pressed her fingers there where she throbbed and felt how wet she was even through her jeans.

She rolled off the bed, her mind scrambling with disjointed, half-formed thoughts, her heart tripping. She walked slowly across the bedroom and opened the top drawer of her dresser, removed the dildo inside. She looked down at it in her hands for a moment, heart racing so fast she felt lightheaded.

She found her purse where she'd tossed it onto the floor and pulled out the lengths of rope. She'd never been a rope slut, but she had to admire this rope—soft, silky, resilient. She slid her hand down the length of one.

How did Carter know that she knew what to do with it? The self-bondage she'd learned years ago wasn't exactly something they'd discussed.

She stood trembling, undecided, fierce need warring with stubborn resistance inside her. Her breasts grew heavy and her pussy ached. She set the objects in her hand on the floor and her fingers went to the buttons of her blouse. One button. Two buttons. She pressed her lips together. Then let the blouse slide off and float to the floor in a silky whisper. She shimmied out of her jeans and let them drop to the carpet too. She reached behind her to unfasten her bra and as she did so, turned to face the mirror on the back of her door.

Face flushed, hair wild, eyes glittering with arousal—the reflection of a woman on the edge. The bra dropped off and she stood before the mirror in lilac lace panties. For a moment she paused then slowly cupped her breasts. Her eyes drifted closed, her insides shivered, both hot and cold. She pulled at her nipples, sensation sizzling from there straight to between her legs, and moaned. She drew the sensation out, let it build and grow with her fingers at her nipples, the heat inside her swelling with exquisite pressure, spreading with a calescent glow until she ached and burned.

She forced her eyes open and dragged air into her lungs, then slipped her fingers beneath the panties and removed them, feeling the wetness on her thighs. She gazed at the rope and dildo on the floor at her feet.

Her lungs strained for air, her heart threatened to burst of out her chest. Then she sank to the floor and spread her legs, watching in the mirror, just as Carter had told her to, the sight of her fingers in her pussy like watching an erotic movie. She spread her lips and when she saw the pale cream accumulated in the opening, her heart fluttered, her tummy clenched. She touched a fingertip to the moisture there. Licked her lips. Then lifted her finger to her mouth and tasted herself. As he'd told her to.

She had to put the dildo inside her. She began working it in, stretching herself wide, the sensation burning. Cold rubber filled her and she longed for heated flesh inside her. Her muscles clenched and pushed the toy out again. How was she going to hold it inside her when she was tied? She bit her lip.

She had to try. She wanted to try. She'd have to keep her legs tight together. She flicked the vibrator on, and the buzzing inside her almost raised her off the floor. With the dildo moving inside her, sending pleasure ricocheting through her body, she picked up one of the ropes.

The cool drag of the skein against her skin, the sharp bite of it as she pulled it taut. Slowly, like a dreamy ritual. Ankles. Wrists. Tight. Secure.

She squeezed every little internal muscle she had to hold the dildo in place, and sensation ripped through her. She trembled with the need to come, wanted to touch her clit and bring herself off, to get that relief. But she couldn't.

He'd said to wait exactly thirty-five minutes. She glanced at the clock beside her bed, then closed her eyes and let the feelings take her. The helplessness of being tied, the need clawing inside her, the heat shimmering over her body.

Perspiration beaded on her skin as the burn intensified. She began to float, lost in edgy pain and voluptuous pleasure. Heat simmered at her wrists and ankles, muscles began to tighten from holding the position, and she reached for what she knew she needed—strength. The strength to face the past. Face the truth. Face herself. Could she do it?

She let herself go, a quietness filling her head. She floated. She drifted. She flew.

Images twisted and built in her mind. Images of Carter. The beauty of his naked body, the power of his muscles, the strength of his mind. Images of him holding her down, spanking her ass 'til it burned with pleasure, fucking her mouth with hard, demanding strokes. The smell of his hair, his groin, the texture of his skin against her fingertips, against her body. And images of him bringing her to orgasm with his tongue, the tender licks and sucking pulls of his mouth on her pussy, always making sure she had her orgasm before his, always making her feel beautiful and special and desired.

Carter was not a bully.

And while his domination might take her to the edge, he would never really hurt her. More than she wanted to be. Or more than she could handle. She knew that.

As everything else fell away, it all became clear to her, like shards of glass, like crystals, like drops of rain.

She was in love with him. The knowledge struck her sure and true.

And as the exquisite edge of sweet pain and fierce pleasure stripped away the past and all the encumbrances left by someone else, digging deep inside herself she knew too that not only did she love him, but she trusted him with everything—her body, her soul, her heart.

When her eyes fluttered open it had been nearly forty minutes since she'd begun. Her entire body glowed with a delicious ache, vibrating, pulsing, shivering. She wrenched her wrists against the ropes, the burn of the rope on her skin a wicked pleasure. When it didn't loosen, panic flared in her, sending a new heated rush through her veins, softening her knees. Another yank, and her hands were free and she reached for her clit. She cried out when she touched it, used her other hand to push the dildo in farther, so far it hurt, filling her. She buzzed and burned and then exploded, her body bowing as she spasmed with pleasure. And when she came, Carter's name was on her lips.

He was the one she wanted to belong to.

* * * * *

Saturday night was Sexpresso Night at Karma Coffee.

Carter glumly surveyed the busy shop, knowing he should be happy business was so good, but feeling cold and hollow inside.

A million times he'd changed his mind about calling Danya, or just going to her place to see her. But she had to choose. Choose to submit. Choose to recognize the truth. And if she didn't? What would he do then?

He didn't have a hot fucking clue at the moment, and would deal with that if it didn't happen. He hoped that she would look inside herself and see what she was and what they'd had together. And what they *could* have together. In the meantime it was killing him, because…dammit, he was in love with her and she was his. His. She *had* to see that.

He carefully built a macchiato, focusing on the creamy swirls to create a thing of beauty. When he lifted his head to hand the drink to the customer, Danya stood there at the counter. His gut tightened.

Face pale, mouth tremulous, she watched him with steady eyes.

He handed over the macchiato and turned back to her even as Juliet asked to take her order.

"Skinny vanilla latte," he said.

Danya met his eyes. "No."

He lifted a brow. "No?"

"No vanilla. I'd like something more…exotic."

His body clenched and his face felt tight and hot.

Juliet looked back and forth between them as if sensing the sizzling current. "Uh…"

"What would you recommend?" Danya asked, voice husky.

"Tonight's special is a Shot in the Dark," Juliet offered.

Danya smiled. "That sounds perfect." Then she muttered, "Whatever it is."

A smile slowly spread Carter's mouth. "It's our house blend with a double espresso shot added to it. You'll be awake all night."

"That sounds perfect too." Her eyes never left his.

His cock swelled. Jesus.

She accepted the drink Juliet handed her and when she reached for her purse, Carter waved a hand to tell her to put it away.

"Can we talk?" she asked.

"Yes." He glanced around the crowded shop.

"Um...not here," she said.

He pinned her with a look. "Downstairs? My office?"

"Okay."

He held out a hand to let her precede him through the door and down the stairs.

"Call if you need me," he tossed over his shoulder at Juliet, just catching her grin.

He followed Danya into his office. She stopped, turned to face him, and then she reached into her big leather purse and pulled out the rope he'd given her last night.

His breath stuck in his throat and his heart lurched to a stop.

"I did it," she said in a low, tight voice. But she held his eyes.

He could barely get the words through his stiff lips. "Tell me."

"I tied myself up like you asked. I knew how to do it."

Her eyes searched his and he nodded, a feeling of pressure in his chest.

"In front of the mirror. Naked. With the vibrator in my cunt."

His entire body clenched hard, his dick a steel rod in his jeans.

"It emptied my head," she continued. "Of all the crap that was getting in the way of who I really am. And what I really want."

"And what is that?"

His heart thumped. Once. Twice.

"I want to belong to you."

Fuck, she'd just about sent him to his knees. Gratitude and relief swept over him, but he held onto his control firmly with both hands.

"What do you mean by that, Danya? Do you know who I am? What I want?"

"I…I think so. But maybe you should tell me."

"Why did you freak out last night? Were you afraid of me?"

"No."

"You didn't trust me."

"I trust you. I just…got mixed up. I should tell you some things too. About my last boyfriend."

"Chris?" His eyebrows shot up into his hairline.

"Oh. No. Not Chris. I meant my last…Dom boyfriend."

He gave a slow nod. Ooookay.

"C'mere." He took her hand and led her to the big leather chair behind his desk. He sat down and tugged her onto his lap. She curled into him, one arm around his neck, and he held her waist. He had to shift her just a bit with a wince as she sat on Big Dick and the twins, engorged and kinda hard to miss.

"Okay, tell me about him."

"I met him just after I came back from South America. He was older than me, confident, commanding…dominant. I fell under his spell, I guess you could say. He pulled me into that lifestyle."

"You didn't want it?"

She bit her lip. "I did want it. I was learning things about myself I hadn't known. I learned that I was a submissive, that there are some things I want...need...that excite me. I wanted to belong to him, to do things for him. I wanted him to...to hurt me. To dominate me."

"Were you his slave?"

"No. But we were Dom/sub pretty much 24/7. Then he started doing things to me that I didn't like. The physical domination got more and more intense. He kept telling me he was pushing my limits, but...it was too much. And he started trying to control everything in my life—what I wore, what I ate, who my friends were, what courses I took. He'd call me a fat whore in front of other people. He made me think I *was* fat."

"Jesus Christ."

"He'd make me crawl to him in the clubs. I wanted to submit to him, but I did *not* want to crawl on the floor to him."

"You went to clubs with him?"

"Yes. And then...one night...he hit me."

Carter's gut rolled unpleasantly. Somehow he knew she didn't mean he'd spanked her.

"He s-split my lip open and gave me a bloody nose," she said, voice choked, her body trembling in his arms. "I was horrified. And terrified. I couldn't believe he would do that to me. I showed up at Marina's place in the middle of night covered in blood. She almost had a heart attack. She and Jenny both wanted me to call the police, but I..." She shook her head minutely. "I didn't want to have to tell them...everything."

"Who was this guy?"

"Evan Bradshaw."

Carter almost knocked Danya off his lap his body jerked so hard. "Jesus, Danya, I know that guy! He's a sick sadist." He tipped her face up and looked down at her.

"How do you know him?" she asked.

"I was part of that scene too. Years ago." He shook his head. "I probably dropped out of it around the time you were with him."

"Why?"

He frowned. "Why what?"

"Why'd you drop out?"

He hitched one shoulder. "It wasn't fun for me anymore. I guess you could say my heart wasn't in it. No satisfaction, no thrill." No emotional connection, he now knew.

"Then why do you still have all that stuff?"

He eyed her. "I still like it, Danya. I'm still a Dom inside. That will never change. I just needed the right woman."

"But..."

"If you're thinking that every Dominant guy is like Evan, forget it." His voice came out gravel-rough. "He's not a true Dominant. He's only in it for his own sick pleasure. That's not what it's about."

"Then I guess I don't really know what it's about." Her small voice made him want to protect her, care for her.

"Oh Danya." He laid a hand on her cheek. "It's about everything we shared the last few weeks. Don't you see that?"

She gazed back at him. "I swore I would never let a man control me again."

"And yet...you know you want to let go of control."

She nodded.

"*That's* what it's about. It's you giving it up, me taking and giving it back, the sharing, the exchange. It's not about me controlling your whole life. Have I tried to do that?"

She gazed back at him.

"When you didn't know what to do about your job offers, did I try to tell you what to do?"

She shook her head, eyebrows pulled together.

"Evan didn't like me to be with my friends," she said slowly. "He really drove a wedge between us. I hated that. But you liked seeing me with my friends."

"Yeah. I like seeing you happy. Didn't you and Evan talk about this stuff?"

"Well, no. We talked about scenes and toys and what he wanted to do to me and what he wanted me to do for him. He knew I liked...some pain. That I liked to submit. But he abused that. He kept saying he was helping me grow, but really he was...destroying me."

Carter wanted to punch a hole in the wall. If that asshole had been standing there he'd be showing him some punishment all right. What had he done to beautiful little Danya?

He slid his fingers through her silky hair and cupped the back of her neck. "I am Dominant," he said. "It's who I am. You have to know, though, that I would never hurt you...like that."

He met her gaze and she nodded solemnly. "I do know that. I realized that last night when I was tied up." She gazed back at him with clear, open eyes.

He bent and kissed her lips, a soft kiss of gentle reverence. Then he wrapped his arms around her tightly and breathed in her sweet scent. "I want to take care of you. I want to show you what Domination and submission really mean. Come home with me."

She paused only a heartbeat, then slid off his lap and stood.

"Will you take me into your dungeon?"

* * * * *

She burned.

Flames twisted inside her. Heat simmered over her skin, damp with perspiration.

"This is the ultimate submission, Danya." Carter's voice drifted to her through an erotic haze.

She was utterly helpless, completely at his mercy. Vulnerable. Exposed. He could do anything to her.

And yet the bindings at wrists and ankles gave a sense of security. She was safe. She was with Carter. And with the helplessness came freedom. She didn't have to feel guilty for loving what he did to her, for the wicked things she wanted. She didn't have to be afraid of letting go.

She tested the restraints, couldn't move. A thrill of adrenaline coursed through her veins. Flames licked at her.

"What are you going to do to me?" she whispered. The blindfold obscured her vision but she heard his chuckle.

"I'm going to give you what you want. I'm going to hurt you, Danya."

Another sizzle of excitement. A surge of white-hot lust and longing.

"You like the burn, Danya. You told me that before."

"Yes."

Anticipation built, hard and hot. Her skin tingled. Her pussy grew wet. Her breasts ached.

"I love your ass," he murmured, stroking a hand over it. She twitched. "Have I told you that?"

"Um…once or twice…I think." It was difficult to form words, her mouth dry. She tightened, awaiting the touch that would bring the sensation she wanted. Needed.

He laughed softly. A gentle touch…a wet touch. His mouth. His tongue. Kissing. Licking. She moaned.

And then a flash of fire. She cried out.

His hand? No. The sting was too precise, too sharp.

Another stinging kiss.

Her ass caught fire and heat radiated over her body in an edgy, transporting rapture that sent her up, up, up. She gave herself over to it, let it consume her as he laid another fiery caress to her buttocks. And another. And another. A hazy glow surrounded her, lights sparking behind her blindfolded eyelids, as every last doubt fled from her mind and only trust remained.

With the pain came strength. The strength to submit. The strength to be helpless and vulnerable. The strength to take the pain and transform it into pleasure. The strength to take what he gave her.

Which was everything.

* * * * *

"We're going to have to talk."

They nestled together in his bed, her body still tingling, her heart full and warm in her chest. "About what?" she asked.

"Limits. Stuff like that. We need to make sure we understand each other."

"Yes. Okay." She lifted her head and looked at him. "And maybe some time I can tie you up."

His eyes flew open. He blinked. "You want to switch?"

"Maybe. Why not?"

He put his hand on the back of her head and pushed it back down to his chest, but not before she saw the corners of his mouth twitch. "We'll talk about it."

After a short pause, he said, "Thank you, Danya."

"For what?"

"For the gift of your submission. It is the most precious thing you could ever give me and I want you to know how grateful I am."

"That doesn't sound very dominating." She pressed her smile to his chest.

He gave her ass a gentle swat. "You have a lot to learn, woman. We both get something out of this. When you submit to me, I feel honored. I feel loved. Trusted. How do you feel?"

She thought a moment. "I feel safe. Loved. Taken care of. But I feel strong too." She sighed. "I know I have a lot to learn."

"I'm still learning too. When you submit to me, I learn from you."

"What could you be learning from me?"

"New levels of self-control. I have never been tested like I have with you. God. You make me almost lose it, time and time again. When I get past it and stay in control, I feel stronger. You make me feel so powerful. When I see your obedience, I see respect. When I see your submission, I see trust." He paused, closed his eyes briefly, got ready to leap. "Respect and trust and love. I'm falling in love with you, Danya."

"Oh." Her breath quivered out of her. "I'm falling in love with you too, Carter."

He kissed her forehead and she felt the reverence, the devotion.

"The fact that you get pleasure from my submission excites me," she said. "And makes me feel...empowered." She'd never felt that way with Evan. Or with anyone—until Carter. The very thing she'd been so resistant to, that terrified her, had in fact given her strength and set her free. "I guess that means you've given me a gift too." Her throat tightened and her eyes stung.

"Love," he said softly, touching her cheek. "We give each other love."

The End

JEMIMAH'S GENIE
Ainsley Abbott

Dedication

To my husband, Peter, who has brought true magic into my life.

Chapter One

Jemimah Murphy was devastated when her grandmother Louise died. She'd moved in with Granny Lou over five years ago after Gran broke her hip. At the time, Jemi thought she'd done it to look after Lou but in fact they'd looked after each other. Granny Lou was the only family Jemi had and was more of a mother than grandmother.

"When I'm gone," Gran would say in her most imperative tone, "you must get on with life. There's someone special out there for you, you just have to find him."

Jemi hated hearing her grandmother speak of dying. And as to "getting on with life", her life was already hectic enough. She worked long shifts as a nurse at the public hospital, then hurried home to housework, chores and the tender but demanding care of Granny Lou.

She didn't consider her work tedious. She adored her grandmother and loved spending time with her. Once in a while, she'd meet with friends for a drink after work but she rarely stayed long. At night, she'd fall into bed, exhausted, knowing she'd have to be up at the crack of dawn to start the routine over again.

As to men, she may have blushed when a handsome guy looked her way, or one of the doctors complimented her efficiency but she wasn't interested in finding anyone. She'd already had enough unfulfilling relationships to last her a lifetime. Given her experiences, she no longer believed she'd find a man who could satisfy her sexually, let alone emotionally. So she poured her energies into her work and her grandmother. If there was something missing in her life, she refused to acknowledge it. She believed dissatisfaction was the curse of an idle mind, so she kept her nose to the grindstone and her thoughts focused on her responsibilities.

But when Granny Lou died peacefully, though unexpectedly, in her sleep, Jemi felt lost and abandoned.

According to her grandmother's wishes, Jemi organized the cremation, then scattered Granny Lou's ashes at the base of the prolific elderberry bushes in their backyard. The thicket of shrubs was revered by both Jemi and her gran, since the bushes had survived over four generations of Murphys and produced fruit for countless pies, wines and meads along the way.

Jemi gazed at the well-tended plants. Sibyl, Gran's black and white cat, looked on. "I guess that's it, eh, Sib?" She reached down and stroked the cat who instantly got up and began to weave herself between Jemi's legs, purring. It was late autumn and the red-yellow leaves of the elderberry bushes were dropping, though some of the branches still boasted purple berries. Gran's ashes made a pathetically small pile at the base of one thick trunk. A cool breeze stirred them gently.

"There's one thing you must promise me, Jemimah," Granny Lou had said only a few short evenings ago.

Kneeling next to her grandmother's bed, Jemi sighed impatiently. *Here we go again,* she thought. "Yes, Gran," she said, "I'll be sure to drink a toast to you when you're gone. Can we not talk about that, please?" How many times had Gran made her promise this? And why did it matter so much?

But her grandmother was adamant. "Sweetheart, listen to me," she said. "All things change and pass on. I won't be an exception. It's important you do exactly as I say."

Jemi sighed. "Okay, Gran, tell me again, what you want me to do."

Granny Lou smiled and held Jemi's hand. "You're to get the two silver wine goblets from the china cabinet. Then fetch one of the bottles of elderberry wine dated October 31, 1865. It was bottled by your great-grandmother Jemimah—who you were named after. Are you listening?"

"Yes, Gran," Her grandmother's hand was cooler than it should be and Jemi wished she'd finish the instructions so she could fetch her some hot tea and another blanket.

"Once it's dark outside, put the goblets on the table, light the candles in the silver candlesticks and pour the wine. You won't need much—it only takes a little." Granny Lou chuckled to herself. Her rheumy eyes grew distant.

"So, I wait until night, pour two glasses and drink a toast to you, right?"

"Hmm?" Granny Lou refocused then nodded. "Oh, yes. Then you drink a toast to me."

"Is that all?" Jemi got to her feet. But Gran's hand clung more tightly.

"Just one thing, sweetheart," she said. "Whatever happens is destined. Don't hold back on anything. And remember, sometimes if you truly love someone, you must set them free." She loosened her grip on Jemi's hand, patted it lovingly, then winked. "Now, run along and put the kettle on. The blanket can wait."

Jemimah cocked an eyebrow. It was uncanny how her grandmother knew things before being told but Jemi was used to it.

Now, the memory of that moment was all it took to bring tears to Jemi's blue eyes. The breeze was picking up and she realized she was cold. She turned back to the house and hurried in through the patio door. She'd light a fire in the fireplace. The house was old and drafty and even the relatively new furnace in the basement couldn't completely take the chill off.

It wasn't until nearly eight p.m. that Jemi remembered her promise. She'd been staring at the fire, her thoughts wandering this way and that, stroking Sibyl who was curled in a ball on her lap.

There was money, Granny Lou had seen to that, enough for Jemi to take a long vacation if she wanted. But what fun was a vacation alone? She sighed, gave Sibyl a quick kiss on the head before putting her on the floor, then stood up, catching her reflection in the mirror over the fireplace. Shoulder-length wavy blonde hair caught back in a ponytail, white pixie face, puffy red-rimmed blue eyes and a small mouth turned down at the corners. She was probably too thin and there were dark circles under her eyes.

She was nearly thirty and what did she have to show for her life? She realized now her dedication to her grandmother and obsession with her job left her isolated from the rest of the world. She had very few memorable moments from her smattering of sexual encounters. Boyfriends? Well, if you called Steve or Dan or Butch boyfriends…she'd dated each of them less than five times and none was memorable for the right reasons.

Jemi made a moue in the mirror. Maybe Gran was right to tell her to get on with her life. But how and where should she start?

Jemi pulled one bottle of wine after another off the rack in the basement cellar. They didn't seem to be in any order and not all were elderberry, which made the process tedious. The single bulb dangling from the ceiling was too far away to make it easy to find what she was looking for.

While Sibyl chased shadows nearby, Jemi squatted down and squinted at the bottom row of bottles. These were obviously older. The glass was thick and oddly shaped and the labels were like parchment. Finally, after searching randomly, she pulled one out and smiled.

"October 31, 1865. Gotcha." Sibyl stopped her play and looked at Jemi with wide eyes then, in a fit of frenetic energy that only cats understand, she shot up the stairs and disappeared.

Jemi stood up and blew dust from the heavy, blue-tinged bottle. She rubbed the label gently. There was a signature and even though it was faded and blurred, she could make out the name, Jemimah. Interesting to think she held a wine made by her great-grandmother's own hands.

She took the bottle upstairs and wiped it with a cloth, then placed it on the table in the dining room. She found the silver goblets in the breakfront and grabbed a corkscrew from the kitchen.

With a minimum of difficulty, she managed to extract the cork, then sniffed the brew to make sure it was fit for consumption. She poured a bit into each goblet, sat down and lifted one in the air.

"Here's to you, Granny Lou. Life won't be the same without you." Before the tears could come, she put the goblet to her lips and sipped.

What happened next Jemi couldn't really say. The room seemed to suddenly fade into a grayish mist, while the strangest sounds reverberated—a sort of crackling, like electricity, followed by a large poof and whoosh, as if air had been sucked out of a receptacle leaving no sound at all.

Oddly, Jemi wasn't frightened. She sat, unmoving, in her chair, the taste of the wine still sweet on her lips, the liquid warm in her stomach. She watched, amazed, as the mist seemed to dissipate and a figure appeared.

"Gran?" she whispered hopefully.

"No. Brian, actually."

Jemi stood up and stared. The most beautiful man she'd ever seen stood at the end of her dining table. He was dressed in a peculiar fashion—very tight black pants and a thin red satin vest that hung open to reveal a superb six-pack and bulging pecs. Jemi's eyes moved from his chest to his face, stupefied. His hair was blond, thick and slightly tousled, his face was strong-jawed, his skin bronzed. His eyes were a sapphire blue, fringed with heavy lashes. His mouth... Jemi licked her lips, feeling as if she were suddenly on fire.

"Where did you come from?" she managed to croak.

He came around the table and smiled at her. "You summoned me."

"I what?"

He gestured to the bottle.

She stared, then laughed, then stared again. "I'm sorry." She sat down abruptly. "Are you telling me you're a..."

"Genie, Jinn...I suppose either would apply," he said, smiling and showing twin, endearing dimples. "They really mean the same thing. And yes," he made an extravagant bow, "your wish, Jemimah Murphy, is my command."

Logically, Jemi knew this couldn't be happening. She'd obviously passed out, or fallen asleep and it was all a dream. So why not enjoy it?

"So," she said slowly, trying unsuccessfully to keep her eyes from roaming to the large bulge in Brian's tight pants. "If I summoned you, what exactly do I do next?"

"You, my lovely," Brian said, "needn't do anything." He grinned, picked up the other goblet, drank it down in one gulp, then moved closer so the mesmerizing bulge was within inches of Jemi's face. Her cheeks burned but she felt no need to retreat. A languid fascination had enveloped her. *Yes,* she thought, *dreams are like that.* She leaned back in her chair and closed her eyes, feeling his fingers touch her cheek, then trail down the side of her neck.

She shivered, feeling him deftly unbutton her shirt. She opened her eyes to find his face within inches of her own, his eyes glittering, a slight smile touching his lips.

She felt she should speak but at the same time knew it wasn't necessary. Why ruin the dream? In any case, his mouth had gently covered hers in a soft, sensual kiss that made speech impossible. He tasted of elderberry wine and she felt her cunt moisten as his tongue flitted about her lips and mouth, teasing.

By now he'd completely undone her clothing and before she knew it, he'd lifted her in his arms and was placing her on something very soft and very warm. She opened her eyes again and realized she was lying on a thick, white faux-fur rug before the fire in the dining room. But wait, Gran had no fur rug.

She pulled her mouth away. "Where…"

He simply winked, then snapped his fingers and the room was instantly filled with glowing candles and soft, sweet music.

"Oh, very nice," she cooed. "I'm liking this dream."

Slowly he removed her clothing, his lips following where his fingers unbuttoned, unzipped and removed. Her hands gripped his upper arms as her bra disappeared and he fastened his mouth on one of her nipples. Goose bumps rose all over her body as his tongue teased the nipple to a tender peak then moved to its twin to do the same.

Her hands lifted to his head, her fingers losing themselves in the thickness of his hair as his mouth trailed down, down, his fingers gently lowering her panties.

She felt her abdomen clench as his tongue circled her navel then moved even lower. Her cunt was wet and flaming. She squeezed her eyes tighter, automatically lifting her hips so he could remove her panties altogether. She waited for his mouth to find the hot, throbbing spot between her legs. She opened her thighs to accommodate him but instead, there was nothing.

She opened her eyes and saw he was standing over her. His vest was already gone and he was slowing unfastening his pants.

In the flickering light, he looked like a god, perfectly proportioned, his muscles defined by shadow and light, his eyes lit with passion, lids half-lowered. She watched as he slowly removed his pants and kicked them away. His penis, fully erect, was huge. Jemimah blinked and swallowed, then as if dazed, got to her knees. She wanted to feel it, taste it. He seemed to know her thoughts and moved closer, his fingers warm and strong in her hair.

She stroked and gripped his shaft, feeling the fiery heat and steely hardness against her palms. She'd never held a cock so thick. Without thought, she put her mouth over the tip, letting her tongue taste and savor. Salty. She heard him groan and smiled to herself, taking it even further into her mouth. She must be good at this if she could make a genie moan, she thought absently.

But he obviously wasn't going to settle for self-gratification. Within moments, he'd pulled his cock from her mouth and gently lowered himself over her, so they lay flesh to flesh, his penis hot on her abdomen, his elbows propped so he could find her mouth again with his own.

She gripped his shoulders, suddenly desperate to feel that hot cock inside her. But instead, he moved lower, his hands grasping her buttocks and lifting her to his face, his breath warm on her pubic hair.

Her cunt was pulsing with desire, as if a hot coal had been placed inside. She could feel herself clenching in anticipation. She stared down at him and he looked up. "I want to taste you," he said simply. And suddenly his warm lips covered her clitoris, his tongue flicked once, twice, then moved lower and plunged into her opening, deep, moving sinuously, licking the wetness, then flicking out again to circle her clit.

Jemi was lost. She couldn't speak. Her hands grasped his hair so tightly her fingers hurt. She moaned shamelessly as his tongue ravaged her—sliding into her hot cavern, licking, licking, then out and flicking her clit. Again and again, faster and faster. She felt her world closing in, spinning out of control, as she came closer and closer to a monumental climax.

"Oh...God," she groaned, moving her head back and forth. Any moment, any second...

Then he stopped. Tiny anticipatory shockwaves filled her as the cooler air replaced his hot mouth. "Shit, don't stop!" she moaned.

Then he was over her. "Look at me," he said.

She opened her eyes. His azure eyes were very close. They were so beautiful, so gentle—hypnotic. His hands gripped hers and pulled her arms up over her head. His fingers curled between her own. His chest was warm on her breasts. He lifted his hips and she felt his cock touch the entrance to her gaping, desperate vagina. But even though her mind was lost to her need, his eyes still held hers.

Then he slipped inside her, slowly, gently and she let out her breath in a gasp of sheer bliss. He moved even deeper, his eyes becoming darker with his own pleasure. She felt her opening stretched to the max, his cock so far inside her, she was completely filled. Yet he didn't move and instinctively, she began to rotate her hips, wanting more, feeling that mounting need turning to fire.

Then he lifted a hand, snapped a finger and a tiny button vibrator appeared in his palm. Grasping her to him, he rolled sideways, holding her close, keeping his rod tight inside as his hand moved between them.

The vibrator found her clit and she was lost to the added sensation. She held him hard, burying her face against his chest, panting. He began to move his hips, pushing his cock slowly in and out.

The combination of the vibrator and his movements brought her to a peak she'd never reached before. Her mouth hung open and sweat bathed her body. His thrusts increased and suddenly the vibrator was gone. He rolled her once more onto her back and she automatically wrapped her legs around his waist. He held himself up with his arms and his movements became more rapid. He pushed her legs forward to get more purchase and she cried out with pleasure as he plunged even deeper.

Faster, harder he pushed, her slickness making it easy. She gripped his buttocks tightly, sensing the brink of release coming closer. He drove harder, slapping against the back of her thighs until, in an unbelievable eruption, her entire body burst into orgasm, every muscle clenching, her cunt spasming magnificently against his hardness. She was still in the throes of climax when he came. She felt his cock jerk inside her, his entire body tensing as he stopped his movements, a low moan emanating from deep in his chest.

Then slowly, he rolled again to one side and pulled her to him. She snuggled her face into his chest and the last thing she thought before falling into a deep blissful sleep was, "This is one dream I'll never forget."

Chapter Two

೮

Jemimah woke slowly, coming out of a deep dreamless sleep to find herself lying on the worn gray carpet in front of the fireplace with Sibyl curled close to her. The fire had died down to mere cinders and the room was chilly.

She sat up abruptly and looked around, memories flooding in. "Brian?" She said the name tentatively, feeling silly. There were no candles, no music, no white fur rug and most importantly, no man lying next to her.

She rubbed a hand over her face. Was she going crazy? Then she remembered how it all began—the toast to Granny Lou and the ancient bottle of elderberry wine.

Of course. The wine was so old it'd probably gone off and caused some psychedelic reaction. She stood up then stopped stock still in surprise. There was stickiness between her legs. She put a hand down to feel, staring at the irrefutable evidence that more than a dream had brought her to a pinnacle of pleasure the night before.

Her mind ran back over what happened and she felt a rising heat at the mere recollection. She glanced at herself in the mirror. Her cheeks were pink, her eyes soft, sated. She put a finger to her lips. She could still feel his mouth on hers.

She pushed her tousled hair back and frowned, more puzzled than anything else. She must be going crazy.

She sighed. "Well, if this was crazy," she said aloud, "bring on the straitjacket." Sibyl meowed plaintively in reply.

* * * * *

"Just try it," Jemi said to Ruth. They'd just finished the evening shift and sat on the old saggy couch, shoes off and feet up, in the staff break room.

Jemi held a flask of the elderberry wine out coaxingly. She'd only brought a small amount of the alcohol, not wanting to waste it or get caught with it at work. The flask fitted inconspicuously into her purse.

Dark-haired, no-nonsense Ruth was about the same age as Jemi but happily married with a daughter. She eyed the bottle skeptically. "You say it's over a hundred years old? I don't know."

"You're in the right place if you get food poisoning," Jemi said, smiling. "Honestly, I've already had some myself. I just want you to try it, see if you think it's as good as I do." She lied. If Ruth had a reaction, at least it would solve part of the puzzle. And she didn't think a reaction like the one she'd had would harm anyone.

Ruth cocked a brow, then took the flask, smelled the contents and took a tentative sip, then another larger swig. She smacked her lips and smiled at Jemi. "Hey, it's very good. Sweet but not bad. You say your great-grandmother made it?"

"Yes. My great-grandmother Jemimah." She watched Ruth carefully but there was no poof, no mist, no sound of air being sucked out of the room. "How do you feel?" she asked.

Ruth handed the flask back. "What do you mean, how do I feel? I feel like I've been here forever, my feet hurt and my back is aching. They brought a new one in this afternoon—skiing accident. I think I wrenched something when I helped get him onto the bed. I should listen to Rick and leave the heavy lifting to the men."

Jemimah listened with half an ear, absently swirling the wine in the flask. She was thoroughly confused, now. Obviously the potion hadn't worked its miracle on her friend.

"Anyway, kiddo, I've got to get home," Ruth said, standing and stretching. "Rick's probably close to tears by now. Amelia's having one of her not-so-good days." She sighed, "What about you, Jem? Are you doing okay?"

Jemi looked up and forced a quick smile. "Yeah, sure. I'm okay. Still trying to get used to the empty house, though. How is Amelia?"

Ruth shrugged and a deep sadness rose in her eyes. "About the same. She's getting weaker. She won't eat, so we're going to have to put in a feeding tube."

Jemi stood and hugged her friend. Amelia was Ruth's seven-year-old daughter. She'd been diagnosed a year ago with terminal leukemia.

Ruth hugged Jemi back, then put her at arm's length. "Hey, girlfriend, I'm okay. It's you I'm worried about. Listen, any time you want to get out, you just call me. If I'm home, you can come over and we can sit around and gab, or better yet, if Rick's home, we can go out for a drink. You need to get out more."

"Thanks," Jemi said. "I'll do that." She watched as Ruth gathered her belongings and headed for the door. "Give Amelia a kiss from me," Jemi called.

"I will." Ruth smiled, waved and was gone.

Jemi gazed at the silver container still in her hand. "So, you're just a one-night stand, eh?" She shrugged, lifted the flask to her lips and drank. It tasted very good, sweet, soothing.

Had she fallen asleep?

"No, you're not asleep." It was Brian.

She realized she was stretched out on a couch. She tried to sit up but felt far too lethargic, as if in the soft embrace of a warm, relaxing bath. She was still in the third floor staff break room. Nothing was different except now she felt Brian next to her, the breath of his whisper tickling her ear.

"So, you can read my mind now?" she said.

"Of course," he said. "How do you think I know what you really want?"

"Did you say something, Jemimah?"

Jemi turned her head slowly. It was Martin Phillips, one of the new interns, who spoke. He sat at a table on the other side of the room with Nancy Fremont, one of the matronly nurses she worked with, cups of steaming coffee between them.

"Uh...sorry," Jemi said, "I must've dozed off. Talking in my sleep..."

She knew logically she must get up and go home but her body simply wouldn't respond.

"Just lie still." Brian's voice, this time she felt his breath on her mouth. She closed her eyes. She could feel him lying next to her, his body touching hers.

"Why can't I see you?" she thought.

"Because what I am going to do to you here, isn't for anyone else's eyes."

Jemi felt a thrill run up her spine.

"And just what do you intend to do in front of these people?"

She heard him chuckle. "You have a wonderful imagination, Jemimah, remember, my wish is your command."

"That's so Hollywood," Jemi began, then stopped with a quick intake of breath. She felt his warm hand slide slowly up her thigh and beneath her nurse's uniform. His lips were making small butterfly kisses down her neck, sending more chills racing through her.

"You can't..."

"Jemimah?" It was Nancy this time. "Are you okay, dear? Are you sure you're comfortable there?"

"Yes...sorry. I'm just tired," she said aloud. "Just need a quick catnap."

Brian's fingers had found the top her pantyhose and he was pulling them slowly down. She raised her hips to accommodate, trying to make it look to Martin and Nancy as if she were simply becoming more comfortable. She fumbled with the blanket folded on the back of the couch for doctors, interns and nurses who used the couch to catch a few winks between shifts. She managed to pull it down and cover herself, just as she felt Brian slip her panties down and push her thighs apart.

"Jesus," she thought. "This is insane." She should be horrified but oddly she merely felt an alien sort of excitement.

Brian's mouth touched hers very gently but firmly. "Relax," he soothed. "Just relax and enjoy."

She wanted to lift her arms and hold him but she knew she mustn't. How would it look? She lay very still, her heart beating, her vagina pulsing and wet with wanton need. She felt his fingers delicately outlining the shape of her cunt, moving just inside her labia, touching her clitoris, making it begin to throb with desire. Her entire focus was between her legs, that molten needy core. When he slipped a finger inside her, she sighed aloud. She didn't care what her work companions thought. Her eyes were shut. They'd think she was asleep.

His finger moved deeper, his thumb gently circling her clitoris, bringing her higher, higher, almost to the brink of orgasm. She realized she was clenching her teeth and forced herself to relax into the feeling, making herself prolong the pleasure.

"I know you like this," she heard Brian whisper. His tongue circled her left ear as he removed his finger from her cunt, gathering her wetness and trailing his finger lower, following her crack, placing his finger over her other opening. Then gently, very gently, he inserted his finger into her anus.

It was everything she could do not to groan aloud. She realized her fingers were clutching the fabric of the couch. But she daren't move, daren't gasp with the delight of it. Then she felt him on top of her. Some part of her mind protested that this wasn't possible but she ignored it. She could feel his hard cock between her legs, hot against her inner thighs.

His finger moved deeper into her anus, crooking gently. At the same time, he slipped his penis into her, not quite all the way.

"Teasing..." she thought.

"Yes," he replied. She could sense his own excitement, his breathing was more rapid. She could feel the heat of him, small droplets of sweat from his brow. She mustn't open her eyes, afraid if she did, it would all end before the magical journey was completed.

"I've never done this," she thought.

"It's time you did," he said. She could hear the smile in his voice. He pushed his penis in all the way, stretching her opening and filling her, then moved his finger, pressing through the thin barrier between rectum and vagina so she felt so full of him she couldn't move for fear of disturbing the exquisite sensation.

Ever so slowly, he began to move inside her. She curled her fingers more tightly in the couch fabric and hung on for dear life. Was she moving? Was she making any noise? She opened her eyes a crack and saw Martin and Nancy had now been joined by Dr. Jergensen, one of the ward doctors.

"Jesus, God," she thought.

"Relax..." Brian's whisper forced her to do as he said. She felt herself sink into the couch as she forced her muscles to loosen. She felt his movements continue, slow but steady, his finger now moving carefully in and out of her rectum in rhythm to his penis. His lips moved from cheek to lips to neck to ear, then back to her lips. His tongue pushed past her teeth, delicately touching her inner mouth.

Jemi could hear the others talking.

"Snow predicted..."

"Sister coming to visit..."

"New patient in room sixteen..."

It all flowed over her like water. It meant nothing. But her awareness of their presence kept her still, kept her from groaning with the pleasure of her rising passion.

"Do you like it?" Brian's mouth, now at her ear once more as his gentle thrusts became more demanding, his shaft driving even deeper.

"God, yes."

"How about this?"

She felt a second finger gently ease its way into her anus and she thought she'd scream with joy. Instead, she felt her entire being become primal. Her mouth hung open in abandon, her mind, though aware of the others in the room, was completely obsessed with the unbelievable pull of desire that mounted with each thrust of Brian's ample shaft.

She probably would've prolonged her explosion for a few more minutes if Brian hadn't taken his other hand and touched her clitoris. It was too much to withstand and she orgasmed so hard, she thought she'd shatter, her spasms gripping his cock and the fingers in her anus hard, again and again.

Brian removed his fingers gently, then thrust once more and she felt him gasp and his body go rigid as he shot his semen inside her. Together they pulsed, his cock and her cunt gripping in aftershock. She felt his arms tight around her and he pulled her onto her side, putting a leg over her and kissing her gently.

Jemi's mind wandered in a blissful half-world. The murmur of the others in the room lulled her. She nestled her face against Brian's chest, his breath warm in her hair. She fell asleep with his cock still inside her and the scent of him filling her with a sense of complete and utter security.

* * * * *

"Jemimah?"

"Hmm?"

"Dear, it's nearly midnight. Maybe you should get home and get some proper rest."

Jemi opened her eyes with a start. "Nancy?"

The older woman was stooped over, looking concernedly into Jemi's eyes. "Yes, it's me," she said. "Darling, I think you must've been having some strange dream. You've been crying out in your sleep. Are you all right?"

Jemi was suddenly fully awake. She blushed profusely as she first felt the telltale sensations of having been pleasured both anally and vaginally, then realized with relief her panties and pantyhose were miraculously back in place.

She sat up carefully, adjusting her nurse's uniform.

"You do look flushed," Nancy was saying. "Maybe I should take your temperature..."

Jemi shook her head and tried to smile. "No, really, I'm okay. I can't believe I fell so soundly asleep here. I must be more tired than I realized." She thought her words sounded lame but a part of her knew no one would ever believe or understand what had truly taken place on this couch.

"Maybe you need a holiday," Nancy said gently. "How long has it been?"

Jemi pushed her hair back, fastening the pins on each side. She considered. "I can't really remember," she said, surprising even herself.

"Well, there you are." Nancy stood up and clucked. "Some time off. Maybe a trip? You spend far too much time here." She smiled. "Give it some thought, dear."

Jemi nodded. "I will," she said. She stood up carefully, aware of Brian's semen dampening her panties and the phantom sensation of his fingers in her anus. She shivered with delight at the memory.

Nancy picked up the blanket and folded it automatically. "You go home, now and get some proper rest. And if you're still flushed and shivering in the morning, stay home. The rest of us can run this place while you recuperate, you know."

Jemi laughed lightly. "Yes, yes, of course. Thanks, Nance." She grabbed her purse and sweater and hurried out before dear, matronly Nancy could suspect the shivers and flush weren't from any illness but from thoughts of pure unadulterated lust.

* * * * *

"You want to talk." It was a statement, not a question. Brian sat in the chair opposite Jemi. She was back home at the kitchen table, the now empty flask of elderberry wine between them.

Jemimah's curiosity and confusion had convinced her to drink the little bit of wine left in the flask she'd taken to work.

"Yes," she said. "I have to know what's going on."

Brian smiled. She looked at him, feeling her cheeks automatically flush and her crotch begin to throb. He was unbelievably gorgeous. A lock of his thick blond hair fell across his brow and when he smiled at her like that, his dimples showed and his eyes danced mischievously. In so many ways, he was like a little boy. Yet in so many other ways, he was all man.

"I think you're pretty fine yourself," he said.

Jemi blushed more deeply. "That's not fair," she protested.

"What's not fair?" He raised his brows innocently. He reached across the table to take her hand in his, rubbing his thumb gently over her knuckles.

"You know my most intimate thoughts," Jemi said, "but I don't know anything about you."

He studied her for a moment. "What do you want to know?"

"Well, anything," she replied. "I want to know what's happening. I assume it's the elderberry wine, right? Is that what summons you?"

He frowned, then nodded. "Yes, I think so."

"What do you mean you think so? Don't you know?" Jemi stared at him in surprise.

"No, I don't know for sure. All I know is when you drink the wine, I live and breathe again—and I do it for you."

"For me?" She considered. "So that's why Ruth had no reaction."

"Yes," he said. "I can't explain it. All I know is when you call me...that is, when you drink the wine...it's as if I wake up and feel like I'm a part of you. I know your deepest desires and every part of me wants to fulfill them." Jemi cocked a skeptical brow and he shrugged. "I know it sounds crazy," he said, "but it's the truth."

"So," Jemi tried to hide the sarcasm in her voice, "what do genies do when they're not fulfilling wishes?"

Brian's eyes bored into hers and she felt as if she were being drawn inexorably into him. She shook her head to clear it.

"When I'm not with you, I don't exist."

"What?"

He sighed. "I don't know—how do I explain? I'm in this heavy darkness, like I'm sleeping but awake. There's nothing except the feeling of being trapped, or lost."

Jemi frowned. "That sounds awful."

He lowered his eyes and continued to rub her hand gently. "Yes, it is."

They sat silently for a moment while Jemi tried to make sense of it. "So, is this like in the books? Am I supposed to have three wishes?"

Brian looked up and she was ridiculously glad to see his face had cleared and he was smiling again. "Yes, I believe that's how it works."

Jemi smiled back. "Okay, so how many wishes do I have left?"

"Three," he said.

"But you've already... I mean, didn't you say you know what I want? Doesn't what you've—we've—done count as a couple of wishes?"

"No." He got up and came around the table, standing behind her and laying his hands on her shoulders, then gently kneading so she closed her eyes and let the worries of the past weeks melt under his ministrations. "You see, you have to actually say the words," he said. "You have to say 'I wish' or it's not official."

"Hmm." Jemi thought about this, as he continued to massage away tension. What could she wish for? Should she wish Granny Lou...

"Sorry," he said. "There are certain limits. I can't bring back the dead. And I can't grant you wishes that wouldn't be good for you."

"Well, who's to decide what's good for me?"

He shrugged. "It's just the way it is." He bent and kissed the back of her neck. "You smell so good," he said.

"Do I?"

He knelt down next to her chair and took her hands in his. "You have no idea how magnificent you are, do you?"

"No," she said, blushing again at the intensity in his blue eyes. "And you're just saying that. I'm sure it's part of your job."

He shook his head. "No, it's not a job. I don't know what it is but it's not that. When I'm with you," he said, "I feel...I don't know, I feel like I've come alive."

Jemi smiled and lifted a hand to push the hair back from his face, letting her fingers linger. "Are you telling me you have real feelings for me?"

He lifted her hand to his mouth and kissed it. "I think, somehow, we're meant to be together."

A thrill shot through Jemi at his words, then she remembered. "You can read my thoughts. You know it's what I want to hear."

He stood up and began to pace. "No…no, that isn't it. It's true. It's how I feel." He stood at the kitchen window looking out into the night at the elderberry bushes bathed in moonlight and rubbed the back of his neck distractedly. "I can't lie even if I wanted to. I think it's one of the limitations. I mean what I say."

Jemi got up and came up behind him, putting her arms around his waist and laying her cheek against his back. "I don't understand what's happening, Brian but I feel the same way. I feel… I feel as if I've known you all my life. Like we're meant. Is that just the wine, or the effects of the trance?"

He turned and put his arms around her, pulling her close and resting his cheek against hers. "I don't think so. I sure hope not."

"Okay," she said, her lips tasting his neck as she spoke, "tell me what I can wish for."

"You can wish for anything. But like I said, it has to be something that won't affect you in an adverse way. Having your grandmother back would put you right back where you were before—working too hard and having no life of your own. You need to let her go. She's in a wonderful place and you know she wants you to be happy."

Jemi nodded. He was right. She pulled away from him reluctantly. "Well, three wishes is a pretty tall order." She sat down again and cupped her chin in her hands, considering. "There is one thing," she said finally.

Brian sat down too and nodded. "Yes, I think that's a good idea."

Jemi laughed. "God, it spooks me when you do that. Okay, so I have to say the words?"

Brian nodded.

Jemi looked at him and smiled. "I wish Amelia Preston was completely healthy and well."

As soon as the words left her mouth, Brian snapped his fingers and a popping sound reverberated throughout the house. He smiled at her. "Your first wish, Jemimah Murphy, has been granted." He glanced at the window where the sky was beginning to turn from black of night to gray dawn. "And now I have to go." He got up and came to her, pulled her to her feet and into his arms, kissing her deeply.

But before she had a chance to put her arms around him and reciprocate, he'd disappeared.

* * * * *

"I just can't believe it," Ruth was saying on the phone. Jemi could hear the pure joy in her voice. "Amelia just got up this morning, came to the kitchen and said, 'Mommy, I'm hungry.' Well, she's been too weak to even get out of bed, let alone eat. I took her in right away for testing and the initial signs say she's completely clear of the leukemia. Jemi, it's just a miracle!" The last word caught on a sob.

Jemimah gripped the phone tightly, her heart pounding. "Ruthy, I'm so happy for you," she said. *Thank you, Brian,* she thought fervently.

"Of course, they still want to do more tests," Ruth said, then laughed, "I think Dr. Runyan is in shock. Hold on..."

Jemi heard her put the phone down and blow her nose, then she was back.

Anyway," Ruth said, "I just had to call to let you know. Rick and I are both taking some time off. What about you?"

"Well," Jemi said, "I've decided to listen to everyone's advice and take a holiday."

Jemi heard Ruth's quick intake of breath. "Truth? That's fantastic. Where? When?"

"I'm not sure where...definitely someplace warm. As to when, starting today. I'm only going for a week."

"I'm so glad, Jem. You deserve some time for yourself. Grab a bottle or two of that elderberry wine, find a warm beach and some hunky guy and really live it up."

Jemimah smiled. *If only she knew!* "Yes, that sounds like a plan," she said. "I'll call you when I get back. Ruth, I'm so happy for you and Rick...and especially for Amelia. It just goes to show miracles can come true."

"Yeah, you said it, kiddo. Call me as soon as you get back. Have a wonderful time."

After Jemi hung up, she stood momentarily staring out the window at the now leafless elderberry patch. How could this be happening? She knew in her heart this was no dream. But none of it made any sense.

She sighed. If she let herself worry, she'd wind up in a mental hospital. *The best thing to do,* she said to herself, *is to accept what's happening and enjoy it while it lasts.*

* * * * *

It was a Thursday. She spent most of the day shopping for her trip. She went to the mall to buy some much needed lingerie, sleepwear and a new, tiny aqua bikini. She treated herself to a haircut, style and manicure.

She delivered a reluctant Sibyl to the kindly next-door neighbor, along with a week's worth of gourmet cat food and plenty of litter.

By the time she was ready to leave, it was past four p.m.

She picked up the precious bottle of elderberry wine and smiled to herself. There was no point spending money on airfare and accommodation when she had Brian.

She poured and drank. Nothing happened. She frowned and took another, larger swig. Still nothing.

A wave of fear ran up her spine and she stared at the glass. She swirled the purple-red liquid and drank more. There was no pop, no sound of rushing air. There was no sound at all except the steady tick of the clock on the wall.

So, that was it? All over? The fantasy was finished?

Carefully she put the glass down and as if sleepwalking, she trudged up the stairs and into her room, falling onto the bed and turning her face into the pillow. The tears came, slowly at first, then in an unstoppable torrent. All the pain of Granny Lou's death, her empty life and now the loss of her greatest experience poured out of her in a flood of despair.

Finally, exhausted, she slept. When she woke, the room was dark and the house was cold and empty.

Making her way downstairs, she turned on the lights, lit the fire in the fireplace and rummaged in the cupboards for something to eat. She'd already disposed of any perishables but found a box of crackers and some peanut butter. She'd sit in the living room and watch old movies.

The thought of being comfortably decadent lifted her mood slightly, so she grabbed a glass and the half empty bottle of elderberry wine and brought it with her.

She took the first swig just as Cary Grant was lowering his lips to Audrey Hepburn's.

"I've missed you."

Jemimah would have leapt up, startled, if not for the strange euphoria that overcame her whenever the wine worked its magic. Instead she turned her head, looked at Brian and said, "Where were you?"

He moved around the sofa and sat down next to her, his arm going automatically around her, his lips touching her ear. "You've had your hair done. You look wonderful."

Jemi controlled her rising need to surrender and pulled away, determinedly fighting the dreamlike sensation from the wine. "Where were you this afternoon?"

"Hmm?" His hand was finding its way into the opening of her bathrobe and down the front of her panties. "I don't know."

Jemi forced herself to stand up, knowing she wouldn't be able to resist if he kept on. "I summoned you. I drank the wine. You didn't come."

Brian looked up at her, his eyes dark with longing. Then surprise registered. "You drank the wine?"

"I drank the wine."

He looked at her more closely. "You've been crying."

Jemi put a hand to her face, embarrassed. "Where were you?" she said again, her voice catching.

He stood up and wrapped her in his arms. "I don't know," he said. "I told you, when I'm not with you, I'm in this dark place. I'd know if you summoned me." Then he paused and realization hit. "What time was it?"

Jemi thought. "Around four in the afternoon." She felt him relax.

"That's why," he said. "I can only be summoned after dark. Didn't your grandmother tell you?"

Jemi's mind began to work. Yes, of course. Gran had told her it had to be night. Relief flooded her and she felt her knees go weak.

"Oh, Brian, I thought you'd gone forever." She threw her arms around his neck and kissed him unashamedly. His arms went around her and he kissed her back, sensuous, lingering.

Eventually he pulled back to look at her, running a finger over her lips. "I'm here now," he said. "I forgot to tell you about the time. That's why I've always left before the sun came up. I thought you knew. I'm so sorry."

Jemi smiled at him. "It's okay. I'm just so glad you're here." She pulled away from him and clicked off the television, then turned back and smiled seductively. "What do you say to a little vacation?"

Chapter Three

☙

Jemi gazed around her, dazzled. The room was beautiful with thick white carpet, a huge bed with white draperies and black satin bedspread. There were gold framed mirrors on the ceiling and across one wall, while half the room was floor-to-ceiling windows. The door to a very large bathroom stood open. The fixtures were rich gold, the basin white and black marble, the tiles glossy black. A huge spa took pride of place in the center.

It'd been a strange experience when Brian snapped his fingers. One second Jemi was standing in her living room, clutching her suitcase and the bottle of elderberry wine, the next she felt a hot rush of air and she was here.

"Where are we?" she asked, completely awed and just a little dizzy. She let go of her case and placed the wine carefully on a nearby glass and gold coffee table. She could see the moonlight dancing on the ocean beyond the windows, stars sparkling in a clear inky sky. The rhythmic, calming rush and roar of surf filled her ears.

"Our own special island," Brian said. He snapped his fingers and a fire came to life in a gold and black marble fireplace. Lights dimmed and the most intoxicating aroma filled the room—a sweet yet musky scent. Jemi breathed deeply, closing her eyes.

"You like?" Brian stood behind her, his arms came around her waist, his fingers gently untied the belt of her fleecy bathrobe.

She leaned her head back and closed her eyes. "I like," she said. She felt wonderful. She let her mind wander as her robe disappeared leaving her naked and Brian's mouth and hands began to stir her smoldering inner fire.

Then she heard him snap his fingers again and she opened her eyes. With an intake of breath, she saw another man, dark-haired, dark-skinned, sultry, muscled—and completely naked. His ample appendage was obviously ready for action. She looked at Brian and he smiled. "Your wish, Jemi, my sweet, is my command," he murmured.

She puzzled for a moment, then realized she'd been fantasizing in her head. Was this what her imagination conjured? "Who is he?" she asked, feeling suddenly hot and cold all at once, her skin tingling. "And why is he here?"

The man spoke for himself. "I'm Rowan," he said, in a deep soothing voice, "and I'm here to pleasure you."

Jemi's fingers clasped Brian's arms where they circled her waist. "Is he real?" she whispered.

"He's as real as I am when I'm with you," he replied, kissing the tip of her ear, then pulling her hair to one side so he could kiss the nape of her neck.

"But...you're not real," she said.

"Is this real?" He pulled her back against him tightly.

Jemi couldn't answer. She felt his hard cock pressed against her back, while his fingers drifted down to that spot between her legs. He inserted a finger deep into her vagina and her knees turned instantly to jelly.

Rowan came closer. She was helpless under Brian's ministrations, his finger moving in and out of her opening, his arms holding her or she would've fallen. She gazed into Rowan's face and his dark eyes seemed to draw her into their depths. He reached out a hand and stroked her cheek, trailing his fingers down her throat to her chest. With both hands, he cupped her breasts then lowered his head. She closed her eyes in delight as the wet warmth of his mouth engulfed first one nipple, then the other, his hands gently kneading her flesh.

He moved even closer and she was sandwiched between the two men, their bodies hot, muscled, hard, their cocks pressing like molten steel against her, front and back. She was unable to speak or think.

Brian removed his finger and turned her gently to face him. He cupped her face with his hands and kissed her mouth, teasing her lips with his tongue. He lifted her, still covering her mouth with his and laid her on the soft bed, the satin bedspread slick and cool against her flushed skin.

Brian lay next to her and pulled her over on top of him, his mouth hard and demanding on hers. Rowan knelt on the bed close behind her and gently lifted her hips. She felt his lips and tongue kissing, flicking, over her lower back and buttocks.

Brian's cock was between her legs. She spread them, wanting his cock inside her. But Rowan held her hips up so only the very end of Brian's penis touched her aching opening, making her squirm with unbridled desire.

Then she felt Rowan's hands from behind. He was using a fragrant lubricating oil to gently massage her buttocks. He moved one hand into her crack, circled her anus, then gently inserted a well-oiled finger. Jemi gasped and thrust her butt back, wanting more. Rowan's hands slid between her legs to gather the viscous wetness there, then back to her anus, inserting a greased finger even further. She moaned. Every orifice of her body ached for penetration.

Brian slid down her body, his mouth trailing a warm, wet kiss down her chest to her belly. He pulled her legs further apart and she felt the stubble from his cheeks pressed against her inner thighs. His lips found her clit, sucking gently and she cried out with joy.

The men held her or she most certainly would've collapsed. Her muscles were completely useless. Her entire focus was on riveted to their actions—Brian's tongue, flicked her clit, slowly circled, then repeated the process, while Rowan's fingers slipped into her vagina then out and up, gently prodding her anus, circling it and repeating.

They continued this way, driving Jemi to distraction. Finally, she couldn't take the anticipation any longer. "Fuck me!" she cried out, her voice catching, "fuck me hard!"

"You want us to fuck you?" Brian's words were breathed against her throbbing clitoris. "You want us both?"

"Yes, yes. Please. I want you in me—both of you." She was nearly sobbing from the exquisite pain of anticipation.

Brian moved back up and his mouth found hers. She could taste her own musky juices on his lips. She felt his penis touch her opening. At the same time, Rowan's hands raised her hips again and she felt his shaft push gently between her butt cheeks.

She held her breath. Gently, so very gently, Rowan's well lubricated cock began to slip into her anus. There were no thoughts as it penetrated deeper and deeper. When he'd inserted it to the hilt, she was completely lost to the sensation of her rectum, completely filled with his cock.

Barely able to register the bliss of this feeling, her focus shifted as she felt Brian's shaft prodding for entry. She felt him push past her labia and slip easily into the burning heart of her swollen, wet pussy.

"Fuck!" she cried out. Every fiber of her body was screaming with need. She was completely impaled. Her body was no longer her own. She was jelly, held together by the hard, relentless cocks inside her. She couldn't move, though she wanted to—wanted to thrust her buttocks back hard, or push her pussy down over Brian's shaft even further.

And with that thought, both men began to pull slowly out, out. Jemi held her breath. They stopped and slid back into their respective openings, seeming to go even deeper. She sobbed with rampant emotion.

They continued gently, making sure Jemi was completely wet at both ends. She felt her juices dripping. Rowan's finger circled his cock, adding oil to her entry so it slipped easily in and out. Bent over her back, his free hand kneaded her breasts, one after the other, so her nipples stood up. His fingers teased them, sending tiny electric shocks directly to her clit.

Gradually the men's movements gathered momentum. She could feel their cocks coming together inside her. Only a thin barrier separated them. Her cunt gasped for more, her clitoris felt swollen, twitching with need. Her abdomen tightened as her body moved inexorably toward a knife-edged pinnacle.

She threw her head back, panting and moaning like an animal as their tempo increased. Brian's cock plunged into her ever-tightening core, while Rowan's filled her over and over from behind. Both men were panting, dripping with sweat. Jemi's own sweat slid from her body to blend with theirs.

When she thought she could go no higher on this journey of bliss, the men increased the intensity their movements. Now, Rowan's thighs slapped hard against her buttocks, pushing her forward but Brian's grip on her shoulders held her steady, his own upward thrusts making her gasp and sob with a demented desire.

The tension continued to grow with each thrust of their cocks, bringing her closer and closer to climax. Then suddenly she knew she was beyond the point of no return and she grew very still. She forced her mind to blankness and relaxed, letting her body take over completely. She began to tighten, her insides tensing of their own accord. She dropped her head, panting to the rhythm of their thrusts. Finally, as if in slow motion, she slipped off the precipice and her body burst into an orgasm so intense, she screamed like primitive creature with the unbelievable spasming of her entire being.

Both men continued as her muscles clamped hard on their steely shafts. Then first Rowan, then Brian, cried out and stopped their movements. Jemi felt the canon-like explosion when they came inside her and she moaned, her insides gripping their cocks in orgasmic pulsations.

She collapsed on top of Brian, completely spent, his arms wrapped around her. Rowan rested his hot forehead against her back. Sweat bathed all three.

Some minutes later, Jemi was vaguely aware of Rowan removing his penis and gently apply a cool, soothing ointment to her anus. Then he was gone.

She didn't move, didn't flinch. She felt completely sated, totally secure in Brian's arms. She knew without thinking she was now a new person. Brian had introduced her to an unbelievable world of pure bliss she'd never known existed.

* * * * *

It was the caw of a seagull that woke her. It was still dark but the sky beyond the windows was beginning to change from ebony to hazy slate. She wasn't surprised to find herself no longer atop the bed but cozy between satin sheets. Brian lay beside her, his arm still beneath her head. She gazed at him, wanting to memorize every feature, feeling a surge of emotion at the way his long lashes lay against his cheeks and his lips parted softly in sleep.

Had she ever been alive before Brian? She felt the pleasant ache in her rectum and vagina and flushed with automatic desire at the memory.

"It was good for me too," he said, his voice sleepy, his eyes gazing at her lovingly.

She laughed. "Oh, Brian! I'm so happy." She sighed and stretched blissfully.

He sat up and leaned over, kissing her gently. "I'm glad," he said.

She pulled back to look at him. "What's wrong?"

He smiled. "I thought I was the only one who could read minds," he said.

She took his hand and wrapped her fingers between his. "Tell me."

He sighed. "It's nearly dawn. I have to…"

"No." She put her fingers over his mouth. "Please, don't say it."

He smiled. "Not saying it won't change things."

"But what will I do here without you?" she cried. A tear ran down her cheek.

Brian was silent, his face showing his own distress. Finally he spoke. "I'll be back tonight—if you summon me." He gestured to the elderberry wine on the table.

Jemi sniffed. He plucked a scented handkerchief out of thin air and handed it to her. It was something a two-bit magician would do and it made her laugh despite herself. She blew her nose. "Oh Brian, I wish you could stay with me all week…"

No sooner had the words come out of her mouth when there was a pop and whoosh, then silence.

Brian looked at her in amazement.

"What was that?" Jemi's eyes darted around, startled, half expecting to see Rowan.

Brian gathered her into his arms and kissed her head, her cheek, her nose, her eyes. "My darling," he said as he continued to drop kisses, "you've just made your second wish."

Jemi blinked then smiled. "What? Oh! So does that mean you can…"

"Yes," he said. "All week." And with that, he rolled her onto her back to claim more than just her mouth.

* * * * *

The days passed gloriously. Jemi had never known such complete happiness. They made love everywhere imaginable—on the beach under the hot sun, in the ocean with waves swelling around them, aboard a yacht Brian conjured for a day, in the coolness of shade and soft grass beneath coconut palms, in a delightful glade with a freshwater waterfall, in the huge bathroom spa—more than once. The only rule she knew they had to adhere to was to sip some elderberry wine each evening. Brian knew it was important but wasn't at all sure why. Jemi didn't care—whatever was needed was worth it.

Sometimes Rowan would join them, sometimes it would be some other hunk of a man. Jemi realized it was her own imagination that brought the others. They were fleeting—there to pleasure her then go. But it was Brian who held her heart. It surprised and baffled her that so much untapped desire had been lying dormant within her for so long.

Still, she didn't mind the feel of more than one hard penis bringing her to pinnacle after pinnacle of ecstasy in every way imaginable.

And she also soon realized she enjoyed giving as much as she took.

* * * * *

She found the stilettos, black mesh stockings, leather garter belt and bra in the bathroom one evening. Lying beside them was a riding crop. She smiled. She was learning that when Brian said, "Your wish is my command" it meant even her unspoken ones.

She put the gear on, applied red lipstick and ample mascara, then admired herself in the mirror. She flicked the whip and enjoyed the snapping sound. She felt a sudden surge of power and confidence.

Brian was naked, propped on one elbow on the bed. He smiled when she appeared. "You look magnificent," he said.

She snapped the whip again and pointed with it to the bedhead. "I want you tied," she said. "We don't want you escaping your...mmm...punishment."

He rolled over languidly and instantly his hands were secured, his magnificent body stretched out before her, completely at her disposal. His cock was already hard and he watched her from beneath lowered lids.

She climbed onto the bed, putting her knee between his legs, taking the whip and running the strands down his face, neck and chest. "So," she said, "how shall I deal with you?"

He sucked in his breath as the whip strands circled his cock and trailed over his balls.

She smiled. "Don't worry," she said. "I won't hurt you — if you're good."

"I'll be good," he said. His voice was low, husky.

She put the whip aside and trailed her fingers over his face, neck, chest. She loved the feel of him, she loved knowing he was completely at her mercy and she loved the way his eyes glittered with anticipation.

She circled his cock with her fingers, then grasped it with one hand, gently cupping his balls with the other. She smiled as he groaned. His penis was hot and rock hard. She licked her lips and put her mouth very close to the tip of his cock. "What do you want?" she whispered, her warm breath causing his rod to jump of its own accord.

"Suck it," he said. He was watching now, pure desire glittering in his blue eyes.

She smiled up at him, then bent her head and touched the end of his cock with her tongue, circling it one way, then the other, still gripping it with her hand, feeling it dance with primal need.

He groaned again, pulling on the bonds.

"Is that what you want?" she asked. She flicked her tongue over the tip again.

"Suck it," he cried. "Take it all."

"Maybe I will," she said, moving her mouth to his scrotum, "maybe I won't." She took one ball very gently into her mouth, savored it, then repeated the action with the other ball.

"God..." Brian moaned.

She loved teasing him. Loved knowing she could make him as weak as a kitten. She ran her tongue down the inside of one thigh, then the other, then moved back up to his engorged shaft and placed her lips over the end.

Slowly, she took it into her mouth, opening her throat so she could slide it in almost to the hilt.

She could hear Brian's ragged breathing and felt him shifting with the agony of delicious anticipation. She could feel her own juices flowing. Her pussy was wet and ready, swollen, hot, wanting to be filled. She moved her mouth up and down, letting her tongue circle and flick as she went. At the same time, she rubbed her clit against his thigh, her hands moving to grasp his firm buttocks. His hips rose so she could take him even deeper into her mouth.

She continued sliding her mouth up and down until she felt a change in him—knew he was close to ejaculation. His body was taut, his eyes shut, a muscle in his jaw worked.

She stopped and sat back, smiling as his eyes flew open and the desperation of his need showed clearly in his face.

"Shit, don't stop!" he breathed, thrusting his hips up with his need.

She didn't reply but repositioned herself so she was straddling him. She knelt over him, her labia just touching his penis. "Stay very still," she said.

He did as he was told, though she could feel the tension in him like a tangible force. Slowly she lowered herself, closing her eyes in delight as his hard shaft entered her. She stopped halfway and knew it was all he could do to prevent himself from thrusting up into her. "That's good," she purred.

She teased him, moving herself down, down, until he was all the way inside her, then up, up, stopping just before he came out. His body glowed in the soft light with sweat. Her own body was beaded. She reached down and fingered her clit as she slid slowly down, then up, feeling the familiar mounting passion, savoring the sensation of being completely in control.

His hands gripped the wood of the bedhead, his knuckles white. Jemi could feel herself climbing to that exquisite height. Without thinking, she increased her tempo, moving up and down faster and faster, her finger on her clit bringing her closer and closer to the edge. Finally, she gasped as she felt herself slip over the edge into breathtaking release. At the same time she heard him cry out and he arched his back, driving his cock up and into her hard as he shot his semen into her.

Together they orgasmed. Bright colorful lights exploded behind Jemi's eyes and she collapsed on top of him. Time seemed to stop as she was completely caught up by their synchronized spasms pulsing inside her.

* * * * *

"Is it good for you too?" she asked some time later, her cheek resting on his chest, his arms around her.

"Christ, Jemi, how can you ask?" he said.

She shrugged. "I'm still learning how this all works. I wonder sometimes if you just seem to like it because it's what I want."

He sat up and pulled her up too, taking her chin and making her look into his eyes. "That's not part of the deal," he said. "I don't lie—and that means I don't pretend."

She smiled and kissed him on the mouth. "I think I knew it," she said between kisses. "I just wanted to be sure."

He pulled her down and rolled her over. "Be sure," he said and she could feel his cock, rock-hard again, pressing against her, his knee gently opening her legs. "Be very, very sure."

Chapter Four

Seven days passed all too quickly. Jemi'd lost all track of time. It was Brian who brought it up. They lay sated in the afterglow of lovemaking. It was early, the rush and roar of the waves lulled Jemi into a semi-sleep. Dawn would be breaking soon.

"I'll have to leave you soon," Brian said, kissing her forehead gently.

She blinked and sat up, peering at him in the dark. "What? No! Why?"

"It's Friday, Jem. Our seven days are up."

A sense of utter sadness filled her. "No," she protested. "Brian, how can I let you go?"

He fingered her hair and she could see his own eyes were moist. "I don't want to go," he said. "But I have no choice."

She lay back down and snuggled into his arms, twin tears finding their way down her cheeks. "I've been thinking," she said, "about my third wish."

His fingers stroked her back. "I know," he said.

She smiled poignantly. "Right," she said. "You probably know what I want to wish for?" She felt him nod. "So what do you think?"

He was silent for a long time. Finally he answered. "I don't know, Jem. I don't know what it will do. I wish I could tell you." She sighed and he pulled her even closer. "But whatever happens, I want you to know how much it means to me. If you go through with it, it'll mean I'll never have to go back to that dark, lonely place again."

She nodded. She couldn't bear to think of him there. Even if she lost him forever, it would be worth it—just to know he'd no longer have to live in some limbo world when he was away from her.

"I still have the elderberry wine," she said.

"True. But if your wish is granted, I won't be as I am now, so it may not work."

She digested this. She'd thought about already and it was hard to imagine what life would be like if he wasn't there. But it was a risk she had to take. Granny Lou's words came back to her, "Remember, sometimes if you truly love someone, you must set them free." She knew in her heart, this was what her gran meant.

So, despite her reservations, her mind was made up. She stroked his face gently, feeling his fingers tangle in her hair. "Brian?" she said.

"I know," he replied. "And I love you too, Jemimah Murphy."

She felt a wave of heartbreaking joy flood her, then, still holding him she breathed, "Brian, I wish you were real."

* * * * *

Jemi sat at the kitchen table in her grandmother's house. The bottle of elderberry wine and empty goblet stood before her. She'd sipped the warm, sweet stuff every morning and night for the past two days. She was certain, now, her wish had been granted and Brian was no longer a genie. She could no longer summon him. And she had no idea where he was in this huge world.

After the initial realization and subsequent tears and anger at whoever was in charge of these things, she'd drifted into dull acceptance. At least she'd always have the memories of the past few weeks to relive. Life would never be the same for her again. And she knew no man would ever fulfill her the way Brian had.

She got up from the table and went to gather her purse and coat. She glanced in the mirror. There was a different woman there now. Her skin glowed a golden bronze, her hair was sun-streaked and curled softly about her face. She looked younger...maybe even beautiful. Brian had done that. Brian had brought her a new lease on life. She tried to smile. It was her first day back at work and it was important everyone thought she'd had a good time. How could she explain to them why she was filled with such an utter, endless sense of loss?

* * * * *

"I must say, Jemimah, you look so refreshed. I don't know what it is but wherever you went it certainly agreed with you." Nancy pushed open the door to room number sixteen.

"Thanks," Jemi murmured.

"Now I think we brought Mr. Jordan in just before you left," Nancy said. She grabbed the chart from the bottom of the bed and handed it to Jemimah. "Skiing accident. He's been in a coma for weeks. Dr. Forbes says he'll have to be removed to a more suitable facility if he doesn't come out of it in the next couple days."

Jemi gazed at the chart. Age—thirty-six. Height—six foot two inches. Weight... Wait," she said loud.

"Pardon?" Nancy turned. She was at the head of the bed, a cart nearby with warm water and a washcloth.

"Name—Brian Jordan."

"Yes, that's right, dear. A shame, really. He's quite a handsome young man. We've all been hoping he'd come out of it but there's been no sign..."

Jemi dropped the clipboard with a clatter and rushed to the bed. "Brian!" She nearly fainted with joy. It was him, right here, right in her very hospital. His face was pale, his eyes shut. She reached out a shaky hand to touch him.

"Jemimah," Nancy said, "do you know this man?"

Jemi paused, then turned to her and smiled, a shaky smile. "Yes, yes I do, Nancy. Can you give me a few minutes with him alone?"

Nancy eyed her, puzzled but nodded. "Certainly, dear. You have as long as you want. He'll need a sponge bath and..."

Jemimah hurried the other woman to the door. "I'll take care of it all," she said. "Thanks."

Finally alone with Brian, she sat down next to the bed and lifted one of his limp hands. It felt warm, alive, as if he were just sleeping.

"Brian," she said urgently. "Brian, you have to wake up. It's me, Jemi. Please."

But there was no response, no flicker of eyelid, no twitch of muscle.

Jemi's mind was working fast. "Brian, if you were in this accident before I met you, my third wish was unnecessary — you've been real all along. Don't you see?" She squeezed his hand gently. "I still have a third wish, Brian. And I wish you'd wake up."

She waited. There was no pop or whoosh of air. The monitoring machine on the other side of the bed continued its regular "ping". As the minutes passed, tears filled her eyes. "Didn't you hear me," she said angrily. "Whoever you are who's in charge, you have to grant me my third wish. It's part of the rules. And I wish Brian Jordan would wake up." Still nothing. Jemi stood up and raised her face to the ceiling, her fists clenched at her sides. "Goddammit, are you listening to me?" she cried vehemently.

"I heard you."

She looked down and began to laugh and cry at the same time. "Brian!" His blue eyes were open, droopy but open. He moved his head slightly.

"Thirsty," he said. "Nurse, could you..."

Jemi grew rigid, her jubilation brought to a screeching halt. He didn't know her. And why would he? He'd been in a coma. How could he possibly know her?

She gathered her wits and grabbed the jug of water and poured him a glass with shaking hands. "Here," she said, lifting his head gently, "I'd better help you."

He sipped gratefully, then lay back on the pillow, obviously exhausted.

"We were worried about you, Bri—Mr. Jordan," Jemi said, trying desperately to hold back the tears that threatened to spill. "You've been unconscious for three weeks."

He frowned as if trying to digest this. "Three weeks," he repeated. Then he closed his eyes and Jemi put the water jug back and turned to go. She'd have to inform Dr. Forbes.

"They were the best three weeks of my life, Jem," he said, his voice barely a whisper. "Come kiss me. I have the worst headache."

Jemimah's heart was pounding so hard she felt it would burst. She gave a small cry of joy, then went to him and kissed his forehead, his cheeks, his eyes, his nose. And when her lips found his and his hand came up to pull her closer, she knew for certain he remembered everything.

Also by Amber Skyze

eBooks:
Body Shots
Dante's Desire
Gettin' Lucky
Ignited
Play With Me
Pretend with Me
Research Required
Spend the Night with Me
Splashing Good Time
Submit with Me

Print Books:
Ignite the Flames

About the Author

From a very young age, Amber Skyze began making up stories—the only child syndrome. Had anyone asked her back then if she would write when she grew up, she'd have laughed. It wasn't until raising children and reading all those romances that she decided—hey, I can write these. Then she discovered erotica and found her calling.

When not crafting hot, steamy tales, this New York transplant now resides in Rhode Island with her husband (the inspiration behind her stories), three children who force her to work a day job, and three dogs. She's thrilled to join the authors of Ellora's Cave.

Also by M.A. Ellis

eBooks:
Ellora's Cavemen: Jewels of the Nile IV *(anthology)*
Filigree and Fantasy
Hallow's Eve Hunk
Just Press Play
Love's Ally
Love's Choice
Seducing the Siren
Shaken and Stirred
The Cake Babe
Twisted Steel and Sex Appeal

Print Books:
Aquamarine Allure *(anthology)*
Ellora's Cavemen: Jewels of the Nile IV *(anthology)*
Hard as Nails
Love's Choice

About the Author

M.A. Ellis is a firm believer that everyone should pursue their dreams…no matter how long it takes to achieve them. She wrote her first short story, *What I Want To Be When I Grow Up,* more than a few decades ago. It was read by a total of seven people. (For those who are interested, the answer to that intriguing statement was a toss up between a veterinarian and a nun.)

Thanks to the encouragement of a creative writing guru at Northern Kentucky University, she stepped out of her neat little writing boundaries and penned an erotic poem, which ultimately led her to the vastly stimulating world of erotic romance. It's a vocation she truly loves — equally as rewarding as furry, four-legged creatures and a heck of a lot more entertaining than Friday nights at the nunnery.

When not devoting her time to crafting tales of hot encounters and steamy romances that always have a happy ending, M.A. concentrates on the delightful task of honing her master baking skills, eagerly focusing on the realms of cheesecake and chocolate which are, in her humble opinion, the only 'c' words that matter.

She lives in northwestern Pennsylvania where temperatures rival those of *Ice Station Zebra* a good portion of the year — making it the perfect arena for devising stories where one spark can ignite a welcomed inferno.

Also by Helen Hardt

eBooks:
Loving Eve
Pianist Envy
Slow and Wet

About the Author

୨୦

Helen Hardt is an attorney and stay-at-home mom turned award-winning author. She's been writing stories since the first grade, when her aspiring writer father encouraged her and gave her a small metal file cabinet with "Helen's Story Box" written on it in permanent marker. She began her first novel, a young adult romance, in the eighth grade. Although it will never see the light of day, she still has the manuscript that she typed on the old IBM Selectric.

She stopped writing to attend college and law school. She met her real-life hero in law school, and they in Colorado with her two teenage sons. Helen writes contemporary, historical, paranormal, and erotic romance. Her non-writing interest include Harley rides with her husband, attending her sons' sports and music performances, traveling, and Taekwondo (she's a blackbelt.)

Also by Kat Alexis

eBooks:
Berry Bliss
Candy-Coated Passion
Ice Cream, You Scream
Set Me Up

Print Books:
Creamy *(anthology)*

About the Author

Kat Alexis is the brainchild of best friends and multi-published authors Eve Savage and Allie Standifer.

Born in a bar on a cool February evening in New Orleans, Kat emerged as the perfect combination of Allie's flair for dialogue and storytelling and Eve's love of sensuality and strong characters.

Together with the bent sense of humor they share and an obsession with all things paranormal, Kat is definitely unique.

Also by Kelly Jamieson

eBooks:
Conference Call
Irish Sex Fairy
Power Struggle
Rigger
Sexpresso Night
Taming Tara

About the Author

೨

Kelly Jamieson is the author of several sexy romance novels. Her writing has been described as "blisteringly sexy" and "a spicy delicious read". If she can stop herself from reading or writing, she loves to cook. She has shelves of cookbooks that she reads at length. She also enjoys gardening in the summer, and in the winter she likes to read gardening magazines and seed catalogues (there might be a there here…). She also loves shopping, especially for clothes and shoes. But her family takes precedence over everything else (yes, even writing). She has two teenage children who are the best kids in the world, not that she's biased, and a wonderful husband who does loads of laundry while she plays on the computer writing stories. She loves hearing from readers.

Also by Ainsley Abbott

eBooks:
Catey's Capture
Jemimah's Genie

About the Author

Ainsley was born and raised in Michigan. She majored in English at university, receiving a Bachelor's in English, with Creative Writing Emphasis. Her first publication was at the tender age of nine. She's now published in other genres, and teaches creative writing to adults and children.

Ainsley's love of travel brought her to Australia, where she met and married the man of her dreams. She now resides in Victoria, on the southern coast, with her true love, her son and daughter, and a medley of cats and dogs. Besides writing, she enjoys rainforests, the sound of the surf, rip-roaring thunderstorms, crackling fires and exotic locales.

The authors welcome comments from readers. You can find their websites and email addresses on their author bio pages at www.ellorascave.com.

Tell Us What You Think

We appreciate hearing reader opinions about our books. You can email us at Comments@EllorasCave.com.

Why an electronic book?

We live in the Information Age—an exciting time in the history of human civilization, in which technology rules supreme and continues to progress in leaps and bounds every minute of every day. For a multitude of reasons, more and more avid literary fans are opting to purchase e-books instead of paper books. The question from those not yet initiated into the world of electronic reading is simply: *Why?*

1. **Price.** An electronic title at Ellora's Cave Publishing and Cerridwen Press runs anywhere from 40% to 75% less than the cover price of the exact same title in paperback format. Why? Basic mathematics and cost. It is less expensive to publish an e-book (no paper and printing, no warehousing and shipping) than it is to publish a paperback, so the savings are passed along to the consumer.

2. **Space.** Running out of room in your house for your books? That is one worry you will never have with electronic books. For a low one-time cost, you can purchase a handheld device specifically designed for e-reading. Many e-readers have large, convenient screens for viewing. Better yet, hundreds of titles can be stored within your new library—on a single microchip. There are a variety of e-readers from different manufacturers. You can also read e-books on your PC or laptop computer. (Please note that Ellora's Cave does not endorse any specific brands.

You can check our websites at www.ellorascave.com or www.cerridwenpress.com for information we make available to new consumers.)

3. *Mobility.* Because your new e-library consists of only a microchip within a small, easily transportable e-reader, your entire cache of books can be taken with you wherever you go.

4. *Personal Viewing Preferences.* Are the words you are currently reading too small? Too large? Too... ANNOYING? Paperback books cannot be modified according to personal preferences, but e-books can.

5. *Instant Gratification.* Is it the middle of the night and all the bookstores near you are closed? Are you tired of waiting days, sometimes weeks, for bookstores to ship the novels you bought? Ellora's Cave Publishing sells instantaneous downloads twenty-four hours a day, seven days a week, every day of the year. Our webstore is never closed. Our e-book delivery system is 100% automated, meaning your order is filled as soon as you pay for it.

Those are a few of the top reasons why electronic books are replacing paperbacks for many avid readers.

As always, Ellora's Cave and Cerridwen Press welcome your questions and comments. We invite you to email us at Comments@ellorascave.com or write to us directly at Ellora's Cave Publishing Inc., 1056 Home Avenue, Akron, OH 44310-3502.

Make each day more *Exciting* With our

Ellora's Cavemen Calendar

www.EllorasCave.com

Ellora's Cave Romanticon

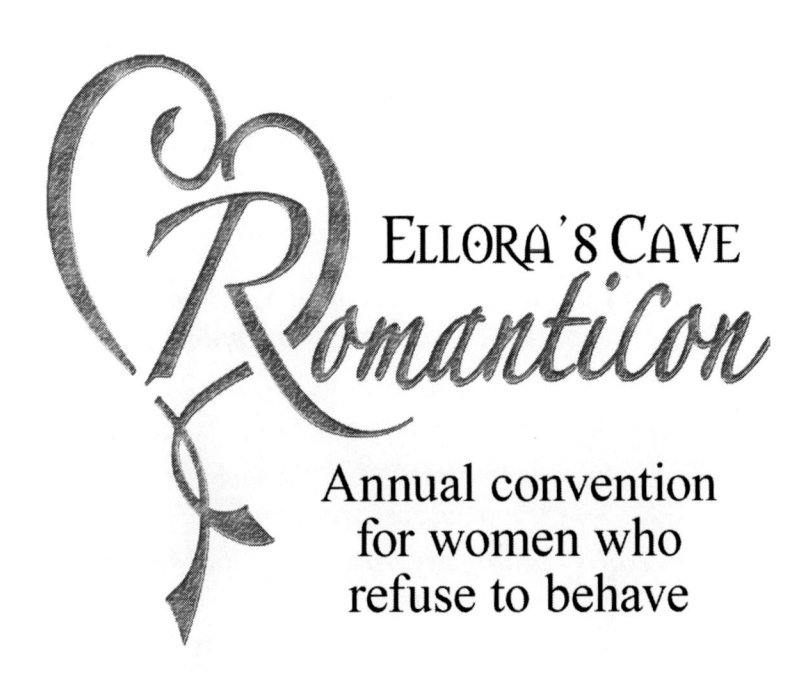

Annual convention for women who refuse to behave

www.JasmineJade.com/Romanticon
For additional info contact: conventions@ellorascave.com

Discover for yourself why readers can't get enough
of the multiple award-winning publisher
Ellora's Cave.
Whether you prefer e-books or paperbacks,
be sure to visit EC on the web at
www.ellorascave.com
for an erotic reading experience that will leave you
breathless.